as she left it

For Diane Nelson,
with love and thanks and no apologies,
because you're not superstitious.

as she left it

A NOVEL

CATRIONA McPHERSON

MIDNIGHT INK
WOODBURY, MINNESOTA

FIRST EDITION
First Printing, 2013

Book format by Bob Gaul
Cover design by Kevin R. Brown
Cover image © Woman: iStockphoto.com/Jaroslaw Wojcik
Cover illustration: © Dominick Finelle/The July Group
Editing by Nicole Nugent
Neighborhood diagram by Llewellyn art department

Midnight Ink, an imprint of Llewellyn Worldwide Ltd.

This is a work of fiction. Names, characters, places, and incidents are either the product of the author's imagination or are used fictitiously, and any resemblance to actual persons, living or dead, business establishments, events, or locales is entirely coincidental.

Library of Congress Cataloging-in-Publication Data
McPherson, Catriona, 1965–
  As she left it: a novel/Catriona McPherson.—First edition.
    pages cm
  ISBN 978-0-7387-3677-8
1. Homecoming—Fiction. 2. Kidnapping—Fiction. 3. Family secrets—Fiction.
4. Leeds (England)—Fiction. 5. Mystery fiction. I. Title.
  PR6113.C586A89 2013
  823'.92—dc23
                              2013001264

Midnight Ink
Llewellyn Worldwide Ltd.
2143 Wooddale Drive
Woodbury, MN 55125-2989
www.midnightinkbooks.com

Printed in the United States of America

In a cottage in a wood,
A little old man at the window stood,
Saw a rabbit running by
Knocking at his door.
"Help me! Help me!" the rabbit said,
"Or the farmer will shoot me dead."
"Come little rabbit, come with me.
Happy we shall be."
                    —Traditional children's song

The outhouse, the outhouse,
The hold your nose and shout house.
Grab thee by thy lug-hole,
Put thee down the plug-hole.
Grab thee by thy left hand,
Put thee down the muck pan.
Pull the chain, pull the chain,
Wash back up again.
The outhouse, the outhouse,
The hold your nose and shout house.
—Children's skipping song

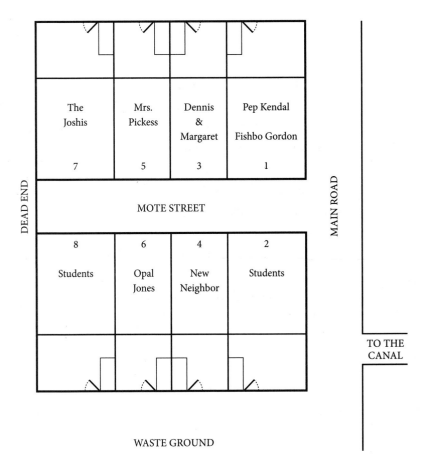

DEAD END

The
Joshis

7

Mrs.
Pickess

5

Dennis
&
Margaret

3

Pep Kendal

Fishbo Gordon

1

MOTE STREET

8

Students

6

Opal
Jones

4

New
Neighbor

2

Students

MAIN ROAD

TO THE
CANAL

WASTE GROUND

PROLOGUE

17 May 2000

There's a line on the yard wall that shows where the outhouse used to be. Red bricks above it, white paint below it. That's where the roof started. That's where the jaggedy castle top was, where the arrows came from. Or the path along the fort walls to shoot baddies off of, or the top of the mast where the sail was tied to.

Except now it's gone.

And here on the ground there's another line too. That's where the door was (or the drawbridge, or the gates where the stagecoach came galloping in, or the hole in the hull where the gangplank went through).

All gone now. So there's nothing to do.

But outside this yard is the lane, and up and down the lane are all the other yards with their castles and forts and pirate ships still there. Only steps away. All the houses joined together in a big long row and easy to run and play at any of them. And then there's the van. The van's best of all. Sometimes it starts moving. And it's a train, an army tank, a spaceship that goes to the moon.

In here, there's nothing.

But if he stretches up as far as he can stretch and wiggles his middle finger under the little hook there and stands on his very, very tiptoes maybe … the gate swings open. Quick look back at the house. No one shouts his name.

So out he goes.

And all the other gates have handles he can reach. And when he swings on a handle, the gate falls open. And the outhouses aren't locked. One's been cleared, all the stuff piled up outside in the yard and inside the stink of new paint. One's so full of boxes there's hardly space to wriggle in there. The van's not locked either. It's empty today—a cannibal cave where his feet boom and his voice is like monsters!

Then he remembers what's down the end. The canal! Full of sharks and submarines and shipwrecks.

So he's limping on his peg-leg when an angry voice says, "Hey!"

Turn round, head down, ready to cry if it means less trouble.

But it's not who he thought it would be.

ONE

21 July 2010
Tuesday

It's all connected. Everything's joined to everything. You think you can keep things out of your head, if you concentrate hard. You think your brain's in charge. And then blammo! *From nowhere, one little thread starts to fray, one little rock gets lifted, and the light shines in. That's when you know it's your blood that runs the show. Your bowels. Your guts and your glands. When you're shaking so hard you can't talk and you're breathing so fast you can't think and all of your careful stories have blown away.*

"Tell me," he says, as the van rocks along. There isn't another car or a single house in sight. No sign of life. The moor fog's coming down. "Start talking."

"Dunno where to start. Dunno if there's time."

"Make time," he says. "Talk fast. Tell me now."

"Okay … Okay … Well, it's all connected, see? That's the main thing. I see that now. The mum and the dad and the boy and the girl."

1

"Who's this?"

"And the little old lady and the poor old man. The baby that's lost and the baby that's ... " Big breath. Try again. "They're all the same."

"Start at the start and tell me," he says. "Keep on talking right till the end."

"The start?"

"When does it start?"

"I suppose ... I dunno."

"So ... once a upon a time," he says, and the words make goose-flesh pop out on her arms.

"No! No more stories. No way. It's ... a month ago, I guess."

"So," he says, "once upon a month ago then."

TWO

19 June 2010
Saturday

Opal came at the house the back way—old habit, that. Along the lane, over the waste ground, in at the yard gate, bolting it behind her. She put down her big bag and stretched her fingers, shrugged off her small bag, and fanned her tee-shirt, looking round. Of course it seemed smaller; she'd been ready for that. She hadn't been here since she was twelve. But she wasn't prepared for just *how* small: three strides from the gate to the back door, and nearly narrow enough to stretch her arms out and touch both sides. When she was little, she played here for hours. What did she find to do? And was it always this shabby? Flaking red brick walls, water-stained from blocked gutters, peeling paint on the door, the wood underneath cracked and greying?

Even still—she couldn't help it—there was a little lifting up inside her, as if she was glad to get home. Maybe she'd have been glad to get anywhere. Her head still ached and stomach still churned

3

from the journey—the train carriage getting to the end of its long, hot day, coming back from the coast, food and drink and bodies, everyone who'd dozed and sweated, slipped swollen feet out of shoes, tucked sandwich wrappers down the side of the seats and left them there. The bus up here from the station had been worse: still all the food and sweat but with perfume too, from the first of the Saturday-night crowd.

If the key wasn't where it had always been, she would wrap her hand and smash the kitchen window. She would listen to make sure the neighbors weren't out in their yards first, but then she would do it quick and confident and mend the glass herself. It wouldn't be the first time. But when she wiggled the loose brick down by the side of the step, there it was the same as ever, and she fitted it into the lock and shoved the door with her shoulder as if she had never been away.

Inside, in spite of the heat, a shudder went through her and left her tingling. It was a smell. Or it was the ghost of a smell—cigarettes and old coal—just wisps of it that memory could fan until it grew and grew, strong enough to choke her. She reeled back out into the yard again, sinking down and pulling her knees up close under her chin.

It wasn't empty! She'd thought everything would be gone. She'd imagined getting an airbed and sleeping bag to tide her over, taking the bus out to Ikea or scouring the charity shops. But there was the kitchen table with the stools that fitted under it, there was the arm of the big couch and the dark pattern of the carpet through the open living room door, and she'd seen dishes upside down on the draining board, the same brown Pyrex mugs and Nicola's glass—a good heavy tumbler that sat square on its base no matter how carelessly you set it down, that never tipped over no matter how hard you knocked it, reaching out in the dark, your rings clinking against its sides.

For two pins, whatever that meant, Opal would have gone straight back to Whitby. Or if she'd had a car, or if it hadn't been so hot and Saturday night ... but the thought of lugging those bags back into town, through crowds of dressed-up girls clacking around on high heels, flipping their shiny hair at the boys in their shiny shirts, doused in cologne ... the thought of finding the right train, and then Steph and Baz, and asking Jill for her job back ...

And she had to pee.

Anyway, when she stood up and went inside again, the ghost had vanished out through the open door. She hauled herself up the steep box stair from the kitchen to the narrow landing and the sliver of a bathroom sliced off the back bedroom (which didn't have it to spare), smelling nothing except the ordinary staleness of a house left closed too long. *My house*, she thought, putting her hand out and trailing it along the bumpy gloss of the bathroom wall.

My home.

———

"It's a cottage," she had said to Jill at the salon on her last Saturday, because once, on holiday with Steph and her dad in Norfolk, when Michael was a baby, she'd seen terraces of flint houses, one window beside the door with one window upstairs, and *they* were called cottages. "In a wood," she had said to Jill. Meanwood, the district was called, after all.

"Watch out for the little old man then," said Jill. Opal stared at her in the mirror and forgot to pass her the next square of foil.

"You know ... *in a cottage, in a wood*," sang Jill. Her lady, whose hair was half-covered with folded foil, joined in. "*A little old man at the window stood*." Then they both stopped with their mouths open, before laughing.

"I forget the rest of it," said Jill.

"I've never heard that," Opal said.

"Your mum never sang it to you?" said the lady, then shut her mouth and opened her eyes wide.

"It's okay," Opal said. "I don't mind talking about her. It. Her."

Jill and her lady both shook their heads, and, instead of poking her with the handle of her tint brush like usual, Jill gave Opal a gentle nudge to restart the supply of foil.

"Poor mite," said her lady. "When did she die then, love?"

"About eight weeks ago," Opal said.

Jill's lady tutted. "Early days yet. You'll have had a lot to do. Funeral and paperwork and all that."

Opal nodded, but Jill flashed a warning look.

"Don't you think about the funeral again, Opal," she said. And then into the mirror. "It nearly floored her. She came back here a physical wreck. Didn't you, love?"

The lady clucked in sympathy. "Well, it's a lot to ask of a young girl. What about your dad? I mean, I take it they were divorced, but even so ... "

"My dad died five years ago."

Now Jill's lady made a kind of whooping noise, like the audience at a circus when an acrobat falls into the net. "Eh, dear," she said. "Both your mum and your dad gone, and you only ... "

"Twenty-five," said Opal. "I've still got my stepmother. I could stay here. Be near her."

"Is this Stephanie?" said Jill, as if Opal could have more than one stepmother, and she frowned as she paddled the tint onto the foil and crimped it shut like a pasty. Opal hadn't realized Jill knew Stephanie's name.

"But a *stepmother*," said the lady. "No, you go, love. Make your own way. Bright lights, big city." She made it sound like London or something. Opal wished it was: hundreds of miles away, the farther from Whitby, the better. But an hour away in Leeds would have to do.

She smiled into the mirror.

"You can't pass all that up to stay put here," the lady was saying. "Not with nobody but a wicked stepmother to tie you."

Opal nodded, but inside she was blotting the words out. She wasn't running away. Baz was nothing to her. Baz was the mayor of Nothingtown in Nowhere County. *Free as a bird*, she told herself, *moving on to better things, plenty more fish in the sea.*

———

Where to sleep though? she asked herself, back out on the landing again. Her old room—what was left after indoor plumbing had replaced the outhouses on Mote Street and the bathroom had been carved out of it—didn't seem to have a bed anymore. She stopped in the doorway and stared. The pink woodchip was the same and the fuchsia-pink nets crossed over the window and held with ruffled ties, but her pine bed with the drawers underneath was gone and with it the white unit that made up her dressing table, homework desk, and wardrobe. The room was full of nothing but black sacks with that lumpy shape Opal knew so well. She kicked one gently and felt the scrape and clunk of the bottles inside it. So upstairs she went again, up to the attic, telling herself her bed would be stored there.

But before she reached the top of the stairs, she could see the rough sea of bin-bag tops stretching all the way across to the front wall. There was the odd cardboard-box island, but no furniture at all. If her old mattress was on the floor under a bag of empty brandy bottles, it could stay there.

And so she would have to sleep in her mum's room, in her mum's bed. She came down the attic stairs and edged along the corridor. The door was ajar, and she stretched out a foot to push it all the way open.

The curtains were shut, like always, and the bed was heaped up with pillows and cushions, like always, piled high with quilts and blankets. A nest, a lair. Magazines and a toilet roll, some clothes, some bottles of course, an ashtray and a big soup tin without its label for emptying the ashtray into. Where the quilts and blankets were pushed back and the pillows and cushions were flattened, was a round hole. Tiny. Big enough to hold her mother? Must have been.

She hadn't died here; she had gone to the hospital, admissions, acute medical—or that bit of acute medical that was basically the drying-out ward really—then HD, ICU, and *there* she had died. But it had started here. One night—or one morning more probably—Nicola had climbed in, and she had never climbed out again.

But looking at it, it was her dad dying Opal couldn't get out of her mind. She could picture him, lying in the hospital with a mask over his face, tubes in him, needles on the backs of his hands. Steph would have had to bend close to his mouth to hear him whisper.

"Tekk care ot lass."

Except that was her granddad's voice she was hearing, and it was her granddad who had had the mask and the needles. Her dad never even made it to a bed, pronounced dead on a trolley in Accident and Emergency—or maybe even in the ambulance. Couldn't have been at the house, or they would have taken him straight to the mortuary. And it was A&E Steph had phoned from to tell her.

"Look after Opal," her dad would have said. "Tell her I love her. Let her have something of mine to remember me by."

Which Steph completely hadn't. And Opal wouldn't have chosen anything big—like his camera or bird binoculars or the sound system from the house or anything like that—but by the time his funeral came round, everything was gone. Every last thing. His clothes and his jewelry, even his scratchy bathrobe that hung down to Opal's ankles, that she would have curled up in whenever she wanted to remember him. Although, thinking about it, that bathrobe must have been long gone because he'd got it when he was still with her mum.

Missing out on a keepsake wasn't the half of it, though. And she'd never have known the rest if Steph hadn't gone off for a long weekend and left Michael in charge. One of the envelopes had come that very weekend and Michael, who didn't know he shouldn't, or maybe because he missed her and wished he was still her brother...

Well, he'd phoned to tell her anyway.

THREE

"WHEN'S SHE GETTING BACK?" Opal had asked, the cheap handset creaking from how hard she was gripping it.

"Monday teatime," Michael had said.

Opal took the afternoon off to be on the safe side and was there at three o'clock. At four, Steph came huffing in with her little case on wheels and three carriers of shopping she'd done, and Opal was sitting there with the big brown envelopes—seven of them, still unopened—on the breakfast bar in front of her.

Stephanie's eyes literally bulged as she took in the scene.

"Did Michael give those to you?" she said and then bellowed with her head back. "Michael! Get down here."

"Michael's not in," Opal said.

"Where's he gone and left you here on your own?" She was darting looks all around the kitchen as if Opal might have stolen her knickknacks or spray-canned the walls.

"I let myself in," Opal said. "And I found these in my room."

"Let yourself … ? *Broke* in, you mean?" Steph's voice faded as Opal slid a single Yale key towards her.

"I'll not be needing this again, under the circumstances."

"How long have you had a key to my house?" Stephanie said.

"How long have you been hoarding my mail? I can't make out the postmarks." She bent over and squinted at the nearest one.

"It'll all be junk," Steph said. She had turned up her lip as if she could smell something, but her eyes were still wide. "It wasn't worth sending on to you."

"That's fraud," Opal said. "Letting yourself into your childhood home with your own key isn't breaking and entering, but this here is postal fraud." She tapped the envelope, thrilling at the brisk, snapping sound it made.

Stephanie flinched, then her eyes narrowed. "Childhood home?" she said. "You were no child when you landed here, lady."

"I was nine," said Opal, and for a minute Steph looked confused.

"Nine?" she said and looked down at her spread fingers, curling them back one at a time, counting. "You were going on thirteen."

"I was nine the first time I stayed under this roof."

"Aye, but that was visiting. You were twelve when you moved in and pulled your little stunt."

"Stunt?" Opal repeated, frowning at Stephanie, who flushed.

"Just go," she said. "Before—"

Opal stood, lifting the bale of envelopes and hugging them to her.

"It'll be flyers," said Stephanie. "It'll be nowt."

"We'll see," said Opal. "I'll take my time deciding whether to report the fraud."

"Who'd listen to you? People keep records, you know. You'll have a big, fat file somewhere. All the juicy details."

11

"Juicy?" Opal repeated, frowning again.

"Look, just get out before Michael comes back and sees you."

"Poor Michael," Opal said. "Having you instead of a mother."

"What would you know about mothers?" Steph had said, but her voice was cracking. Opal tried to make her eyes as hard as pebbles, as flat as coins on the front of her face, but she kept hearing those two words—*stunt, juicy*—and she could feel her face tugging to make a frown again.

No way would she remember. Time to go.

———

Would there be spare bedding? When she was small, her one set of Bambi covers was taken off, washed, dried, and put back on again between one night and the next, and Nic's nest was never dismantled and reformed. She looked around the room anyway, wondering where her mother might have kept some extra sheets, and her eye caught the edge of her old single mattress peeping out from beside the wardrobe where it had been stored.

As she hauled it out, the curtain dragged away from one end of the window and although she didn't want to be seen—not tonight, not yet—she couldn't help herself, and she lingered there.

Who lived here now? Who had come in the thirteen years since she'd been gone? Strangers. And they'd stay that way. She'd smile but no more. No chummy chats, no cups of tea. No prying. That was the best of a city. You could be all alone in the crowd. If there was nobody looking, there was nothing to see.

Except . . . straight across at number five, she saw something that troubled her. Because how many people hung those plastic strap things at their doors these days, or put jam pots on the window sills

12

to catch the wasps? How many people polished their windows until they glittered, right into the corners, and had one of those wide flat vases—made for windowsills, she supposed—dead centre in the living room window and another one exactly the same, precisely above it in the bedroom window, as if she'd dropped a plumb line down to make sure they were even? Not many. And how many people had a shopping trolley with a plastic cover to keep it clean as it parked outside their door on its own little plastic mat? Not even as many as that.

Mrs. Pickess, wicked witch of Mote Street, was still around.

Well, she could handle Vonnie Pickess, and at least the others would be strangers. As Opal shuffled farther in to the window to look at the top house, though, a car turned in at the foot of the road, roared up it, braked hard, and turned, coming to a halt crossways on the cobbles. She watched as the driver's door and the house door both opened. A woman crossed the pavement and held out a folded cloth bundle to a young man (in slipping-down jeans and a vest so loose and baggy he might as well have been topless), who was crossing the cobbles to take it from her.

It was Doolal Joshi, she was sure of it. He was the same age as her and they had walked to school together, until they were nine and he turned into a boy and decided he couldn't be seen with a girl. And that was Mrs. Joshi, for sure. She hadn't changed one iota, not a jot—which was the same thing as an iota, whatever they both were. She was still making those sandwiches—Opal scrabbled in her memory for the right word ... *dosas!*—and she must still be running the taxi business, because she had a headpiece on.

So Mrs. Pickess and the Joshis. Not great but not the end of the world.

Doolal got back into his car, revved the engine as if he was getting ready to launch a space rocket, backed up a bit, and roared off down the street again.

Opal turned and pressed her face against the glass, watching until he had gone, and she was still looking when a red Transit van chugged impossibly slowly round the corner and pulled in across the street in front of No. 1. The driver's door slid open and one after the other, four old men climbed down. She laughed out loud. It was the Mote Street Boys, still dressed in their shiny suits and narrow ties. Opal took hold of the rings at the bottom of the window and slid it very quietly open.

"That piano stool's like a bed of nails," said Pep Kendal, knuckling his back.

"It's a good gig," said Big Al. "Steady money."

"Tea dances!" said Jimmy D, the drummer.

"I'll rustle us up some dinner," said Pep. It was his house, Opal knew. His kitchen.

"You're going to cook?" said Mr. Hoadley. "I'll maybe just shoot off home."

"I'm going to *phone*," Pep said. "Pizza."

"Aye well, all right," said Mr. Hoadley. "No olives, mind." He lowered his double bass case carefully out of the back of the van and stepped down.

"Fish!" shouted Big Al. "Pizza?"

Opal caught her lip and waited. The passenger door rocked slowly along its rail and then, hat on the back of his head, white hanky foaming out of his breast pocket, battered trumpet case clutched in one hand, out stepped Fishbo—Mr. Gordon, her old music teacher. How in hell was he still alive? He had already been an old man when she was tiny, and he looked truly ancient now, mummified nearly, all battered and leathery and so skinny that his suit hung off him like Doolal's jeans.

"*Mooooon Reeeeebah*," he sang. "*Wider dan dee miles*."

"Fish!" Pep barked at him. "You know the deal."

"That's the worst of letting him finish with 'Moon River,'" said Mr. Hoadley. "It could be days now."

"Might as well ask my blood to stop flowin' in my veins," said Fishbo.

"Could be arranged," Jimmy D shouted from inside the back of the van. Still complaining, the old men filed into the house and closed the door.

Opal slid the window back down and leaned her head against it. How could it be that they were all still here? Thirteen years, half her lifetime. She'd been to hell and back—well, Whitby—and yet here they all were as if it was yesterday. Just as she left them. People who knew her. Knew her mother was a drunk and her dad had walked out and she'd not been home since she was twelve. So much for being alone in a crowd in the big bad city.

But she couldn't go back. To her old pals at the Co-op coming round with their questions; Jill at the salon and her sympathy; Steph and that look she always had on her face. Baz, the scumbag, most of all.

She had to stay in Mote Street. Those seven brown envelopes she'd got at Steph's house that day, they were a sign that it was meant to be.

———

Back in her bedsit, away from Steph's scorn, she had laid all seven envelopes out on the floor and knelt in front of them. The address was copied out in the same handwriting on the front of each:

Miss O. Jones
c/o 7 Upgang Close
Westcliffe, Whitby
YO21 3DT

It wasn't her mum's writing, even though—she flipped one of the envelopes over—the sender's address was Jones, 6 Mote Street, Leeds. It had made her heart jump up high into her throat, hardening like bubble gum spat into cold water, imagining her mum making these parcels for her, filling them with mementos and gifts for after she was gone. But Nic would never have spent—she peered at the label—three pounds forty-eight on postage, seven times over, and a brand-new envelope each time too, one that hadn't been through the post already with the old address scribbled over.

Holding her lip in between her teeth, Opal worked her thumb under the flap of the first one, and ripped it open.

Not junk mail, but no video of her mum's dying wish either. No velvet roll of diamonds passed down the Jones line through generations, no sepia photographs of flappers and soldier boys, no treasure map, no magic beans, no safe deposit key, no ransom note of pasted newsprint letters—nothing that Opal had ever dreamed or dreaded finding. Just endless letters for Nicola, all opened out flat, envelopes gone. From the gas and the electric, the coal man and the hospital, the poll tax and the phone, the dole and the insurance and the housing assoc—

Opal blinked. Those letters—seven of them from the housing association—were addressed to her. *Miss O. Jones,* and her name had been gone over in highlighter pen.

They were from a woman called Sally Smith at West North West Homes (Leeds), which she knew was what the council was called now it was sold. Opal skimmed through them: condolences, advise, notification, warnings—endless guff about the tenancy, like it was any of her business. As for the rest ... She looked at a gas statement and an electric, and her eyes widened. They weren't reminders and red reminders and threats. These letters were receipts. Even the coal was paid, as far as Opal could tell, which must have been a nice change for the guy after all the years of Nicola trying to settle her debts with anything but money.

But who the hell was paying Nic's bills? And why did Sally Smith and the whole of the rest of West North West Homes (Leeds) think that Opal still lived in Mote Street? She looked at the last letter again, read it properly this time, and saw what it would mean. Then her attention snagged on something else she had missed before: the date in black numbers in the middle of the last letter, highlighted in yellow was 11 June 2010. Today. Opal blinked. This was the last day. She looked at her watch. It read 16.51, and she thought it was slow.

She leapt over to stand beside the window, where the signal was best, and keyed in the number—Sally Smith's direct number—waiting for it to ring and the recorded voice to tell her the office was closed for the day.

"Transfers," said the voice.

"Hello," said Opal. "It's Opal Jones."

"Uh-huh?" said the voice.

"You wrote to me?"

"Uh-huh?"

"Seven times," Opal said.

"And what was this in connection with?"

"The house in Mote Street?"

"Number?"

"Six."

"I meant the case number, flower. It should be on the letter."

Opal had let the paper slip out of her hand, and she knew if she bent to pick it up she'd lose the connection.

"It's umm ... " she said, trying to read it upside down where it lay on the floor.

"Oh, hang on, here it is," said the voice. "It's right here on top of the pile. You've cut this a bit fine, haven't you?"

"Sorry."

"I'll send you out an appointment letter," the voice said, sounding as if she was going to have to write it in her own blood. "Get you in to sign up. Mind you answer this one."

"Sorry," Opal said again.

"Right."

"And sorry you won't get the house back too. If you wanted it. For someone else, I mean."

"Six Mote Street?" Opal could hear the curl in the voice, and she remembered Steph's face from an hour ago. "You're welcome to it, flower. Nobody's exactly queuing up to move *there*, are they?"

———

So here she was. And it would be okay. Because even at twelve, Opal had been good at hiding. Mrs. Pickess and Mrs. Joshi and the rest of them didn't *really* know her and wouldn't have believed it anyway.

In fact, it might not be so bad. Opal raised her head and looked over the road towards No. 3. If the Joshis and Mrs. Pickess and Peppermint Kendal and the Mote Street Boys were still here, was it stupid to hope …? The net curtains covered the windows. And they were thicker than Mrs. Pickess's nets. The house looked blinded by them. Impossible to see inside. Impossible to know who lived there.

Then movement at the edge of her vision made her turn and squint down to the corner again. She blinked and put her hand flat on the glass. It was a tiny little woman, thin as a stick, nylon shopper in hand, almost-finished cigarette in mouth, orange tabard fluttering in the warm evening breeze.

Opal leapt across the bedroom floor, clattered down the stairs, sprinted across the living room, and threw the front door wide.

FOUR

"MARGARET!" SHOUTED OPAL, BOUNDING across the cobbles like a puppy.

Margaret Reid let out a screech like a demon. "*Aaaiiyee!*" She threw her cigarette down on the pavement and opened her arms. "Opal Jones, as I burp and fart! I cannot believe it. Is it truly you?" Her accent, fifty years after she had left Ireland as a bride, was Meath and Leeds curdled together, and Opal let out a clear peal of laughter like a bell as she threw herself into Margaret's arms and hugged her.

"The size of you!"Margaret said. "Have you been stood in a bag of peat all this time? You're a giant, Opal." Opal held on and hugged even harder, drinking in the cocktail that took her back twenty years to when she sat on Margaret's lap for stories: pink floor soap and Elnet hairspray, setting lotion and chip fat, nicotine and a hard day's work in a nylon overall.

"But where had you put yourself? Why were you not there for Nicola's sendoff? I couldn't believe it."

Opal hesitated, but before she could answer, Margaret gasped, making herself cough.

"Lay me down dead!" she said. "What am I thinking? Opal, my soul, I'm so sorry for the loss of your dear mother. You're in my prayers."

At last Opal drew back, so she could look Margaret in the eye.

"For real?"

"Jesus, no!" said Margaret. "If I prayed for you, black sinner that I am, you'd be struck by lightning for sure."

And so Opal managed to dodge the question of where she had been when Nicola, her own dear mother, had been laid to rest—or turned to ash actually—never mind where she had been for the thirteen years beforehand.

"And how are you, Margaret?" she said. "Still working, anyway. How many jobs have you got now? And how's Denny? Is he at the track? Have you still got your dogs? I haven't heard them."

Margaret walked backwards and rested her bony bottom on the painted windowsill of her living room. Her eyes, magnified behind thick glasses and always a bit watery (whether from the smoking, the Elnet, or the floor soap, who could say), were glistening and glittering now, fat tears trembling against her lower lashes.

"Margaret?"

"You don't know?" Margaret said. "You never heard what happened?"

"No," said Opal, faltering. "At least, I don't think so."

"Oh, you'd know if you knew," Margaret said. "Your mother never told you?"

"We didn't ... What is it?"

"And maybe your father didn't *want* to tell you. It's nothing for a child to hear."

"I'm not a child now," said Opal.

"Come inside." Margaret lowered her voice. "Only don't go jumping in the air and cursing when you see Dennis, mind."

Opal shook her head, not understanding, and Margaret fitted her key in the lock and opened the door.

"Here I'm back, Dennis, my soul," she said, "and you will not guess if you live to be Nancy who I've got with me."

"I heard through the window," said Dennis. "Opal Jones has come home."

Margaret's living room was right through the front door, right off the street like Opal's own. She followed her in and turned, peering towards where his armchair had always been. Then the smile froze on her face, and she was sure he must have noticed in the split second before Margaret slammed the door and shut the sunlight out again.

The Dennis Reid she remembered had a blue car and a moustache and two greyhounds called Bill and Ben. He worked in a mattress factory and kept sweeties in one pocket, dog treats in the other, and he used to pretend to mix them up all the time.

And maybe that man was still in there somewhere, but around him, in the last thirteen years—and it must have taken all thirteen, surely—had grown another man. A hulk of a man, a mountain. He was wedged, lapless, into a two-seater settee, beached there; legs splayed wide but still packed hard together, a broad expanse of hairless bloated ankle showing between his trouser hem and slipper top; arms like gammons, elbows pushed out by the bulging ring of his girth, hands—inflated surgical gloves, white and shining—resting dully on the wooden arms of the couch, fingers—uncooked sausage fingers—hanging down.

"Hiya, Mr. Reid," Opal said, shocked out of friendliness by the sight of him.

22

"Cup of tea?" said Margaret. She was hopping about, putting her bag away, getting her fags and lighter out of her pocket, patting at her hair as she peered into the mirror over the fireplace. "Come on through, Opal, and we'll let himself be in peace." But when the kitchen door was closed, her routine flagged, and she gave Opal a look of pure misery as she sank down into a seat at the kitchen table and clasped her hands together on its top.

"What happened to him?" Opal whispered. "Is this the thing you thought I'd have heard?"

Margaret shook her head. "There was a tragedy here on Mote Street, Opal," she said. "Ten years ago this summer. Feels like a lifetime and feels like the blink of an eye." Margaret shook a cigarette out of the packet and lit it. "Ten years of shame and sorrow. Killing Dennis there. And killing me."

"Shame," Opal said, picking on the only word that didn't fit with her idea of a tragedy.

"Remember my daughter, Karen?" Margaret blurted it out, startling Opal. She nodded. "And her husband, Robbie?"

Opal nodded, less certainly. She didn't remember Robbie Southgate. Didn't want to.

"Remember Karen and Robbie's little lad?"

"Craig?" said Opal, brightening. "Of course I do." Craig Southgate was the first baby she had ever been trusted to carry about in a shawl or wheel up and down in a pram, and she had spent the last summer before she left Mote Street watching out for Karen dropping him off and then hotfooting it over to the Reids' to ask if she could take him.

"He's gone," Margaret said. "Disappeared."

"Ran away?"

"Ten years ago," Margaret said. "He was three."

"*Taken*?" said Opal. She hadn't thought about Craig Southgate once in thirteen years, but she could see him as if he was standing in the kitchen beside her. She was imagining reddish hair cut in a short back and sides, tiny teeth like white kernels of corn clenched hard together when he smiled, head tipped right back, like Michael used to do. Margaret hadn't spoken. "Do you mean he was taken?" Opal said again.

"That's what they said. The Mote Street Snatcher. All over the papers it was." Opal watched her take a deep drag, hold it inside her, and then let it out through her nostrils, like a dragon. She had only known Margaret as a grownup while she herself was a child, and she wasn't used to this swimmy feeling of being the one who should think of things to say. She spoke very gently.

"Margaret? You said 'shame.'"

"Aye," Margaret said.

"I can see the tragedy and the sorrow … "

"It was all in the papers," Margaret said again. "Toddler vanished. Snatched in minutes flat. Never seen again." She took another drag, let it out through her mouth this time, blowing it so hard out of her down-turned lips that the jet of smoke kicked back off the tabletop in rolls.

"There's no shame in that," Opal said. "That would make people sorry for you, not make them—"

Margaret was shaking her head. "They don't know," she said. "People left flowers and sent cards, Opal. People sent *money*. They don't know."

Opal didn't want to ask, but she couldn't help herself. "Know what?"

"And if I don't tell *someone* I'll run mad with it pressing on me."
Margaret lifted her head and turned those magnified, headlamp
eyes on her.

"No," Opal said.

"You coming back is a sign," Margaret said. "You've been sent
to me."

"No. I haven't. It's not."

"Let me speak before I burst."

Opal screwed her eyes shut, thinking *no, no, no*. She was escap-
ing—she could admit it inside her head. She was running away. *Free
as a bird, free as a bird.* And if she tried to fit a secret as big as Margaret's inside herself beside all her own secrets, something would
spill over. *Alone in a crowd, free as a bird.*

But Margaret spoke anyway.

FIVE

"Karen..." Her voice cracked on the word, but she cleared her throat and tried again. "Karen went back to work full-time." Opal opened her eyes again. That didn't sound too bad. She had room for that inside her.

"After Craig was...?"

"Before. And if I'm to be fair, she didn't have to. To listen to Karen, you'd think he kept her without two ha'pennies to rub. But Robbie was a good man, a wonderful father. You'll remember him Opal; he was a great friend of your mother's at one time."

"Just a pal," said Opal, shaking her head. "Not a friend. I never knew him really."

"Well, I looked after little Craig for her anyway. I was on early mornings over at Immaculate Heart, and then afternoons for my old girl in Headingley, and in between I used to have the baby."

"I know," said Opal. "I helped, remember."

"Ah, it's no toil to look after a tiny baby, but by the time he was walking, he was a handful. So that's the first thing. Karen went to work and I jiggled and juggled and we just about managed, you know. Most of the time he played out in the yard there. He loved to play in the outhouse."

"In that black hole?" said Opal. She got a cold feeling inside her to think of a little kid in there.

"He liked it," Margaret said, then her voice dropped to a gravelly whisper. "Then the second thing. Dennis decides he wants more space for the dogs, see? And he knocks it down."

"Jesus!" said Opal. "With Craig *inside*?"

"No, Christ! But once his little wee playhouse was gone, Craig started to wander. Any time the back gate wasn't chained shut, he was at the latch. If I took my eye off him, he'd be away.

"And then one fine day—it was a Friday in the middle of the summer, a hot summer just like this one's getting—Karen dropped the babby off and went to work. Now Dennis wasn't feeling too well that day—a hangover is what it was—and he come home from work about ten in the morning—waste of time going in. Craig was in the yard, and when Dennis come back, I said to him that I'd go up and lie on my bed for a sleep and would he . . . " Margaret paused and once again her eyes swam with tears. "What I said was, would he mind out for the babby. Meaning, you know, keep an eye on him. But what *Dennis* thought I meant was would he not go out until Karen had brought Craig, so he could answer the door. That's what Dennis thought I meant. That's what he's said for ten years, and there's no shifting him."

"Jesus," said Opal again. "Denny didn't know Craig was there?"

"No. And he didn't feel like sitting around waiting either. He thought a bit of fresh air would help his head, so he got the dogs and went away along the canal.

"When I got up, Denny was back and Craig was gone and I thought nothing of it. 'Karen's got the babby then?' I said to Dennis.

27

And he said, 'Looks that way' or 'she must have,' or something like that, thinking I was pestering him. And I was mad at that, thinking why was he being rotten to me when *I'd* not poured the beer down his neck. So we never spoke another word to each other the rest of the day. And I thought Karen had come and got the babby and took him to the nursery same as ever."

"So what happened when Karen went to the nursery to get him at the end of the day?" Opal said.

Margaret closed her eyes and shook her head slowly from side to side. Her cup of tea was growing cold, untouched, in front of her, and it felt wrong to Opal to sip at her own even though her mouth was dry and foul, a metallic taste beginning.

"Karen—God love her," Margaret said. "This is the third thing, see? That very day, Karen got asked out on a date. Her and Robbie were over and done with by then. Anyway, this fella she'd been getting to know asked her if she was doing anything that night. And she thought 'Ah, why not,' and she called the nursery and left a message, would her mother hang on to little Craig, keep him overnight and she'd pick him up in the morning. Hoping the date would go well, you know? That was her way. Flesh and blood of my own as she is, I cannot deny that that was the way of her."

"Then what?" asked Opal, the bad taste in her mouth growing.

"And the nursery thought 'hang on to him' meant . . . Ah, it was all garbled and third-hand."

"But why didn't Karen just phone you?" Opal said, before remembering that Margaret and Dennis hadn't had a phone then. Hard to believe now when everyone had mobiles and had everyone's number in them, but when Opal left Mote Street, Margaret had still been knocking on Mrs. Pickess's door to use the telephone when she needed to.

28

"I'm never away from one now," Margaret said, patting the big pouch pocket in the front of her overall. "Ten years too late to be any good." Her voice wobbled, and she sniffed hard before she went on. "It wasn't until the next day, Saturday, going on for eleven in the morning, when Karen turned up here looking for Craig."

"Oh, Margaret," said Opal.

"We searched. All through the house and the yard and lane, all the other yards. The waste ground, the canal path, everywhere. The road up to his nursery, all round there. Shouting and yelling for him."

"But you didn't find him?"

"We asked the neighbors all up this side and your mother and next door. The student houses were empty, but Dennis broke in and searched them too. And everyone kept saying he'd turn up and he wouldn't go far and he was such a right little wanderer—a nomad, old Fishbo called him."

"And what about the night before?" said Opal. "Nobody heard anything? Saw someone?"

Margaret said nothing for a long time, and when she started to speak again, it was very quietly, with her head down.

"We didn't tell them. Couldn't. I couldn't bring myself. Karen—she was hysterical. And Dennis was like a zombie. The thought of looking into everyone's face and saying... We couldn't face the... the..."

"The shame," Opal said, so softly she didn't know if Margaret had heard her. Then she stirred. "Didn't the police tell the neighbors, though? When they were taking statements?"

Now Margaret squeezed her eyes shut as if she was trying to disappear. Like a baby, thinking if she couldn't see anyone then no one could see her.

"The police came, sure enough. But the thought of it. His mother out on the town with a fancy man, Dennis hungover, and me in my bed there. Nobody speaking to each other. We couldn't ... We just ... Opal, you've no idea how they were looking at the lot of us and the questions they were asking, even from what they *did* know."

I've got a pretty good idea, Opal thought, saying nothing. She knew exactly how people looked at you when they had your form in front of them and they knew the worst things about your life and you knew not the slightest thing about theirs.

She put her hand out and took hold of Margaret's, squeezing it gently. This made the tears finally start to fall. "Poor Karen," said Opal. "And you. And poor Dennis too." She turned her head and looked at the living room door, thinking about him sitting there.

"Karen got so she was a stranger to us," Margaret said. "Came round less and less and now we haven't seen her for five years. Not a call, not so much as a card at Christmas. We've lost the both of them. My sister Annie tells me she has a daughter now. I have a grand-daughter, Opal, and I've never clapped eyes on her."

"Margaret," said Opal, "I understand, I really do."

"It's killing me." She leaned forward, her skinny bust flattening against the tabletop.

"But if you tell people now ... " Opal said. "It won't bring him back, and it might make it worse. For Denny and you."

"I don't tell *people*," Margaret said. "I told *you*." She sat up and pulled at her neck as if her overall was strangling her. "No one ever got over it, you know. Mr. Kendal next door and Mrs. Pickess. It's changed her, no matter what you think of her. And the Joshis. The Taylors next to your mother moved away. And your mother was never herself again. And as for Dennis ... he's just going to sit there and die. If I lose Dennis after I've lost Karen and Craig ... "

"So what are you going to do?" Opal said. Margaret only shook her head slowly, more to show sorrow than anything else. Then she sniffed again, stubbed out her latest cigarette in the brimming ashtray, and stood up.

"I'll tell you what I'm going to do," she said. "I'm going to cook the tea. Will you stay?"

"I'm really tired," Opal said, "and not hungry."

"Chips and egg," said Margaret, as if she was dangling a real treat.

"How are you still okay?" said Opal. "How come you're still you when Denny and Karen are lost?"

"I don't know, and that's the truth," said Margaret. "Tough as old boots, me."

But as Opal let herself out the back door, she saw the prescription bottles lined up on the kitchen windowsill, getting on for a dozen of them—bottles, boxes, and blister packs—and she wondered if Margaret, just like Denny, had found a way to dull the pain every day.

SIX

SHE STOPPED IN THE lane and leaned her back against the cool brick of Margaret's yard wall. It made her dizzy to think of the thread that kept life strung together and joined one thing to the next. If Margaret hadn't said "mind out," or if Denny hadn't been hungover, or if the nursery people had paid more attention, or Karen's new man had asked her out on the Saturday night instead of the Friday, Craig would be at his mother's house right now. Or maybe up here at his granny's eating four fried eggs and a pound of chips with his laughing granddad.

And look at how she'd landed back here. Nic didn't ever tell the council that Opal was gone, and someone sent the mail and paid the bills, and Stephanie was gone from the house at the right time, and Opal still had her key, and everything lined up so that exactly when she needed to escape, here was somewhere she could escape to. Another thread, as delicate as a single strand of spider's web, stringing things together, leading you through the forest, but only if you squinted hard enough to see it glinting and held it lightly, barely touching, in case it broke and everything drifted away.

She pushed herself up off the wall and strode down the back lane, across the bottom of the street, up the lane behind her own side, avoiding the front and the sharp eyes of Mrs. Pickess, still second nature after all these years. In her own little yard again, she glanced for the first time at the outhouse door and her pulse quickened. He *played* in one of those? How could any little kid not be scared even *thinking* about going in there, getting stuck in that pitch black, freezing cold, stinking hole? Deep inside her, something shifted, as if a single drop of water had fallen on something dry and tight and a tiny of piece of it had softened, spreading into a bigger part of her.

She shook her head. She was grown up now, and there was nothing to fear. So she put her hand on the outhouse doorknob and twisted it. It turned, but the door wouldn't open. She frowned and tried pushing instead of pulling, even though she was sure it opened out, or it would have banged against your knees when it opened in. Still it wouldn't move. Opal let her breath go; she hadn't realized she'd been holding it.

Back inside again, she started cleaning. She threw out all the food, jars of jam and treacle and lemon curd, then the ashtrays. There was going to be no more smoking in this house, she decided, even though that had been Steph's rule and she would rather it was her own. Opal hadn't smoked since she was fifteen, since Steph had stood over her and made her finish every last one in the packet, making her retch.

"Steady on, love," her dad had said, hovering in the doorway, looking out at them. Opal was on a garden seat on the patio with a bucket in front of her. There were eleven butts and the ash from them in the bucket.

"She needs a lesson, Sandy," Steph had said. "She'll throw up on top of them and then bloody well clean it out."

"Is this supposed to be traumatic or something?" Opal had asked. "Shock to my system kind of thing?" She managed a laugh. "Well, eight of ten for effort, Steph, but you'd need to do more—" then she had belched, a thunderclap, and leaned over the ashy bucket, and her dad had gone inside and closed the door.

Opal shook the memory out her head and dropped in the last of the ashtrays, the Stella Artois one that had been on the non-nest side of her mum's bed for as long as she could remember. "Who is Stella Artois?" she had once asked, rhyming it with *tortoise*, and Nicola had cackled with laughter and made Opal ask it again in front of all of her friends.

Then, looking around the kitchen for more things to chuck out, her eyes landed on the big iron key hanging on its hook at the back of the door. "Duh," she said out loud. No mystery after all. The outhouse door wouldn't open because it was locked. And it could stay locked too. She didn't need to go in there. That soft spreading feeling inside her was only hunger. She should have stayed at Margaret's. Had some tea.

But now she had noticed it, the key was in the corner of her eye every time she moved. Black against the white paint, enormous. She remembered reaching up for it with both hands and the feel of it cold against her skin. But she was grown up now. No reason on earth she shouldn't go and look in the outhouse, just as part of settling in.

So she took the key outside, tried to fit it into the lock on the outhouse door, wiggling it and shoving it, bending down to look through and see what the problem was. The lock was bunged up with something. She stepped to the side and peered in at the high window, amazed that she was tall enough; this window had been far above her head anytime she'd wanted to see out of it when she was a kid.

She had no more luck this time, tall as she might be. The window was completely covered with a layer of fine grey dust. She rubbed, but it was all on the inside, turning the glass milky, showing only her own reflection back to her. The window still opened, but the way it worked—the top half dropping inwards until, about twenty degrees from upright, it hit a metal bracket that stopped it going any farther—meant that she couldn't see a thing even with it as wide as it would go. She rattled the handle one more time then took the key back into the house with her and hung it up, only realising when it took three goes to get it on the hook that her hand was shaking. She breathed in and out, shrinking that feeling down like she'd learned to, twisting it hard, making it so small and so tight that soon it was gone as if it had never been there at all.

Then she locked the back door, went through and locked the front, went upstairs, and dragged her single mattress downstairs into the living room, the coolest room in the house, and lay on it with a cushion off the couch for a pillow and her jacket over her shoulders for a cover.

But some things just won't shrink. Try as she might, Margaret's voice was booming in her head. *You were sent to me, Opal.* Deafening her. *It's a sign.* She turned over on her other side and shut her eyes. She hadn't been sent anywhere. Her little thread wasn't twined to Craig's, not at all.

Then a new thought washed through her with a shudder, like from swallowing aspirin. She rolled onto her back and opened her eyes. What if there was only one thread? And it had dragged little Craig away all these years ago and everything that had happened to her had only happened so she would catch hold of the other end and

35

follow it home? And what if little Craig was still hanging on there somewhere?

She sat up. Margaret was right. This was all about Craig. It wasn't Opal's story at all. Those strange soft feelings inside her? She knew what they were now. She knew what to do.

She was going to find Craig Southgate. Or at least find out what had happened to him. Find his body if that was all there was left of him. That's what she was here for and all the rest of it meant nothing.

Now she felt sleep pulling her. As she drifted down into it, she could see the pink face and wisps of red hair, four ice-white little teeth in a row along the bottom and three along the top. She could feel his hot, fat hand clutching a fistful of her tee-shirt as she tried to balance him on one skinny hip. And once fully asleep, she followed him up and down the aisles of the Co-op, never finding him, calling his name—except it wasn't his name she was calling and it wasn't Craig she was looking for. It was only a dream.

SEVEN

"Fffffsssh," said the woman at Tesco's information desk. "Bad time of year to be looking for a job, love, if I'm honest. All the students have been in last week in front of you."

"I'm not a student, though," Opal said.

"That's a start, right enough," said the woman, twinkling.

"And I'm not looking for a summer job," said Opal. "I'm looking for a real job. I don't mind what shifts I do, I've no kids or owt, and I've got five years of experience."

"With Tesco?" the woman asked.

"The Whitby Co-op," Opal said.

"Why'd you leave?"

"The Co-op or Whitby?" said Opal. "Well, it's the same answer. My mum's from Leeds—I grew up here. And she took ill in last winter, and I had to give up my job and move back to look after her."

"So no kids, but you do have a dependant?"

Opal took a big breath before she answered. "Oh yeah, no. She died. Eight weeks ago."

"Eeh!" the woman said, pressing her hand to her chest. Opal noticed her name badge for the first time—Charlotte. "She died?" Opal's kept her eyes wide open, thinking that would make them stay dry, but they filled up with tears just the same, brimming and spilling in one second flat. She gulped, turned away, and only turned back when the woman pulled gently on her arm.

"Sorry!" Opal said.

"Eeh, love."

"I'm sorry," Opal said. "I'm fine, really. I wouldn't do this at work, I promise." She could feel a flush starting to spread over her neck. She was going to blow this if she couldn't stop crying, but the tears were pulsing out her now, hot and prickly, and everything swam together: her mother and little Craig and *Charlotte* printed there like some kind of sign. "God, I'm so sorry. I just saw your name, that's all."

"Oh, little love," said the woman, putting her hand over her chest and hiding the badge. "Was that your mum's name?"

"No," said Opal. Why hadn't she said yes? Why couldn't she stop crying? People were looking now. Two girls in uniforms standing flirting with the security guard in the doorway broke off and turned to stare at her. Even Charlotte was frowning. "I'm an only child," she said, at last thinking of something sensible. "But I had a little sister, and she died and ... "

"She was called Charlotte," said Charlotte. Opal nodded and, because she was concentrating on imagining a fake little sister and there was no reason that would make her cry, at last the tears started to slow down until, with a huge sigh, she managed to stop them.

"Here," Charlotte said. "Here's a form. You go up to the canteen and get yourself a cup of tea. Mind and put sugar in and get yourself a bun. And in ten minutes, on my break, I'll come up and go over it with you." She patted Opal's hand. "You've had a right bad of time of it, haven't you? But let's see what we can do."

And despite the time of year and the flood of students, despite the crying in front of everyone and having her hair in three plaits because she'd forgotten her straighteners when she moved back home, Opal was as sure as she could be when she left the form behind—with promises from Charlotte to take it up to the office and give it to HR when her shift was over—that she would soon be working again. *Yes*, she had said to nearly all the questions on the form—experience, flexibility, cash handling. Except where she said *no*—sick days, criminal convictions, allergies. She was sure enough to take a hundred pounds out of the machine at the front door and get the bus out to Ikea. She wasn't going to spend another night on a mattress on the floor. Not her, not anymore.

But when she totted it up—the flat-pack bed, the mattress, quilt, pillows, and a change of covers for it—a hundred pounds wasn't nearly enough. She would need to choose what to keep of Nicola's stuff and what to buy of her own, but the thought of moving the nest to a new bed or spreading fresh new things over that sagging old box base gave Opal a sick feeling inside, like when a lift takes all of you up except your stomach. And standing in the Sunday afternoon scrum, the smell of the hotdogs, the wreckage of burst open packing, the rumble and hiss of a hundred families arguing, all the bright certainty from Tesco was gone and this place seemed as broken and hopeless as Mote Street with its bin bags. Opal didn't want to sleep in a bed from here.

———

Back in the city again, she headed for the big charity shop that sold furniture at the far end of North Lane. Of course it would be closed on a Sunday, but she could look and come back in the morning. She had seen a couch in there once—green leather with a back that was the same height all the way round, a fat roll studded with buttons—and anywhere that had that couch would have a good bed too, she was sure of it. Except when she was halfway along the street and could start to focus on the stuff in the window, it wasn't like that green couch at all; it was just tired and flimsy and exactly the kind of furniture lives go wrong on, exactly the ratty old tables people sit around worrying about their little boys who've wandered away and not come back again. And when she got even closer she could see a single bed the very same—the exact same!—as her single bed in her bedsit in the shared house, a bed she'd lain and ached on, cried her heart out on, dragged herself to and from on endless shuffling bathroom trips in her dressing gown. She turned her head to look at the other side of the street and walked on past without stopping.

Only now she was lost, or almost lost—more than she thought she could get in the middle of Leeds, anyway—and her feet were throbbing from the heat and from walking so far in her rope-soled shoes that she could only keep on by curling her toes up and down again with every stride. So when she saw an open doorway and heard music from a radio inside, all she thought of was asking directions. It wasn't until she was picking her way to a counter that she noticed what kind of shop it was.

"Help you?" said a man. He was winding a rope into a coil around his forearm, breathing hard. Opal heard a toilet flush somewhere in the background.

"Hope so," she said. "I think I'm lost."

"Where were you headed?" the man said. He was dressed like some kind of nutty professor—a bow tie and one of those knitted things with no sleeves and all the wavy stripes, brown shoes as shiny as conkers.

"Well," said Opal, "I've been at Ikea, and I'm going to Meanwood."

"Blimey," said the man with a laugh. He finished winding the rope and put it down. "What are you doing down here then? And *what* were you doing in Ikea?"

"I thought we'd agreed not to use that word," said another man, appearing from the back shop, pulling up his zip. This one was wearing paint-splattered overalls, but he talked like the boss. "Flippin' Ikea," he said. "If everyone buys *their* overpriced junk, who'll buy *ours*?"

"I was looking for a bed," said Opal.

"Tah-dah!" said the first man, spreading his arms wide and finishing off with a flourish of his wrists and a flick of his fingers.

"Yeah, right," Opal said, looking around at the burnished wood and smoky velvet upholstery everywhere. This was a proper antique shop—no prices on anything and everything gleaming in the light from the gold and crystal chandeliers.

"Unless…" said the scruffy man, stroking his chin and arching one eyebrow. The dapper man behind the counter scowled, and Opal thought he blushed a little.

"Unless what?" she said.

"What do you think of this?" said the toilet man, beckoning her. "Come through the back and have a look, sweetheart."

Opal hesitated for a moment, but she was pretty sure they were a couple, these two, and that they wouldn't be taking her through the back to tie her up with that blue rope and have their wicked way. She edged round a table piled high with china and followed him.

In the back corridor, he switched on a bare light bulb and nodded at something stacked up against the wall. Opal waited for the bulb to heat up and then snorted.

"Yeah, right," she said again. It was a bed, sure enough, or all the bits to make one anyway. The headboard and footboard leaned against the wall and the side-rail things lay on the floor. And it was magnificent: it was made of some dark wood, halfway between red and black, like the oxblood shoe polish they used to always have in the shoe cleaning box for some reason, even though neither Nicola, Sandy, nor Opal (or anyone else she knew) ever had oxblood shoes. The headboard, almost as tall as she was, had a mop of heavy carving along the top—feathers and blobs and things that looked like pennants snapping in a breeze—and the footboard had studs shaped like chrysanthemums and roses. All four corner posts were fluted and had bulges and skinny bits and looked like posh park railings on the top, or like the plumes you saw on horses at a parade.

"Well?" said the scruffy man.

"Wow," said Opal. "How much is that then?"

"Hundred quid," said the man.

Opal turned to stare at him. "Get out."

"Seriously."

"Why?"

"Can't you tell? Have another look."

"Bog off, Tony," shouted the first man from the front shop. Tony put his hand up in front of his mouth and laughed—tee-hee-hee—shaking his shoulders. Opal turned back to look at the bed again.

"Is it fake?" He shook his head. "Stolen?" He mimed outrage, and Opal grinned. "Um … woodworm?"

"A touch," Tony said. He took a pencil torch out of his back overall pocket and shone it at one of the side bars, showing Opal a tiny round hole there. "Signs of historical infestation," he said. "But they've long gone."

"Will they come back?" Opal said.

"They're not salmon, sweetheart," Tony said, in a way that told Opal he had been asked that silly question a hundred times before and had delivered the same clever answer to everyone.

"I give up then," she said.

"Quitter," said Tony. "You can only have it if you can guess why it's so cheap. Come on: it's staring you in the face."

But Opal only shook her head. "Sorry," she said. "I don't know anything about antiques. But it's really lovely. I would pay more than a hundred pounds if I had it, honest I would."

"Don't be so rotten, Tony," said the man's voice from the front again.

"But I want to keep it!" Tony said. "It'll be fun. Like a game. Guess the... We could call it: Guess the... like one of those, you know."

"Dolly's birthday," Opal said.

"Exactly," said Tony. "Number of beans in the jar. In the window."

"Bog off and *die*!" The other man was hissing now, and Opal started to make her way to the front of the shop.

"Good luck with it," she said. "I'll come back if I have a brainwave," then she let herself out and was walking away when she realised that she hadn't asked them directions. She turned back just as Tony was coming out of the open doorway.

"Yoo-hoo," he said, waving. "You can have it. You don't need to guess."

Opal jogged back. "Really?"

"I might have to share it with you," Tony said. "I'm in the right doghouse."

She followed him back inside again. The other man was sitting on a chair that looked a lot like a throne, his arms folded and his legs crossed, one foot jiggling, making his bow tie quiver. He looked close to tears.

"Does it have a mattress?" Opal said.

"It's in the van," said Tony, "but you *seriously* don't want to see it."

"That's not what's wrong with it, is it? No mattress?"

Tony grinned again and then, shooting a quick look at his partner, he frowned and shushed her.

"It was a crowded room," the man in the throne said. "Anyone can make a mistake."

"It is *safe*, isn't it?" Opal said. "I mean it seems like a right bargain, but if I'm going to get … I don't know … poisoned or something as I sleep—"

"Poisoned?" said Tony.

"Or something. Squashed?"

"Yes, of course it's safe. It's just not something we want in the shop, is it dear?" He smiled at his partner. "Billy went to an auction all by his own little self. I usually go too."

"I didn't have time to have a proper look," Billy said.

"Because you got lost," Tony said.

"I'll take the mattress too," Opal said hurriedly, thinking that Tony was one of those people who didn't get how annoying they were being, even when the person they were annoying was nearly in tears.

"Sight unseen?" said Tony. Opal nodded, thinking that no mattress could possibly have had a harder life than Nicola's, then she took her wallet out and handed over a hundred pounds in crisp twenties. "Do you deliver?" she said. "It's only Meanwood."

"Go on then," said Tony, pocketing the twenties. "Since you're a cash buyer. I'll bring it round for you tonight."

44

Billy recovered then, snapping upright in his throne.

"You dare," he said. "You just bloody dare deliver the damn thing tonight. Where's your sore back now that couldn't even sit in the passenger seat and navigate?"

"Never mind," Opal said quickly. "One of my neighbors has got a van."

EIGHT

She was hoping for Mr. Kendal, of course, when she knocked at No. 1 (he was the only one of the Boys who ever drove the van), but when the door opened, Fishbo was standing there. He squinted into the low sun, and his eyes flashed an unmistakable look of pure panic. Then he put a hand up like a visor, and his faced cleared.

"Baby Girl!" he said. He stepped forward and folded Opal into an embrace, quite crushing considering the bony twigs that his arms were and the grating feel of his shoulder joints, as though all the muscle and gristle—never mind fat—had wasted away.

"Mr. Fish," said Opal. "It's lovely to see you. Who did you think it was then? You looked like you'd seen a ghost."

"You're no ghost," said Fishbo, holding her at arm's length and beaming. Opal could see his teeth slipping, and he clamped his lips down over them and worked them back into place with his tongue. "Now come in and visit with me, girl. Tell me where in the world you've been. Lighting out that way! Leaving us all!" Opal followed him inside, dragging her feet a bit. She had a lot to do and when

Fishbo got enthusiastic, he would start serving drinks and cooking funny food and then he'd get his trumpet out, and it would be hours before you could escape without offending him.

Except she quickly realized that those days were gone. Fishbo went into the living room—these big houses on the corners had a hall behind the front door and a room to either side—and sat down by putting his hands on his knees and letting himself fall into the chair, groaning.

"I went to live with my dad," she said, sitting opposite him.

"Well, ain't that nice?" said Fishbo, although his face clouded briefly. Then he grinned that enormous grin again. "What about your old granddad?"

"He's—" Opal was going to say *dead,* but she remembered just in time how Fishbo used to joke about her being *his* grandchild, on account of how she had what he called "a touch of the tar brush", which he said slapping his knee and wheezing with laughter. It made Opal think of being touched by a wand at her christening, but her mum had flown into a rage when she repeated it. Nic had stormed over the road and shouted things ten times worse through the window of Mr. Kendal's other front room, where Fishbo gave his lessons.

"How come you missed your mama's funeral?" Fishbo said, once he was settled.

"I was in hospital," said Opal. She knew she was safe to tell this to Fishbo. Not many people in the world would hear such a thing and not ask questions, but Fishbo was in the dead centre of his own little world.

"*That* was a fine day," he said. "'In the Sweet Bye and Bye' when they wheeled her in and 'When the Saints Go Marchin' In' when they closed the curtains on her. I set some toes tappin' that day."

"You played?" said Opal. "All of you?"

"Damned crematorium," said Fishbo. "Rules and regulations ten ways from Friday. No, I didn't get to play, but I chose the numbers and it was a fine day. Except for you missin' it." He stopped and stared at the floor for a moment then he went on, skewering her with a look. "You keeping up your practising, Baby Girl?"

"I haven't played for years," Opal said, feeling a bit guilty in spite of herself.

"That's a pity," said Fishbo, shaking his head. His gaze had turned very speculative. "But you could sure pick it up again."

"Maybe," said Opal. "But anyway, how have *you* been?"

Fishbo sucked his teeth and hung his head, the picture of sudden sorrow. "Not good, Baby Girl," he said. "Nothin' but bad news here these days. I've been a-wandering in the wilderness for more years than I can tell you," he said. "But I always thought I'd find my way home." Opal waited, not sure what to say. Fishbo glanced at her. "Norlins," he said.

"Sorry?"

"That damned hurricane! Ain't nothin' left to go home to now. Ain't nowhere to lay down and rest my sorry head now. I'll die here, and that's the end of the story."

"I didn't know you were from New Orleans," said Opal.

Fishbo twitched as if she had pinched him. "What the hell you talking?" he said. "Where did you think I come from? I've always come from Norlins. Everybody knows I do. Why, where would you throw me off to, huh?"

"Sorry!" said Opal. "Blimey, Mr. Fish, I was only twelve the last time I saw you, remember. You don't think about where people are *from* when you're twelve. I thought you were from Mote Street, from Leeds."

"I *sound* like I'm from Leeds?" said Fishbo, scowling.

"No, fair enough, but neither does Margaret and neither does Zula Joshi. I didn't know everybody was supposed to sound the same and look the same till I went to Whitby. God knows I found out quick enough there." At least he was laughing again.

"Yes indeedy, it's a melting pot and no mistake. Meltin' in Mote Street—sounds like a number." And he started snapping his fingers and shaking his shoulders up and down, one at a time, turning his head to watch the shoulder that was rising as if he was surprised.

"So did you lose family?" Opal said.

Fishbo stopped dancing and sat back in the chair, tired out by it already. "Not in the hurricane," he said. "Long, long ago. Lost touch, lost heart, lost everyone."

"Maybe not," Opal said. "I bet you'd have a better chance of getting in touch with them now than before, even. I bet they've got all sorts of agencies, or whatever, trying to sort people out who've got displaced. Hm? Mr. Fish?"

"Long, long ago," said Fishbo. His eyes were closed and his voice was gravelly.

She waited until she was sure he was sleeping and then rose quietly and left the room. She stopped in the hall and wrote a note for Mr. Kendal on the pad of paper by the phone—Mr. Kendal still had a telephone table; who still had a telephone table?—asking if he would mind fetching something heavy in his van if she promised to help lift it.

———

The head and foot of the bed only just went up the stairs, with a lot of creaking from the banisters and a lot of swearing from the three men, while Opal and Fishbo hopped about at the bottom, Opal telling them to mind their backs and Fishbo telling them to be cool and quit the cussing.

When all the bits were upstairs in the front bedroom, the three of them stood panting and looking at it, Jimmy D giving it his gunslinger stare, Big Al squinting and kicking it as if it was a second-hand car, and Pep Kendal grinning.

"Guess how much it was?" said Opal. It looked even better here in the bedroom, twice the size and three times as fancy. She would either have to get rid of the wardrobe or put it where it would stick out over the window, but she didn't care.

"Sorry about all the effin and jeffin, Opal love," said Big Al.

"Go on, guess," she said.

"Pretty penny," said Jimmy D. "You've come up in the world if you've bought the likes of this."

"More to life than dough," said Fishbo. "Lucky for me, cos dough I ain't got, but an idea I surely do."

"Somebody guess," Opal said.

"A grand," said Jimmy D.

"A hundred!" said Opal. "I got it for a hundred quid. Because there's some kind of secret thing wrong with it that only an antiques expert would know, but I've been all over it with a whajcallit, and I can't find any problems."

"Hundred quid?" said Big Al.

"The guys in the shop couldn't get rid of it quick enough," Opal said. "It's like they were embarrassed or something."

Pep Kendal turned right round to stare at her, giving her a screwball look, one eyebrow up and one down. "Are you kidding?" he said. "You really can't see what's wrong with this?" Opal half-smiled, thinking he was joking. The bed looked perfect to her, enormous and extravagant and the kind of bed that lives go right in, where mysteries are solved and lost children found, where tangled threads are spun out into straight strong lines of gold.

"Nope," she said.

"Don't you wanna hear my idea, Baby Girl?" said Fishbo.

"It's not a bed," Pep said.

"What do you mean?" Opal asked, staring at it.

"I'm not gettin' any younger," Fishbo said. "And man-oh-man I do not have the lungs I useta!"

"Oh, yeah!" said Big Al, suddenly striking one of the bedposts with the flat of his hand. "I see it now."

"And jest when I was gettin' to frettin'," said Fishbo.

"Mr. Fish, hang on," Opal said. She turned to Pep. "What do you mean it's not a bed? What is it?"

"It's half of one bed," said Pep, poking the pennants and feathers on the headboard, "and half of another." He pressed the chrysanthemums and roses on the footboard as if they were lift buttons. Opal blinked, then laughed.

"God, yeah!" she said. "That's why it looks so completely mad. It's got twice as many different things as it should have. Fantastic!"

"The more the merrier," Fishbo said. "That's what I'm saying. Two for the price of one."

"Is that what Billy in the shop was so embarrassed about?" Opal said. "I think it's even better."

"Oh, but for a *dealer*," said Jimmy D. "What a red face it would be."

"Well, lucky me," said Opal. "Except—do you think it'll fit together?"

While Jimmy D, Al, and Pep started manhandling the side bars, grunting and softly swearing, Fishbo perched on Nicola's Ali-Baba basket and put a cigarette between his lips, starting to pat his pockets, looking for his lighter.

"No," said Opal. "No smoking."

"Oh, sweet baby," said Fishbo. "You said a whole lot there. If I had never got the taste for these damn things...but I practically growed up in a tabacca fiel', you know." Opal thought the swearing got louder then. "Which brings me back to my idea. I'm a song and dance man, much as a trumpet man, always was. All my life I did all three—singin', dancin', blowin' my horn. That's my life. That's Fishbo. Now, I gotta choose. I don't got the puff no more."

Pep Kendal was sitting back on his heels inside the bed frame—it had gone up without a hitch, iron balls dropping into sockets like putting nuts back into their shells; nothing from Ikea would have slotted together that way—and he stared at Fishbo as if his eyes were taking X-rays of the old man's thoughts before he could turn them into words and speak them.

"And suddenly, here *you* are!" Fishbo said. He put his unlit cigarette behind his ear and gestured broadly, beaming at Opal. "A girl who can blow a horn just the same style as I blow mine and who ain't gonna go takin' over my band on me. I'll be the band leader, the song and dance man, and you be the trumpet. You got the puff for it, Baby Girl. Whaddaya say?"

"Are you getting this?" said Pep to Big Al, who was moving the spring, walking it, bouncing and jangling, over the floor towards the frame.

"Me be in the band?" said Opal. "I haven't even practised for—"

"It's a job," Fishbo said. "I'm offering you a gig."

"Eh, hang on now," said Pep. "You can't just add another member into the band. We're splitting our take five ways already. No offense, love."

"It's okay, Mr. Kendal," Opal said. "I couldn't anyway. I've *got* a job. They phoned me yesterday. Thirty contracted hours and as much overtime as I want." Of course, as well as her job she had her mission; she couldn't take on trumpet practise and travelling to gigs.

"It's Saturdays and Sundays, mostly," Fishbo said.

"If we're looking for a trumpeter, we should hold auditions," said Jimmy D. "No offense, Opal."

Al finished squaring up the spring to the frame and let it go. It fell slowly at first, and then, with a rushing, tinkling sound, it crashed onto the base like a dropped piano and sent up a puff of rust and dust that filled the air and set them all off coughing.

"Jesus, Al!" said Pep. "JD, get Fishbo out of here."

Right enough, Fishbo's eyes were watering and his coughs grew deeper and richer, rattling and gurgling from far inside him. He stood up and put out a shaky hand to take Jimmy's arm and together they shuffled out of the bedroom and closed the door.

"Sounds like you might need those auditions," Opal said. "Is he really still playing the trumpet with that chest?"

"Barely," said Big Al. "Sorry about the dust."

"You're all right," Opal said.

When they were gone, she fetched a duster—she wished she had one of those proper yellow dusters that were edged with red stitches, but she made do with an old tee-shirt—and ran it lovingly all around the swooping lines of the head and footboards, smoothing it over the dips and swells of the four corner posts, and winkling it into all the dark places between the carving. Once, a corner of it snagged and got stuck on a foot post and, pulling on it, she felt something grate. She held her breath, suddenly certain that the bed was going to collapse and she would have to haul it outside and phone the council to take it away, but the duster came free and the bed stood just as before.

That evening she lay in it, banked up on three pillows—they were Nicola's pillows and it was Nicola's covers she was under, but in this bed it was all right somehow. This was the kind of bed people were born and died in; this wouldn't be the first time a young woman had lain under inherited blankets in this bed and put her head on the same pillow where her dead mother had rested hers. But something about the foot post troubled her. She shut one eye and then the other. She looked to the left-hand side and then the right and then she sat up straight and stared.

That right-hand foot post, the one where the duster had snagged, was squint now. The main column was straight like the left one and the big square blob with the vines carved into was still square too, but the ball on top of that had four roses carved on its four sides. And she was looking down the length of the bed at the *left* edge of one rose and the *right* edge of the next one round, instead of at one whole flower, face-on. And the horse-parade plume thing on the top was facing the window, its narrow side to her instead of showing its three feathers like the other one. Opal knelt on the crackling mattress—one look inside the plastic had convinced her she wouldn't unwrap it—and shuffled down to the end. She grabbed the squint plume and twisted it back. It turned without protest back to its proper place. Opal gave it a rub with the hem of her pajama top and started shuffling back up the bed again. Then she stopped, returned to the foot, and twisted the plume the other way.

It turned, and turned, started to wobble and then, without warning, came off in her hand—impossibly heavy—and clunked a chrysanthemum as it fell onto the bed beside her. She stared at the brass threads revealed on the thick peg that had held it in place and peered at the matching brass threads inside the stump of the post, standing decapitated now. Then she rose up on her knees and peered down into the bedpost itself, into the brass-lined cavity there. In it, curled round into the shape of its hiding place, was a thick sheet of yellowed paper folded in two.

Opal reached in to grasp it but then drew her hand back, snapping it against her chest and staring around the dark bedroom, her heart walloping. She could hear something. Somewhere—she couldn't have said if it was above her or below—someone was very quietly weeping.

NINE

FIRST THINGS FIRST, OPAL made damned sure the weeping was real and not some mad ghost-crying she had released from the little brass hidey-hole where it had dwelt. She reached in, grabbed the paper, and pulled it out. The crying just carried on, not any louder or any softer than before.

It was bad enough, though, and she hopped out of bed and put her head round the curtains, looking out into the dark street. Maybe one of the Joshi boys had dumped a girlfriend and she had come to moon under a streetlamp and stare up at his window. But there was no one out there and anyway, the sound was definitely coming from inside. She followed it out into the passage and along to the back of the house and the attic stairs, then climbed them as quietly as she could. She didn't know whether her ears were getting attuned or if she was really getting closer. *Warmer*, as they used to shout playing hunt the thimble. (It was never really a thimble. Who had thimbles? But hunt the ring pull didn't sound the same.) Yes, she was getting *warmer,* and her mouth had gone dry. She would much rather be getting *cooler, cold, stone-cold, in the deep freeze, up at the North pole, Opal.* If there really was someone crying in her attic, the farther away she was, the better. But her feet kept moving her forward all the same.

She was halfway up there now. Who the hell would have broken into her house, gone up to an attic full of bags of booze bottles, and sat down to weep there? The sniffs and sobbing were louder than ever. A tramp? An old friend of her mum's? Then a thought came crashing in so hard and fast she could almost taste it and now her feet *did* stop moving, frozen to the carpet, legs like columns of stone.

The thought was so loud inside her head she couldn't believe it hadn't clanged out all around: it was Craig Southgate. She raced up the rest of the steps and fumbled for the attic light switch. Little Craig—nearly fifteen now—had come to a house he thought was still empty, across the road from his granny's, to look out and . . . but there was no one there. And there was no window up here to look out of anyway.

Then a throat was cleared, and Opal heard footsteps cross an empty space. That was no teenager and there was no empty space to walk across in her attic. It was next door.

She stared at the dividing wall, a single course of bricks. It seemed like she'd got a new neighbor then. Moved in to his dream house and gone straight up to the attic all alone to cry his eyes out. *Welcome to Mote Street,* she thought. *I wonder what brought* you *here?*

Opal slumped for a moment, as the adrenaline left her and a foolish feeling washed into its place. Then she remembered the note in the bedpost and raced back downstairs again. *The piece of paper,* she told herself sternly as she clambered back up onto the bed. *Who said it was a note?*

But it was—or part of one at least. She opened the paper very gently, easing the brittle fold apart, and held it up under the ceiling light (she hadn't got as far as lamps on bedside tables yet). It was handwritten, in pale ink, old-fashioned writing from when children were taught how to write and all used the same loops and curls and the same little flicks joining each letter to the next, like toy elephants nose to tail. *South*, it said at the top of the page. Underneath were these words:

Because bad things happen to little girls

Opal let the note fall onto the bedcover and stared at it. She said it aloud: "South—because bad things happen to little girls." The night was as hot as ever and the dash up the attic stairs to where it was even hotter under the rafters had left a film of sweat across her back, but she shivered now. It was horrible, even though she didn't know what it meant. In fact, it was the worse for that. What was *South*? Someone's name? And what about the rest of it? She couldn't tell if it was a threat or a motto or some kind of…what was the word…*incantation*. As soon as she had it, she pushed *that* thought away.

And the note just stopped there. It started up in the middle of a thought and then it stopped again. She looked inside the bedpost, but she knew it was empty. So where was the rest of it?

Opal smacked her head with her hand and rolled across to the other side. She twisted the left-hand foot post hard, but it wouldn't budge. *Maybe*, she thought, *it goes the other way, mirror-image to its partner*, and she tried reversing. Now there was some movement, but she had tightened it with her first twist, and she had to get up and stand on the floor, bracing herself, wrestling the plume in a two-handed grip before she felt the thread start to give way and could spin it clear.

There was another sheet just like the first. *East*, it said.

when someone finds this after I am gone

But what did it mean? Opal put the two sheets side-by-side, first *east-south*—*when someone finds this after I am gone because bad things happen to little girls.* And then *south-east*—*because bad things happen to little girls when someone finds this after I am gone.* Neither order was all that great. And there was no capital letter to say where it was supposed to start and no full stop to finish it off. Even with both bits, it started in the middle and stopped before the end, only just a bit longer.

Then she smacked her head again. She didn't *have* the start and the end. *South east* was the middle. *North south east west*, it went, round the compass, round the four posts of her bed.

Except her bed wasn't a bed, was it? She stood at the head and squinted hard at all the undulations of the carving, looking for a join. The grain of the wood bloomed and withered in a pattern like a flame and—she had missed this before—there was a tiny hairline crack running up the inside of this top right post. Right the way up, no joins, no secret compartment, no more of the note there. The rest of it, the start and the end, north and west, were with the other headboard, wherever it might be.

She stared down at the footboard again. It looked grotesque with its heads lolling on the covers, and she picked up one of the tops to replace it, wondering whether to put the note back too. *when someone finds this after I am gone.* What if no one had ever found the rest of the note in the headboard? What if it had been destroyed and that's how the foot came to be matched up with the wrong partner? What if she—Opal Jones—was the only someone who had ever found anything?

And suddenly the brass threads screwing shut the secret place where the note had lain for years and years, since little girls learned to write in that loopy way, were glinting in Opal's mind like the golden thread that had brought her here and made Margaret tell the secret that only Opal knew. And in a picture in her head, the little lost boy and the little girl—who sounded pretty lost to Opal—had joined hands and were walking away into darkness, maybe going to be lost forever, unless Opal followed them and brought them home.

Could she do both? She had told Fishbo she didn't have time for another job. Turned him down like a bedspread, as Margaret used to say.

But that's different, she thought, laying the pages of the note on the dressing table and going to screw the tops back onto the bed again. There was no golden thread tying her to Fishbo. He thought there was, of course, because of her suddenly appearing, his old pupil, but he was just an old man who needed a stand-in if he was going to keep up with the rest of his band and not ... what had he said? ... lay down his sorry head and die.

Two mysteries was more than enough, she told herself, getting back into bed and burrowing down. Plus a job. Two mysteries and two jobs would be crazy. Things didn't come in fours, everyone knew that. Things came in threes. Craig Southgate, the little bed girl, and ... a job at Tesco. Except that didn't sound like three; it sounded like two of something and one of something else.

She sat up, punched her pillow (releasing a faint trace of old tobacco), and lay down again, finding herself wondering if Fishbo had really worked in a tobacco field when he was a boy. Big Al and Pep Kendal had rolled their eyes when he said it; Opal had seen them and thought it was pretty mean, when he was old and he thought he was dying and would never go home again because everyone he had to go home to was—

Sitting up this time, she scraped the back of her head on one of the outcrops of carving on the back of the bed; she'd have to watch out for that. She rubbed it roughly as she got up, shrugged out of her pajama shorts, and pulled her leggings back on again. She slid her feet into flip-flops and buttoned her camisole top up to make it look like a tee-shirt if she was lucky.

Things came in threes. Not jobs—unless you were Margaret Reid—but special things. Golden thread things. And she had hold of all three ends now. She was going to find out what happened to Craig, solve the mystery of the little bed girl, and get Fishbo back with his family.

She let herself out of the front door and trotted over the road to tell the boys she was ready to join the band.

TEN

BUT THE TROUBLE WITH having three fine threads of gold twined together to form a rope tying you to three separate quests—one tragic, one mysterious, and one pretty urgent, if Fishbo's cough was anything to go by—was that the induction and training process for a full-time job as a cog in a machine as mighty as Tesco took up a pretty big slice of your time.

And for the first two weeks or so, even when she lay in bed at night, the pick and the rumble, the trays and the dollies, the codes and symbols and substitution rules were all her skull could contain.

She had expected to find herself stacking shelves and she wouldn't have minded. But on her first proper day, she was told that she was shadowing a picker.

"What's that?" Opal said.

"It was in the induction," the team leader said (like anyone had listened). "Picking" turned out be the Tesco word for shopping—they had to have a special word for it. Doing the shopping for all those people who sat at home at their computers instead of coming

62

out and doing their own. Pat, the picker Opal was shadowing to see if she was any good, had been in it since the beginning.

"Twelve years," she said. "Started when there were only two of us and one van. You stick wi' me, love."

"Like a shadow," said Opal.

"Charlotte's got you in here," Pat said. "Put in a word for you. So let's crack on."

Opal turned to look at the device clamped to the edge of the trolley, concentrated hard on the buttons and the little screen.

"You scan the team pad, scan your own badge, scan the customer's badge, and then you're ready to start the pick," said Pat. "It goes frozen, ambient, and then chilled. No booze or fags. If they're on your picking list, they shouldn't be, and you just ignore them."

"Frozen, ambient, chill," said Opal, looking over the list. "What if you can't find something?"

"Substitution rules," said Pat. "Now, I'll find the right shelf and you do the picking."

"Right away?" Opal said. "Whatsisname—the team leader—said we were just to watch at first."

"You're a bright kid," Pat said.

And they wheeled around the quiet shop as smooth as if they were on casters just like the trays. Frozen, ambient, chilled. Round and round, up and down, out to the warehouse, onto the shop floor, tray after tray. By lunchtime, by the time of the postmortem up in the canteen, when Opal was filling in shift sheets, Pat said she could do the afternoon on her own.

"Just go to Customer Services and buzz me if you get stuck. But you won't. You'll be fine. She'll be fine," she called over her shoulder to the team leader, who was checking the substitutions. He stood and came over.

63

"You'll be fine," he said. "The two-packs of cinnamon raisin dan-
ish on special offer instead of three individuals was genius … What's
your name?"

"Opal," said Opal, trying to sound as cold and uninviting as possible. She hadn't missed the way he swept his gaze from her feet up
to her neck and down again.

"Tell Opal about that worst ever," said Pat.

"Aye," said the team leader. "This wasn't training, mind. This was a
live pick, went out to the customer and all." He pulled over a chair and
sat down backwards on it. Pat chuckled in advance. "First thing, the
list said fat-free creamy Greek yoghurt, and this kid picked full-fat
creamy Greek frozen yoghurt dessert instead. But that you can nearly
see if you turn sideways and half shut your eyes." Pat laughed again.

"Wait till you hear this," she said.

"The worst was Silvikrin lemon and lime conditioner for oily hair."
He paused. "That was what the customer asked for. Guess what she
got."

"Lemons and limes?" said Opal.

"If only," Pat said, bursting with it. "Tell her, Dave."

"A baguette," said the team leader. "A crusty baguette. She phoned
us up."

"I'll bet she did," said Opal. "Still, it must have gave her a laugh."
Dave turned to look at her. "And I bet she'd rather have pudding instead of yoghurt than the other way around."

"A laugh's not the point, love," Dave said, the spark of interest
gone from his eyes again. "We had to issue a refund and send a
replacement."

"I dunno," Opal said. "I bet if you entered the mistakes in like a
prize draw or something every week, people wouldn't get so fed up.

If the baguette woman had got a hamper for best mistake of the week kind of thing."

"Anyway," said Dave, standing and replacing the chair, giving her a stern look. "Just to be clear, we do carry out random checks on your work while you're on probation. Checked and double-checked it is." He clipped their pick sheets inside a folder and strode away.

"Poor Dave," Pat said. "He'll fret on that all afternoon now. You're a right live wire, aren't you?" Opal grinned. "Charlotte said you were down in the dumps last week."

"Yeah, no, I was just stressed out," Opal said. "Moving house and all that."

"Have you? Where to?"

"Meanwood," Opal said. "Mote Street." And she watched Pat's round face cloud as she tried to remember what that name meant and then winced when the memory came.

"Mote Street!" she said. "And is it just you? No kiddies or owt?"

"Nope," said Opal. "No kiddies. No no one. Just me." And a lost boy and a lost girl and a lost family in a hurricane.

"Oh well, that's fine then," Pat said, as if the Mote Street Snatcher would still be there ten years later. Would be back again. *They're not salmon*, Opal wanted to say. She glanced at her watch.

"Aye, I suppose we'd best get a move on," Pat said, draining her coffee. "You've only got four picks for the rest of the shift. I'll take a look at each one as you go, if you like."

"Okay," Opal said. "But about that—wouldn't it make more sense to have more than one list up at once?" She had thought so in the morning as they had rolled down *Sugar, Preserves and Home Baking* for the third time to pick up one jar of jam. "If there's two trays can go side by side, anyway, wouldn't it be quicker to have two customers' frozen up and then both of their—"

"Bright kid," said Pat again. "You've cracked it. Depends what's on if you get done, mind. You can either pick slow and fill your shift, or you can pick quick and flatten boxes for an hour at the end."

"Ah," said Opal. "Right. And I suppose you'd get mixed up easier too, eh?"

"Exactly."

And as the days passed and she started working alone, she changed her mind anyway. It would take all the fun out of it to be juggling two or three lists, all mixed up in your head at the same time. Because the fun was the lists themselves, like windows that Opal was allowed to breathe on, scour a clear patch in, peer through, and watch what happened on the other side, where people breakfasted on live yoghurt and blueberries and put prawns in their baked potatoes, drank glass bottles of water called Pellegrino, and spread their bread-machine bread with Breton butter. Or lived on Chunky Monkey ice cream at home but took individual muesli bars and 250ml Innocent smoothies to work where people might see them.

And slowly, as she got the hang of it, her brain freed up again and she could shop for the week for a family of four and spend the whole pick thinking about Fishbo's relatives, or where a kid of three would wander off to if he had his way or—this one had *really* been bothering her—who had paid Nicola's bills and forwarded all the mail on to Whitby.

One of the neighbors, obviously. Who else would have a key? And who else could go in and out without some other neighbor's nose twitching. But which one? Not Mrs. Pickess. She would open letters, right enough—steam them, most likely—but she'd never cough up for gas and electric. Not Pep and Fishbo—they were men and men (as far as Opal had ever seen) didn't go in for much taking care of things. And if Margaret had sent parcels, they would have had letters in them full of love and blessings. The house next door was empty (or had been until that crying man came), and that left only the students (say no more) and the Joshis.

So on Friday night, Opal brought home a bunch of lilies near their date, since she knew that Zula Joshi liked them, took a deep breath, and knocked on the door.

ELEVEN

"I DIDN'T DO IT to get thanked," Zula said, burying her face in the flowers.

"Is that why it was anonymous?" said Opal.

"But these are lovely." She came up with lily pollen all over her cheeks and nose, like bronzer. "Come in, love. Have a cup of tea."

Opal had always loved the Joshis' house when she was small, saucer-eyed at the elephant god in his shrine and the smoking joss sticks, the carpet on the walls, the spangles on the carpets, the mirrored glass droplets on the fringes that hung above the doors. Her favourite thing of all was in the kitchen, where, from hooks suspended underneath the top cupboards where other people might have mugs or ladles, the Joshis had garlands of plastic flowers with light bulbs instead of seeds. Opal had always thought when she grew up she would do without ladles and have lit-up flowers hanging in her kitchen too. So she was pleased when Zula took her past the living rooms to the back of the house, but she stopped dead in the doorway.

"It's changed," she said, taking in the glass cupboard fronts with their silver handles and the grey laminate on the floor. There was a glass table too and stools with suede tops and silver legs.

"About time," said Zula. "I was straight off the plane when I came here, you know, and then I started popping the babies out before I was over the jet lag. Twenty years later when I lifted my head and looked around, I was living in a pantomime."

"I loved your house," Opal said. "Not—I mean, it's lovely now too. What did you do with all the Indiany stuff? The flower lights and all that."

"Scrapped the lot," said Zula. "Tea or coffee? Mind you, I see them on eBay now. Should have kept them."

"And the door things?" said Opal, pointing.

"I still put them up for Divali," Zula said, "but I've got nicer ones now. Not so flashy."

"Coffee," Opal said, trying not to let her disappointment show.

Zula held up one finger and pushed her earpiece in, concentrating, then spoke into the microphone suspended in front of her mouth. "Sanj? Can you go out to Roundhay to Mrs. Pelham. The usual do, only she's a bit early. How long? Thanks, son." Then she smiled at Opal again.

"That's a bit space age, innit?" Opal said. "You were sat at a great big machine before."

"Changed my life, this has," Zula said. "It was like coming off dialysis when I got rid of that switchboard."

"And so anyway, yeah, thank you," said Opal. "About sending me the stuff."

"I was glad to help," said Zula. She was looking at her reflection in one of the glass doors, and she swiped at herself. "What's that on my face?"

"And I think I owe you some money too, don't I? I'll pay you back, but it'll have to be slowly."

"Oh get out," said Zula. "Least I could do."

"What do you mean?" Opal said. "The least you could do how?"

Zula waited with her hand on the kettle and then filled a proper glass coffee pot and put it down on the table with two mugs.

"I always liked Nic," she said. "She was a laugh. And I knew she had never told the council you'd left home."

"Yeah, why was that?" Opal said. "She'd have got a rebate for living on her own."

"Opal," said Zula, looking up at her from under her brows. "Your poor mother." She had great brows for frowning, shaped into blobs in the middle, down to little black spikes at the ends.

"You know what I think?" Opal said. "I think she didn't say owt when I first went because she'd have lost her child benefit and then by the time that stopped, she was too far gone."

Zula was still frowning, then she flipped her microphone out away from her face and seemed to give up the argument.

"Yes, you're right," she said, blowing into her mug. "She didn't go out much to take care of any business towards the end. The last while got a bit … what's the word?" They were quiet for a moment, sipping their coffee, before Zula spoke again. "Where were you, Opal love?"

"Eh?" said Opal. "You forwarded my mail. You know exactly where I—"

"When she was fading, I mean," said Zula. "When she died."

"Why?" Opal said, and she knew her tone was arch but couldn't make it not be. "Did she ask for me, like?"

Zula shifted her eyes away from Opal's face before she answered. "She wasn't herself."

Opal laughed. "Oh, yes, she was. That *was* herself."

"No, it was worse at the end," Zula said. "She was more … distressed. Bad in the night. She used to phone people. Police, Samaritans. Just someone to talk to."

"How do you know?" Opal asked. "Did she phone *you*?"

"I used to stay with her," said Zula. "Sometimes. When she was really upset, I would sleep over there."

Opal could only stare. Zula Joshi left her own comfortable bedroom with its en suite bathroom and stayed all night with Nicola? And Opal knew what Nic was like when she was "distressed" in the night too.

"Is that why the single mattress was stashed in Mum's room?" she said. Zula nodded. "So why the hell do you want her daughter back in the house after all that? I might have been the same. I might have been worse, if I'd had a good go at it."

"But you're not, are you?" Zula was smiling. "And nothing would be as bad as someone coming in and gutting the place to rent out to more rowdy students."

But there was something she wasn't saying, Opal knew. Zula didn't care about rowdy—her own five sons had been rowdy since the day they could walk: football and boom boxes, parties that spilled out into the street and fireworks in the backyard, not to mention the taxis roaring up and down and even, in the early days, getting mended right there outside her front door, Mr. Joshi bent over the bonnet and yelling to a son to floor it while the fumes filled the air.

"How's Mr. Joshi?" Opal asked. "I haven't seen him."

"Buggered off," said Zula and then laughed as Opal choked on her coffee. "To Huddersfield to look at a new motor. He'll be back for his tea. He's fine. Talking about retiring."

"And was he as keen as you to get me back again?"

"I wasn't *keen*," Zula said. *What are you not telling me?* Opal thought, trying to see Zula really clearly without showing how hard she was looking at her.

"Going to all that trouble, " she said. "The highlighter pen."

"No more than I'd do for any friend," said Zula, and Opal was sure she wasn't imagining the flush, the lily pollen yellow against Zula's skin. Because for one thing, Nic was a neighbor, not a friend. And for another, paying the phone and gas and insurance was more than *anyone* would do for a friend. Zula was definitely blushing.

"Phew," she said, fanning herself. "It's my age—hot flushes."

"Power surge," said Opal. "That's what they call them now."

"Bloody hope not," Zula said, tapping her headphones. "These things'll electrocute me."

And because it might have been a hot flush and nothing more, plus because there were more important things to ask about, Opal changed the subject. But she didn't miss the fact that after they stopped talking about the mail and the bills, the hot flushes were gone.

"So how's it been?" she said. "Your lads must all be cracking on now? Any of them married? Any grandchildren?"

"Ha!" said Zula. "That's a laugh. They're all still here! In their twenties and me slaving after them. You should see the size of the washer and dryer I've got out the back there. They're meant for hotels."

"Doesn't that cramp their style a bit?" said Opal.

"What?" Zula said. "Not them. Every Sunday morning I'm tripping over some poor lass that's been sent down to make them tea."

"What does Mr. Joshi say to that then?" said Opal.

"Past caring, same as me," Zula said.

"Better than never seeing them," Opal said, trying to work the conversation round to Margaret and Denny.

"Sure is," Zula said, and as she put her coffee mug down and pulled her black brows together again, Opal realized, just too late, the blind alley she had walked herself into. "I mean, I'm pig sick about Birbal being here at twenty-eight, true enough, but leaving home when you're twelve, Opal. What happened?"

No, Opal told herself. *This is about Craig Southgate. Not about me.* And she rubbed her hands up and down her legs. They were sweating.

"Nothing happened," she said. "No one big thing. Anyway, Mote Street was no place for kids, it turned out."

"Craig," said Zula.

"Yeah," said Opal, trying to sound casual even though she was cheering inside to have finally got the talk round to where it needed to be. "Little Craig. Margaret told me about it. That must have terrible for *you*."

"Me?" said Zula, and she fanned her face again.

"With five kids, on a street where a little boy had gone missing."

"Oh!" said Zula. "I see. Well, Vik was ten by then and he was always tagging along behind Advay and Sanj. Little Craig was a toddler. A baby."

"It must still have been bad, though," Opal said. "Margaret told me how hard you took it."

"Me?"

"Everyone," Opal said. "She said none of the neighbors ever got over it. Even my mum." Zula was staring at her with tears beginning to well up in her eyes.

Margaret *had* said that, hadn't she? Opal hadn't dreamed it. But thinking about it again, it was peculiar. Of course, Craig disappearing was sad—it was tragic—but would neighbors really be so much affected? Ten years on? One of the tears splashed down Zula's cheek. She scrubbed at it and then looked into her hand.

"What *is* that all over my face?"

"And the investigation," Opal went on. "I can hardly imagine it. Poke, poke, poke."

"Now *that*," said Zula, "were hell. Sheer hell. All these coppers. You hear a lot about how they keep going off on courses all the time, learning how to talk to folk, but I never saw any of it. Not ten years ago. Not that day. They had all our lads, one by one; where had they been and who was with them. Even Vik. Ten years old."

"Jamie Bulger," said Opal. "Those kids were ten that took him, weren't they?"

"Aye," Zula said. "I suppose they had to. And I sat in with them, all except Birbal because he was eighteen. And with it being a Saturday morning, of course, they'd all been hanging about, no proper whatyoucallems."

"Alibis."

"That's them. If it had been the Friday they'd have been at school and then football and we picked them up and went straight to a party at my auntie's, and they'd not have had to go through it."

"If it had been the Friday," Opal repeated.

"Aye," Zula said. "But seeing it wasn't, the police had a hundred questions. Had they seen him and did they ever play with him, did they ever make him do things for a laugh, play jokes on him, had they ever made him cry."

"Jesus," said Opal.

"And Doolal lost it. Said how come they were coming down like a ton of bricks on us instead of going out trying to find the little lad. And—oh, Opal, he said some terrible things."

"Like what?" Opal said.

74

"He said they were only pestering us because we were Indian and instead of trying to make something out of nothing with five lads, how about the other end of the street and all those single men that hung around together."

"My God," Opal said. "Did Pep and them ever find out he'd said it?"

"No," said Zula, grimly. "And neither did his father, I can tell you. But I gave him a belt across the backside he's probably still feeling now. Sixteen and six feet, just the same. I'd *die* if Pep and Fishbo ever knew about that."

"That's right," said Opal. "Mr. Fish was a friend of yours, wasn't he. Didn't he work for you?"

"He did," said Zula. "He drove one of our cabs."

"Until he had a smash-up and stopped again, right?"

"Right," said Zula. She was giving Opal the hard, head down stare again. "Fancy you remembering that after all these years."

"Anyway, Margaret said the police reckoned Craig was snatched, because he didn't have time to wander off," Opal said, and she was glad to see that Zula seemed happy to talk about Craig some more. "So he couldn't have been snatched by a neighbor. They wouldn't have had time to take him away and then get back here again. In time."

"That's right," Zula said. "Not in the time." Then, to Opal's horror, she gave a sly glance from the corner of her eye. "Because only minutes after he was gone, Margaret and Karen were turning the streets upside down looking for him."

"Yeah, that's what Margaret told me," Opal said.

Zula nodded. "Me too."

And then the silence between them stretched until it was singing, until it seemed it would have to snap, both of them waiting.

Opal had been nursing her empty cup, but she put it down now, cursing inside as it rattled on the glass top of the table.

"I better go," she said, trying to keep her voice steady. "I'm keeping you back."

But Zula put a hand out and laid it firmly on Opal's arm "So what are you going to do with yourself then? Got a job lined up? What plans?"

"I've got a job, and I'm going to start my trumpet up again. Talking of rowdy."

"Still on the trumpet, eh?" said Zula. "No other hobbies?"

Opal shrugged. Zula was still holding on to her and her grip was impressive. Opal had to work at not pulling her arm away.

"Not got a canoe in that backyard, eh?" Zula forced a laugh out from behind a stiff smile.

"A canoe?"

"Or—I don't know—a mountain bike or a potter's wheel... I thought all you young ones went in for hobbies with loads of fancy equipment these days. You should see our garages. That's why we always have three cars parked up here. The lock-ups are full of sailboards and BMXs."

"And potter's wheels," said Opal. "I haven't even got my own trumpet anymore. Fishbo's going to lend me one."

"He's a good neighbor," said Zula, walking Opal to the front door. "Him and Pep."

"They helped me out bringing my new bed home," Opal said. "Took it upstairs, put it together and everything."

"But if you've any work wants doing, proper work I mean, you come to us, love." She had hold of Opal's arm again. "The Mote Street Boys aren't boys any more. You get my lads on it."

"On what?" said Opal.

"Like if you want any renovations doing," Zula said. She had let go and was pleating and repleating the curtain that hung in front of her alcove where the coats were. "Any DIY. If you want anything doing out in the yard. Any improvements."

"I thought you didn't want a lot of noise," said Opal, but Zula didn't smile back at her.

"Just that nothing's ever been done at your mother's, has it? And I was thinking if you wanted to make any big changes in the house or out in the yard or anything, the lads could help you."

"Thanks," said Opal, "but I don't think I'll be getting the builders in just yet. I'm saving up for another two plates so I can have a tea party."

"So no major works in the pipeline," Zula said. She let the curtain drop and opened the door. "Still, let us know if we can ever help you. Don't go struggling away on your own."

"I won't," said Opal, stepping out. "Bye."

TWELVE

The door shut right on her heels. Opal knew Zula felt the cold, never found Leeds warm enough to leave her front door open, even after all these years. Even tonight when the evening air settling down over Mote Street made Opal think of the way Steph used heat up a dish of stew and then roll a disc of raw dough over the top of it, pressing the edges down, trapping the steam inside. She blew upwards into her hair and downwards into the neck of her shirt. It wasn't *just* the heat of the evening making her prickle all over. That she knew. It was the memory of that firm grip on her arm, that hard look right into her eyes, and that wretched failed attempt at a light voice and laughter. *Anything doing in the house. Or out in the yard. Changes in the house. Or out in the yard.* The house made sense. But that tiny little square of concrete? What would want doing there? All it was, was a place to hang the washing and keep the bins. Plus the outhouse.

"Oi!"

The voice made Opal start and sent her pulsing thrumming. She looked wildly round and saw what she'd missed before: a red, white, and blue Tesco van parked outside her door. The driver hopped down and wiggled his eyebrows at her.

"You were miles away there!" he said. "Are you number four, love?"

"Six," said Opal.

"Well, can you tekk these for number four?" He had opened the back of the van and dumped out three of the flimsy carrier bags at his feet. "There's nobody in."

"Are you supposed—" Opal pressed her lips together to stop the end of the sentence coming out. Of course, he wasn't. The customer was supposed to be there for the delivery; if they weren't, the driver certainly shouldn't leave it with any Tom, Dick, or Harry next door to be poisoned. Or even someone who lived on packets and would leave a seafood salad on a sunny windowsill for five hours, not thinking. But she didn't want to turn into Dave, the team leader.

"Aye, fine," she said. "Should I sign for them?" And she scrawled her name, Opal Jones, and tried to remember that thing Steph always wrote on her paperwork from the social club when she signed instead of someone who wasn't there, the same thing people wrote on your formal letters to let you know you weren't worth the boss's attention and it was the tea lady or janitor or someone looking after your case. But she couldn't remember, so she just left Opal Jones signed beside the name FF Gilbert, with nothing to explain.

Once the driver had gone, she wished she hadn't had that thought about poison and salmonella. Because now she couldn't bring herself to leave the bags behind the front door, and she couldn't fit them all into her little fridge, even bare as it was, so she was going to have rummage through them. Through someone else's stuff, someone's private things. An only child—Michael was so much younger than her and was kept as far from her as Steph could get him—Opal had never had her clothes borrowed, felt-tips left to dry with their tops off, hair mousse used up before a big party. If she had ever kept a diary, no one would have forced the little gold lock and read it. Plus, Nicola never even hid stuff that no kid would want to know—wafting about in the mornings with her kimono flying in two wings behind her, contraceptive pills kept in the soap dish to remind her to take them, letters from the rent office sitting on the kitchen table with Nicola's planned disputes over the sums written in red to help remind her what to say when she phoned them, ranting, from one of those public phones like big plastic helmets in a row down at the Arndale Centre where anyone—even someone from Opal's class—might hear her.

So on two counts, Opal hated poking and prying so much it was like a phobia nearly. She didn't mind asking questions—people could always decide not answer them, after all—but pawing through private *things* made her feel queasy in the same way she'd sometimes get in Baz's car with its soft suspension and dirty engine.

Standing up straight, with her eyes and nose as far away as they could be and still have her hands reach to where they needed—the way nurses stand to change dressings, keeping out of it even when they're in it—Opal untied the bag handles and looked inside. There were no dirty magazines, no three-litre bottles of cheap cider, nothing like that. Just white sliced, polyunsaturated, mild cheddar type of thing. Oven chips, lasagne, and peas. A lot of tins. But Opal didn't look at the ambient; she packed the chilled into her fridge and managed to squeeze everything frozen except the chips into the ice-cube bit at the top, so she wrapped the chips in three issues of the free paper, planning to swap them over with the peas if the crying neighbor was more than an hour or two.

And then back to Zula, that look she had given Opal from right in the corner of her eye. She hadn't imagined it. She might have imagined the rest—or picked it up wrong, made something of nothing—but that look had been real, quick and furtive as a little mouse dashing out of sight when the lights came on.

But how could Opal suspect Zula, or any of those five boys that she might be protecting, of knowing something they shouldn't about Baby Craig? How could she even *think* those things about the woman who had—face it—given Opal a home? Except that was one of the things she might just be imagining: that niggling question of why Zula so much wanted Nicola's daughter back in Mote Street, why she made out like Nic herself was such a saint all of a sudden, why she cared so much about Opal having fun—mountain biking?—and what would make her offer free labour for the very "renovations" she said she couldn't face if new people came to live there.

Opal was staring out of the kitchen into the yard, moving from foot to foot, making the evening sunlight dazzle through the smears on her just-washed window, when a soft noise—hardly a knock at all—came at the door. Had someone tried the handle? She stepped quietly towards the front of the house, and the knock came again.

For some reason, when she opened it, the words Jill had sung to her in the salon on her last Saturday came back to her. *In a something, something wood, a little old man at the window stood.* Of course, he was at the door and he wasn't really old, she realized when she looked properly at him. Forty maybe, but tired with it. It was just the way he was standing, planted on the step as if he'd been there for hours. (*Had* he tried the door?) Or as if he'd been placed there, like a statue, for decoration. *Or actually*, Opal thought, *not a statue, but a carving.* Like the chainsaw carvings at the garden centres, eagles and warriors and three monkeys one on top of the other to make a totem pole.

"Hello," said Opal, trying not to let her voice go up at the end.

"Hiya," said the man. He rubbed his hand up and down the leg of his jeans before holding it out to her, and some kind of reddish dust flew out in a cloud from either his skin or jeans, Opal couldn't tell which.

She took his hand and let him shake hers up and down once each way, feeling herself flushing. She had hardly ever shaken anyone's hand in her life and always hated it, not knowing how it was supposed to be done, when to stop, but this man's hand was as sure and steady as the latch that swung up and down on her cart at the Co-op, locking the cage.

"I think you've got something for me," he said, making Opal blink. Was he one of Nicola's friends? A boyfriend? Had he left something behind here, something that she'd heaved into her wheelie bin without looking at and that he could sue her for?

"I don't think so," Opal said, noticing over his shoulder that one of the Joshi boys—not Doolal, one of the younger ones she hadn't sorted out again yet—was standing watching. She relaxed and went as far as to lean against the door jamb. "I can't think what it is, anyway."

The little man frowned and looked down at a piece of paper in his hand. As he moved his head, more of the red dust flew out of his hair.

"The driver's note says next door," he said. "And the other side's empty."

"Oh God, yes!" said Opal. All the puzzling over Zula had driven it clean out of her brain. "God, sorry. Your shopping. Mr. ... Gibson, was it? I've got it right here." Vik or Advay or whoever it was nodded slightly and turned away. "I'm Opal, by the way. Pleased to meet you." He stuck out his hand again and shook hers up and down like before, like someone at a slot machine.

"Hiya," he said again.

"I hope you don't think I was being nosy, but I just split it up a bit and put the cold stuff away. This weather, you know?" She was calling over her shoulder, hopping like a bird around the kitchen, shoving the three bagfuls back together. She brought them to him, then remembered the chips and went back again. He smiled as she handed over the newspaper parcel.

"Thanks," he said. "It won't happen again."

"I don't mind," Opal said, thinking that anyone who cried as much as this man, all alone in his house at night, could do with a friend. She looked closely at him to see if his eyes were red or his nose swollen, now that she knew who he was, but the bags under his eyes might have been from tiredness or age. Or from that red dust he had all over him. "In fact, you know, you can enter up to nine alternative delivery addresses. You don't have to do it on the nod. The next driver might be a stickler, or what have you."

"Nine?" said the man, his eyebrows shooting upwards, turning his forehead to corduroy and showing white crows feet at the corners of his eyes where the dust had missed. He looked over his shoulder. "We've only got seven neighbors."

Opal laughed. "And the students don't count," she said. "Even when they're here. They'd eat the lot and deny it! But Mrs. Pickess over there's always in. And Denn—"

He nodded but he wasn't smiling, and he was stepping away from her.

"Thanks," he lobbed at her, which shut her up. She was only trying to help. He went inside No. 4 and closed the door firmly. Opal was still standing there, hands on her hips, face blank, when Vonnie Pickess pushed aside her fly curtain and peered out.

"Did I just hear my name?" she called.

Opal managed not to groan. She'd had a good run, going in and out the back and washing her front windows *after* she'd seen Mrs. Pickess going for a bus, but she'd have to face it sometime.

"Hiya, Mrs. P.," she said. "The new neighbor was just wondering about who could take in deliveries."

"I wouldn't want to push myself forward," said Mrs. Pickess. "I've tried to be friendly already and got my nose bitten off for me. Never even got his name out of him." Opal shifted her weight from side to side; Mrs. Pickess was speaking very loud, probably hoping her voice would carry in and he'd come out with some letters of introduction. Then she lowered it. "What is it? What's he called, Mr. Hoity-toity?"

Opal opened her mouth to tell her but then closed it again. He hadn't said, had he? She'd said hers and he'd just said hello. That was a bit funny.

"I didn't catch it," Opal said. But something else had snagged Mrs. Pickess's attention now.

"What did you use on these blessed windows?" she said. "Look at the state of that."

"First pass," said Opal. She had used washing up liquid and dried them with a towel.

"A home can tell between a broom and a cat's lick," Mrs. Pickess said. Opal thought she couldn't have sounded more like a witch if she'd tried, never mind what did that even mean? "My mother," Mrs. Pickess continued, "used nothing but vinegar and newspaper, cleaned her step every day with a nub of— What's that?" She was bent over looking down at Opal's step, which had probably once been as red and shining as Mrs. Pickess's and her mother's before her, but which had been bare grey in the middle and faded orange at the edges as long as Opal could remember. "What have you been putting on here, Opal?" She crouched down and dabbed a finger into the film of crumbly red dust the neighbor man had shaken off himself, standing there.

Opal bent down too. Mrs. Pickess was staring at her finger as if there were bugs crawling on it, but Opal brought a pinch of it up to her nose and breathed in the scent she hadn't noticed when the little man had been standing there.

"It's sawdust," she said, thinking again about the garden-centre carvings.

"Well, it wants sweeping," said Mrs. Pickess. "This int a butchers. You get that swept up and I'll do over your windows."

"Tomorrow," said Opal, firmly. She wanted to speak to Mrs. Pickess—of course she did, living right next door to where Craig had gone missing and always watching—but not tonight. "It's my day off. Come over and have a coffee then." Mrs. Pickess's eyes flashed with sudden fire at the thought of getting a good look inside Opal's house and not having to content herself with what she could pick out through the window, so she trotted back over the road without protesting.

Opal went to close up her ice cube compartment and her fridge—left hanging open and whirring away in the hot kitchen—and from next door she heard the unmistakable grating pop of someone stabbing the film on a tray of food for the microwave. Lasagne. Then she listened again at the sound of gulps and a rough, sawdusty sob that turned into a cough. *Lasagne and bitter tears*, she thought. *Why in the name of God did he move here?*

THIRTEEN

A FULL-TIME PICKING SHIFT for dot com was six to two, which was terrible for buses on a Saturday morning—Opal thought about getting a bike, maybe even a mountain bike to startle an explanation out of Zula Joshi—but ideal for working on quests in the afternoons. Saturday afternoon saw her back at Billy and Tony's—Walrus Antiques, it was called—waiting for a break in the customers so she could pick brains. She sat in the chair where Billy'd had had his sulk and she pretended to read her magazine, but no makeup tips or keep-your-man quiz in the world could compete with the problems pressing down on the lives of the other half: a cleaner who couldn't be trusted with crystal droplets, twins who would have to be kept away from satinwood, a kitchen in a cellar with a turn in the stairs that no chapel pew could get round even if you greased it with butter. Tony gave up explaining how to measure the cubic space of the tightest corner and went through the back to saw down a piece of doweling for them to take away. Meantime, one of the other couples had fallen out over a print of some sheep in a gold oval and left, so

Billy turned to Opal with rolling eyes and asked if she'd slept well. He gave her a good look up and down, like you'd expect someone in cuff links and brogues to give to someone in leggings and flip-flops, but he was smiling.

"Excuse me," said a tall thin woman with those brutal rectangular glasses. "We were first." Her partner, Opal decided as she looked at him, had been hounded into the same specs and a haircut that looked like a mop spread out to dry on his head. He seemed as unhappy about it as he was about the set of six dining chairs his wife was standing guard over with her arms folded and her chin high.

"Madam?" said Billy, and Opal raised her mag to hide her face. The preamble "Well, aren't you a right little—" hung in the air.

"What's your best price?" the woman said.

"Yes, they are beautiful, aren't they?" Billy said. "Arts and crafts, eighteen nineties."

"They need reupholstered," she countered.

"The tapestry *is* original."

"The stuffing's coming out."

"Some attention wouldn't go amiss."

The male part of the pair chipped in: "They're bloody uncomfortable, Ash."

"Posture," said his wife.

"Piles?" said Billy. Opal snorted. "I do beg your pardon. Hemorrhoids, I should say."

"And they won't go with the table," the man threw in.

"Well they'll juxtapose, of course."

"Right," said Billy. "That's it. You've said the J word. Thanks for stopping by."

"What?" said the woman. "Is that a joke?"

"Seriously," Billy said. "We don't do juxtaposition here. We do matching, fitting, nearly fitting, toning, and clashing. Take your pick. What kind of table is it you have, anyway?"

"Ikea," said the man.

His wife hissed like a cat. "Modernist," she said, but the fight had gone out of her. They took a card from the till and left.

"Poor bugger," said Opal when they had gone.

"Who me?" said Billy. "I know. What I have to put up with."

"No, him," Opal said. "You don't have to put up with *her*."

"I have to put up with you, though. What is it now?"

"I worked it out," Opal said.

"Congratulations. Have you come back for a table with four piano legs? Chaise longue with some wardrobe doors?"

"At least you're laughing," said Opal. Tony ushered the couple, their diagram, and their length of dowelling back through the shop and out of the door.

"It took Billy all night, a curry, and a crate of stout to see it," Tony said. He hung his little hacksaw from one of the loops on his overalls and wiped the dust off his hands with a red bandana. "Are you sure they weren't going to buy those chairs, Billy-boy? I heard you at that poor cow."

"Best price!" Billy huffed.

"I've told you before, we're not an adoption agency," Tony said, sinking down onto one of the arts and crafts chairs and pulling another forward to prop his feet on. "Make us a cup of tea," he added. "Ooh, that fellow was right, you know. They are a bit hard on the old bumbeleary. Maybe we should sell them in twos as hall chairs. I'll take four out the back and stash them."

"Can I just ask?" Opal said, not sure whether to be offended that they so obviously didn't think she was a customer or flattered they had given up the shopkeeper pose and funny voices they had used when the real customers were here.

"Sorry, love," Tony said. "What are you after today?"

"Where did you get the bed?"

"No good, flower, we phoned," said Billy. "They haven't got the other halves. Don't think it didn't occur. Oh, we weren't above that lark at one time, were we Tone?"

"What lark?" said Opal.

"Remember those poxy antique fairs?" said Billy. Tony was carrying a pair of chairs, one upside-down on the other like a Jack in playing cards, and Billy leaned after him, shouting, laughing again. "Tony? Remember? We used to take two stands instead of one—a table or a grotty little stall in a community centre and we'd each take a pile of separate stuff, only I'd take one of a pair of vases and Tony would take the other. I'd put mine in a box with a load of crap, stick a fiver on it, and Tony'd have his front and centre, fifty quid. You wouldn't believe the bidding that went on. Three hundred for Italian majolica sometimes. And as soon as whoever had left the room we'd each take out another one and start again."

"Should you be telling people that?" said Opal.

"What people?" Billy said, looking around. "Oh, you mean *you*! Well, it was a long time ago now."

"When times were hard and friends were few," said Tony coming back with three mugs of tea. "That's not what this auction was up to, anyway. They had a laugh at us, but they haven't a clue where the other pieces are."

"Did they try to track them down?" Opal said.

"Track them ...?" said Billy.

"I want to try to find them. So—thanks for the tea, by the way— can you tell me what auction place it was?"

89

"Find them how?" said Tony.

"I don't know," Opal said. "I've never done it before." Which made both of them laugh at her. "But I'll tell you this: if I do it, I'll split them with you. You get one bed and I get the other."

Billy and Tony shared a look, eyebrows high and lips pursed, sizing up the deal.

"You're on," Tony said. "In return for telling you where the two halves came from—"

"And buying the other two halves when I find them," Opal broke in. "If they're for sale. I don't have that kind of cash."

"Cheeky!" said Billy. "Oh, fair enough, go on then. You find the bits and we'll stump up. It was Claypole's at Northallerton."

"Aw, great," said Opal. "How am I going to get all the way up there? You're not going back for any reason anytime soon, are you?"

"Forget it," Billy said. "I took enough of a slagging for that bid. I'm not going back up there with my bloodhound and magnifying glass like—"

"Miss Marple," offered Tony, smirking. "So which bed do we get anyway, love? If you find them. Are you particular?"

"You get the headboard we've got already and the new footboard," Opal said. "I keep the foot and take the new head. And the side bits and the spring. And the mattress."

"Which was which again?" Tony said. "I can't remember."

"Oh, let it unfold," said Billy. "Chances are it'll never—no offense."

"None taken," said Opal and finished her tea. The door dinged and another couple in retro clothes and ugly haircuts come in.

"We're looking for a pair of chairs to stand either side of a coat stand in our front hall," the woman said, and Billy stood to help them.

FOURTEEN

SHE SHOULD HAVE GONE straight home and waited for Mrs. Pickess. Of course she should. For one, it was rude not to be there good and early; for another, Craig Southgate was the most important thing she had to do. He was *now*—or not too long ago, anyway—and the little bed girl was in antique times for all Opal could tell from the brittle yellow paper and the loopy writing. But the problem was that if Zula Joshi really did know more than she should about what day Craig went missing and if Mrs. Pickess remembered something useful, Opal would have to tell someone. And then it would be the police and the papers and wondering for the rest of her life if she'd done the right thing. So she stopped at the bottom of Mote Street and knocked on Fishbo's door before Mrs. Pickess could see her.

At least finding someone's long-lost family wasn't the kind of thing you'd ever kick yourself for.

"Baby Girl!" said Fishbo. "I thought you'd forgotten me. Now step right in. I'm all ready." He shuffled aside and pointed Opal towards the right-hand room, the music room, which was away from the shared wall so that Fishbo's pupils could squeak and honk their way towards a tune all day, and the Mote Street Boys could squeak and honk their way back again all night and blame it on jazz. It was just the way Opal remembered it: last decorated by the last resident who cared about wallpaper, only more rusted now with another ten years of nicotine clinging to the cornice and the lampshades. She looked at herself in the mirror hanging by a chain above the tiled fireplace, remembering when she had been too small to see anything in it except the reflection of the opposite wall. The sideboard was still loaded with sheet music, skeletons of dismantled trumpets, scrabbled tangles of guitar strings, and a bent cymbal with a rash of apple and bananas stickers spreading over it. There was the same old couch and the same three chairs, ashtrays on the arms, shoes kicked off half under the frills, folded newspapers sliding down the sides. There was the same coffee table covered in opened mail, tea mugs, smeared plates with drying bacon rinds.

The little table beside Fishbo's armchair was the same too—a brimming ashtray, a bottle of something Opal had called "Mr. Fish's medicine for his throat" but that she now saw was Southern Comfort, three cans of coke left in a plastic noose made for six, and a sticky glass almost empty. His chair itself had flattened and sagged and been bolstered up again with new cushions, too bright against all the fawn and beige of spilled coffee and tobacco. In the centre of the room, as always, there was a music stand, a hard chair, and an open trumpet case on it, the horn itself glittering with polish.

"Can I tidy up a bit for you?" Opal said, before she could help it. It never used to bother her, the cans and the bacon rind, but now a little thrill of something unwelcome went through her, like running past railings with a stick and letting it rap against them. It was too much to be in this room again, as if she would go back across the road and find Nicola there, glass sticky with brandy, different ashtray just as full.

"Women!" Fishbo said. "All the same! Cain't let a man *be*."

"I'm just saying," said Opal.

"Well, save your damn breath to blow your damn horn," said Fishbo. He let himself fall into his armchair, put one claw on each armrest, looking like some kind of Bond villain or something, and nodded at the trumpet, waiting there, pulsing with the late sunlight filtering in the window.

Opal picked it up and tried the keys. They were smooth and free and she bit her tongue to keep from asking how come they could all keep their instruments like new pins and live in such a pigsty. That was one of Vonnie Pickess's expressions—"like a new pin"—familiar from when she used to regale Margaret or Nicola or anyone who would listen about what a palace No. 1 had been before Mrs. Kendal gave Pep up as a bad job and moved back to Derby.

It had been ten years since she had put a trumpet to her lips, but everything about it was as familiar as if she played for an hour every day: the nudge of the rim against her bottom teeth, the crackle in her ears as she built up the pressure of her breath ready to blow, the forgotten—until remembered with a jolt—reflection of her own face in the back of the flare. She wiggled her eyebrows at Fishbo, cocked her elbows, and started softly to play.

Not good. What leapt to mind was Pinocchio trying to speak and finding out he was a donkey. She took the mouthpiece away with a jerk, apologised to Fishbo (who was sitting bolt upright with the shock), and tried again. Another sliding, farting groan belched out of the flare and ended with a screech like nails on a blackboard.

"Man, oh man," said Fishbo.

"Bloody hell," said Opal. "Scales?"

93

"Scales, baby."

"And I'll put a baffle in."

After twenty minutes, it wasn't so bad. Her fingering and her breath control were coming back to her, the notes were holding steady, and the rasping had stopped, but her cheek muscles were aching. She took the mouthpiece off, polished it, emptied the condensation from the spit valve, and placed the trumpet flare down on the seat of the hard chair.

"I wish I'd practised," she said, remembering Steph and Sandy nagging her and the trumpet case sitting in the shoe cupboard day after day, month after month, until Steph got sick of dusting it and moved it to the loft.

"You'll be jes' fine," said Fishbo. "End of next week, you'll be good as new."

"Why? What's on at the end of next week?" Opal said, but he must have heard the nerves in her voice, and he waved the question away. "What age did you start at?" she asked, leaping on the first way she could think of to get him talking about the past.

"I was nine," said Fishbo. "Little nappy-headed critter. Nine years old with a little toy trumpet my daddy gave me."

"Was he a trumpet player too?" Opal asked, and Fishbo slapped his knee, making his foot lift up off the floor in a reflex.

"Daddy? Not hardly, Baby Girl. He worked on the railroad. He had no music in *his* soul. Somebody left that toy trumpet in the railway car, see, and so he wrapped it up as a gift and gave it to me for my birthday."

"He told you that?" said Opal.

"Not right then," Fishbo said. "Later, when I wanted to git me a full-size horn, I tried to hawk it. Daddy hit me upsides and down saying I didn't get a good price, y'know? Drive a hard bargain. He said it was a fine little horn, worth more than I sold it for. See, I'd been thinkin' if *I* got it for *my* birthday, it must be bottom of the damn range, cuz I knew how dirt poor we were." Fishbo was laughing and shaking his head as if this was the funniest story he'd ever heard, but it made Opal feel as if she might cry. Then Fishbo himself seemed to hear a different strain in the air of it too, and he grew sober. "Aw, Daddy," he said. "Long gone now. Little nappy-headed critter won't be too long following him home."

"Did he die while you were still there?" Opal said. "Or after you moved over?"

"Long, long gone," Fishbo said, too cryptically to be much help really.

"What about your mum?" Opal said. "Sorry!" He had looked up at her with a sudden sharp look. "I suppose mums are in my mind."

"My mama was jest a chile when she had me," Fishbo said, "and she lived to a fine age. Clean-livin' woman, Baby Girl. She died five years ago."

"Wow," said Opal, hoping that he would take it to be one of those meaningless expressions her generation went in for (awesome! fabulous!) and not what it was: amazement that someone so decrepit could have had a mother alive as recently as that. She gathered herself. "So you were still in touch with them *then*?" Fishbo nodded in that slow measured way of his that looked more like yoga than communication. "But you didn't go back?" He began shaking his head. "And you really think there's no way you could get in touch now?" Fishbo stopped shaking his head and looked at her, through her, through the wall behind her and the one beyond that.

"You cain't never go back," he said. "Life is a one-way ticket. Ain't no road home."

Opal was doing the slow yoga-nodding too now, thinking how much she used to love listening to Fishbo when she was a little girl; the slow rolling sound of his voice and the sudden flights up-tempo where his words were as sharp as his snapping fingers and his smile flashed like a light show, but now … Now everything he said sounded like something off a movie trailer or like it might be printed under the title of a trashy paperback, and his voice didn't thrill her the way it used to. She thought of Margaret and Zula and how they sounded so mixed up and chopped about. Leeds and Meath, Leeds and India, all jumbled together. Why did Fishbo still sound exactly the same?

Then she took a long, hard look at him, sitting there on his chair with its extra cushions, looking like a bundle of clothes with a head on top, like a scarecrow, and her heart melted again.

"Did you have brothers and sisters?" she said. Let him talk about the past in any voice he wanted to.

"Our house had more bunk beds than a dog has fleas."

"You've probably got nephews and nieces then," said Opal. "And great-nephews and -nieces. Gordon can't be that common a name in New Orleans."

And Fishbo's eyes seemed to swim back into focus again and fasten on her face again.

"What you …" he said. "Why you—who *are* you? You some kind of ghost come to haunt my last days? What's going *on*?"

"What?" said Opal. "Mr. Fish? It's Opal Jones. It's me."

"I'm tired," the old man said, leaning back in his chair and closing his eyes. "You leave me now, chile. Let me be."

Opal crept to the door and let herself out, closing it softly behind her. She was the master of getting silently through a door. Started learning how at ten, had it down pat by the time she was twelve. Steph used to lock up and take the key out after Opal moved there. But by then she was thirteen, her sneaking about days already over. "I was a prodigy," she had said to one of the torn-faced social workers she used to sit with every week, the pair of them bored to tears. "Doing things way earlier than the rest. Like that Mozart bloke, yeah?" And she got written up for an uncooperative attitude, just because the miserable cow had had no sense of humor.

The doorway at the end of passage darkened and she turned to see Pep Kendal standing there.

"Is Fishbo all right?" she said, and even in her own ears she sounded like a tearful child. Pep beckoned her, and she went to join him. "Is he, though?" she said when the kitchen door was shut behind them. "He got confused there. Like an old person."

"He *is* an old person," said Pep. "They're called senior moments, love. Yours'll be along someday too."

"I don't mean like that," Opal said. "He didn't know who I was for a minute."

"He doesn't eat enough," Pep said. He was cooking, and he waved his spatula over the frying pan as if a brown, frilly egg and a few links of sausage were just what the doctor ordered. "And he's got a chest infection, keeps him up coughing at night. He's just tired."

"That's what *he* said," Opal agreed, glad to let the worry go.

"I heard you practising," said Pep, watching the sausages. He pushed his lips out, making his moustache bristle. Opal laughed.

"Yeah," she said. "What's this thing at the end of next week?"

"Silver wedding," said Pep. "The Mote Street Boys played at their reception, and they want us back again."

"Great!" said Opal, feeling a trickle of cold down between her shoulders at the thought of a function room full of people, all dressed up, all staring slack-jawed at the stage where she was trying to play a scale.

"They moved away from Leeds, obviously," said Pep. "Mote Street means nothing to them. They've been down in Coventry."

"Is it really that bad?" Opal said. "The 'Mote Street' thing? Why didn't you just change the band's name?"

"Ah, the youth of today," said Pep. "Got an answer for everything, eh?"

And because it was far too close to the truth—the way Opal had waltzed back in here and decided she could fix all the problems, solve all the mysteries, make life perfect for everyone—she didn't give him any backchat. He went over to a cupboard and got a plate out, then looked over his shoulder. "One or two?" he said.

"Plates?" said Opal. "Well, he's out for the count, I think."

"I was inviting you to dinner," said Pep. "You want it engraved?"

"I want my egg broken," Opal said. Pep brought two plates over to the counter, picked up the spatula, and drove its edge into the middle of one of the eggs.

"Hey," Opal said. "That was the good one. What a waste! You shouldn't break the good egg." Pep put an arm around her shoulders and gave her a quick squeeze; Opal couldn't tell why.

"He's really upset about his family too," she said when they were sitting opposite one another at the little kitchen table. Opal rolled a sausage up in a slice of buttered bead and squirted in ketchup, like a hotdog. There was a lot to be said for single men who didn't care about manners. "You know, since the hurricane."

Pep chewed and swallowed, then ran his tongue around the outside of his bottom teeth.

"Ah yes," he said. "The hurricane. New Orleans and the French Quarter and the Gordon family scattered to the four winds and poor old Eugene who cain't never go home."

"What?" said Opal.

"We've been hearing a lot more about Norlins again since Katrina blew through."

"So who's Eugene?"

"Eugene Gordon, my lodger," Pep said. "Fishbo!"

"Look who's talking," said Opal. "Pep!"

"Here," said Pep. "I was called Peppermint since primary school—after Kendal Mintcake."

"Who?" Opal asked.

Pep stared at her. "Mean to say you've never had a bar of Kendal Mintcake? On a day at the lakes?"

"When was *I* at the lakes?" said Opal. "Nicola wasn't exactly the type for picnics, you know."

"But I'd bet you all the money in my pockets," Pep said, going back to the subject, "that Gene Gordon made up 'Fishbo' for himself."

"Why are you being so mean?" asked Opal. Pep screwed his tongue into a back molar and worked it round there, saying nothing. "He's supposed to be your friend."

"He is my friend, the old fart. I wouldn't change him, which is just as well because he'll never change now. Just nod and smile, love. Like we all do, while he's looking. Nod and smile."

"I don't know what you're on about," Opal said.

"Well, do me a favour and don't try to work it out," Pep said. "He'll be enjoying having you back and telling you all about it. Don't spoil it for him, eh?" He shook his head then and laughed. "Louisiana!"

"What about Louisiana?" said Opal, sounding scrappy even to her own ears. Once again, Mr. Kendal was hitting far too close to home. "We've all got to come from somewhere."

"Exactly," said Pep. "Well put, love. I wish you could convince her next door. She had a right go about the Joshi boys *again* to me yesterday. Terrorists, she reckons. Or on their way to it."

"God, I know," said Opal. Then she dropped her knife and fork. "Christ, I asked her over for tea."

FIFTEEN

OF COURSE, MRS. PICKESS was up on a chair at Opal's window, scrubbing away at the glass hard enough to go through it to the other side. *And* she didn't miss Opal coming out of Pep's either.

"Oh, there you are," she called over. "I thought I'd just crack on while the light was still good."

Opal didn't say that it was the first week in July and the light would be good until ten o'clock, she just mumbled apologies and stood with her head down until Mrs. Pickess had finished telling her how fine it was and how she was quite happy to get on with it on her own and how Opal shouldn't feel bad and her hip was hardly bothering her in this warm weather anyway.

"I'll put the kettle on," Opal said.

"See and empty it out," Mrs. Pickess called in the front door after her. "Refill fresh from the tap."

It does look good, mind, Opal thought staring out while the water boiled for the tea, even if the view through the sparkling glass was of Mrs. Pickess on her chair, polishing madly with a page of crumpled

101

tabloid, her skirt hem lifting to show the frill of her underskirt and her shirt collar slipping aside to show its shoulder straps. Who wore full-length underskirts anymore, never mind in a heat wave? "Are you not roasting?" Opal shouted. "Would you rather have something cold?"

Then she had to sit through the explanation of how hot tea cools you down on a warm day, as well as a lecture about putting hot tea-bags in the bin and how it would attract vermin and how she would look out for a little teabag dish for Opal next time she was down at the city markets, but until then she should use a bowl, next to the kettle, with a folded square of kitchen paper in the bottom to stop it staining.

"I haven't got any kitchen paper," Opal said. "I'll use toilet roll." And Mrs. Pickess looked as if she might gag.

"Well," she said, looking round, once she had recovered. "You've made a start." Opal fixed her eyes on Mrs. Pickess's face, refusing to look around her kitchen and see where she might have failed. A start! She had been up until after midnight last night making sure the kitchen and living room would pass muster. She would never have invited Mrs. Fussy Knickers in after just a *start*.

"And now with my windows so nice and clean, it looks lovely," was all she said. "You came round and did the back first, didn't you?" The evening sun was blaring in through the clean glass and bouncing around the kitchen like a pinball. Opal thought she better not say that she had quite liked the softness that came from the dust and smears.

"I did," said Mrs. Pickess. "I knew you wouldn't mind."

"I'm very grateful."

"Well, I've done what I can," said Mrs. Pickess, "but my days of going up a ladder are behind me."

"Of course they are," said Opal, hoping it wouldn't have been more polite to disagree. "I'll ask the Joshis if I can borrow a ladder. They're bound to have one. One of the lads might even offer to hold it steady for me."

"If you can catch them in between *prayers*," Mrs. Pickess said.

Opal smiled. Pep Kendal was right. "Prayers?" she said.

"Five times a day," said Mrs. Pickess. "I saw something on the telly about it. A big curtain down the middle of the room."

"They're not Muslims, Mrs. Pickess," Opal said. "They're Hindus."

"*Pffft*. It's all the same," said Mrs. Pickess. "They can't fool me."

"You're right," Opal said. "We're all the same. Good for you." Mrs. Pickess's eyes narrowed to slits, but she said nothing. "Where do you come from, originally?" Opal went on. "I've never met anyone else called Pickess. Where's that from?" Mrs. Pickess put her mug down on the table with a crack, making Opal think that if she'd used cups and saucers, like Mrs. Pickess said, she'd have six cups and five saucers now.

"My husband's family—the Pickesses—were greengrocers in Osmondthorpe since Queen Victoria," she said. "You can still see their name on a gable end. And my family were called Thirsthwistle."

"Bloody hell," said Opal.

"Which is a fine old Yorkshire name."

"You should have gone hyphenated," Opal said, which wrung a laugh out of Mrs. Pickess at last.

"I was so glad to get rid of it," she said, "I'd have married Mr. Pickess if he'd had a glass eye and wooden teeth." She heaved up a sigh like a load of wet washing from a twin tub and huffed it out again, slumping. "We had thirty happy years and he left me well set. There's not much more you can ask for."

"Did you never have children?" Opal said, only realising that minute that she had never seen youngsters visiting No. 5 when she was a kid.

"We never did," Mrs. Pickess said, taking another biscuit and snapping it in two. "But Mr. Pickess never cast it up to me. Not a word." Opal nodded, but she couldn't help thinking he must have semaphored his feelings somehow, or else why did Mrs. Pickess assume the guilt and feel humbled and lucky instead of never casting it up to *him*. "And they're not all joy, not by a long chalk." She put one of the pieces of biscuit in her mouth and chewed it steadily, with a circular grinding motion, her gaze fixed on the tabletop.

"Margaret would agree with you there," Opal said, and Mrs. Pickess shifted gladly to someone's else's troubles—as Opal had known she would.

"Poor Margaret," Mrs. Pickess said. "And as for Denny—have you seen Denny?" Opal nodded. "Poor Margaret."

"Karen really never comes near her? Never at all?"

"Not for over five years now. She was always a funny one. Not family-minded. But after Craig went, it was more and more strained and longer and longer in between and then she just stopped coming."

"You'd think it would be a shared thing, wouldn't you?"

"And that's not all. She's moved house now, and Margaret doesn't even know where she's gone."

"And she was an only child, Karen, wasn't she?"

"The only one." Mrs. Pickess ate the other half of her biscuit. "Margaret wanted a big family, of course ... *you know* ... and one time her and I very nearly fell out over it. She was going on about it—Karen would be five, then—about how she was cursed and her arms ached for another baby and there was no justice in the world when all her sisters had such crowds of them. Well, Opal, I snapped. Just the once, mind. I told her she was blessed, not cursed. That she had a beautiful little girl—and she kept her lovely when she was a child, just like a little doll, always in a dress and white socks and gloves for church, like a little doll in a box. I'd have given…" Mrs. Pickess grappled with another sigh and got it out of herself. "But look at us now. I wouldn't swap with Margaret *now*. Karen gone and Denny just sitting there in the living room."

Opal knew that for years *Mr.* Pickess had just sat there in the living room too, in an onyx jar in the alcove beyond the fireplace, with his British Legion medal in an open box in front of it. It had fascinated her when she was small and she had hatched numerous plans to get Mrs. Pickess to leave her alone in there, planning to open the top of the jar and peer inside to see if there were any big bits. Teeth, maybe. Or a toe, that you could grow a new Mr. Pickess from.

"Opal?"

She shook herself back from the memory. "And Craig," she said.

"Hm?" said Mrs. Pickess.

"Denny just sitting there, Karen gone, and Craig disappeared who knows where."

The sun was having its last gasp before it set behind the trees in the back gardens of the big houses over on Grove Lane, and as Mrs. Pickess looked up, the light shining through the scoured glass showed a face not even just naked, but *peeled*, suddenly stripped of a mask no one knew was there until it had gone. Opal blinked and in the time it took to shut her eyes and open them, the look was gone; the sun had slipped below the highest little twigs and leaves on those far-off trees, and Mrs. Pickess was herself again.

"It must have been terrible for you all," Opal said, steeling herself, hating herself for dredging it up. Mrs. Pickess said nothing. "I didn't know about it until I came back, you know. Margaret told me.

Just the bare bones. And I didn't want to keep on at her." Still nothing. "But it's just so hard to imagine. It's such a quiet street, for one thing. And everyone's always looked out for everyone else. How could a little boy just suddenly be gone that way?"

Mrs. Pickess spoke at last. "The bare bones?"

Opal thought about Mr. Pickess's toe on its bed of ash again. "I mean, just that he was playing outside and then he was gone and no one could find him."

"That's right," Mrs. Pickess said. "Only minutes it was, and the whole street out on the hunt for him. And give them their due, those..." she waved over her shoulder towards Zula's corner of the street, "they all pitched in just like the rest of us."

"And you never heard anything?"

"Me?" said Mrs. Pickess. The light was fading fast now, so Opal stood and turned the light on. "You'll need to shut your door else you'll have flies all through," Mrs. Pickess said, but Opal sat down again and left the door to the yard open.

"Right next door like that, I mean," she said. "If Craig was playing in his yard and your back door was open with the fly curtain like it usually is, you might have heard something."

"I was upstairs," said Mrs. Pickess. "In the front bedroom. I was putting ironing away."

"When?" Opal said.

"That day," said Mrs. Pickess. "When do you think?" Her voice was growing rough now, and just a little unsteady.

"But *when* that day?" said Opal.

"When Karen came to the door," Mrs. Pickess said. "I saw her standing on the step and in she went. I heard her shouting, screaming really, and then banging in and out the back and front, all three of them. Up and down the lane in back, up and down the street in front. I went straight down to see what was wrong. Anyone would have. Even her at the top was out. And that lot down the bottom. And your mother. And the Taylors at number four. You'd not know them. They hadn't been here long and they didn't stay long after, I can tell you."

Opal returned, on tiptoe, to the point Mrs. Pickess had raced away from. "But Mrs. Pickess, even if you were putting your ironing away when Karen came, you might not have been upstairs in the front bedroom when Craig actually . . . you know, if he left the yard or if someone came in. Do you put it away as soon as you're done?"

She did not want to answer, not one little bit. But Opal had played a masterstroke: she'd asked about housework. More than that even, she'd hinted that Mrs. Pickess might not set about it with order and precision.

"Of course I do!" she said. "I don't know what's worse between pressing stuff that's too damp and having to hang it back up on the pulley again after, or leaving it dried out in a basket for days, waiting. I iron when it's dry enough to iron, always have, never fail. And then I put it away. Catch me leaving a batch of shirts hooked over the door to get food smells in them!"

"Food smells," said Opal. "You iron in the kitchen then."

Mrs. Pickess stared back at her, her eyes wide and her lip quivering. "I never heard a thing," she said. "I told the police. I heard not a voice nor a step. Didn't hear the gate. Didn't hear a car. Nothing."

"A car?" Opal said. "Do they think a car came up the lane? Did someone else see one?"

"No!" Mrs. Pickess said, shouted almost. "I'm just saying, I heard nothing. And I saw nothing. All morning. It was as quiet as a grave. I had my door open all morning, and there wasn't a peep from him."

Of course not Opal thought to herself. And it was hardly surprising since he'd disappeared the night before. Why then would Mrs. Pickess be so swimmy and quavering that way?

"It must have been dreadful," she said, taking pity at last.

"It was," Mrs. Pickess said. "They searched everywhere, you know. The police. Searched the houses and all over. Searched right through my house, took the bath panel off and went up to the attic, into the eaves, everywhere. They turned *this* place upside down." Opal looked around, picturing coppers moving about her mum's kitchen, too big for the little rooms, all starched serge and squeaking shoe leather, opening cupboards, their faces set like cement, not reacting to anything they had to sort through. But they still knew how to tell you what they were thinking.

"Mrs. Taylor," Mrs. Pickess was saying, "she told me they took up the floors."

"Well, no wonder they left!" Opal said. "They didn't take up your floors too, did they? What for?"

"No, not the Taylors' floor," Mrs. Pickess said. "In here. Your mother's." She sat back and folded her arms, watching the news settle into Opal, waiting to see how it would land. Then she gave it another little nudge. "Because Karen's ex used to knock about with her."

Opal nodded. Made sense. She read the papers, sometimes. A kiddie goes missing and its mum and dad aren't together anymore, the first thing you check is the dad. And if he's got a girlfriend, of course you're going to have good long look at her, and if she looks like Nicola, then it would be criminal not to go over the place carefully. She was still nodding, but there was something going on her chest, like when you put a clean trainer in the dryer to stop your pillow going lumpy.

"And who told them?" she said. "About Mum and Robbie Southgate. Margaret?"

"No!" Mrs. Pickess said. "Don't you go saying that to Margaret, she never said a word about it."

"Karen then? She'd a bloody cheek. Margaret thinks Robbie walked out on Karen. I know she does, and I wouldn't poke my nose in to put her right, but that's not what my mum told me."

"Well, who's to say?" said Mrs. Pickess, desperately. "It was all such a long time ago."

"Me, for a start," Opal said. "My mum didn't lie to me. I wish she bloody had—there were things she told me that no kid should have to know. If she said Karen kicked him out, then Karen kicked him out, okay?" She could hear her voice, harsh and ugly, and she could imagine the face to match, but she couldn't help it. Except she would have to help it, wouldn't she? If she was going to find out what really happened to little Craig, she would have to handle anything that came along, listen to anything anyone told her without getting angry.

"Sorry," she said, managing to smile after she had swallowed hard. "It's just, she was still my mum, even if she was . . . troubled."

"I know, love," said Mrs. Pickess, and as well as a bit of kindness in her voice, there was something else. Opal turned her head to one side and looked at the woman. What would you call that other thing in her voice?

"How did you know it wasn't Margaret?"

"What?" said Mrs. Pickess. The look was gone now and Opal had worked out what to call it as she watched it go: relief. Relief at an awkward moment got by.

"Was it you? Did you tell the cops that Mum knew Robbie? Did you set the police on her?"

"I thought Margaret would have told them already," Mrs. Pickess said, shrugging. "I mentioned it. I thought they'd already know."

"You thought my mum would have hurt a little kid?" Opal said. The trainer was thumping around in the tumble dryer again.

"She had no time for him," said Mrs. Pickess, finding reserves of courage from somewhere.

"So you said 'go over the road, Mr. Policeman, and take up the floors'?"

"They didn't *find* anything," said Mrs. Pickess. "It's better to know, innit? It's better than wondering."

"Nobody would have *been* wondering if you hadn't started them."

"Best to get everything out in the open," said Mrs. Pickess. "Not let things fester. And it wasn't your mother I was thinking of. It was everyone else in the house. In and out, like Piccadilly Circus, and Friday nights were always the worst of all."

"I remember," Opal said. But she didn't remember. She *wouldn't* remember. She was going to concentrate on Craig and Craig alone. And the little bed girl. And Fishbo. And then there would be no time left to think about anything else and that was the best way.

"I better go," said Mrs. Pickess. "I'm sorry I upset you." Opal said nothing. "Put it out of your mind, eh? It's all a long time ago now even if it is new to you. Don't go raking it back up when everyone's taken years to get it behind them, eh?" Still, Opal didn't speak. She stood and walked through to the front with Mrs. Pickess, opened the door and stood while the old woman stepped down onto the street, holding the door jamb to help herself keep steady. She was rattled, for sure.

"I hear what you're saying, Mrs. Pickess," Opal said. "I can't agree that Denny's got it behind him though. Or Margaret. Or Karen, wherever she is. And you just said yourself, it's better to know, better than wondering."

Mrs. Pickess only blinked at her.

"So here's what I'm wondering," Opal said. "What's wild Friday nights at my mum's got to do with anything if it was a Saturday morning when Craig went away?"

SIXTEEN

THE NOTES FROM THE bedposts weren't exactly a lullaby, but Opal read them over just before she went to sleep anyway, because in the morning she was going to forget Craig for the day—she whispered an apology to his ghost, in case it was listening—and forget Leeds too. It was a surprise how much she hankered to get up out of the city and see the moor. Probably because a moor would do the same job as the sea—letting her eyes fix on something long and low stretching across in front of her instead of little houses and buses and lampposts, shelves and cages and boxes, all right in front of her nose. And marching into an auction room held no fears for her, not after Walrus Antiques.

But Claypole's Auctions was in a different league from Billy and Tony with their cups of tea and flirty quarrels. For one thing, it was huge—some enormous grey stone building that had obviously once been something else, only Opal couldn't work out what, since it wasn't fancy enough for a church or plain enough for a factory. And the reception that you had to go through to get to where all the stuff was looked like a bank or something, with a blue carpet and a little coffee table and leather chairs, big plants in pots and glossy brochures fanned out everywhere.

She was dozy and hot from rocking along on the bus—she'd picked the shady side in the station, but as soon as they swung out onto the road the sun had come hammering in at her, and one side of her face had been baked all the way so that it felt as tight and shiny as a bun—and everyone else strolling round the viewing rooms looked so very respectable, not like people you'd think would go to an auction at all. Men in blazers and hairy green jackets, women in striped shirts and navy jackets and—God almighty—pearls. And it was Sunday, which meant they'd all been at *church*, and here was Opal in her jeggings and a cami with her hair scraped up in a bundle. She skulked around at the back of a room full of chairs—same as Walrus, nobody seemed to care much for chairs—and kept away from the glass cases where the respectable people were peering in at jewelry, some of them even screwing monocles like little lengths of copper piping into their eye sockets and leaning in so close that their heads kept bonking on the glass. They all had stapled sheets of paper too, and Opal couldn't tell where they had got them.

Looking around, what she did see was a lad in a brown overall whisking across the top of an aisle lined either side with dressers and chests and, hopping every few steps to flick her flip-flop back on, she plunged after him.

"Excuse me?" she said. "Pal? Oi? Scuse me!"

He turned round and gave her a swift up and down, then he stuck his pen behind his ear and folded his arms.

"Can I ask a question?" she said.

He smirked at her, leaned against a sideboard, and crossed his ankles. She smiled up at him.

"I bought a bed from here a couple of weeks ago and ... "

"Bed problems, eh?"

She managed to keep smiling. "No seriously, listen! I didn't actually buy it from here, I bought it in a shop and they got it from here, but what I'm wondering now is—"

"You'd have to take it back to the shop if you've changed your mind, doll," said the lad.

"No, it's not that," said Opal, thinking it wouldn't take half as long if he'd just let her tell him instead of guessing. "What it is, is I want to know where you got it from. Claypole's. Where it was before it came here."

"Why?" he said.

"Well," Opal said. Billy and Tony had coached her on this. "Provenance."

"Can't help you," said the lad. "Can't pass out customer info. However—"

"Okay, not provenance," she said. "How about this? I found something in it that I think the original owner might want back."

"In a bed?" he said. He was smirking again and he leaned forward, close enough so that she could smell his aftershave, one of the cheap ones that smells like sherbet. "What did you find?" He was practically leering now.

"Behave," Opal said. "If you tell me the name, I'll tell you what it was." She put her hand up to twirl her hair but remembered it was in a scrunchie.

"No way," he said. "I couldn't divulge that kind of information from one customer to another. However ... " This time Opal decided to let him finish, smiling up at him; if it cost her going out for a coffee with him it would be worth it. "What I might let slip in the throes of passion ... know what I mean?"

Opal stopped smiling and took a step backwards.

"Half an hour in the van?" he said.

Opal stepped another pace away from him, staring.

"Oh, come off it, love," he said. "You trying to make out I've shocked you? Sod off out of it." He laughed again, a very different laugh this time. "Bloody pikeys!" Opal had lowered her head, but she could see from the corner of her eye another pair of black doc shoes and the hem of another brown coat coming up to join the first one. Her stomach did a flip forward. Where were all the church people in their pearls now?

"That's no kind of language for the floor, Jordan," said the new man. Opal raised her head again. "And no way to talk to a young lady, even on your own time. Get out the back. There's two vans want tidying."

Jordan swaggered away with one last leer at Opal. She looked at her knight in armour.

"What was that all about?" he said, but Opal couldn't speak. He looked so much like her dad, or at least in the dim light of this ware-house he did, and her eyes filled. "Hey, now!" he said. He reached forward, but of course he didn't really touch her, not her bare arm or bare shoulder. He'd never. "What's to do?"

"It was my own fault," Opal said. "I was being cheeky, asking for a favour. I walked right in to it."

"Wait, no! Stop that," the man said and this time he did just touch his knuckle to the outside of her arm. "There's nothing you could have asked that would have earned you that."

Opal sniffed and nodded.

"Sorry, yeah, you're right," she said, and she raised her fists to her face, quickly reviewed her morning to remind herself whether she had mascara on, and scrubbed at her eyes.

"So what was your cheeky favour then?"

"I asked him to tell me where you'd got something you sold on," Opal said. "Confidential customer information. I should have known."

"Confidential?" said the man. "You want to be here on a sale day, love. If the auctioneer thinks there's any swank about where summat come from, you can't shut him up. We had a cabinet in that had once been in Newburgh Priory a while back, and he were practically giving out Lady Wombwell's knicker size. No holding him."

Opal giggled. "Who's Lady Wombwell?" she said. "Is that a real name?"

"Oh, she's a big noise round here. Her *and* her knickers. Anyroad, it'll have been an estate sale, more'n probably, and so there's nothing to be confidential about. Aye, most of Claypole's best clients are dead."

And he took her back through to the reception with the blue chairs and pot plants and used a key from his big bunch to open a filing cabinet and find the records from the right day.

"Hmph," he said, reading off the page. "Not an estate sale, as it goes. Looks more like somebody clearing out the attic. Silver, silver plate, some medals, bit of furniture, fox fur." He flipped through the pages a bit more. "It's all the way in Leeds. Says 'N Fossett, Far Headingley.'"

"That's just up the road from me," Opal said. He was reading out the address and, grabbing a biro off the desk, she wrote it on her hand.

"Most of it's gone," the man said. "No reserve, see? Funny that." He was talking to himself more than Opal now, flicking the pages and running his fingers down the inventory. "No reserve," he said again.

116

Opal made a mental note to ask Billy and Tony what that meant and why it was funny, then thanked the man and left, stepping back out into the muggy, stale heat of the day, holding her hand stretched out like a starfish to stop the ink from smudging.

SEVENTEEN

ALL DAY AT WORK on Monday, she was thinking about N Fossett of Far Headingley and what she would say if she actually plucked up courage to go and knock on their door. Especially, she was thinking about what connection there might be between N Fossett and the little bed girl. Would they even know her? Would she be an old, dead relation maybe? Or did N Fossett buy the bed at an auction too, years ago? And now they'd changed their mind about furniture and gone all modern? And would it be Mrs. or Mr. N Fossett? Opal didn't think there were that many N names for girls, same as O. She had been the only O girl right through school, although there were always a few Olivers and Osmans on the boy side.

So what would she say to Mr. Neil or Norman or Neville Fossett? That she had found something that belonged to him? She didn't want to get that nice man at Claypole's into trouble. She could say Jordan had given her the address; she didn't mind what trouble he got into. But what *exactly* she would say depended on what N Fossett told her. If his mother or his granny had slept in the bed, she'd probably keep quiet about the letters. It was bad enough reading what a stranger long ago had written in secret on dark frightened nights. If it was someone you knew …

"Earth to Opal." It was Kate and Rhianne on their way back from a break, and Opal's heart sank. They had seen her the day she was crying at the front desk when she came for the job—stopped flirting with Security to watch her—and they'd got interested in her right then. But it was the dinner break they heard her talking back to rude boys that really meant she'd never shake them off.

"Opal, isn't it?" one lad had said, from the next table along in the canteen.

"Op-al Fruits, made to make your mouth water!" his friend sang as if he was some kind of genius for thinking it up.

"Congratulations," Opal said. "You're the millionth person to crack that joke today. You've won a smile." And she moved the corners of her mouth up and down again, for about a second.

It got rid of them, but it attracted the attention of two girls who looked familiar. They started clapping and came to sit beside her.

"That's told him, the scuzzo," said one of them. "He thinks he's God's gift to the world."

"Which one?" Opal said.

"Both," said the other girl. "Jan and Paulo. *Yann* and *Paaooouulo*. I'd love to get into their HR files. I bet they're called John and Paul, really."

"Or George and Ringo," Opal said, kicking herself when the two girls started giggling. But she told herself it was fine. She would only see them at work, and she didn't need to talk about anything she didn't want to. But still she was jumpy. Pat and Charlotte were easy. Like Jill at the salon. They didn't really ask you stuff. If they wanted to know something, they *told* you. "So Opal, I bet you've got a fella, pretty girl like you." But with Kate and Rhianne, proper girlfriends, the same age, it was harder to keep things light, harder to stop the questions and get them to swallow the answers she could handle giving them. They were at it already.

"Where did you go to school?"

"Round here?"

"Still at home?"

"Or got your own place?"

Opal couldn't cope with both of them at once and ended up telling them about breaking up with Baz and leaving Whitby.

"Is that why you were crying?"

"We saw you, you know."

So in case they thought she was heartbroken over Baz and kept asking questions and she started crying again—it wasn't that unlikely—she ended up telling them about her mum dying and moving back into her old house, and then she'd gone back to work five minutes early off her break to get away from them.

They were at it again now.

"Good weekend?"

"Thought you were coming to Yates's?"

"We bagged three lads and were left with a spare one."

"Where were you?"

Opal thought hard. "I went up to Northallerton with pals of mine, Billy and Tony. To a club. Claypole's. Great night. Sorry."

"Billy and Tony with Ys?"

"Where's Northallerton?"

"Can we come next time if we find a third boy?"

Opal said of course they could. It seemed to satisfy them and she could go back to thoughts of N Fossett again.

After her shift, when she got to the right street, she could hardly believe she was in Leeds at all. High grey stone walls on both sides of a quiet road with trees almost meeting in the middle and every house with two sets of gateposts—one at one edge of the front garden and one at the other and a drive that was half a circle, so you could come in one side and out again without stopping. Opal wondered if lads in cars ever came up here and wove in and out for laughs on a Friday night but decided probably not, with it being so quiet and a dead end—just like Mote Street, except not really—and probably everyone in the houses was in Neighborhood Watch and would call the cops at the first rev of an engine.

She walked up one side (2, 4, 6, 8) and down the other (7, 5, 3, 1) and stopped. Number 9 she was after. She turned and looked along the street again. You couldn't even see the houses from here, set so far back behind the walls and trees like they were, but she counted the gateways and there were definitely eight of them.

For another long moment she just stood there, thinking. False address? Or just a typo, maybe. And then she noticed that at the dead end of the road the black railings with more of those gnarled, enormous trees behind them weren't railings at all, or not all the way across, anyway. There was a gate there too, taller than she was, twice as tall, and curved over at the top, with a lamp hanging in the middle, in a fancy black iron thing like a little birdcage, just above where one gate met the other. Opal walked back down the middle of the road—so quiet, just like Mote Street only without the Joshi boys—and peered through the railings.

There wasn't a drive as such, or even a path, but between the trees on one side and the trees on the other, between the big bushes with the stiff shiny leaves (that Opal thought might be azaleas although she couldn't be sure because there were no flowers on them), there was a space that was just grass. Mounds of it, old stuff from last year bent over and looking like great big clods of hair fished out of a drain, and this year's growth too, tall and stiff, more like reeds than grass really, with heads on it like corn. And there were spindly little trees as high as her shoulders that looked as if they might have just decided to grow there instead of someone planting them.

Was there a house in there? Could there be? No one would put a gate in if it led to nothing. And if she squinted at the join between the maybe-azaleas and the drain hair, she thought she could see a line sweeping round and disappearing. She put her face right up between the railings and stared at the trees hiding where the line disappeared to. Nothing. The bushes were too thick and the dazzle of sun off the dead clumps of grass was too bright.

Opal took hold of the handle on the black lock plate of the gate and rattled it. No chance there. She looked up, wondering if the railings were really too high to be scaled and that's when she saw the design on the cage where the lantern still hung, broken and dusty. The iron hadn't just been bent into fancy shapes for decoration like she'd thought, but into a number nine. Four number nines, one on each side of the lantern, that must have stood out against the light when it was on. She'd found N Fossett's house. Now, did she have the nerve to clamber over these railings and knock on the door?

She didn't. And anyway, there must be another way in, from another street that Ned or Nicholas or Norbert—she laughed out loud when she thought of that last one—used every day. He couldn't possibly hack his way through the undergrowth and unlock this rusty old gate when he needed a pint of milk and a paper. So she turned away, keeping her eye trained on the tallest of the gnarled old trees, hoping she would recognise it again if it popped up from another angle on the next road over.

But it was confusing, these looping roads and walls and all the bushes, and Opal had lost her sense of direction by the time she'd gone round two corners. She couldn't even find her way back to the dead end road and the iron gate now. She needed a street map, she decided. And so, hungry and hot, she turned for home—or crossed a road or two anyway, hoping she'd see something familiar if she kept walking.

She was standing on a corner, wondering which way to go, when a little whispering voice behind her spoke so softly she had to turn to be sure it wasn't just the wind in the trees.

EIGHTEEN

"Excuse me?" the little voice said. "Are you going to the party?"

It was a tiny woman wearing slippers and an apron. She peered up at Opal from eyes that were pale blue and pink, almost no lashes, just a thickened rim, sore-looking, making her blink every second or two.

"Eh?" said Opal, looking down at herself, at her strappy top and cotton pedal pushers—the coolest, lightest clothes she owned, washed out every night for the next morning, because jeans in this heat would have killed her. They weren't scruffy, but they weren't party clothes either.

"I was at a party," said the little woman. "But … " she looked past Opal and shook her head. Her hair was short and straight, pure white, showing her scalp at the parting. "They're supposed to come today, you see, but I was at a party and I must have missed them."

"Shouldn't you be at home?" Opal said, looking down at the slippers.

"Yes, but I missed them," said the little woman, her voice climbing higher and beginning to sound wavery. "They always come today."

"Maybe you should wait for them at home," Opal said.

"Oh! Yes," the woman said, clapping her hands as if Opal had had a brainwave, and she stepped down just as a car went sliding past, only twenty miles an hour, if that, but Opal clutched the woman's arm as the horn blared and she dragged her—practically lifted her—back up onto the pavement again.

"Sorry, sorry," the woman said in her whispery voice. Her pink eyes swam, making her blink even harder. She rubbed her arm through her blouse where Opal had grabbed.

"Oh God," said Opal. "I'm so sorry. Don't tell me I hurt you."

"Sorry," said the woman again, and she bowed her head as if Opal had threatened her.

"Look," Opal said. "How about if I walk home with you? And we'll see if they're there, waiting." Without thinking, she had slipped back into that same old way of talking, learned early—agreeing, picking up on whatever she could and batting it back, whether she believed it or not.

"Thank you," said the little woman, slipping her hand through Opal's arm, making Opal think of the way the smallest birds, blue-tits and finches, slipped into the holes in the nest boxes in Steph's back garden.

"Which way?" Opal said, but the little woman hesitated, humming a bit under her breath and looking up at Opal, blinking.

"My house," she said. "Home."

Fantastic, thought Opal, and they set off along the nearest side street. "Is it this way?" she said. "Does this look familiar? Are these your neighbors? Who lives here?" And she kept it up, coaxing and pecking, while the little woman trotted along at her side, thanking her, asking if they were too late, if they'd have missed them, that little hand resting soft and light in the crook of Opal's elbow until at last she stopped and let out a cry.

"My house," she said, pointing up a lane towards a row of garages behind the street they were standing on. "But … " she blinked at Opal. "I wanted to go to the party. Are you going to the party?"

"Why don't we go to your house?" Opal said. "See if anyone's there." The woman's little face crumpled, and she put one of her hands up to cover her mouth.

"They come today," she said. "I'm supposed to be there for them."

"Best hurry then," Opal said, and together they trotted up the ash lane, past the lockups, and into a garden gate. Behind it was a kind of covered tunnel with vinyl walls and a cloudy vinyl roof to match, covered in moss and dead leaves; the little woman bustled along it like a white mouse in one of those puzzle runs. *Must be a care home*, Opal thought, following her, planning to give the staff a good slice of her mind, but when the woman trotted up the five steps to the door at the end of the passageway and opened it, disappearing inside, and Opal followed her, it wasn't an institution of any kind—*that* was clear.

They were standing in a kitchen, quite small and very dark from the fact that the tunnel outside covered over the only window, but it wasn't that that made Opal shiver. It was the smell of food going off in warm air. All over the little table that took up most of the floor were polystyrene trays of food—stew and soup and mash-potato-topped pies—and plastic tubs of boiled vegetables and wilting salad, the sliced raw onion reeking. Opal looked away.

All around the walls there were fitted cupboards, not like ordinary kitchen cupboards with a worktop and a row of cabinets above, but floor to ceiling with drawers and doors, some of them so high you'd have to stand on a chair to reach them, and all painted with blue gloss except for their matching shiny black handles. But what grabbed her attention wasn't the cupboards themselves but the signs all over them; clipboards with tick sheets and pieces of paper pinned on cork strips with thumbtacks. **Do not take more than one meal out of the fridge** one of them said in thick black letters. **Lock the door** was another. And then the one that Opal was really glad to see: **In an emergency, call Shelley** and a local phone number.

"I'm going to call Shelley," Opal said. "You sit down."

"They're not here," said the woman, but she sat and waited, no sign of her making another break for the door.

"Hi," said Opal into her phone. "Is that—Can I speak to Shelley? Oh, hi, yeah. Listen, I just found this little old lady wandering about and brought her home, and it says on the wall—"

The woman on the other end of the phone made a sound half-way between a groan and a sigh.

"Not again," she said. "Home to your house? Or home to hers?"

"We're at hers," said Opal. "But, like, she just let me walk right in, and I don't think I should leave her here."

"Beggars belief, doesn't it?" the woman said. "I'll be there in two ticks, if you can just hang on."

"Shelley's coming," Opal said, hanging up, and the little woman's eyes lit up into sparkles.

"She might take me back to the party."

"She might well do," said Opal. She was snapping the lids back onto the polystyrene trays, wondering whether to put them in the bin and let the little woman starve or put them back in the fridge and poison her, when the back door opened.

"Shelley!"

"Hell-o!" She was a young-ish woman, thirties maybe, dressed in that rich-mum uniform of linen trousers and a floaty top cut to hide the baby spread around her middle. She shook her head and rolled her eyes at Opal. Then, seeing the tubs and trays, she groaned again like she had over the phone. "Don't tell me!" she said and turned to where the little woman sat with her hands clasped between her knees, slippered feet swinging. "How many times, Miss Muffett? Hmm? Did you take everything out again?"

"To give them when they come," the woman said.

"They don't come on a Monday now." Shelley turned back to Opal. "They used to come every afternoon and now they come three full days. They say it's better, but she can't…"

"I missed them when I was at the party."

"It wasn't a party," Shelley said to Opal, dropping her voice. "I was taking my little girl and her friend to their ballet class and I made some sandwiches." She rolled her eyes again, but Opal couldn't help thinking that it wouldn't be that bad, thinking life was a party just because two toddlers put tutus on and gave you a sarnie.

"Does she live on her own?" Opal said in the same quiet voice Shelley had used to her.

"Beggars belief," she said again. "I mean you could have—" She stopped and flushed a little.

"No, yeah, you're right," Opal said. "I could have been anyone."

"She's got a niece," said Shelley. "And two greats—not sure if they're girls or boys—and doesn't that say it all?"

"One of each. A girl and a boy," the little woman said. "And my nephew."

"I didn't know you had a nephew."

"A niece and nephew and a great-niece and a great-nephew."

"And where does *he* live?"

"Here," said the woman. "Leeds."

"Really?" said Shelley. "Well, he could at least—" Again she stopped. The little woman had bowed her head again at the change of tone.

"Sorry," she said. "Sorry."

"Come on, Norah, my love," said Shelley, taking both her soft little hands and pulling her to her feet. "Let's go and put your tape on. She's got a video of Billy Smart's circus. Watches it every day. That and a Trooping the Colour parade, until she wore the tape out."

They disappeared through the kitchen door and Opal stood staring at it as it swung shut behind them, listening to the footsteps growing fainter and fainter. *Norah.* Was it possible? But that Shelley had called her Miss... Opal scrabbled to remember and then laughed when she did. Miss Muffett, because of the way she was sitting there with her hands together and her feet swinging. But that couldn't really be her name. *Was* it possible? She stepped to the kitchen door and, opening it a crack, peered along the passageway beyond.

It had to be fifty feet long, door after door on either side, and the ceiling so high it felt like being in church or something when Opal stepped softly along the length of it. Church because it was dark too, and dusty, but at the end light dazzled down and the motes danced and—was that a pulpit?

It wasn't. It was just the fancy bottom of the stairs before they turned and started for real. Opal couldn't see out of the front door, stained glass onto the vestibule and frosted glass beyond, so she went up the first few stairs to peer through the fanlight, and it was right enough. This was N Fossett's house. There couldn't be two drives choked like that with the bushes grown up like Sleeping Beauty's vines.

She dropped back down from her tiptoes and that was when she saw Shelley, standing at the bottom looking up at her.

"Big house, eh?" she said. She tried to sound innocent, but Shelley's face had gone wooden. "Why would a single woman buy a house this size?"

"She didn't," said Shelley. "She was born here. Where were you going?"

"Wow," Opal said, her thoughts tumbling. *How old was she? When did they stop teaching kids that loopy writing?*

"Were you needing to find the loo?"

"Nah, just nosey," Opal said skipping down the stairs and landing with a jump on the thin carpet. "Must be nice, living in the lap of luxury like this. It would do me."

Shelley said nothing.

"Tell Miss Fossett I said bye," Opal called over her shoulder. As she let herself out and went back along the weird tunnel to the gate, she punched the air and shouted "Yes!" making a long fierce hissing sound. Miss N Fossett, who *had* to know who the little bed girl was and who might even *be* her! Locked and loaded!

"Hey!"

It was Shelley, standing at the back door. Opal turned.

"What are *you* so happy about?" Her face was just as wooden and her eyes were narrow too.

"Good deed for the day," Opal said. "Little old lady home safe and sound."

"That's what you said when you called me," said Shelley. "A little old lady." She was walking towards Opal, slow and steady. "But, just then, when you were saying goodbye, you used her name. Miss Fossett."

"Yeah?" said Opal. "So?"

"How did you find out her name? Were you snooping? Upstairs?"

"Yeah, that's right," said Opal. "You got me. I got into her house but before I went snooping round I called up a neighbor so I could get caught red-handed."

Shelley flushed.

"*You* told me her name," said Opal. "On the phone."

And now Shelley put a fluttering hand up to her throat.

"Did—Did I?"

"None taken," said Opal and went on her way. She was unstoppable. Take more than Shelley to slow her down. And she wasn't just coming along after the little bed girl was dead and gone and telling her story either, because she was still *there*, alive and kicking. Well, alive anyway.

And, okay, whoever had done bad things to Norah when she was little might be dead by now and past punishment, so you could ask what was the point. But Miss Fossett had put her head down and said "sorry, sorry" when Opal grabbed her arm. *That* was the point. She was a white-haired little old lady who'd told no one except her bedposts what was wrong, and a hundred and fifty years later (or however old she was), she was still apologising if someone hurt her arm.

And, Opal told herself, it might have been some horrible schoolmistress with a bamboo cane or a priest or something. There might have been a coverup, and it might have happened for years and years or even be happening still.

In fact—she was marching along by now, jaw set, flip-flops smacking against her heels with every angry stride—she knew "it" was happening still. "It" happened to little girls all the time. And "it" had happened to Craig Southgate, in Mote Street, just ten years ago. Some "it" or another anyway. Close enough.

"Cool down, Curly," said a voice. Opal swung round. There were two lads sitting on the low wall by the bins on the corner of Monkbridge Road, coke cans and cigarettes in their hands, laughing at her. Opal bared her teeth and made a noise like a cheetah, rasping from deep in her throat, making the lads shrink back, just for a moment, before they shook themselves and started again, whooping with laughter. Opal didn't care; she'd scared them.

She'd seen it in their eyes.

NINETEEN

AT THE BOTTOM OF Mote Street, she crossed her fingers and hoped that Fishbo wouldn't see her and grab her for more practising. This silver wedding gig made her mouth turn dry every time she remembered. But she was out of luck. When she peeped round the corner of Pep Kendal's house to see if the coast was clear, it was only to meet his eyes looking back at hers from where he was sitting on a dining chair set out on the pavement ten feet away.

"She's at her book group," he said, twinkling.

"Who?" said Opal

"Vonnie," he said. "Who else?"

"A *book* group?" said Opal, coming round to join him. "For real?" Pep nodded. Opal hitched her backside up onto his living room windowsill and whistled through her teeth. "Sometimes it feels as if I've never been away and sometimes … Mrs. Pickess in a book group." Pep laughed and stretched out in his chair until he was only touching it with his shoulder blades and the backs of his thighs, before relaxing again. "Anyway, it was you I was dodging, if you must know."

"What have *I* done?" he said.

"Well, Mr. Fish, anyway. Roped me in for this weekend. I'm shitting bricks."

Pep waved his cigarette at her, his eyes screwed up, until he had caught his breath, exhaled the smoke, and could talk again.

"You're safe enough," he said. "It's off. Cancelled."

"They heard about me!" said Opal, and Pep laughed again.

"Naw, *we* cancelled it, Opal love. The boys and me." She told herself it was silly to be hurt, told herself it was their job and their reputation and of course they'd cancelled rather than let Opal makes fools of them all. "And don't look like that, softie," he said. "We cancelled on account of Fishbo."

"Huh?" Opal said. Pep held up one finger and cocked his head telling her to listen, so she cocked her head up too, to the same side, and found that she could hear a rattling, burbling cough drifting down from the open front bedroom window.

"I had to get the doctor in," Pep said. "Chest infection. No way he'll be fit for Saturday."

"Cool," said Opal and then flushed. "I mean—" She stopped to listen to another cough, or maybe a new phase of the same one. It was deeper now, each spasm of it making a clapping, hacking sound that Opal couldn't imagine happening inside someone's body, in their chest, without bones breaking. Nicola had sometimes had a hell of a cough in the winters, smoking too much and not eating enough, and one coal fire never really got the house really warm right through to the brick. But Opal had never heard a cough like this one, and she swallowed hard, trying not to shudder as she listened to it ebbing away at last, leaving Fishbo retching and moaning.

"Okay?" Pep shouted up to the open window.

"*Hoo-yah!*" said Fishbo's voice, faintly. "Okay."

Opal noticed that Pep's face was pale above his stubble and, in spite of the heat, the hairs that usually lay like a pelt all over his arms were standing up, stiff and fuzzy. He rubbed his hands over them as if warming himself and shuddered too.

"I wish he'd move downstairs," he said. "I didn't get a wink last night with that racket. Never mind up and down all day with cups of tea."

But he didn't sound annoyed. He sounded worried and for the first time—funny how you just accept things when you're a kid—Opal thought about the fact that Fishbo had moved into Pep Kendal's house, taken over a room to give music lessons in, and just stayed put there.

"How long have you lived together?"

"Eh?" said Pep. "We don't *live together*. Bloody hell. He's my lodger. Nineteen eighty-five, he moved in, more or less as soon as he gave up driving taxis and joined the band. Live together!" He lit another cigarette, flustered.

"I didn't mean *that*," Opal said. "But come off it with the lodger bit. You wouldn't be running up and down with tea or calling the doctor if he was a lodger, would you?"

Pep blinked, considered it, and then acknowledged the point with a nod of the head, lips pushed out in a pout.

"Call him a pet, then," he said. "Like a parrot. More annoying than a bloody parrot, that's all."

"Yeah, yeah, you can't stand the sight of each other," Opal said. "Lived in the same house my whole lifetime cos you *annoy* each other."

"Nothing annoys Fishbo," said Pep. "That's one of the things that makes him so irritating." He looked up at the open bedroom window again. "I hope he can hear me, the old fart."

"But you must be fond of him," Opal said. "All these years. You must be." She was hoping to get the conversation round to his past, New Orleans and his family again; she couldn't have predicted where it would suddenly swerve off to.

"He's been good to me," Pep said, and for this he dropped his voice. In case the old fart heard him, Opal supposed. "Stuck by me when times were hard."

"And friends were few," said Opal. She couldn't remember where she had heard that, but it made Pep smile.

"Certainly seemed that way," he said. He had his cigarette in the corner of his mouth, making him squint, and with the low sun making him squint as well, he was grimacing like one of those old cowboys in the films, all screwed up against the desert dust as they stared into the distance. Except Pep wasn't staring into the distance; he was looking up and down the street, letting his eyes rest on one house after another, like he was doing some kind of stock-take. When he was done, he shook his head slowly. "Fewer than I'd reckoned, anyway. Can I ask you something, Opal love?"

She nodded. He cleared his throat and wet his lips with a smacking sound.

"I know you didn't come to visit," he went on, "but maybe you talked to your mother on the phone? So I was thinking maybe you could clear it up for me."

"Clear up what?' she asked.

"Something that's bothering me for years. Ten long years, if you must know."

"Ten years?" Opal echoed.

"Since Craig Southgate died. Disappeared." Opal had flinched at the word and hoped he hadn't seen her. It didn't mean anything.

Everyone thought he had died, didn't they? Everyone knew deep down that he must have. Pep saying it didn't mean a thing.

"What about it?" she said. He threw his cigarette down onto the pavement in front of him and ground it away to shreds with his heel.

"You shouldn't do that with slippers on," Opal told him.

"What about it"—Pep was bringing his foot up to rest on the opposite knee, craning to see his slipper sole and then flicking at it— "was that one of my dear neighbors in this close-knit community here told the police I was a kiddie-fiddler. That's what about it."

"No!" said Opal. That wasn't what Zula Joshi had told her Doolal had said. Not so clear and harsh as all that. It had just been a hint— bad enough—about all the men in the band, living together. Or maybe Zula couldn't bring herself to tell the whole truth of it. And no wonder. "No," Opal said again.

"Oh yes," said Pep, grimly. "Wife left, Fish never married, kids in and out for music lessons … you wouldn't believe what a couple of coppers can make of that if they've a mind to."

"*I* was in and out for music lessons," Opal said. "Jesus!"

"Aye and when you left, your mother came over more than once asking Fishbo why you'd upped sticks. What had he done to you to make you go. Asked me too. That's what made me think, years later, she might have said summat."

"What was she on about?" said Opal. "I never said anything about not being looked after over here. Was she drunk?"

"Well, she was breathing, love, put it that way," Pep said. He paused then. "Sorry."

"Don't be," said Opal. "It's a fair comment. What a nerve, though, blaming you for me leaving. That wasn't exactly Disneyland, was it?" She nodded across at her own house.

"So she never mentioned owt about it?" Pep said. "Never said to you who she suspected? When Craig d—disappeared?" He had checked himself, making Opal think he'd noticed her flinching before.

"We weren't in touch," she said. "I didn't even know about Craig till I got back again and Margaret told me the story."

"Right," Pep said, and he slumped a bit in his seat. Opal wished she could have told him different. It had to hurt, him not knowing who'd said something like that. Maybe she could explain. Tell him that Doolal was angry and lashing out, and that his mum was mortified and if his dad knew he'd get a thrashing. Then she shook the thought away. Her granddad always used to say to her—when she was scared of ghosts in her cupboard at night, this was—that it was the living you had to mind out for and forget the dead. Nicola was past caring now, but Doolal could still get his beautiful teeth knocked down his throat if Pep had a mind for payback.

"Wouldn't put it past her, mind you," she began. "If she'd fling that kind of accusation about after I left home, she'd do the same after Craig went, wouldn't she? I mean, she was pally with his dad, and I think the police took a long hard look at her."

"Yeah?" said Pep.

"Oh yes," Opal said. "Mrs. Pickess sent them over."

"Like pass the bloody parcel," Pep said. "Vonnie set them on Nic, Nic set them on me?"

"And then Fishbo set them on someone else to get them off your back?" Opal said, thinking that there was no one much left, since the Joshis had had their turn without anyone pointing the finger.

"Eh? Fishbo?"

"I thought that's what you meant about him being good to you."

"No, not Fish. Not his style at all. Wouldn't harm a fly. He just kept his trap shut, that's all."

"What about?" said Opal, thinking of the way Pep Kendal had said *died* like that.

"Little Craig," Pep said. "About what really happened that night." Then he stopped and turned right round in his seat to face her. "You're a sensible girl, Opal, aren't you? You'd not get any daft ideas?"

Opal stared at him.

"What night?" she said, because Craig disappeared on a Saturday morning, so far as anyone knew. But Mr. Kendal was back in the past, and he didn't hear her.

TWENTY

OPAL'S HEART WAS BANGING in her chest again, and she wondered if the pulse in the soft part of her throat was showing.

"He used to hide in the van, see?" Pep said. "Not just the van—he'd hide anywhere he could—but the van was a big draw. Many's the time we'd find him in there mucking about with our kit and have to drag him out by the scruff. And once he got locked in there on a hot day and he was like a little grease spot by the time we found him." He gave a snort that might have been laughter. "Fishbo wanted to throw a bucket of water over him, but I talked him down to a wet flannel and a suck of an ice cube. Margaret and Denny just laughed and gave him a clip round the ear."

"But surely, that Saturday morning, you checked the van," Opal said. "I don't see what's worrying you."

"Well, see, once or twice we *didn't* find him, that's the trouble," Pep said. "Once we didn't find him until we'd got all the way to Bradford and started unloading. Margaret and Denny weren't on the phone, and I didn't want to get Mrs. Pickess involved and have her wagging her finger at Margaret forevermore, so we just drove him back again and dumped him out in the back lane. I brought him once—the Bradford time—and the boys just had to do without a piano till I was back again. And another time we were out at Pudsey, and it was a short set, just a spot at a festival, so we just bought him a coke and a bag of crisps and … "

"What did Margaret say?" Opal asked.

"She didn't know," Pep said. "It was two hours all told he was gone. And when I took him back in the gate from the lane, she just seemed to think he'd been hanging around out of sight for a while."

"You must have wondered why they were in such a state the morning he disappeared for good then," Opal said.

"Yeah," Pep said. "I was that. At first anyway. The thing is, we'd been away out to a gig in Shipley the night before."

"The night before?" said Opal.

"And Craig had been in the van the night before. Sometime the afternoon before anyway."

"How do you know?"

"A wrapper," said Pep. "From an ice pop. You know those things? A blue one. It was tucked right down the side of the wheel arch."

"Yeah, but you said he ducked into the van a lot. He could have left that anytime, couldn't he?"

Pep shook his head.

"Margaret still had five more in a box in her freezer. And she'd never bought that kind before. The police made quite a thing out of that blue ice pop. They looked all over for the wrapper. Never found it."

"They didn't find it in the van?"

"I told them we'd been late back from Shipley Friday night and didn't even unload the gear. Just locked it up tight and didn't open it again until Karen came out shouting and wailing on the Saturday morning. No more than the truth. It was later, next day, when I found the wrapper."

"But…" Opal couldn't see her way through this at all. "If Craig disappeared on Saturday morning, it's no matter where he ate an ice pop on Friday night. The cops wouldn't have been interested anyway."

"True enough," said Pep. "*If* he disappeared Saturday morning. But he didn't, did he?"

Opal was sure she could hear the beat of her heart even over the rasping in and out of her breath. What was he saying? How did he know when Craig went missing? What exactly had Fishbo covered up for him?

"Why are you telling me this?" she said. She heard the old dining chair he was sitting on creak as he turned to look at her again, even more sharply this time.

"You okay?" he said. "I didn't mean to upset you. Shouldn't rake stuff over, I suppose."

Of course she wasn't *okay*. It was happening again. Zula knew when Craig went missing. She grudged her boys being questioned about Saturday morning when she *knew* little Craig had gone missing Friday night. And Vonnie Pickess knew too; she'd let it slip that Friday night parties might be part of the story some way. And now here was Pep Kendal saying it straight out. Craig had gone missing on Friday.

And how did they all know that if none of them had anything to do with where he'd gone?

"I'm fine," she said.

"I thought you said Margaret told you all about it," Pep said.

"She—She did."

"Of course she did," Pep said. He started a laugh that ended up as a sigh and shook his head. "She can't help herself."

"Oh!" Opal said, and she sat back against the living room window so hard she could hear the putty grating. "*That's* how you know? Margaret told you?"

"What did you think?"

"Margaret told me it was a secret. She said she had to tell someone or she'd burst."

"She probably says that every time," Pep said. "Or maybe she's lost track. She's on six different pills for her nerves, you know. She told Fishbo first and you want to be sure she said it was a secret to him. Of course, he came straight out and told me. Said he'd sooner die than tell the cops Margaret's secret and get me into trouble."

"*Would* you have got into trouble?" Opal said.

"If I'd told the police he'd been in the van the night he went missing? I think that would be enough, don't you? And if I told them I'd had him away to Bradford and out at Pudsey and never told his granny? Added to someone round here telling them I was ... What do you think?"

"But he didn't actually stow away with you that last night, did he?" Opal said. Pep sat forward and clasped his hands, staring at the pavement, where a short line of ants was rippling along a crack in the concrete, scaling a crown of dandelion and disappearing down its far side.

"I've gone over it and over it," he said. "And there's no way. The van was open when it was empty, but when it's empty there's nowhere to hide. As soon as we'd put the gear in we locked it up, and the next time we opened it was at Shipley in the function room car park, and I stood in the back the whole time while the boys were unloading. It's a rough old place; I'd never leave a van open and no one watching."

"So he couldn't have been in there."

"Couldn't have been. And that's what I told Fishbo. And that's why he kept the ice pop quiet for me."

At that moment, the coughing started again upstairs in the bedroom, and Opal and Pep listened to it in silence for a while. The retching was worse at the end of the bout this time, but eventually he quieted again.

"*Hoo-yah!*" he said. "Still down there, old friend?"

"You okay?" Pep called up to him.

"I'm okay," the voice came back down. "Lost my damn lunch on my damn pee-jays, all the same."

"Lovely!" said Pep, getting to his feet. He shook his head and laughed, looking down at Opal. "Can't say I'm not repaying him."

"No-o," said Opal slowly. "But if you want to say thanks in a big way, I've thought of how."

"Bigger than putting up with him for all these long years? Listening to his yakking on and acting like a nurse in a striped pinny?"

"Well, nicer," Opal said. "A what do you call it—a grand gesture. Not just housework and stuff."

"Yeah?" said Pep.

"He really wants to see his family again," Opal said. "Or at least hear some news from them."

But Pep was shaking his head, that same twisted smile on his face as the last time Opal had tried to talk to him about Fishbo going home. "You just keep out of it, Opal love," he said. "Take it from me and don't go meddling."

"Pep?" came Fishbo's voice, high and querulous.

"I'm coming, I'm coming," Pep shouted. "Just having a word with Opal Jones."

144

"Don't you bring me any visitors up here." Fishbo sounded panicked now. "I ain't fit for comp'ny. You tell her to git gone. No visitors today."

"Looks like you're on your own changing the pajamas," said Opal. She waited until he had gone inside and shut the door before she went over the road and in at her own.

It was cool in the living room—or as cool as anywhere would be tonight anyway—and it was pleasant to stand there halfway back where she could see all four houses across the way without any chance of being seen. Even more pleasant to let herself feel the relief of understanding.

Margaret had told them all. *That* was why Zula looked so shifty, and why Mrs. Pickess had tried to cover her slip. They knew, but they didn't know Opal knew. She nodded to herself and turned towards the kitchen to go and make her tea.

She never got there. She stopped in the doorway and felt the relief drain out of her, could have sworn she could feel it literally pouring out through the soles of her feet, sucking her in to the carpet, leaving her heavy and soft like she'd never move again. Margaret told them to keep the secret, but why *had* they?

Pep Kendal was keeping his head down. Fishbo was being a good friend, keeping his down too. But why had Zula Joshi not told the police it was Friday instead of Saturday morning? Friday, when her boys were safely at school. And Mrs. Pickess! Mrs. Pickess, who tattled on Nicola for no reason at all. Would Vonnie Pickess ever have kept Margaret's secret in a million years?

Opal put her two hands on the frame of the kitchen door and pulled herself forwards, setting her feet moving again, making herself stumble out onto the linoleum. *It's the heat,* she told herself. *I'm light-headed from heat, that's all. And I've drunk nothing since dinner break either. I'm dehydrated; that's all that's wrong with me.*

But it wasn't. It was this: if Margaret told Zula, Mrs. Pickess, and Fishbo—all her old neighbors of years and years—wouldn't she have told Nicola too? And wouldn't Nicola have blabbed a juicy story like that to a hundred different people on one of her wild Friday nights? Or down at the pub or sitting on a bus or any of the places she opened her mouth and let every single little bit of her business come dolloping out? Only she couldn't have, could she? Because nobody knew. And so she must have had some really good reason for keeping her trap shut.

Opal stood at the sink, stared out into the yard, and tried to think of some way around it. There wasn't one. If Zula choosing not to get her boys out from under suspicion was weird, if Mrs. Pickess not dropping her old friend right in it and calling it her Christian duty was weirder, Nicola Jones managing to keep something quiet for any other reason except to save her own neck was a million miles the weirdest idea of all.

TWENTY-ONE

ON THE OTHER HAND, though, the new discovery—finding out that everyone in Mote Street knew everything—meant that Opal wasn't *special* after all. She hadn't been chosen by Margaret, there was no golden thread. Which meant she could stop anytime she wanted. No harm no foul, whatever that meant.

Only that would be like saying she was too scared to go on. Scared of what she might find out. About her own mother. Like she was saying she thought her mum might really have hurt a child. Somewhere deep down inside her, like a pit dug under a tunnel that ran below the basement of her memories, something moved. She ignored it. And decided to carry on.

So she cleared off her kitchen table and sat down with a clean pad of paper. If she was going to keep her mind focused on the right questions—not let it drift off around a load of useless old junk that was nothing to do with anything (absolutely nothing at all)—she had to get organised about it. Pep was in the clear. Opal wrote his name at the top of the first sheet and drew a thick, deliberate tick beside it. He was no fiddler. She'd been in and out of his house from when she could toddle over and hold a cornet to her lips. And there were four others who would have seen Craig Southgate in the back of the van when they opened up at the function room in Shipley to take out their gear. She went over the tick again, even harder. Pep had a good innocent reason for keeping his head down and not telling the police how long the kid had been missing before his mum and granny knew.

But what about—Opal turned to a new page—Fishbo? He had heard Margaret's confession—the first time she'd made it, Pep said—and he hadn't breathed a word. Loyalty, Pep reckoned. He didn't want to get his old friend hauled over the coals. But couldn't his loyalty help Pep anyway? If Fish told the cops that Craig disappeared on Friday, he could also tell them there was no way the boy could have ended up locked inside the van. So was it loyalty to Margaret then? Was Fishbo particularly close to Margaret? Or Denny, maybe? Opal didn't think so. Maybe he just didn't want to get involved, or he didn't think much of the law, or by the time Margaret told him it was too late to make any difference anyway and his kind heart didn't want to see her shamed and hurting.

After all, *Opal* wasn't about to tell on Margaret, was she? Why couldn't Fishbo feel the same? She put her pen against the paper by his name, but instead of the big black tick she was planning, she found herself drawing a question mark there.

Because Opal knew why *she'd* never tell the police a single damn thing. She hated the bastards. Hated the way they looked at her mum and the way they spoke, all kind and calm on the surface with their little eyes like pebbles and nothing moving in their faces except their thin mouths. She had never seen a cop with big eyes or full lips. Not one. Asking all their questions, calling her *love* and *pet* and *darling*, and poke poke poking to get her to say what they wanted to hear. "Do you get to school every day, love?" "Do you get your breakfast, dinner, and tea every day, pet?" "Does anyone who comes to the house ever bother you, my darling?"

"Aye, *you*!" Opal had yelled at that one and clattered off upstairs to get away from him.

She went to pour herself a drink of water, letting the tap run and run, waiting for it to come through cold.

Was it the same for Fishbo? It was hard for Opal to think of old men who wore jackets and hats as needing to worry about what the cops might think. Hard for her to think about Pep and Fishbo and the rest of the Mote Street boys except as grownups to her little-girl memories of them, but if she tried—twenty-five and no fool—she supposed that Eugene Gordon arriving in Leeds all those years ago probably hadn't got a hero's welcome and might well have had a few set-tos that left him supporting whoever was on the other side from the boys in blue.

She felt the water start to turn and she put both her hands under the tap, letting it stream over her wrists, like her granny used to do when she felt too hot. It didn't make any difference, though, and it was a hell of a waste of water so she took them out again, held a glass under and drained it in a gulp. In fact, since she was on a meter, she thought, she should probably keep a big jug in the fridge instead of running it cold every time she was thirsty. She'd get herself a jug and start that sometime.

Right, she thought, sitting down again, drying her hands by pressing them against her neck and shoulders, trying to push some of the coolness from the water drops into her skin. *Right then.* New page. *Who's next?*

Vonnie Pickess. Now, *there* was a puzzle. Because for one thing, Mrs. Pickess didn't have a loyal, friendly, generous bone in her body—and never mind a bone: try a cell, try a chromosome, try a *gene* (if that was smaller). And for two, Mrs. Pickess obviously didn't have a problem cuddling up to the cops because she had blabbed to them about Nicola being pals with Craig's dad, hadn't she? A big fat question mark for Vonnie.

Which left Zula, Mr. Joshi, Birbal, Doolal, Sanjit, Advay, and Vikram. She put them all on one page, and for a long moment she sat and stared across the kitchen. Because how was she supposed to know whether all the funny little looks and funny little comments that had freaked her out that day over at Zula's were anything to do with anything? How did she know what to write down and what to ignore?

Start with everything, she decided, and then narrow it down. She had to eliminate people—like Pep already, and Fishbo soon to follow as soon as she could get him to tell her how much the pigs had hassled him when he was fresh off the boat—and she had to eliminate... What would she call them? Inconsistencies? Niggles? Shadows? Knots?

1. Why did Zula want Opal to come back to Mote Street?

2. Why did she sleep in Nicola's room?

3. What was Zula on about with the canoes and mountain bikes?

4. Why did she offer to help with DIY?

Opal sat and looked at the four questions she had written and tried to see any connection to Craig at all. At a stretch, if one of the Joshis knew something they shouldn't, and if Nicola found out, then it would make sense for Zula to chum up with Nicola and make sure she didn't spill the beans. That was fair enough. But what would be the point of getting Opal back here? And what could Opal's hobbies or home improvements have to do with it? No, the more she thought about it, the surer she was that three out of those four...niggles...would be eliminated from her inquiry just as soon as she could think up a way to ask about them without Zula thinking she'd gone off her trolley.

And that left the big one. Question 5: Why did Zula Joshi not tell the police that Craig disappeared at a time her boys had alibis for? It was a straight choice, wasn't it? Protect Margaret or protect her five sons.

Unless it was *after* the police stopped coming that Zula found out. She could maybe ask one of the boys in the course of an innocent conversation. Less suspicious than tackling Zula again.

She could hear the boys right now, at least two of them anyway, out on the street: an engine running, loud voices, laughter. She could go out and say hello. After all, she'd been here nearly a month and only waved at them so far. She went through into the living room and edged around the armchair in front of the window so that she could see who was there—Vik in one of the cars and his dad standing at the kerb, holding a steaming mug, wearing Zula's headset with the microphone pushed away to the side so he could drink his tea. *Perfect*, she thought. *I'll just nip over and say hello.*

But she heard the car leaving as she was smoothing her hair and finding her flip-flops, and by the time she opened her front door, Vikram was gone and Mr. Joshi was standing there on his own.

"Hiya," said Opal, coming over to stand beside him.

"Zuleika's not in, love," he said.

"Well," said Opal, "it'll be quiet on a Monday, isn't it?"

"It is if the dispatch coordinator's not there to keep it busy."

"Right," said Opal, thinking if that was the mood he was in there was no point trying to strike up any kind of conversation at all. "Where is she then?"

"Morrison's," said Mr. Joshi. "Doing the big shop."

"Blimey, I thought she was on a girls' night out, the way you were talking," said Opal, and at last he laughed. He took a last swig of tea and then threw the dregs into the long grass and dock leaves behind him.

"She'd rather be in Morrison's than at the Chippendales any day," he said. "She'll be back here with foot spas and paper shredders and ten new shirts that won't fit me. 'But they were on offer'. The woman's a maniac when she gets her hands on a trolley."

"You should give me a list and I'd bring it home from Tesco for you," Opal said.

"Me?" said Mr. Joshi. "I'm worse, love. That's why Zul goes on her own. I bought a garden shed the last time I went. And a garden table and six chairs. Solid teak."

"You don't even have a garden," said Opal, laughing.

"They were on offer," Mr. Joshi said. Then he sighed. "So you're back again, are you? Back to stay?"

"Yep," said Opal. "Thanks to—" She bit it off. "Thanks to my mum never getting her act together to tell anyone I left, I'm still the official tenant. Unless someone tells them I'm not."

"Bah, that's nothing to do with anyone else," Mr. Joshi said, and the easy way he spoke left Opal almost sure he knew nothing and couldn't care less whether Opal lived there or someone new moved in. And that left her almost sure too that Zula's funny little hints and odd little looks were summat or nowt, as her granddad used to say.

"True," Opal said. "But neighbors, you know. I don't mean you!"

"Ah yes, the Neighborhood Witch," said Mr. Joshi, wiggling his eyebrows at Mrs. Pickess's front door.

"Mr. Joshi!" said Opal.

"She's out," he said. "She won't hear me."

"Yeah, she's at her book club. Mr. Kendal told me."

"Book club! How can you read a book on a broomstick?"

"Stop it! She's not that bad." But Mr. Joshi, for once, had not a trace of a smile on his face.

"I used to think she was harmless too," he said. "But we went through a right bad time here while you were away, Opal love. And she showed her true colours then, I can tell you."

"You mean when Craig Southgate disappeared?" Opal said.

"I never found out for sure," Mr. Joshi said, "but who else would have told the police that Pep and Fish were the type to hurt a little boy? Filth like that when we'd known them for years."

Opal said nothing. Zula was right: if Mr. Joshi had found out it was his own son who poured that little drop of poison into a policeman's ear, he would skin the boy alive.

"It must have been a terrible time," she said.

Mr. Joshi cleared his throat. "Long ago," he said. He cleared his throat again. "I shouldn't be talking to you about old troubles anyway. I should be saying sorry about your mum."

"Yeah," said Opal. She never knew what to say when people said that to her. It wasn't their fault. Why were *they* sorry?

"If there's ever anything we can do." That was another thing. What could anyone *do*? Then she remembered why she'd come over and saw a way in.

"I know," she said. "Zula told me. But"—she took a deep breath and decided to go for it—"she's done enough, really, hasn't she?"

"Zul?" said Mr. Joshi. "Likes of what?"

"Oh, I just mean taking such good care of my mum. I mean, they got quite close towards the end."

"Did they?" said Mr. Joshi.

That's genuine surprise, Opal thought.

"And you're all right, are you?"

"How d'you mean?" Opal asked. "Oh, you mean getting jobs done in the house and all that. Yeah, Zula already told me to ask, but really I'm not planning anything."

"Eh?" said Mr. Joshi. "What jobs?"

"DIY, like I told Zula. Can't afford it and wouldn't know what to do anyway."

"What are you on about?" said Mr. Joshi. Opal could have hugged him. He didn't have a clue about any of those so-called niggles, knots, and shadows. Not a single clue. Maybe she had just imagined all the sideways looks that day. Maybe she could cross off the whole Joshi family. Solid alibis, nothing to hide.

"Zula told me that you and the boys would help me out if I needed any work doing," she said.

"Did she?" said Mr. Joshi, and he looked a tiny bit ruffled now. "Well that's my dear wife for you. If she's not buying stuff we don't need, she's giving away stuff we do." Then he turned and looked over the rooftops in the direction of the main road. "Here she comes, talk of the devil," he said.

"How can you tell it's her?" Opal said. She could hear a car, but it could have been anyone.

"That is the mating call of a two-year-old Mondeo driven in the wrong gear and weighed down by ... ooh ... a hundred and fifty quid's worth of stuff we'll never find a use for, and another hundred quid's worth of food we won't fit in the freezer that's still full from last time."

And right enough, Zula's Mondeo was turning up at the bottom of the street. She waved when she saw Opal.

"Good to see you!" she called through the open window as she drew in beside them. "Stay and have some supper with us, Opal love. I've got three hot chickens off the rotisserie and they won't keep. Sunil, go and sit down. There's sandals for you try on."

"Maniac," said Mr. Joshi to Opal under his breath. "Pop the boot, crazy woman, and I'll start bringing it in." He handed two bags to Opal and told her to take them to the kitchen.

When she was on her way back along the passage to the front door for another load, though, she could hear them talking.

"—needed it for the new garage floor and she never even used the bloody—"

"Sssh, Sunil, she'll hear you."

"—stuff, probably sold it. So why are you starting up the same way with the daughter now?"

"I'm not starting anything."

"DIY. She specifically mentioned DIY. I had to act like an idiot to cover—"

"She's just moved house. Of course, she's going to be—"

"And why is she asking questions?"

"What questions?"

"And talking about you and her mother. Together. Making a link."

"She's going to *hear* you."

And so Opal went back to the kitchen where she couldn't hear a thing and opened up the two bags to start putting shopping away, stacking the fridge with lemon and coriander hummus, three for the price of two; 50-percent-extra flat-leaf parsley; and smoked peppered mackerel, buy one get one free.

TWENTY-TWO

THAT NIGHT, LYING IN her bed, melting into the plastic on her mattress (planning to unwrap it, squirt it with ten big bottles of Febreze, and take her chances), she could hear whatsisname next door sobbing again, worse than ever. She turned over and fanned the sheet. *Too bad pal*, she thought. *Things come in threes and I'm full up of other people's problems already. You'll just have to cry.*

But on the floor the next day she brought up a list for an FF Gilbert and was sure, nearly sure, that that was the name she'd signed beside on the clipsheet the van driver gave her. White bread, olive marg, oven chips, pizza... It sounded like him, and she wondered what the two Fs stood for. Fat Freddy, Franz Ferdinand, Full Fat. He'd asked for Gŭ two-pack individual lemon cheesecakes and there were none. Opal stopped and looked back at the list. Nothing suggested as a substitution. She should check out the back. And she couldn't explain why she didn't, except that thinking about him crying like that the way he did, and the way he stood on her step all crumpled and dusty, she thought he needed a laugh more than he needed a pudding. So even though if Dave chose that day to spot-check her pick she'd get the sack, she did a little substitution of her own. Instead of lemon cheesecake, she gave him a lemon, some cheese—half a pound of mild cheddar, the kind he seemed to like—and a cake. A small frosted occasion cake with a smiley face piped onto the butter icing and *Smile!* written in chocolate under it. Would he get it? Was it worth risking her job on the off-chance that he would? She was just reaching her hand into the tray to take the cake out again when she jumped at a voice beside her.

"Off at two?"

"Want a lift home?"

"I'm at Sandford, in the Broadleas."

"Practically neighbors."

"Kate's coming to mine."

"You can come too."

Opal couldn't think of a reason not to, so she nodded.

"Cool."

"Because we're going out Friday night."

"So I'm going back with Rhianne to try on."

"It's Tuesday," said Opal.

"It's desperate," Kate said. "I haven't had more than a peck on the cheek since Christmas and that was from Uncle Bernie."

"Do you want to come with us?"

"On Friday, she means."

"And today too. We'll stop off, get your stuff, and all go down to mine together."

"I'm going round to my friend's after work today," Opal said.

"Yeah?"

"Yeah."

"Where does she stay?"

"Headingley."

"Bring her!" said Kate, and Opal had to try not to laugh. "Bring her out on Friday too, if she's single."

"Oh, she's single," said Opal, thinking of Miss Fossett's ringless little hand slipping into the crook of her arm. "But she's a bit…"

"What?"

"Quiet," Opal said. "She's got a lot of family stuff going on. That's another reason I was so keen to come back to Leeds, actually. To help Norah. Stop her getting depressed…again."

"Norah and Opal?" said Rhianne.

"Who calls a girl Norah?" Kate said.

"No wonder she's got family stuff going on. Her mum and dad must be psychos."

But Opal was grateful for the lift. It got her home miles earlier than her two buses, and she really did mean to go up to Miss Fossett's, if she could find it again. Only, when the girls saw Sanj and Advay Joshi hanging around outside No. 8, vaccing out the backs of their cars, there was no shifting them. Rhianne turned off her engine and took the scrunchie out of her hair.

"Opal!" she said. "You might have told us. I'd have *bought* something to change into."

"Jeez, imagine a pair of snacks like that seeing us in our Tesco polo shirts."

"Yeah, no wonder you changed into your little skimpy-pimpies," said Rhianne, pulling Opal's strap and pinching a bit of skin along with it.

"There's five of them," Opal said. "That two's actually the ugly ones."

Rhianne gave a long groan and slid down in her seat as if she was melting. Then she sat straight back up again.

"Jeez-us," she said. "Katie, look over there. Look—it's whatser-name's buggy." Rhianne was staring across the street towards Mrs. Pickess's shopping trolley on its little mat under its little plastic cover.

"Oh my God!" said Katie. "The buggy in the bubble. It must be her—what was her name?"

"Oh Opal, go over and knock on her door," said Rhianne and started laughing. "I'm dying to see if it's really her."

"If she's in, she'll be out in a minute anyway to see who's parked and what they're at," said Opal, and sure enough the door was opening even as she spoke and Mrs. Pickess, cloth in hand, started wiping her fly blind.

"It is!" said Rhianne. "It's Lena Martell. It's Lena bloody Martell! Wait till Eric hears this."

"I thought she'd drunk herself to death," Kate said. "We haven't see her for months."

"What did you call her?" Mrs. Pickess had disappeared inside again as soon as she saw that they were talking about her.

"Lena Martell," said Kate, laughing. "One of Eric's. You know Eric on Wines and Spirits? He's got a hundred of them. Carlsberg Cathie, Sherry Lee Lewis. I think Lena Martell was some old country and western singer from when Eric was a lad."

"But Mrs. Pickess doesn't drink," Opal said.

"She might have stopped," said Kate, "but she certainly used to drink. A bottle a day sometimes, remember Rhianne? Eric used to sing it when she came in. At seven o'clock in the bloody morning like all the pensioners do. *One day at a time, sweet Jesus, da-dah, da-dah-dah-dah-DAH.*" They were swaying back and forwards now and kept it up until they saw that Sanj and Advay had noticed them at last and were standing staring, with their dust-busters held up like pistols, pointing into the air.

159

Rhianne screamed and dropped down under the dashboard.

"God almighty!" she said. "The stud brothers heard us singing Lena Martell! Jee-zus. Opal, get out if you're getting out and let me crawl away and kill myself, eh?"

Opal let herself out of the car, and Rhianne backed away down the street.

"Don't tell me you've joined a choir, Opal Jones?" Sanjit said. He always called her Opal Jones like that.

"Nah, Tesco," Opal said. "It's more of a cult."

"Yeah, right, whatever," Sanjit said, making her think of Jan and Paulo and whether there were any boys in the world who wouldn't get annoyed if a girl said something funny. She turned away and let herself in at her front door.

Lena Martell. The song had rung a faint bell even if the name hadn't, but it wasn't the song that was niggling her. Carlsberg Cathie, what was the other one, and Lena Martell. She dumped her bag down and went upstairs. Both bedrooms were clear now and she was making progress in the attic too, but she wasn't finished yet, not nearly.

She went over to the nearest black bin bag, quite far over the floor now, and untied its bunny ears. The smell was enough to send her rocking back on her heels. Hot plastic and hot stale brandy. Worse than stale, really. Dried out, dark and sticky, like burnt sugar on a gas ring. And fumes too as she moved the bottles. She pulled one out and looked at it. Martell VS Cognac. And she thought about all the dozens and dozens of bottles she'd taken away and looked around at the dozens more bags still waiting. It had never occurred to her to wonder why, if Nicola was still going out to the offy, she didn't dump the bottles in the bank on her way like she used to. But then Zula and Margaret had both said she didn't go out much at the end. So how did she get the booze?

Opal should have known there was something wrong with all those bottles too, all the same brand, all the same size. That wasn't Nicola's way. She stuck to brandy as much as she possibly could, it was true, although when she was on a proper jag and the money was low she'd move to sherry, vodka, strong lager, anything she could lay her hands on. But she always bought whatever was the best buy. Litres, flat half pints, own labels—no labels, sometimes from the Sunday market; or at least no label in any language Opal had seen before. And yet there had been a whole attic and a spare bedroom full of 70cl bottles of Martell VS.

And Vonnie Pickess didn't drink.

And the only reason she would go so far from home—two buses, as Opal knew only too well from sitting on them day after day—was surely so that no one she knew would see her buying all that brandy and wonder why.

Opal wandered downstairs again, feeling the start of a headache. Why would Mrs. Pickess land Nicola in trouble, blabbing about Robbie Southgate and her knowing each other, and then start buying her brandy? One thing made sense if Mrs. Pickess suspected Nicola of something, and the other made sense if Nicola suspected Mrs. Pickess.

None of it made sense to Opal, that was for sure.

TWENTY-THREE

So she went to Headingley, to Miss Fossett, where things not making sense was part of the deal and she could handle it from long practise, even though it surprised her how much talking to an old lady with senile dementia was like talking to a woman in her thirties with a good drink in her. It was the stubbornness. Miss Fossett didn't slur her words or sob on your neck, telling you she loved you and then telling you you'd ruined her life and she couldn't get it back again—but the way she went on about how they were supposed to come and how she wanted to go back to the party? That was just the same.

Opal found the back lane and the vinyl tunnel straight away, no trouble at all. Nothing happened when she knocked on the door, but if the room with the DVD was at the front—Opal remembered how long that corridor was, how many doors—someone could stand here and bang the door into splinters without Miss Fossett hearing, especially if she had the telly turned up high like old people always did. So

Opal started looking for a way around the side to try at the front instead.

There was no break in the tunnel walls, just twenty feet of smooth vinyl panelling like a rat-run. Out in the lane there was a garage door, but it was padlocked. Just as Opal let the padlock fall from her hand, she realized someone was watching and turned sharply. There, standing at the mouth of the lane, staring at her, was Shelley, the neighbor. She had a little girl by the hand and her mobile flipped open in the other, and she just stood there.

"Hi," Opal said. "Me again. I came back to see Miss Fossett." She walked towards Shelley, very casual, smiling, but she could tell that her face was red and knew her voice sounded funny.

"Oh, yeah?" Shelley said.

"Hello," said the little girl, staring up at Opal. Opal gave her a smile, eyebrows wiggling.

"But she didn't answer the door. I hope she's not wandered off out again."

"Was it open?" Shelley said.

"I don't know," said Opal. "I didn't try it. Maybe she didn't hear me, if she's got her DVD on, I was thinking. It's a big house."

"You said that before," said Shelley. "You've had a look round, haven't you?"

Opal flushed even deeper. "Look," she said, opening her arms wide. "No bag, no pockets. Do you want to frisk me?"

"Frisky!" said the little girl. "My friend Emily's got a guinea-pig called—"

"Ssh, sweetheart," said Shelley, looking at Opal as she spoke.

"Sorry," Opal said. "I know you're trying to take care of her. But honest, I really just wanted to see her again. I liked her. I—I wanted to hear some more of her stories. About her life. Look, I'll give you my name and address, if you're worried."

"I didn't mean—"

"Look," said Opal again. "You did mean and I know you did and you know I know, so let's just …"

"I'm just being a good neighbor."

"Course you are," said Opal. "It's the same where I live. The young ones look after the old ones, and the old ones help out the young ones. That's how it should be."

"Where *do* you live?"

"Oh, yeah," said Opal. "Name and address. It's Opal Jones, Six Mote Street. I'll give you my mobile number and you can check it right now." She held her phone out in the palm of her hand.

"Mote Street?" said Shelley, and she took a firmer grip on her daughter's hand, pulling the little girl hard into her legs.

"Yeah," said Opal.

"Everybody takes care of everybody else in *Mote Street*?" Shelley took a step away, physically backed away and swung her daughter up into her arms. The little girl, picking up on her mother's mood at last, it seemed, wound her fat fists into the straps of Shelley's sundress and stared at Opal, all smiles gone.

"I grew up there," Opal said. "I live there. It doesn't make me a bad person."

But Shelley was looking at her now like she'd not looked at her before, head to toe, considering, letting her eyes linger on the space between the bottom of her tee-shirt and her waistband—Opal made herself not tug her tee-shirt down—but she sucked her stomach in and felt the material fall down on its own anyway.

"I haven't seen a look like that since I left school," she said. "I bet you were a fucking bitch, weren't you?" The little girl opened her eyes

164

very wide and then buried her face in her mother's shoulder. "Oh, she knows that word then?" Opal said. "Where did she hear that? Ballet class?" And she shouldered her way past the pair of them, nearly touching Shelley's arm, but only because she was standing there in the middle of the narrow lane like she owned the world.

And although her eyes filled up with tears and her nose started running, no one watching her from behind—seeing how she swung her arms and rolled her hips, swishing along with her flip-flops dragging on the ground—would think she had a care in the world.

Plus, she told herself, trying to find a bright side, it would be easier to make pals with Miss Fossett if she didn't have to bother what Shelley thought of her. Now she only had to get round Norah herself—which would be easy. And if anyone else started asking her what she was up to, chumming in with an old lady she'd never met before, she could say she didn't trust Shelley, wondered why she was trying to keep everyone but herself *away* from Miss Fossett, that she—Opal—thought Miss Fossett needed someone *really* looking out for her, in case Shelley was ... but Opal stopped herself. That was the kind of thing Vonnie Pickess would do.

Franz Ferdinand was in when she got home. She could hear his tap running, then the sound of a kettle lid being pulled off and jammed on again, and she wondered if his shopping had turned up yet—if it really was his. Wondered too for the first time what it would be like when the students came back in September if she could hear one sad single neighbor making himself a cup of tea. Then she remembered someone telling her once—when she was little; who was that?—that the big end houses were separate squares of solid brick, and the two small houses in the middle of the row were really like one house cut in half, hardly divided at all. He had stood at the kitchen window and pointed along the back

165

wall—Opal looked out there again now—and showed her how the two outhouses were built as a pair, back to back, and how thin the wall between the yards was. Telling her how, if he had the money, he'd buy two and knock them in together, make a decent place out of the pair of them. And then Nicola had snorted—she was sitting at the table behind them—and said if her place wasn't decent enough, he knew what he could do and that Opal didn't need him to show her round her own outhouse like a bloody tour gui—

Opal jumped. A door had opened, and she swung round thinking someone had come into the house. Then she let her breath go in a rush as she heard the door shutting again. That was exactly what she had just been thinking! It was Franz Ferdi's door, through the paper wall.

Then she jumped again, just a little. Why else would he open and shut his door except to take in a delivery? She went into the bottom of the stairs and put her ear against the joining wall. He was back in the kitchen and surely that thumping sound could be shopping bags being dumped on a counter. Footsteps, and a cupboard door. More footsteps and then silence. Opal waited, her breath held, her lip between her teeth. And then she heard it. He was laughing. Quite loud, gusty whoops of laughter ending in a sigh. Then some silence and another chuckle. Then the footsteps started again and the cupboard doors and another new sound. Franz Ferdinand was whistling as he put his shopping away.

Opal took her ear away from the wall and sat back, resting her elbows on the step behind her and stretching her bare feet out, cooling them against the painted stairway wall. Next door the kettle sang—*he doesn't have a proper kettle either*, she thought, *just one on the cooker top like mine*—and she imagined him getting a mug and dropping in the teabag, opening the fridge for some milk and opening a cupboard for a bowl—no, a bag; he was a man living alone—of sugar. Then sitting down and...

She could hear him chuckling again, faintly, then a series of gasps and gulps. She put her ear back against the wall and listened. Yep. He was crying.

She went out into the yard, right to the end, into the shadows, and leaned her back against the brick wall. Pretty much a failure of a day. She'd let Kate and Rhianne drive her home when she was supposed to be freezing them out. She'd made an enemy of Shelley. And she'd risked her job to make Franz Ferdi cry worse than ever. And then there was the thing she *wasn't* thinking about, which she supposed had gone okay. It was progress, anyway.

She'd found out Mrs. Pickess bought her mum's brandy. Mrs. Pickess, who'd shopped her mum to the cops, had started taking care of her—at least Nicola would see it that way. So Mrs. Pickess knew something, or Nic did. Maybe both. Zula definitely did. Fishbo, possibly. All those people with secrets to keep, keeping Margaret's secret too. How was she going to get any of those secrets out into the open?

Well, she could stop kidding herself for a start.

She remembered exactly who it was who told her about the big houses separate and the small houses in pairs. She had remembered when she heard FF crying again. Something about sitting on the stairs and a man crying in the kitchen. It was Robbie, of course. Robbie Southgate. Craig's dad. He wasn't just a pal, not just one of the Friday night crowd. He was Nicola's boyfriend. He was on the scene when Opal left home—she knew he was, even if she didn't remember anything about him—and if he was still on the scene when Craig disappeared, then he was the obvious person to find if she really wanted answers.

If she wanted answers. If she did. Did she?

TWENTY-FOUR

"I wondered when you'd get back round to us." The voice was soft, like dough, like someone muffled under the covers at night, face pressed into a blanket. He had called out for her to come in and in she came, sat down on the edge of the sofa, and smiled. "Margaret's missed you these last weeks. She's worried she said something to offend you."

"Margaret?" said Opal. "Said what?"

"She worries these days. She's not like she was."

Opal smiled again. How could he sit there saying his wife wasn't how she was, with the change there had been in him? Could it have happened so slowly he didn't know?

"I've just been getting myself settled," she said. "Starting my job, seeing everyone again, saying hello."

"Yes," said Denny. "I heard."

"Heard what?" Opal said. "Off of who?"

Denny flung his head back to the open window behind him.

"I mean, I *heard*," he said. "You. In and out. Over the road and back again. I don't miss much that goes on. Not these days."

Opal didn't know what to say. She had almost forgotten, if she was honest, that all the time she was talking to Pep, shouting up to Fishbo, chatting away to the Joshis, fending off Mrs. Pickess, Denny was right here with the window open. Listening. But surely she hadn't ever said anything she wouldn't want him to hear.

"And I don't like the look of those two girls much, love," he told her. Opal frowned and Denny held up a mirror—it must have been Margaret's; it was one of those ones with a handle, roses on the back of the glass. He angled it over one shoulder. "I can see your house and the Taylors from here."

"Why don't you turn your chair round so can you see out properly?" She was telling herself she'd known Dennis Reid all her life, there was no harm in him, nothing to fear. But the thought of him sitting there watching her house with a mirror made her shudder.

"Keep my eye on the back too, this way," he said, and it was only then that Opal understood. He wasn't spying; he was taking care. Too late—and he must know that—but no harm would ever come to anyone on Mote Street again if Denny could stop it by watching.

"Well, I'm sorry I haven't been in for … however long it's been," Opal said, "but I'm here now. I take it Margaret's working." Denny closed his eyes and nodded his head slowly. "Can I get you anything, while I'm here then?" she said. "Cold drink?"

"You help yourself," said Denny. "I'm okay."

"I'm fine," Opal said and then no one said anything for a moment or two. "Denny?" He must have guessed what was coming because he took in a breath, deep and hollow, almost gasping. "Please tell me to shut up if it's clueless of me, but I've got to say something." He didn't answer. Opal couldn't tell if that was his way of saying it was all

169

right to talk or his way of telling her to leave it alone. So she kept talking. "I can't even imagine what it must have been like for Margaret and you." Nothing. "And Karen." He was as still as a stone. "And Robbie." She couldn't even hear him breathing now. "And I know—Margaret told me—that her and Karen don't see each other anymore. Or you. That's rough. That's got to be . . . But do you see Robbie ever?"

Denny didn't even blink, never mind answer. They sat in silence long enough for a phone in one of the other houses to ring out three times, clear as anything, until someone answered it and the street fell silent again.

"You think it must be bad, eh?" He wasn't looking at her.

"Of course," Opal said. "It must be the worst thing there is."

"Craig or Karen?"

"Both. Well, Craig. But yeah, Karen too."

"How could anyone do that to her own mother?" he said softly.

"I don't know," Opal said. "Anger, I suppose. Hurt."

"*You* don't know?" said Denny. "Well, if you don't know, who does? Where were you, eh? Thirteen years. Where were you when she died? Where were you the day she was buried?"

Opal blinked five times, very fast; one blink after another. How could she not have seen *that* coming?

"What good does it do to come to a funeral?" she said, knowing how it sounded. "It's too late by then."

"No, it's not," Denny said and his voice was loud. "I told myself if nothing else brings her home, at least she'll come to my funeral. I'd never have dreamed for a minute she wouldn't come until you showed me different."

Even as Opal squirmed, though, she was thinking that if he would sit there and die to bring Karen back to her mother, there were other things—less drastic things—he would do as well.

170

"What about just going round to her house and begging her?" she said. Then she took a deep breath. "Or getting someone else to talk to her." Another breath. "I'd talk to her for you."

"We don't know where she is, love."

"How hard could it be to find her?"

"Don't know where to start."

"Did you think about a private detective?"

"Haven't got that sort of money, Margaret and me."

"And then, once you've found her—and someone *must* know where she is—maybe you could..."

"What?"

"I don't know."

"Because nothing's going to bring him back again, is it?"

"No, but wouldn't finding out once and for all what happened to him be better than this?"

"How would forcing Karen to see us again do that?"

"Well," Opal said, "maybe if you were all trying to find out together instead of trying to keep the secret—"

Denny moved for the first time, an enormous movement like whale breaking the surface of still water.

"You don't know what you're saying," he began, but Opal interrupted him.

"I *do*," she said. "Look, I don't mean the police. Or maybe I do. Maybe it's not Craig that's killing you all. Maybe it's the secret. Maybe it would be better if it was out in the open."

"You think we never thought of that?" Denny said. He was restless now, his feet paddling against the floor and his arms flailing as he tried to grip the sides of the settee. "You think I didn't beg Karen to tell the police what really happened?"

"Margaret said you all decided to keep it—"

171

"At first, we did," said Denny. "But you think I cared a damn about my reputation after months had gone by? That's what drove her off. That's what finally sent her packing. Me threatening to come clean. Me saying I'd add shame and gossip and all to what she was carrying already. It was me. I knocked the outhouse down. I went out boozing. I didn't listen to what Margaret told me. And I threatened my own daughter and drove her away."

"But you didn't mean it to be a threat, did you?" Opal said. "You just wanted to find him."

"Karen reckoned I wanted to clear my name."

"Of what?"

"His mammy went to work, his nana went to bed, and I went walking along the canal with the dogs. Who's the only one who *could* have had a babby along and lost him?"

"But that makes no sense," said Opal. "If you'd let him fall in the canal on *Friday,* you'd be the last person to tell the police it wasn't *Saturday.* You wouldn't be clearing your name at all. You'd be ... muddying it. It doesn't make sense what you're saying."

"Karen said I was thinking of myself. Not Craig and not her."

"But that doesn't make any sense either," Opal said. Her head was beginning to pound again like it had when she thought about Mrs. Pickess and Nicola. Who would keep quiet and who would speak up: the innocent or the guilty? Who would bribe and who would threaten? Why would he soil his name to clear it? Why would Karen think that's what he would do?

"None of this ever has made sense and none of it ever will," Denny said. "How can a little kid be there and then be gone? Never come back? How can it be that you love a babby more than your own life and then one day you're hungover and you're in a bad mood and you just don't keep him safe anymore?"

"But someone might have snatched him, Denny," Opal said. "They searched and searched, Margaret said, and dragged the canal. Someone *must* have taken him."

"And what sense does that make, eh? How could someone hurt a little kid? How could anyone?"

But all Opal could think was that Denny, for all his sorrows, was lucky. That he must have had a good life up until ten years ago if he thought that was a mystery.

"I'm sorry I upset you," she said. "I didn't mean to."

"Ah, you're all right," Denny said.

"I'll go now."

"Fair enough, on you go. But leave it, eh? Just let it alone. There's no point in another person starting to fret on it too."

Opal muttered something like an agreement, but there was no way she was going to leave it. She wasn't just going to fret either. She was going to find Karen, she decided, as she let herself out. To get to Robbie, if they were still in touch, and she hoped they would be. She was sure that Robbie must know something. He was Nicola's only connection to that little boy and Nicola definitely knew something, else why was Mrs. Pickess trying so hard to keep her sweet? Only why would *she* care, if it was Nicola's secret? Or Robbie's?

Opal shook the tangle of questions out of her head.

There was another reason to find Karen Reid anyway. Surely if someone told her what was happening to her mum and her dad— especially her dad—she'd come to her senses, bring her granddaughter round, and join what was left of her family together again.

TWENTY-FIVE

It wasn't even that hard. It wasn't as easy as years ago when everyone was in the phone book and you could just look them up, but she got Vonnie Pickess talking about it all again—no problem there—and said she supposed the police had interviewed everyone Karen knew, all her neighbors, everybody at the bank. And Mrs. Pickess had asked what bank, and Opal had opened her eyes very wide and said didn't Karen Reid work at the Nat West, and Mrs. Pickess, triumphant, said Karen had worked for Leeds City College, organising the evening classes or whatever they were called now, from when she had left school. Took maternity leave and went right back again. Bank, ha!

So Opal went along to the college gates on Park Lane at five o'clock and waited outside first one exit and then another and a third, watching. She didn't really expect to see Karen; she was more than ready to pick a woman the right sort of age, one who looked as if she'd been in with the bricks and would remember everyone. Start there. Think up a story, see where she could get to. She was trying to think of what story she could tell—Karen's stepdaughter, Robbie's new wife's girl?—when all of a sudden she was *there*. Opal turned her back, heart hammering. She couldn't help herself, but of course, Karen wouldn't recognise her, not after all these years and grown up like she was now. Opal wouldn't have recognised Karen either, if it wasn't for the fact that she looked so much like her father. Well, like her father used to. The woman walking over the road towards her had the same black hair and wide mouth, the same jaw and shoulders and, as well as all that, she had her mother's walk, hurrying along, looking from side-to-side and a bit of a bounce through the balls of her feet that Margaret always used to have—Opal remembered it now—although these days it was gone.

She walked right past Opal leaning there, didn't give her a glance, and Opal shoved herself up off the wall and fell into step behind. What would she do if Karen went to a car park and drove away? A taxi? Order the driver to "follow that car"? But Karen made for the bus station and joined the queue at the rank for the 84. Opal walked past, let a few more people join, and then turned back and slipped in behind them.

Karen used a pass when the bus came and so Opal, not knowing what fare to ask for, bought a return to Ilkley—the end of the route—and took a seat three behind on the other side of the aisle.

Now she could look properly at Karen for the first time, study her. And the first thing she thought was that no one would know. She didn't look stricken, there was no tension in the way she sat there, swaying a little as if she was tired and taking the chance to unwind. And what surprised Opal most of all was that she got a book out of her bag—a paperback book with a pale picture of someone's legs on it—and started reading.

Opal thought about Denny facing the back door with his mirror for the front, and Margaret with her bottles of pills and telling her secret to everyone, as helpless as a jug that overflows if no one stops the water running. Shouldn't a woman whose child went missing in this city be looking out of the bus window in case he walked by? Wouldn't a woman look out of the window every day, just in case? How could she help herself? Everyone said that Karen Reid was a bit of a cold fish and it was Robbie who wanted a family, but this was beyond a joke, the way she just sat there reading her book as they edged up Woodhouse Lane, stopping and starting in the long snake of traffic struggling home.

And as they got to the turnoff to Meanwood, Opal waited to see if Karen would raise her head and look out to where her parents lived. Lived or died, no odds to her, apparently, because she didn't look up and didn't turn away. Her grip on the edge of her paperback didn't loosen or tighten. The bus went past the junction and kept on out of town and Karen read her book, and Opal stared at the side of her cheek and wondered what it could mean.

Therapy, she decided by the time they'd cleared the bypass. Karen had been to therapy and put it all behind her. Maybe giving up on old Margaret was part of her "recovery." Maybe she'd let go and moved on and learned not to blame herself for anything. Opal had met that type before, and she couldn't stand them. So calm and sure of themselves, they were more like robots than real people. Ask any of them for something you really needed and you were on your own. Big part of therapy, that was—learning to say yes when you wanted and no when you wanted—and not worry about anyone else and what *they* wanted at all. Opal had asked a woman in the Co-op a favour just that spring. Asked if she could borrow her caravan down the coast—pay rent for it and everything—just so she had somewhere to go where she wouldn't see Baz, somewhere to think things through. And the woman had looked her straight in the face and said, "I'm going to say no, Opal. I don't want you to stay in my caravan, so I'm going to say no." She had even smiled. "I don't find it easy to say no. This is a big step forward for me." So Opal had said she really needed somewhere quiet to be on her own for a while and she couldn't see what harm it would do anyway, and the woman had said that she was very comfortable with her decision and it would be a better world if everyone said what they thought. And so Opal said she thought the woman was a selfish bitch, and that was the end of that. Opal ended up in that crappy little bedsit, and then she left the Co-op anyway.

She blinked and came back to the present again. The bus was slowing and Opal looked out of the window to see where they were—not that she would know; somewhere in the suburbs—then she looked back towards Karen and her leg kicked out so fast that she banged it hard against the back of the seat in front. Karen was standing. Opal stood up and, limping a bit, followed her to the front of the bus. They were the only two getting off here.

"This int Ilkley, love," said the driver, seeing her waiting there. Opal smiled and said nothing. "You've paid through to Ilkley," he said. "You don't have to change." Karen was listening, not quite turning round but paying attention. Opal smiled again. The bus had stopped now and opened its doors with a hissing sigh. Karen stepped down.

"You all right?" said the driver.

"Not feeling very well," Opal said. "Just the heat. I'll get back on the next one along."

"You can't use your ticket," said the driver. "You'll have to buy another one. Maybe if you moved to the shady side? Or here—have a mint."

Karen had turned a corner out of sight, and the driver's hand was hovering over the lever to close the doors again, so Opal just took both steps in one and launched herself out onto the pavement.

"Thanks," she said, but the driver was already looking the other way.

She trotted to the corner and stepped boldly round the wall and hedge that hid the side street from view. Karen was still in sight, walking along at a good pace, past pairs of neat little semi-detacheds with cherry trees on the verges outside the gardens, even if most of the gardens themselves had been paved over to make parking for cars. Karen turned another corner, not looking behind her, not seeing Opal, but still Opal thought she had better hang back a bit. When she did finally start walking again and turned into the new street—more pairs of semis, and some bungalows too—she couldn't spot Karen at first. Then, from the corner of her eye, she saw one of the front doors opening and there was Karen on the step. Opal slipped a few paces onto the hard standing of the house she had stopped at and ducked down behind the car parked there. She gave one quick glance at the front window—if the car was there someone must be in—but what choice did she have? Up the street, Karen didn't go inside but just stood on the step waiting. Then, after a minute, a little girl about three or four, dressed in a pink sundress, bounced out of the door and down the path to the road. Karen followed, rummaging in her bag. She found something, took it out, and pointed it—*like a gun*, Opal thought—but then the sidelights on a car flashed on and off, and the little girl opened a back door and climbed in. Karen got into the driver's seat and pulled away, passing where Opal was crouched, the little girl staring out at her and then twisting round in her seat to keep her in view as long as she could before they disappeared on their way.

"Shit!" Opal said. She stood up and, still limping a bit from where she had banged her knee, hurried to the corner. Karen's car was out of sight already, well gone. "Shit!" she said again. "Bugger it!"

She could walk all round the other streets of this suburb—or whatever it was called—and hope to see the car, but for one, Karen had headed back towards the main road, and for two, if she lived close by she probably wouldn't bother with her car anyway.

She could give it up, catch the next bus back to town and come again another day, wait in a taxi at the end of the street and … except taxi drivers probably wouldn't follow a car in real life. Or borrow a bike from someone. One of the Joshis, except how subtle would that be, following Karen on a bike, pedalling like a maniac trying to keep up? She'd be seen for sure.

Then Opal stopped her pacing, hobbling, whatever it was. Idiot! Why did she need to keep from being seen? What was she going to do, anyway? She was going to walk up to Karen and ask her a load of questions. She could have sat beside her on the bus and started then!

"Stupid arse," she said out loud, and she went back to the car she'd hidden behind and leaned her bottom against its boot, like it was home base or something, shaking her head and calling herself more names. She'd forgotten all about it being in someone's front garden and the possibility that they might come to the door and start throwing plates at her. Or—since this street wasn't really a plate-throwing kind of place—might come to the door and take a photo of her to show the police so she'd get done for trespassing.

TWENTY-SIX

AND THAT'S WHERE SHE was, leaning there, when Karen's car came back around the corner and stopped in front of her, pretty much blocking her way.

"I told you!" said the little girl, craning to stare at Opal. "She was hiding. Like a baddie. I *told* you she was here." Karen turned round and said something Opal couldn't hear. The little girl sat back sharply, taking herself out of view, and Karen turned round and smiled at Opal through her open window. An awkward smile, with a bit of swallowing.

"Sorry," she said. "My little girl." She rolled her eyes. "Too many cartoons! She said you were—"

"I was," Opal said, not taking a moment to think it through. Karen was so embarrassed that she might just put the car back into gear and slide away again before Opal could stop her. She pushed herself up off the boot and walked over to the open window. "I was waiting for you, Karen," she said. Karen blinked, and Opal thought she swallowed again.

"Do I know you?"

"You haven't seen me for a while," said Opal. "Maybe you don't remember me." This time Karen definitely swallowed, pretty hard. "It's about—" She stopped, dropping her voice. That little girl wasn't even old enough for school yet; maybe she didn't know. "It's about Craig."

Karen whipped her head round so fast Opal almost missed her expression.

"You sit here, Jodie," she said. "Mummy's going to talk to this lady."

"Wanna come," said the girl, whining and wriggling in her safety seat.

"You just sit here like a good girl. How many times do I have to tell you?"

Jodie instantly stopped moving and clasped her hands together between her chubby knees. Opal had a flash of Miss Fossett, perched on her kitchen chair.

When Karen turned back, the look on her face had been smoothed away, but she was pale, Opal thought, looking yellow behind the tan or makeup that gave her face its colour, and she fumbled a little as she got out of the car and closed the door again.

"Do you mind if we stay out here?" she said, nodding towards the front door of the house. "I don't want to be out of sight of her."

"Oh!" said Opal. "No. I don't live here. Your little one—Jodie?—was right enough. I was kind of hiding out here, watching for you. I live—"

"You were on the bus," Karen said, as if just remembering.

"Yeah," said Opal.

"You followed me?"

"Yeah," Opal said. "Sorry, but I really want to talk to you."

"About"—Karen moved away from the car—"about Craig?"

"Yeah. And his dad." Now, for sure, Karen Southgate—if that was still her name—changed colour, and Opal thought it was definitely makeup on her face, not tan, looking bright and streaked now as all the blood faded away from under it. Her lipstick had mostly gone over the course of the day too so that her lips, turning blueish, only had a bit of red left on the outside edge at the top, like a little red moustache.

"Who *are* you?" Karen said.

"Opal Jones," said Opal. "From Mote Street. You probably don't remember me."

"Mote Street." Again, it wasn't a question, just an echo.

"I live across the road from your mum and dad and, Karen, I don't know if anyone's told you but—"

"Did they send you to find me?" The sound of her voice was like nothing Opal had ever heard before, somewhere between terror, rage, and the mumbled sleep talk of someone coming round after anaesthetic.

"I'm really sorry," Opal said. "No, they didn't send me. They don't know I'm here, but I've got to say, if you want to see them—especially your dad—if you want to make sure you see him again, you better not leave it too long."

"I don't—" she said, but it came out as a yelp and from the car a small voice said, "Mummy?"

"One minute, Jodie!" Jodie stopped straining against her belt but kept staring out at the pair of them with round eyes. Opal could see the white all the way round the blue, the clearest part of the little girl's face inside the shade of the car.

"Okay, that's one thing," Opal said. "I think you should come and see Margaret and Denny. That's one thing, yes." She was steeling herself. This woman was really hard to talk to—barking at her kid, couldn't care less about her parents. "But also, I want to talk to Robbie if you can help me find him. Tell me his address maybe? If you know it?"

"But who *are* you?" Karen said.

"I told you," said Opal. "Opal Jones. I live across the road from your mum and dad. I'm Nicola's daughter. You must remember Nicola." Karen nodded, but very vaguely. She was studying Opal hard, or maybe just staring at her and thinking hard; Opal couldn't say.

"But you were long gone by then," she said. "Why are you asking me all these questions?" Opal thought to herself that she had only asked one question, really, but she didn't say so. "What's Robbie to you?"

"Nothing," said Opal. "Except him and my mum were friends. Good friends. And after ... what happened ... because of them being friends, the police were at my mum. Like she was a suspect. Nearly."

"And are they still?" said Karen. She was staring very hard at Opal and her chest was starting to heave again.

"The police?"

"Friends. In touch. Together."

"No," Opal said. "Or otherwise I'd know his address, wouldn't I?"

"Right," Karen said.

"And actually my mum died."

"But before she died," said Karen. "Did she tell you anything. Did she know anything?"

"No!" said Opal. "Jesus! Of course, she didn't. But the police thought she did. They searched her house and everything. Ripped it to pieces." Karen was blinking hard, and Opal realized she shouldn't have made it so clear she was thinking of a thing hidden, not a boy hiding. She hurried on, trying to cover up the horrible pictures she might have conjured with more and more words. "And now I can't ask her why the police did that, and I just want to know, and I thought Robbie might be able to help me."

"My husband would never have harmed a hair on his head," Karen said. "I've never said any different."

"Of course he wouldn't," Opal said. "I just want to find him and talk to him."

"Where do you get the nerve?" Karen's voice was loud.

"Mummy?" The little girl had undone her belt and was kneeling up on the front seat now.

"I really didn't mean to upset you," Opal said. "I know you must—"

"You don't know *anything*," Karen yelled at her. "You weren't even there."

"I know, I know," Opal said. "I'm sorry. I didn't think how it would sound. Look, like you say, I wasn't there. I went away when I was twelve. I never saw my mum again before she died. I must have flipped out or something to be bothering you like this. But look—that's what I'm saying to you. If you don't go and see Margaret and Denny and let them see your little girl, you might end up with all these things you want to know and want to say but it'll be too late. How can you be right here and go past them on the bus every day?" Karen was staring, stunned, her arms hanging at her sides, and it was Opal shouting now. "I was a little kid, and I had a good reason. I must have, eh? And at least I was in Whitby, which is a half-decent way away, but you could be there in ten minutes in your car and how *can* you?"

Something very strange was happening to Karen's face now, red patches climbing up out of her shirt collar and spreading over her neck, creeping around the corner of her jaw and bringing her face back to rosy life, instead of the yellow mess it had been. And since her chest was heaving up and down, Opal couldn't help thinking that it

184

was those gulped panicky breaths that were pumping the colour up into her face. And she wanted to tell the woman to slow down, calm down, before all her blood ended up in her head and the rest of her just fell in empty crumples onto the ground.

"Mummy, *please*!"

Jodie was sobbing, with both her fat little hands pressed on the front glass, but Karen stood, frozen, nothing moving.

"And I know more than you probably think I do," Opal said. Karen started backing away from her towards the car, and Jodie's sobs rose and quickened. "Go and see your mother. For God's sake, before it's too late. She's talking. She's so unhappy she can't help herself. She needs to see you." Karen had got to the car now and she opened the door and sank into the seat. Jodie immediately clambered over and wrapped herself around her mother, arms and legs, burying her face and pretty nearly screaming. But she might as well have been hugging a tree. Karen didn't stroke her hair or rock her, but just stared at Opal until *Opal*, sickened with herself, tore her eyes away. She walked past the car back towards the main road, not looking in as she passed, but saying a soft apology she hoped Karen would hear over the muffled crying.

It was twenty minutes before a Leeds bus came along, but the car still hadn't appeared by the time Opal climbed on board and took a seat by the window. Maybe there was a different way out of that little scheme of houses somewhere. Or maybe Karen was still sitting there.

TWENTY-SEVEN

"HIYA," SAID OPAL, WHEN Miss Fossett opened the kitchen door. "I'm glad you heard me knocking this time. I wouldn't want to just barge in."

"Hello," Miss Fossett said.

"It's Opal."

"Opal!" said Miss Fossett. "That's a pretty name."

"So's Norah," said Opal. "Can I come in?"

Miss Fossett's face clouded a little.

"I'm not supposed to," she said.

"I know," said Opal. "Strangers. Shelley told me."

"Shelley!" said Miss Fossett, and it was like open sesame. She stood back and let Opal walk in.

The kitchen wasn't quite as bad as before, but Miss Fossett had been making cocoa, so between the milk that had boiled over onto the cooker top, the sprays of dry cocoa powder over the table, and the wet clumps of cocoa all over the draining board, it was bad enough.

Opal looked into the pan at the thick blackened layer coating its bottom.

"Did you get your cup of chocolate?" she asked.

Miss Fossett screwed her face up and shook her head. "It tasted funny," she said. "I put it down for the cat." She nodded at a plate sitting on the floor half under the sink that had a dribble of pale pinkish liquid in it, flecked with burnt bits.

"Have you got a cat?" Opal said, thinking what a poor bugger it was if so.

"Smoky," said Miss Fossett. "We got him when he was a tiny kitten you fed off a spoon, and I used to dress him up in my bonnets and push him in my pram."

"Your dolly's pram?" said Opal. She was running hot water into the cocoa pan and wiping up the worst of the dribbles.

"Emerald," said Miss Fossett. "She had green eyes and red hair. I got her for my birthday." So Opal lifted the long-gone cat's dish and added it to the hot water filling the sink.

"Let's try again," she said. "Where's the co— Oh, I see it." Inside the tin, it didn't look too good, but she dug around and managed to get enough for two cups without having to use any of the lumps. That would have to do. "Milk in the fridge?" She didn't look too closely at the shelves, just took a carton out of the door, sniffed it and filled another pan. "So were you allowed to take your kitten to bed at night? Or did you take Emerald with you?" She had been thinking on the bus—as soon as she decided to make up for upsetting Karen by going to Miss Fossett and giving her some of the company she was so obviously pining for—that she should try to get the old lady to talk about the past, the very distant past when she was a little girl. It was easier than she'd been expecting.

"Smoky wasn't allowed upstairs," Norah said. "And Emerald's hair was too pretty to let her get jumbled about. I had my teddy bear. Binks."

"Because it's a big house, this, innit?" Opal said. "A little girl could get scared at night in a big old house like this, without something to cuddle." She was watching the milk beginning to shimmer in the pan and didn't look around until the silence had gone on for a minute or two. When she did glance up, Miss Fossett had wrapped her arms around her shoulders and was hugging herself hard. She had a sleeveless dress on, baggy and loose in the armholes—it was that hot this summer; even old ladies were wearing clothes with no sleeves—and her little fingers with their horny fingernails were digging deep into her skin, the little bit of flesh so soft her hands seemed to be squeezing right down to her bones.

"Hey," said Opal. "You'll hurt yourself."

"Milk," said Miss Fossett in a tiny voice and Opal jerked her hand away from the pot handle as it boiled over again and the foam doused the gas and sizzled on the burner.

"Bugger it," she said, and Miss Fossett giggled. "There should still be enough for one." She poured a cup, whisking hard with the spoon trying to make it as nice as it could be, a treat to take the nasty memories away. Or maybe she was just salving her own conscience because she knew she was going to bring them back again.

"Where will we go?" she said. "Where do you sit?"

"In the morning room," said Miss Fossett. "I'll show you the way."

She trotted off along the corridor Opal had glimpsed before, past door after closed door, past large paintings all thick with dust so the people in them looked like ghosts. And there were ropes of cobweb hanging from the lights, reaching like swags to the tops of the picture frames. And the carpet was dark and flat in the middle where feet passed up and down, and only at the edges and in the corners could you see that once it had been red and had a pattern cut into it of swirling leaves. It rustled underfoot as if it was laid over straw or something. Opal couldn't remember feeling that before.

Miss Fossett had trotted to the front of the house and turned to look back at Opal, waiting.

"The morning room," she said, sweeping her arm out to the side. She stood against the light coming through frosted glass panels at the front door—or a vestibule, anyway—and Opal could see very soft pale hairs in her armpit. Beside her, lined up behind the vestibule door were three shopping bags on wheels. The first of them was wicker with a curved bamboo handle and black metal wheels. Then a tartan one with black vinyl sides. The last one was made of rucksack material, bright green with a logo and a handle made of chrome with a rubber grip.

"Are these all yours?" Opal said. Miss Fossett turned and looked at where she was pointing.

"All mine," she said. "I was going to get a new one, but I don't ... they come now, so I don't ... " She shook her head as if she had got water in her ears and was trying to get it out again. Then she smiled at Opal. "The morning room," she said. "Do come in and do sit down. It's very nice to see you."

Opal went in, but sitting down wasn't so easy. Miss Fossett's chair was set about three feet from a big old television as deep as it was wide, and there was a tray table on casters pushed to one side, holding the channel changer, a pair of glasses, some tissues, and a tube of lip salve. Every other seat in the room was occupied. There were two full three-piece suites, Opal noted looking round, as well as a round table and six chairs set into the corner bay window, and every chair was packed like a suitcase. It wasn't like stuff just lying around; they really were packed. Linens on one, tablecloths probably, folded to fit the space and heaped up exactly level with the top of the headrest; rolled towels on another, a pyramid of them; and photograph albums—tricky things to heap up that many of, but Miss Fossett had managed it, using the longest thinnest ones to build up the sides and the shorter fatter ones to fill in, like those walls you see out in the country made of stones with nothing holding them together except the skill of the builder. The LP records had defeated her: they were tied together with hairy green string to make blocks and then these blocks had been built up like the photo albums too.

"Mighty me," said Opal. She was still kicking herself about letting out that one rude *bugger*. "You're very ... organised."

"Oh, this isn't mine," said Miss Fossett, sitting down and pulling her tray table in front of her, so that she looked like a baby in a highchair. Opal put the cocoa cup down on it, and Miss Fossett picked it up in both hands and took a sip. "Lovely," she said, smiling up at Opal from under a moustache of cocoa froth. Opal smiled back at her.

There was a footstool round the other side of the armchair, one of those leather cubes, so she pulled it out and sat down.

"Whose is it, then?" she said. "All these photos? And the records?"

"It's theirs," said Miss Fossett. "All of this. I only come in here to watch the"—she waved her teaspoon, scattering brown drops on the carpet—"the thingummy."

"The telly," Opal said. It wasn't worth saying anything about the teaspoon. The carpet, when she looked closely, wasn't *actually* patterned under the tea and soup and one patch that she hoped was cheese sauce or maybe curry, but Miss Fossett didn't do well with getting told off and Opal didn't want to upset her.

"So where are they?" Opal said. "Going off leaving all their stuff for you to work round!" But that was too sideways on, and Miss Fossett only gazed at her. "Is it your family's?"

"They've gone," said Miss Fossett. "They died. Father died and then Mother died."

"My parents died too," said Opal.

"In the war?"

Opal smiled. "No," she said.

"My father died in the war. I was away."

Opal frowned. Away? Shelley said Norah had never left this house in her life.

"When were you away, Norah?" she asked.

"In the war," Norah said. "Father died in the war."

"Right," said Opal. "Were you a nurse or something?" she asked. Miss Fossett put her cup down very carefully and wiped her lips on a tissue, refolding it despite the dark smears, and putting it back down on her tray.

"I'm not supposed to say," she said. "Sorry, sorry, sorry."

"No, *I'm* sorry," said Opal. "And I'm sorry your mum died too."

"I nursed her when I came back, but she died anyway," Norah said. "She had a stroke."

"She must have been very young," said Opal.

"Ninety," Norah said. She tipped her cup right up and sucked out the very last drops of cocoa. Opal nodded. It was hard to follow Norah's elastic sense of time. She put cocoa down for a cat she'd had decades ago and missed out half her lifetime saying something happened when she was away and then something else when she came back again.

"So after your father died, it was just your mother and you?" said Opal.

191

"I'm not supposed to talk about it," Norah said.

"But of course it wasn't!" said Opal, remembering about the niece and nephew. "You had brothers and sisters, didn't you?"

"No," said Miss Fossett. "I was an only child."

"Me too," said Opal. Then she frowned again. "But Shelley said you had a niece, Norah."

"And a nephew and a great-niece and a great-nephew," said Miss Fossett, delighted again, rolling the words around and beaming just as she had the first time.

"So how was that then? Were they your brother's children?"

"I haven't got a brother, I never had a brother, I don't want a brother," Norah said, then she drew a breath and started it over again. "I haven't got a brother, I never had a brother, I wouldn—"

"Or your sister's children, maybe?" Opal said.

"Oh!" said Miss Fossett. "I wish I had a sister. I would play with her all day and tell her my secrets."

Opal smiled at her. This was worse than talking to a drunk. "I wish I had a sister too," Opal said.

"I'm an only child," Norah said again. "It was Father and Mother and me, and then Mother and me, and now me."

"Same here!" Opal said. "Just the same. Mum and Dad and me, and then Mum and me, and now just me." She didn't mention Steph and her half-brother, Michael, but it made her pause and look at Norah even more closely. Maybe they had that in common too. Maybe Father didn't die in the war at all. Maybe he went off and left Norah and her mum and married again, and *that's* how Norah could be an only child with a niece and a nephew.

"And they're helping you out now, aren't they?" Opal said. "Helping you clear out your stuff?"

"Father and Mother are dead," said Miss Fossett. "Father died in the war, when I—Father died in the war and I nursed Mother, but she died too."

"I meant your niece and your nephew," Opal said. "They're helping you clear out the house?" At least, she bloody hoped so. Hope they weren't just waiting until Norah was at some day-centre and then coming round with a van.

"Clear out the attic," Miss Fossett said.

"Right, right," Opal said. "A fox fur and some jewelry and silver."

"Mother had a fox fur," said Miss Fossett. "It's not mine. None of this is mine."

"Right," said Opal.

"My things are in my room," said Miss Fossett.

"Is your bed in your room?" Opal said.

"My bed and my bedside table and my dressing chest and wardrobe."

"I'd love to see it," said Opal. "Is Emerald there?"

"I don't know," said Miss Fossett, brightening up at the idea. "We could go and look for her."

So she pushed away the tray table and got to her feet. There was none of the hauling and groaning you'd expect for such an old lady. She hopped up like a bird and pattered off across the stained carpet to the door. She was part of the way up the stairs before Opal had got up from her perch, shaken the life back into her legs, and followed her.

"Do come upstairs," she said, making that same sweeping gesture as when she'd shown Opal into the morning room. "If you would like to wash your hands, I can show you where."

"I'm all right," Opal said. "Let's see if we can find Emerald."

"And Angeline," said Miss Fossett. "She's got golden hair and blue eyes and she's lovely, but Emerald is my favourite." She was at the landing and she turned and gave Opal a serious look, eye-to-eye since Opal was a few steps below. "I don't want you to tell Angeline," she said, looking first over one shoulder and the over the other. "But I think she knows. I gave Emerald the dress with the lace, and Angeline had to wear the plain one. I heard her crying."

"These are dolls, right?" Opal said.

"Yes," Miss Fossett nodded. "But I can still understand them when they talk to me."

TWENTY-EIGHT

THAT, AS FAR AS Opal was concerned, was just a bit too Bates Motel for her liking. Added to which the staircase was dark and the spaces in between the fancy bits on the banisters were just about choked right up with cobwebs like they'd been sprayed for Halloween and, all in all, Opal decided that if when they got to Norah's room, "Emerald" and "Angeline" had their heads missing or turned round to the back or damaged in any way (or any part of their bodies really, but especially their heads), or if they were doing anything except sitting propped up on a shelf like dolls should, she was going to run away and never come back again.

Miss Fossett was heading towards the back of the house, down a few stairs and round a corner and all of a sudden there was no carpet, just dark brown lino and a door that looked as if it had been made for her. Opal didn't have to stoop—she was only five three—but it was the smallest door she'd ever walked through.

"Here we are," Miss Fossett said. She trotted over and stood beside her bed, smiling but standing up very straight like she was ready for inspection.

Opal looked around the room. It had a ceiling that dipped down at the edges, and there were black bars over the outside of the window. It must have been the maid's room or something.

"This is yours?" she said, wondering how many empty rooms they had gone past.

Miss Fossett nodded, and Opal looked at the painted bed, white with little gold paint droplets along the edge of the headboard like a necklace, one big teardrop shape in the middle. The bedside stand had a gold-painted handle to its single drawer and the dressing table—the dressing chest, Miss Fossett had called it—had more of the droplets round the mirror.

"It's really pretty," she said. It was, but it was puzzling too.

"Thank you," said Miss Fossett.

"And it's very tidy."

"Thank you," said Miss Fossett again, although she sounded troubled this time, and she put her head down. But Opal meant it. She hadn't believed a word of that downstairs about all the stuff being "theirs," but there were no piles of records and bales of tablecloths up here. There was a hairbrush with a comb stuck in it on the dressing table and there was an old-fashioned kind of a little book on the bedside table, soft-looking with leather covers, too small for a Bible. A prayer book, maybe.

"But it's very small." Opal figured that the footboard with the secret compartments (plus its headboard that had to be at least as big) would fill this little room to bursting, if it even got through the door. Maybe the bed wasn't Norah's at all. Her mother's? How old could those pieces of paper be? But looking at the door she saw that it had a bar lock, like a bathroom would have, and she thought surely a little girl wouldn't sleep in a room where she could lock herself in. Not one with bars on the window too and an open fireplace. That just wasn't safe.

"Norah," she said, "has this always been your room?"

Miss Fossett shook her head. "It's the nursery," she said. "We were in here when we were tiny, before we had our own big rooms beside Mother and Father."

"Right," said Opal. "Who's *we*?"

"Sorry," Miss Fossett said. "Sorry."

"When did you move back here?"

"Sorry."

"Was it when you came back? After you'd been away?"

"Sorry, sorry," Norah said, the words getting faster and higher again.

"Do you know what I'd love?" said Opal, clapping her hands. "I'd love to see your other room. The big one."

"I'm not allowed to go in there," Miss Fossett said.

"Yeah, but you could show me the door," Opal said. "I'll just have a peek."

"I can't go in. They told me I wasn't allowed to."

"No, but you just point to the door," said Opal. "And then you wait downstairs. When I come down, I'll put the circus tape on."

"Oh yes!" said Miss Fossett. "We can watch my circus tape."

And she was off again. She got to the head of the stairs and started tripping her way down them, slightly sideways on, one-two-three and one-two-three like a schoolgirl.

"Hey, hang on!" said Opal. "Which one is your old bedroom?" Norah's head was only just above the level of the upstairs floor, but she turned and looked through the banisters.

197

"Dusty," she said. "I'm not allowed to dust."

For the first time, Opal wondered if Norah was capable of having someone on. "Not allowed to dust" sounded about as likely as "not allowed to eat vegetables," which she herself had tried on Steph one of the first times she visited Whitby. She could remember Steph and Sandy laughing at her and the tears filling her eyes.

"Which one, Norah love?" she said, and Miss Fossett pointed one of her skinny little fingers with the dry soft skin and the horny nails before she turned and scampered away.

Opal walked over to the door she'd pointed at, grabbed the handle, and turned. The creak sent a shiver across the back of her neck and she had to tell herself it was a summer evening in the middle of Leeds and there was no one in the house except a little old lady and her. She put her head round the door and then opened it up completely and stepped in, gawping.

It was empty. Totally empty. Not so much as a square of carpet on the floor. The fireplace was very fancy with green and white tiles all around, and the window was hung with nets and paper blinds and stiff shiny curtains covered in green and white jugglers or minstrels or something. They looked completely ridiculous in the blank space, like wedding dresses at a funeral, Christmas trees on the beach. But at least it was an answer. Opal knew exactly the kind of over-the-top furniture that would look at home in here.

But where was everything? Well, she knew what had happened to some of it, mixed up and cut adrift, washing up at Claypole's and fooling everyone, even experienced bidders. But the rest?

"Where's all your stuff?" she said to Norah when she got back to the morning room. "Your big bed."

"I haven't got a big bed. I've got a beautiful little bed. White and gold and fit for a princess. Mother bought it for me."

"Yeah, but the one you had before?" said Opal. "Is it in the attic? Did you give it to your niece maybe?"

"She can't have my bed!" said Miss Fossett. "Where will I sleep?"

"Not the gold and white one," said Opal. "Don't worry."

"Where will I *sleep*?" said Miss Fossett. "I'm not supposed to go in the other rooms. I'm not allowed to."

"Sorry," said Opal. "Maybe I meant someone else's. There are a lot of bedrooms, aren't there? Your mum and dad's for a start."

"Please don't give my little bed away. I got it for my birthday and I never sleep anywhere else, ever ever ever."

"Did you take it with you when you went away?" Opal said. "To Filey?"

"Was it Filey you went to?"

"Every summer. We go with Mother, and Father comes and takes his holiday."

"And who's *we*, Norah?"

But Miss Fossett only blinked. "Mother and Father and me."

"Right," Opal said. "Okay. You win. I'll put your circus tape on for you, and then I'll have to go. But I'll come back again and make you some cocoa another day. Have you ever had cocoa with marshmallows on top?"

"On top of the cocoa?" said Miss Fossett, her eyes looking quite like two marshmallows—round and pink—as she took in this amazing idea.

"I'll bring some," said Opal. "And I'll do a bit of dusting upstairs too, if you like." She was fussing with the remote now, trying to work out the video and she hadn't realized, but she'd started talking to Miss Fossett as if she wasn't really there, or as if she was a cat or a baby. "See if I can get things sorted out for you. Track down some of these incredible vanishing beds of yours."

"Not mine," said Miss Fossett. "I've got my bed."

"Right," said Opal. "Not too big and not too small but juuuust right. Ah! Got it. Forward play."

"Goldilocks," said Miss Fossett. She was pulling her tray table over in front of her chair again, settling in.

"Just about," Opal said.

"Who's been sleeping in *my* bed?" Miss Fossett said. She was staring at the screen where the penalties for showing the tape on oil rigs and in prisons were scrolling by.

"You tell me, Norah," Opal said. She put the remote on the tray table and stood behind Miss Fossett's chair, noticing that she had put her thumb in her mouth. "You tell me."

Miss Fossett took her thumb out again with a plopping sound.

"Martin," she said and her voice was slack and dreamy as she gazed at the screen. Fireworks were bursting all over it and then came BILLY SMART PRESENTS picked out in fizzing flares against a black background. Opal could hardly let enough breath go to ask the next question.

"Who's Martin, love?"

"My brother."

Opal came back around the side of the chair and crouched down. Miss Fossett blinked and refocused as Opal's face took the place of the firework writing in front of her.

"Where's Martin now?" But Miss Fossett shrank back in her chair and jerked both her slippered feet straight out in front of her, knocking Opal backwards.

"I haven't got a brother, I don't want a brother, I never had a brother."

"I know, I know," said Opal picking herself up again. "I'm sorry."

"Sorry, sorry, sorry, sorry," said Miss Fossett.

"Look, Norah, horseys," said Opal, pointing at the television. "Look, clowns. And remember I'm going to make you cocoa with marshmallows soon." Norah was still whimpering, the *sorry*s making a shushing sound under her breath. "I'll make it for you and Emerald and Angeline. Hmm? Would you like that?"

But it took another five minutes before she settled down and Opal thought it was safe to go. She paused at the bottom of the stairs and then shook her head. Never mind Norah, she didn't think *she* could take any more today. She let herself out and walked slowly along the tunnel to the garden door.

So. Norah used to have a big bedroom with a great big bed. And she had a brother. And then she got a little bed and she moved to a room where she could lock the door and decided she didn't have a brother and never had one and didn't want one either. Who could blame her?

But Opal couldn't stop thinking about how spry she was for a woman her age, whatever that age might be. If her brother had those good genes too, he might not be dead yet. And he had a daughter, Norah's niece. And a granddaughter too.

So Opal would search the empty rooms and the attics and find the other half of that bed if it was there and put the whole note together and—if Martin was still alive—she would take it and she would . . . but probably the bed would be gone or the man would be dead or he might be as wandered as Norah was now and not understand if everyone got angry. And what would be the use of dragging it all out now? Could Norah still learn, at her age, with her old brain about as sharp as a marshmallow sinking into a cup of cocoa, that she wasn't a bad girl and she didn't have to say sorry?

Worth a try, Opal told herself, *worth a damn good try.*

TWENTY-NINE

That Saturday—the seventeenth of July—was the hottest day yet, the hottest day ever, since records began. Opal woke at five o'clock with the sun already throbbing in at the bedroom window and the air still thick and damp from the heat of the day before. She went for her bus and no one in the queue had a jacket over their arm or an umbrella folded up along the top of their handbag. Everyone—even the men—was wearing sandals. And out at the store two of the assistant managers were putting up parasols next to the doorway. Round in the warehouse, Dave and the supervisor from Wet Fish were dragging an open-front chiller on a trolley towards the flap doors.

"This is one of the turkey chillers," Dave said. "Email from Head Office. It's going to the door for water. We're to fill it with chipped ice off of Fish and hand out bottled water." He was caught, Opal thought, between feeling thrilled at the drama and being troubled by the notion of giving away something people would buy by the barrow-load anyway.

"Whole bottles," said the Wet Fish supervisor. He was already in his white coat and trilby. "Not like samples. Not plastic beakers like a tasting."

"Because we asked them, to be sure," Dave said. "Whole bottles. *For free.*"

That was the start of the day's madness. The barbecue hordes came early. Usually it was gone eleven before they started drifting in, tattooed and topless, filling deep trolleys with charcoal and Polish lager. But that day the first of them arrived before nine and some of the very first bought all of the ice, then the later ones wanted to know where the chipped ice in the open front chiller by the door had come from and why couldn't they get some too. And one of the assistant managers had to be beeped to come and explain that it wasn't edible ice and couldn't be used in drinks, but then Charlotte had a mother complaining that one of the girls giving out the water had said to her little boy that he could have a scoop of it in his empty slushy cup and he'd eaten the lot. And there was no cream in the ten o'clock delivery—none at all—double, single, whipping, clotted, even Chantilly.

And then the UHT and aerosol cans ran out and everyone who had picked up strawberries on a twofer started putting them back again. Only hardly anyone bothered to go back and dump them with the rest of the strawberries; they just shoved them onto the nearest shelf and the store started to fill up with cartons of sweating strawberries. And Kate and Rhianne, detailed to seek them out and bring them home, couldn't do it because the warehouse boys had brought out more and there was nowhere to put them, so they got stickered down and piled up in Reduced but that only started the whole strawberries-and-cream!, but-they've-no-cream-so-put-back-the-strawberries cycle all over again until, as Rhianne said:

"I'm starting to recognise some of these buggers. This is the third time I've moved the carton with that big one like Santa's nose."

And just when it couldn't get any busier or noisier or grumpier, a crow flew in the front door and started swooping up and down just above the Special Boards, setting them swinging, making everyone who'd ever seen *The Birds* put their arms over their heads and scream.

"So how's your friend?" Kate said to Opal in the canteen. She was rolling a cold can of ginger beer around her neck like a massage wheel.

"Huh?" Opal said.

"Norah," said Kate. "The one with the family trouble so you couldn't come out last night."

"Not so good," Opal said. "She just sits and watches the same video over and over again. She hardly leaves the house now."

"Sounds like she needs help. What happened to her anyway?"

"Her dad died when she was a little girl and her mum died a few years ago too and her brother . . . well, he was a total creep. A *real* weirdo. He was the one that needed help, not that he got any."

"Typical," said Kate. "Is he still around then? Is she stuck with him?"

Opal gathered up her plate and glass onto her tray, wiped up the spilled salt with her crumpled napkin, and stuffed it inside her sandwich carton.

"She won't talk about it. Sometimes . . . Well, sometimes she won't even admit she ever had a brother."

"Sounds like the right idea. Change the locks and forget all about him."

"Nah," said Rhianne. "I think it's better to get it all out in the open. Doesn't matter how far down you shove all that stuff, it comes back in the end. Like the strawberries."

"Right," said Opal. "That's what I keep saying. That's why I'm trying to help. It's not just for the sake of interfering."

She truly believed it too. What downside could there be from Karen and Margaret being reunited even if Craig was never found? And Fishbo back in the bosom of the Gordon family? That was a no-brainer too. Norah's story told at last, even if Martin was dead and gone? Absolutely.

But—Opal flipped through the next batch of lists on her pick and saw FF Gilbert—whether or not to try to cheer someone up with grocery jokes if they only ended up crying even harder? Who could say.

When she started picking, though, she saw that he didn't need her cheering him up this weekend. He was having visitors. As well as his white bread and frozen dinners, today he had ordered cocoa-pops, string cheese, mini-Twixes, and fruit shots. But what was going on the bread, Opal couldn't say. He'd ordered half a dozen eggs and a punnet of cress, but no kids like egg sandwiches. He would probably have some mild cheddar left from the week before, but he didn't have any chutney or ham to go with it, and plain cheese sandwiches were going to be too dry for whatever kids were little enough to drink fruit juice shots, weren't they? So she put in a pack of clown-face luncheon meat and a jar of tomato chutney and called it a day.

And after that it was just another two hours of trudging up and down the aisles, keeping out of the way of the hot and possibly drunk barbecuers as the second wave of them came back for more burgers and chicken after they'd burnt the first lot, only to find out there were none left, and no salad left either and for sure there was no ice and the best-deal lager packs were long gone and the rotisserie only had ham knuckles and stuffing balls until at last she could go home.

She *walked* home, with an ice lolly in one hand and a can of Fanta in the other, because the bus was full and everyone on it, looking out through the windows, had boiled pink or roasted brown faces and plastered-down hair. And some of them were fanning themselves with the free paper, and she couldn't face the stale air and her legs sticking to the seat, and if one more person told her it was too hot for them and they'd welcome a shower of rain, she would personally provide them with a shower of Fanta.

As she turned into Mote Street, she thought her day was done. It had hardly started.

THIRTY

THAT DAY, THE HOTTEST day, would also be the longest day she had ever lived through, the one that changed everything from something in Opal's head that she could stop any time she chose, to something outside her, all around her, that there was no turning back from no matter how she tried.

First off, Pep Kendal knocked on her door. She was still opening windows, back and front, upstairs and down, both doors—she even opened the yard gate to see if that would help get the air moving—and she had the shower running cold and the kitchen taps running cold water into the sink too, *anything* to get the temperature down, all thoughts of her water rates driven out by the thumping and pulsing heat and the dread of spending another night like the last one.

"Opal?" he shouted in through the open door. "You there, love?"

"Pep?" she shouted downstairs. "Come in. I'll be right with you."

"You in the shower, love? I'll come back."

"I'm not," she said, arriving at the bottom of the stairs. He was halfway across the living room. "I'm just running cold water. It's like a bloody sauna upstairs."

"Aye well, since you mention it," Pep said. He was wearing a short-sleeved shirt that looked as if it was made out of dishcloths and—Opal could hardly believe it—short trousers. They weren't *shorts*; they were definitely short trousers, creases down the fronts and turn ups at the bottoms and they were the brown of a used teabag, but they only came down to the tops of Pep's knees. Opal tried not to look at his calves, pure white under the pelt of dark hair and knotted with veins, and she felt grateful that he had socks and shoes on; she didn't want to see the feet on the end of those legs.

"Since I mention what?"

"You said you wanted to help Fishbo. Don't suppose you're free tonight, are you?"

"Saturday night?" said Opal. "Course I am."

"Only I want to bathe him."

"Whoa, hang on."

"Give over," said Pep. "I can manage that on me own. What I want you to do is change his bed while I've got him in there. See what you can do to freshen up his room. He won't stand for me meddling with it when he can see me, and I don't want to leave him on his... well, you'll understand when you see him."

"Change his bed and tidy his room?" said Opal. As hot and stale as her own little house was, she could hardly imagine what it would be like in Fishbo's bedroom, where he had been lying, coughing, sweating, throwing up a bit, and probably smoking too, despite the coughing, for nearly a week now. And then she thought of him having to be there, so she relented. "Go on, then. You hose him off and I'll muck him out. But is he no better then? Have you had the doctor back in?"

"Coming Monday," said Pep. "If he makes it that long." He tried to make it sound off-hand, but his mouth kept moving after he closed it again. "Never thought I'd say it, but I'd give anything to hear him sing 'Moon River' for four hours straight now."

"It can't be that bad," Opal said. "It's a chest infection? And he's got antibiotics, yeah?"

"Yeah, you're right," Pep said, letting his breath go in a long hiss. "Look, I better get back over, love. Do you want to have your tea first or are you coming now?"

"Now." If she had to strip Fishbo's bed of sickness, she'd rather get it over with and eat after. If she could eat at all.

———

She *did* understand when she saw him, staring at him from his bedroom doorway, unable to believe he had got that way in just a week. He was a colour no human being should ever be—sort of khaki—and the skin round his mouth was broken and sore-looking, his hands so dry they were ashy and, although his brow ran with droplets of sweat, his cheek when she touched it felt cold.

"Mr. Fish?" she said.

"Baby Girl," he said, and that was enough to set off a bout of coughing. Pep came forward and sat him up a bit and he curled over into himself, pressing a hand against his chest and trying to keep the cough as shallow as he could, his lips spread wide. "*Heek, heek, heek,*" he went, and Pep caught Opal's eye. They could both hear the scrape of the cough, just whipping the top edge of whatever filled his chest, not shifting it, just gently tickling. "*Boahhh!*" Fishbo sank back against his pillows and closed his eyes again.

"Maybe he should be in hospital," said Opal.

"No!" It was gravelly and faint, but no one could doubt how firm he was.

"You've got two nights until the doc comes back, old friend," said Pep. "Try that 'no' on him and see where it gets you."

"Jest a touch of cole," said Fishbo. "Jest need some rest and I'll be good as new."

"Right," said Opal. "Okay, Mr. Kendal. You take him away and I'll dig in."

Pep mimed shushing, but Fishbo wasn't listening anyway and made no reference to the fact that Opal Jones was standing in his bedroom as Pep worked his arms under the bedclothes, gathered Fishbo up, and lifted him, letting the blankets drop away. The movement disturbed whatever monster it was that had made its home in his chest, and it rattled and rasped as they left the room.

"I've drawn a cool bath for you," Pep said. "And I'm not taking no for an answer."

"You leave me be," Fishbo said, and after he had spoken there was a clapping sound in his throat, as if a bubble of something strong and gummy had burst there.

"Don't get agitated," said Pep. "I'm going to wash your hair and then you're goin' to lie and soak. I'm not scrubbing the rest of you."

"You leave my hair be."

"—just about ready to crawl off your head and go to the bath on its own, anyway—"

"—years since *you had* enough damn hair to wash."

And then they were out of earshot, and Opal closed the door.

How long would it take one boiling-hot, tired-out old man to strip, bathe, dry, and dress another one—half an hour? Longer if he was trying not to joggle him and set that nightmare of a cough off again. And he'd said a soak. All in all, Opal reckoned she had time for her chambermaid routine and then plenty time left for the real reason she had agreed to come.

She stripped the blanket off the bed and shook it hard out of the window, but there was no shifting the smell of cigarettes (and worse) out of it. She'd take it over and run it through her machine. She could put it out on the line overnight and it would be dry by morning. Fishbo could have the fleece throw off her couch until then.

Next, the sheets. Opal was an old hand at stripping a bed without uncovering the bottom sheet, without seeing anything she might not want to see. She bundled both sheets and the pillow case into a ball and put them, with the blanket, on the landing. She turned the mattress and then hesitated. She didn't want to shout through the bathroom door and she didn't want to go raking in Pep's cleaning cupboards without asking. Well, it would give her a chance to get the first load of washing on.

Five minutes later she was back from her house again, with her hoover, carpet freshener, a bottle of lemon cleaner, a couple of bin bags, and a roll of kitchen towels. Vonnie Pickess had seen her—she was hovering behind her fly curtain—but Opal had put her head down and scuttled over the road before Mrs. Pickess thought up something to say.

She sprinkled carpet freshener on the mattress and all over the floor, sprinkled a bit on the clean linen Pep had left on the dressing table for her to use, puffed it up the curtains too, then left it to sink in while she emptied the ashtrays—three! She tipped the wastebasket full of tissues into the bin bag with her head turned away, dropped every newspaper and magazine, fag packet and matchbook, every junk mail envelope and empty tissue wrapper in on top of them. She tied the bin bag and put it on the landing. There was a slow and quiet sloshing sound from the bathroom, like the noise of a walrus in the shallows or something. Opal drew back, making sure she closed the door.

Back in the bedroom, she squirted lemon cleaner on every newly bare surface, into the waste bin, all over the mirror and the window, up and down the fireplace of pinkish-brown tiles, and the piece of painted hardboard that covered over where the grate had been. Then with a fistful of paper torn off the roll, she started wiping.

"Bloody hell," she said to herself. "No wonder his lungs are a goner." The swipes of the towel left tracks in the decades of tobacco and hair pomade, and (to be fair) traffic dust from outside and (to be honest) plain old honest-to-god filth. It was like nothing Opal had ever seen. Or at least—she thought this to herself as she scoured the fireplace tiles that weren't not pinkish-brown after all, but pink, pure and simple, the pink of Germolene or cheap baby dolls, the pink of waterproof plasters, what people called "flesh-coloured" before they got a single clue—what it reminded her of was those magic painting books she used to get from the newsagents on a Saturday when she was tiny. The ones where you dipped a brush in plain water and soaked the picture and all the colours sprang out; magic right enough when you were three. She used the whole roll of towels and she had forgotten about the window. The lemon cleaner was starting to congeal there in the warmth of the evening sun. Opal looked around and then made herself a pad of tissues, rubbed it with them, picked off the bits that sloughed away and stuck to the glass, then remembered what Mrs. Pickess had told her. But she couldn't face reopening the bin bag to get a piece of newspaper out again. She slipped her top off, rubbed the window dry with it, and put it back on. Bloody Mrs. Pickess was right about newspaper then. A cotton tee-shirt was no substitute for it. The window was worse than ever. But she was wasting precious minutes now. Never mind smeared windows, it was golden thread time.

She looked around. Where would Fishbo keep papers? Old addresses, letters, that kind of thing. She opened the cupboard in his bedside table, but there was only a tower of magazines in there. She couldn't help herself, even though she didn't really want to know if the mags were *that* kind, but it was okay: on the cover of the top one was a picture of Louis Armstrong with his trumpet at his lips, and Opal could tell that it was the same magazine all the way down.

And in the drawer on top, there was only more cigarettes, more matchbooks, a watch and a spare watch strap, a couple of odd little keys, and a small clay pipe—a Popeye pipe—that Opal had never seen Fishbo using.

Next, the chest of drawers. The bottom drawers were filled with cardigans, knitted tank tops, long-sleeved vests, and long-legged pants. In the middle were summer shirts and short vests, pants that were a bit more normal—but only a bit. And in the top drawer were socks—really terrible socks, black nylon washed without any softener so they were stiff and crackly and all with a row of white pillies along the tops of the heels where they rubbed against his shoes. As well as the socks there was a pile of folded and ironed handkerchiefs, the ones Fishbo always had to mop his face when he was onstage. She was glad he'd graduated to tissues for his cough. Imagine having to wash the hankies after he had used them now! She fingered one of the smooth white squares and felt the embroidered initial. EG—Eugene Gordon. He hated that name, but he had it embroidered on his hankies? Not FG or even just F? She looked quickly down through the pile. Nope. EG, it was. Or GG sometimes. Fishbo might be Fishbo in every other part of his life but he was Gene or Eugene Gordon on his hankies, and it made Opal smile.

There was only one place left now. She lifted the latch on the old-fashioned brown wood wardrobe and tried to open the door. Stuck. She tried again. Locked? Then she remembered the keys in the bedside drawer.

One was definitely a suitcase key, but one looked older and more sturdy and when she fitted into the lock on the wardrobe door, it turned. *Weird*, Opal thought. *That's got to slow you down in the morning—having to fetch a key and unlock your wardrobe.* Then she saw what was inside and understood, because here was where Fishbo kept his private things. His treasures. A trumpet case, a hat box, a cricket bat, about half a dozen flat packages wrapped in yellowed crepe paper and tied with string that she thought, when she felt them, were picture frames. Family photos. They must be! And as well as all that there were newspapers, a whole great big pile of them. *Yorkshire Evening Posts* on the top. A couple from ten years ago. The headline: "Little Leeds Lad Still Missing: Prayer Vigil Tonight."

Opal looked at that one for a long moment, but then told herself nothing would be more normal than to keep a newspaper about the biggest news that had ever happened on the street where you live.

But what if the other papers were about other children gone missing? She checked. The next one was the *Yorkshire Evening Post* again but whatever had made Fishbo keep it, it wasn't front-page stuff. And the next, folded open at the right page, made Opal let her breath go in a big rush. "Mote Street Boys Raise the Roof" it said, and there was a photo of them. They were all slimmer—except Fishbo, who was a tiny bit fatter if anything, not such a bag of bones as now—but they all wore exactly the clothes they still chose today—the leather waistcoats and string ties, the pork-pie hats and deck-chair-striped blazers.

She skipped the rest of the *Evening Posts*—there were only a few—and dug down to a more-yellowed, different-sized paper, not

214

standing up so well to being kept all these years. *The Daily Gleaner*. She lifted the top one—it would be interesting to see a real New Orleans—

"What the hell are you doing?" Pep Kendal's voice froze her like a searchlight on a prison break and instinctively she ducked her head down between her shoulder blades to dodge the blow. None came, so she turned very slowly, hoping against hope that Fishbo was exhausted from his bath and asleep in Pep's arms. It was even better than that: Pep's arms were empty, hanging by his sides as he stared at Opal kneeling there.

"I—" she said. "Is Mr. Fish okay?"

"I came to get him some clean pajamas. I forgot to take them through and he wouldn't hear of me shouting to you to bring them." Pep's face hardened. "He's a private man, Opal. Always has been. No matter how sick he is, he still deserves his dignity."

"It's only newspapers," said Opal, brash as she always was when someone gave her a proper row, and as she said the word she had a brainwave. "I needed some newspaper to finish off the window. Look at the streaks I've left on it!" Pep did look, briefly, but when he brought his gaze back to Opal, it was through narrowed eyes.

"You found the wardrobe key and unlocked it to see if there was any old newspa—*tchah!*"

"No," said Opal, colouring up. "I opened the wardrobe to see if there was a clean blanket in here." She stared back at him as hard as he was staring at her, and at last he faltered. Then she started piling the newspapers back in to the bottom of the wardrobe as she had found them. "But these are all too old and dry anyway. It'll just have to stay streaky."

"I better get back," Pep said, with a glance over his shoulder. Opal stood and opened the second drawer down on the chest, where the pajamas were, and took a pair out. It was only when she was handing them over that Pep's eyes and hers met and they both realized that the only way she could know where they were was if she had been snooping.

THIRTY-ONE

WELL SO WHAT IF she had, Opal argued to herself, stomping back over the road. She was still blushing, and between that and the lather she had worked up getting the hoovering done and the sheets on in three minutes flat before Pep and Fishbo came out of the bathroom, she felt as if she had a coating all over her: lemon cleaner and carpet powder and old tobacco. But she was sure there were answers in that wardrobe, and she would get back in there no matter what Pep Kendal had to say. Because *The Gleaner* must have been kept for the same reasons as the *Evening Post*. Fishbo was in there, or someone he knew, maybe even announcements of births and deaths. Or why else would he have saved them? Never mind saved! Packed them and brought them all this way when he came.

She dumped her hoover down on the step and put in her key.

"Got yourself another little job?" came the voice from directly across the road. Opal blew her breath out and turned.

"Just helping out, Mrs. Pickess," she said. That was all the excuse Mrs. Pickess needed to bustle over and take a good long searching look at what Opal had in her hands.

"You don't want to be wasting your money on that rubbish," she said, nodding at the bottles of freshener and cleaner with her lips pursed. "It's nowt but perfume. It won't budge muck, it just covers it up with a smell."

"Well, it's my money," said Opal.

"Nowt but chemicals," Mrs. Pickess said. "And it's not good for you. Mr. Pickess used to get terrible asthma, every month. It were the oven cleaner. I went back to wire wool and hot suds and he never ailed again."

Until he died, Opal couldn't stop herself thinking. Then: "Great," she said, proud of herself for managing it. "Listen, Mrs. Pickess, I could really do with putting my feet up."

"Young piece like you?" said Mrs. Pickess, scandalised and unbelieving.

Opal knew she should guard her tongue but it had been *such* a long hot hell of a day and Mrs. Pickess was the tin lid on it. She gave way to irritation. "Why not come in and have a drink?" she said with her sweetest smile. "I'm sure there's a bottle of brandy and it's a good make, smooth as anything. D'you like brandy, Mrs. Pickess?"

Mrs. Pickess stood very still.

"I'm no drinker," she said.

"Me neither," said Opal. "I didn't buy it. It's left over from my mum. She must have bought it herself, eh?"

"I've left summat on the ring," said Mrs. Pickess, beginning to move away.

"Oh?" said Opal. "Hope it's not a chip pan."

"Stock," Mrs. Pickess said.

Opal couldn't help laughing, and she thought that maybe letting her tongue run on wasn't such a bad idea after all. She'd just confirmed that Mrs. Pickess really did know about Nic's brandy. Why else would the mention of it freak her out this way?

"Right," she said. "Stock." She looked up at the pale pink glow in the sky, the muggy haze that hung over Mote Street. "It's just the weather for a pot of broth. Wish I'd thought of doing one."

She couldn't face so much as a lettuce leaf, actually. She'd a sick headache like when Steph had been gloss-painting, and she wondered if Mrs. Pickess might be right about the chemicals as well as the newspaper for windows. She sat down at the kitchen table and got her Golden Threads notepad out. She hadn't written in it—hadn't so much as looked at it—for days. And so when she started, she was surprised to see how much ground she'd covered since last time. Lena Martell and finding Karen—finding out that Karen had no suspicions about Craig's dad. She'd just about jumped down Opal's throat for hinting that Robbie was involved. Opal twiddled her pen. That was rock-solid, wasn't it? A woman might protect her husband no matter what he'd done—happened all the time—but if she hit the roof and defended her *ex*-husband, that really meant something. And if she defended her ex-husband to his girlfriend's daughter, when his girlfriend's daughter was poking her nose in, she must be *really* sure.

And why exactly had Opal suspected Robbie Southgate, anyway? Witchy Pickess made her. Hinting and gossiping...

She always acted like she was better than everyone else. Holier than thou. But Vonnie Pickess was a gossip. She shopped Nicola and the police took Nic's house apart and probably gave her a really hard time. So Nic retaliated the way that only she knew how. God knows what tale she threatened to tell to pay Mrs. Pickess back again. *So* Mrs.

Pickess bought the brandy to shut her up and keep her in line. And if *Nic* had threatened Mrs. Pickess's precious reputation with some gossip of her own, that explained why Mrs. Pickess never blabbed Margaret's secret. She didn't dare. Scared of comeback. Of course, it wasn't nice to think that your mum was a bully and a blackmailer, but it was better than what Opal *had* been thinking. Anything was better than that.

So she'd answered three of her questions then. She'd done a good bit to get three suspects off her list. Robbie, Vonnie Pickess, and Nicola. At least, they weren't off the list exactly, but they could be explained away.

And Pep and Fishbo were never on the list.

So did that mean the Joshis were the prime suspects now? Because they had kept Margaret's secret and they alone had no reason to? And because they had whispered—Zula and Mr. Joshi that day—about Opal asking questions and about … what was the other thing? Opal tried to remember what it was she had heard when she was putting the shopping away. Something about offering to help Opal and giving stuff to Nicola that she probably sold anyway. Nicola again. Opal started to let her mind drift, trying to see a pattern, but the sick headache flooded her and she had to catch her breath and swallow.

Something about Nic and Robbie and little Craig and what Mr. Joshi had said and … it just wasn't there, and she didn't want to chase it. Maybe if she thought about something else for a while it would come back to her. Or maybe—and she might prefer this—if she thought about something else, it would sink below the surface and stay there for good.

So onto another thread and again she couldn't help being chuffed at how far she had come with the little bed girl, as she was still calling Norah in her mind. She'd made miles of progress there. She'd found out that whatever happened to Norah, it was her brother Martin that did it to her, and decided that it was absolutely the right thing to do, even after all these years, to try to help. Because Norah wasn't over it; she wasn't okay. She was still scared and sorry and bewildered. And Martin had children and grandchildren, and for all Opal knew they were scared and sorry too. And unless she found out that Martin was dead, she was going to track him down and tell him she knew what he had done.

Once she found out what it was, anyway. And once she had some definite proof too. So she had to find the other half of the bed, and put the whole north-south-east-west letter together again. If you could even call it a letter; it was more like a spell. Or a prayer. She remembered Norah's little leather prayer book sitting beside her bed in the nursery bedroom and wondered if she would have written anything else in there.

Also, she should track down the rest of the family. That shouldn't be too hard. There were contact numbers pasted up all over that kitchen; the niece and nephew had to be two of them.

And as for the third golden strand? Okay, Pep didn't agree about finding Mr. Fish's family for him, but it wasn't Pep's call. Somehow she'd get back into that wardrobe to track down names and addresses. Then of course she'd have to write, which would take forever and Fishbo, even though he'd definitely throw off this chest infection once the antibiotics kicked in, certainly didn't *have* forever. Not if he wanted to take a long plane journey and still be alive and kicking at the end of it. So she could phone, which would be really expensive. But then again, her three golden threads had so far cost her one return bus fare to Ilkley, so she thought she could spare enough for a phone call to America if push came to shove. Maybe some of it could be done at the library on email.

She hadn't ever had email at home. Kate and Rhianne would. But she didn't want to tell them she didn't have a computer and couldn't afford to buy one and didn't have any other friends who had one. If the library didn't work out, she'd ask someone who already knew she had no money. Michael? Steph wouldn't let her back in the house. The Joshis would have the Internet for sure, but she couldn't ask them, because Zula would stand and read everything she was typing over her shoulder. And Margaret, Mrs. Pickess, and Pep would no more have the Internet than they would … Opal tried to think of something less likely … than they would install jacuzzis in their outhouses.

Then another big wave of nausea washed over her and it left the pain in her head sharper and stronger than before, like a drill coming in under her skull. *Cool shower*, she thought. Might as well stand under it since it's on anyway.

And the water had worked. Upstairs was not only not boiling hot anymore, it was almost chilly, so Opal went into the small back bedroom to close the window there. Three daddy longlegs had come in and were rattling about where the ceiling joined the wall; she'd forgotten how her room had always been full of them and she'd not been in there much since she came back. She looked around. This was where she would put her desk and computer if she had one. Maybe she'd get hold of a cheap desk and put it in here anyway, keep her notepad up here. It would be better than leaving her notes lying around the kitchen where anyone might see them. And the view was better too. Or at least you could see a bit farther. She went over to the window and looked out.

The backs of the big houses were dark against the pale pink sky, and the yellow oblongs of their lighted windows made Opal think of advent calendars. She wished she was close enough to see inside to what the families who lived there were doing. Not standing in an empty room planning the incredible luxury of a cheap desk anyway! She took her eyes away and let it rest on the trees instead. It wasn't like her to be so chippy, she thought. Maybe the picking was getting to her: the avocados and pumpkin seed crisp breads, the endless bloody bottles of Cava people seemed to need to deal with a decent summer. But that wasn't fair: Franz Ferdi used the online shop, and he never ate anything fancy.

Thinking of him she flicked a glance down at the yards, hers and his, and jumped. He was standing there.

THIRTY-TWO

SHE HADN'T HEARD HIM because for once he wasn't crying. He was just standing with his head down in the middle of the concrete, looking at something on the ground in front of him. Opal watched him. He didn't move. And now she couldn't stop watching him because if *she* moved, he might hear her, the window being open the way it was and the night being so very still, nothing moving at all except the soft rattling of the daddy longlegs dancing around above her head in the empty room.

When he did move, Opal shrank back, holding onto the window frame. She hadn't seen the thing in his hand, but it glinted when he raised his arms and she was sure she could hear it whistling as he brought it smashing down. When he lifted it again she got a clearer view and she could see it was a hammer, shiny metal with a long slim handle, and he was pounding something bright and brittle that lay on the concrete floor of the yard. Shards of plastic flew around, hitting the walls, and one flew right over and landed in Opal's yard, just by the outhouse door.

And still he kept going, starting to chase the pieces around until he had beaten them all down as small as they would go, little splinters of red and blue plastic, then he hurled his hammer at the back wall of the yard and disappeared into the kitchen, slamming the door so hard Opal could feel her own bedroom floor shaking underneath her.

She waited, wondering if anyone else had heard, if someone else would come to the back gate and look over to see what the noise was, but after the slammed door stopped echoing in her ears there was perfect silence again. She looked at the curved jagged piece of blue plastic lying in her yard, and it jolted her back to life again. If she could see over his wall, then he could see over hers, and if he looked out of his back window and saw that lying there, he might come to get it. Opal didn't want the man who had swung that hammer so fast it had whistled coming into her yard.

But before she could stir herself he was out again. And he went straight to his gate, trampling over the mess of plastic, wrenched it open, and disappeared out into the lane. Opal stepped back and waited to see him fill her open gateway, but he didn't appear. And there were more noises now. She sidled up to the window and listened. He was chucking stuff into his wheelie bin; she could hear it bouncing on its little rubber wheels and the unmistakable hollow thump of the lid hitting against the body every time something landed inside.

She stepped away from the window again and went downstairs to her kitchen. Could she creep out and get her gate closed and locked without him hearing her? She could hear *him*—ragged breaths and scuffing, scraping sounds—and she thought he was kicking the plastic pieces across the concrete, maybe edging the mess towards the bin. She'd chance it. She slipped off her shoes. In bare feet she tiptoed down the two steps and took six of the eight paces before she heard him moving. He was going back inside again. He had closed the door. Opal sprang over to the gate to lock it, but then couldn't resist the urge that took hold of her when she got there. She ducked out into the lane, streaked past his open gateway, and lifted the lid of his bin. She could see most of the front of a co-coa-pops box and the greasy gleam of string cheese. She lowered the lid and shrieked. He was standing there.

"Jesus!" she said.

He was still panting and his face was streaked with sweat and tears, the bags under his eyes bigger and more bruised-looking than they had been the last time—the only time—she'd seen him.

"I thought you'd gone back inside," Opal blurted out before she realized that would tell him she'd been listening.

"What are you doing in my bin?" His voice sounded calm enough, but that in itself made her heart start to pound. He had just been sob-bing and smashing stuff with a hammer and now there was someone raking though his bin. He should be anything but calm. He was trying to fool her. He wasn't going to manage it.

"Sorry," she said and she gave him a sheepish smile. "Mine's full. I was just having a look to see if there's space in yours. I should have asked really. I should have come and knocked on your door."

His eyes flicked over to her bin, but if he was trying to seem calm and normal, he was hardly going to go and check, was he?

"Nah, you're all right, love," he said. "You help yourself if you need to."

"Thanks," said Opal. Then, "Are you okay?"

"Me?" he said. "Can't smile wide enough, me. Sorry about the din." And he took a very deep breath and rubbed his hands over his face. "*Brrrr*," he said, like he was splashing himself with cold water.

"Din?" said Opal. "I never heard a thing."

"Except me going back into the house," he said.

So he hadn't missed that little slip then. "So I thought," said Opal. She looked past him at how far away the house was. She had definitely heard him close the door. She'd never have come out of her yard if she thought he was still around, and yet a moment later there he was again. Opal felt a movement as the hairs on her neck and down her spine crackled, leaving her tingling.

"I was in the outhouse," he answered, and Opal nodded slowly. Of course. He hadn't had time to cross his yard to the kitchen. That door she'd heard closing was the outhouse door. He held up a broom to show her and she nodded again. *The outhouse.*

"Well, night then," she said, and he gave her a look different from all the others before, head cocked, brows high.

"Are *you* all right?"

"Tired," said Opal. *The outhouse, the outhouse.* "This weather."

"Aye," he said.

"Makes it hard to sleep at night." *The outhouse, the outhouse. The hold your nose and shout house.*

"All right if you can keep your doors and windows open," he said. "All right for me. Nobody's going to come bothering me, but you'll be careful, eh love? Lot of funny folk about these hot nights. Full moon too." He nodded over Opal's shoulder, and she turned. A pale, glassy moon as big as a lake was just edging above the roofline.

"Right," she said. "Thanks for the warning."

He blinked. "Advice, love. Just advice. Ignore it if you want to."

Grab thee by thy lughole, put thee down the plughole. Opal felt her stomach roll over.

"Night, then," she said again, but this time she started moving. She took her wheelie bin with her in through the open gate and then

227

shut the gate behind her and bolted it. Waste of time. He no more believed she was "just checking there was space" than he believed she hadn't heard all the commotion, than she believed he was just giving her a friendly piece of advice about locking her windows. *Pull, pull, pull the chain, wash back up again.* She couldn't stop the voice in her head now it had started. She took the piece of blue plastic and put it inside her bin. It looked like a bit of a skittle or a Frisbee or something. Something a kid would use, although she supposed it might be a dog's bed or the bucket part of a cheap wheelbarrow. *The outhouse, the outhouse, the hold your nose and shout house.*

She really did feel sick now and there was no way she'd make it up to the bathroom in time. Her cheeks were pouring with water. She looked at the outhouse door. Could she pull it open? The toilet, as far as she knew, was still in there. How hard had she tried that first time anyway?

She went over and grabbed the handle, hauling on it, bracing one of her feet up against the panels of the door and tugging with all her strength. It didn't so much as budge, but Opal felt *something* give way. Something inside her body had burst and was flooding her. And she didn't feel sick anymore. The sickness came from trying not to see what was in front of her eyes and not join up all the thoughts that were skittering around the edges of her brain. She tugged and slammed, crying now; changed legs and hauled again, ignoring the way her foot slid down the splintered door, ignoring the sting as tiny shards of paint and wood dug into her skin.

Then she gave up, panting. Looked around and picked up the half-brick used for propping the gate open. She stood back as far as she could against the opposite wall and threw it at the outhouse window. It hit the wooden crossbar and rolled away. She picked it up and threw it again, standing closer, not caring about broken glass now. This time it went through, shattering the coated, dusty glass and disappearing. Opal heard a dull thump and a grating sound as it hit something solid in there. She stepped forward and pushed the rest of the pieces in so that one quarter of the window was clear. Then she stuck her head inside and looked down.

The floor—except it wasn't really the floor—was halfway up the door, about three feet below the bottom of the window, as smooth as a pond in patches, uneven in others, rippled at the edges, with crumpled, lumpy shapes half-in and half-out of the tilting plane of it. *Bags*, Opal thought. The bags had been shoved in through the window, the easiest way to get rid of them, and they poked up and broke the surface here and there. In one place, it looked as if a bag was just *below* the surface—not sunk and not floating. Something was there. Opal turned around and sank down, sliding down the wall until she was sitting on the ground with her legs bent like hairpins and her feet, one still bleeding, tucked close in underneath her. There was a noise inside her chest trying to get out of her. A howl. She held on hard and managed to keep it to a low moan that no one would hear.

Cement. Or concrete. Something Mr. Joshi wanted for his new garage floor and Zula gave to Nic instead. And Nic poured it in through the window and left it to set there. And now Zula wanted to know if Opal was planning any renovations, if she had any bikes or sports equipment that needed storing and wanted to make sure that Opal asked the Joshis to help before she turned to strangers.

Zula? Mr. and Mrs. Joshi? They couldn't have.

Couldn't have what, Opal?

And Mrs. Pickess. She told the cops to take Nicola's house apart and she bought brandy and asked Opal if she'd managed to unstick the outhouse door. But she couldn't know.

Know what, Opal? Come on, out in the open.

229

And Pep and Fishbo knew he liked hiding. Liked little dark places, little secret places, vans and sheds and behind bath panels. But that didn't mean they would hide a thing like that.

Like what, Opal? Just say it. These things always come back no matter how deep you bury them.

"No," Opal said, screwing her face up as tight as it would go. No kid could want to be in such a dark, smelly, cold, filthy hole. They were lying. He would have to be lured in there, with a trail of sweets thrown down for him to follow. Bribed in with the promise of a toy.

She jerked her head up, thinking of the piece of blue plastic, a toy smashed to pieces, treats thrown away. And she put her arms over her head and tried again to keep the howl inside.

"This is now," she said to herself. "This is 2010, and you are twenty-five. You're not twelve anymore. Franz Ferdi wasn't here then. He's the only safe one."

But that left the rest of them, all around her; monstrous Denny and Margaret saying it's secret, it's secret, but telling everyone. And Mrs. Pickess watching, and Fishbo ashy and hacking and secrets locked in his wardrobe, and Pep looking at her like she was dirt and telling her not to think, not to ask, just to leave it be. And Zula Joshi—the sly look from the corner of her eye—and Mr. Joshi's whispered questions, and the hammer glinting and smashing down, and Norah taking her thumb out her mouth and saying "Martin".

———

Opal was stiff and, for the first time in weeks, cold. It was pure night now; the moon, much smaller, glittering down from out of a navy blue sky. Had she been sleeping? Please God let it be that she'd fallen

230

asleep and not just that she'd *gone*. That hadn't happened for thirteen years, and Opal had believed it never would again.

Okay, she told herself. *Take another run at it. Breathe deep and stay calm. Stick to the facts.* The main fact was that Nicola Jones lived on a street where a little boy went missing, and that little boy liked hiding in small places, and Nicola Jones's outhouse was half-filled with cement. If Nicola Jones wasn't her mother, what would she think of that?

Zula gave the cement meant for her garage floor to Nicola. Vonnie Pickess kept her in brandy. Fishbo kept Margaret's secret, and Pep Kendal was so grateful he was willing to *bathe* him. And Franz Ferdi came to live on Mote Street, and he cried all the time and smashed up a plastic bowling set (or whatever it was) with a hammer and threatened Opal. Those were puzzles. But the *big* fact was that Nicola Jones's outhouse was half-full of cement and a little kid was gone.

She stood, pulling herself up like an old lady climbing out of a swimming pool, feeling gravity try to haul her back down again, and wincing as the sole of her foot moved, grinding the splinters in. Then she limped into the house and (advice or warning; it made sense anyway) she locked and bolted the back door and went through to check the deadbolt on the front one too.

And that was when she saw the gleam of something white on the carpet just inside. An envelope, lying in a patch of streetlight. It must have come through the letterbox since Opal had gotten home. She picked it up and carried it through to the kitchen where the light was on.

There was nothing written on the front, but why would there be? No one else lived here. She ran her thumb under the seal, opened it, and peered in. It was a photograph and her first thought was that

Pep Kendal had forgiven her and brought over something of Fish-bo's to help her out after all. But then it was far too new to be Fish-bo's family back in New Orleans. This photo was colour. A little girl, pale skin but wild natural hair, sitting on a step in the sunshine, chubby hands clutching chubby knees, round face beaming. Opal looked at it for a minute, and the first thing she recognised was the step and then the wall and the patch of carpet.

It was here, No. 6 Mote Street. And the little girl was her. It was a picture of Opal. Why would someone deliver that with no note?

She turned the photograph over and let her breath go. There was a note after all, written on the back of the picture itself, in black felt-tip printing. Then she read what it said and dropped it, wiping her hand on her tee-shirt.

Curiosity killed the cat. This little kitten is still too young to die.

THIRTY-THREE

OF COURSE HER THOUGHTS were going to fly to Franz Ferdi. Of course they were. His gleaming hammerhead whistling through the air, his sudden appearance at her side, his friendly "advice" that wasn't friendly at all. But it couldn't be him, because how could he have a picture of Mote Street from years ago when he had only just moved here? So Opal put him out of her mind.

But he crept right back in again. Hadn't she wondered why he had moved to a new place when he obviously hated it, crying alone in his house that way? What if he *hadn't* moved to a new place? What if he had moved back to a place he'd been before?

She put him out her mind again, more firmly this time. If he had lived here when Opal was a baby, all the other neighbors would remember him. Not that you needed to live in a place to take a photo there. But why would you take a photograph of a random kid in a random street where you were a stranger?

As soon as she had asked herself the question, she saw the answer plain and clear. And what would she rather believe? That Craig

Southgate was buried under concrete in the earth floor of her outhouse or that the man who snatched him was back and living right next door? It couldn't be both. Unless Franz Ferdi knew Nicola all those years ago and used her yard. And that would explain why he was back again, in a way. Come back to the house with the shared wall where he could take his time, chip all the concrete out, dig up the body, and finally take it away.

Crazy, she told herself. Insane. (As opposed to all the sane thoughts she'd been having, all the uncrazy ways little boys could just disappear? Right.)

But then why would Zula have provided the cement, and why would Mrs. Pickess have bought the brandy? And anyway, Sandy and Nic were still married when Opal had been that little girl with the chubby knees. How could Nicola know Franz when Opal's dad was still here?

And speaking of Vonnie Pickess, Opal had tipped her hand only hours ago, hinting that way about a bottle of brandy. And that photo was taken from right across the street, right outside Mrs. Pickess's front door.

But it was Pep Kendal who had seen Opal actually snooping, going through Fishbo's things, letting her "curiosity" get the better of her. The note made more sense if it was him who sent it.

But if she was thinking of people who knew she was snooping, there was Denny too. He'd more or less told her to stop stirring the pot, hadn't he? Could he have done it? Opal could no more imagine him writing that threat than she could imagine him getting out of his chair, raking through whatever box or album Margaret's old snaps were in, leaving the house, and lumbering over to push the envelope through her door. If he had told Margaret, though... Opal shook her head. Margaret could physically do it, but she'd never write such a thing, threatening someone she still thought of as a child, still loved like a child, when one grandchild was gone and the other one was kept away.

But what if Opal's message to Karen had hit home? If she'd called her parents maybe, or written to them, and hurt them all over again? If Opal's interference had made it worse somehow, could Margaret have been pushed to write the note *then*?

No way. Margaret and Denny just weren't the kind of people who do something so furtive as write a threat and quietly put it through a door. They hated secrets, for one thing—Margaret bursting out and telling everyone over and over again a secret she couldn't keep inside, and Denny wanting so much to let it go and tell the police the whole story even if it came back on his head and ruined him. And for two (and Opal wasn't proud of thinking this), it was too subtle for them. Margaret would just have come over and sat at Opal's kitchen table, drinking tea and begging Opal to stop meddling. That was her way. She didn't go at things sideways.

Then, thinking of sideways made Opal think of sideways looks, sidelong glances, casual asides meant to find things out without ever really asking. Which took her back to Zula Joshi. Made her think—and now her thoughts were racing—of the sideways plan Zula had hatched to get Opal back here; nothing as blatant as phoning her up and telling her about the tenancy that was Opal's if she claimed it. No, just forwarding mail, paying bills, not even saying who was doing it, just letting Opal make the discovery for herself, decide for herself that she was coming home.

But why would Zula suddenly push that photo through Opal's door tonight? It was days since they had even spoken. To stop Opal connecting the warning with what she had said to Sunil about the DIY?

Did that make sense? If Opal couldn't so much as connect the warning to what she was being warned about, how could the warning really warn her? She put her head down on the table and groaned. It was late and she was tired and she couldn't make sense of anything.

She didn't even know what she was being told to stop interfering in. Craig? Fishbo? Some bit of Franz Ferdi's business that was nothing to do with little Craig at all? Some bit of Pep Kendal's business that was nothing to do with Fishbo's family?

The safest thing would be to stop meddling in all of it.

She should concentrate on the little bed girl. The mystery of Norah Fossett and her creepy brother, Martin. At least she knew the photo and the note had nothing to do with *that* golden thread. Then she raised her head.

Did she? Shelley wasn't too keen on Opal hanging around Miss Fossett, and she knew Opal's address. But would she go as far as threatening Opal? Sure, if it was Shelley who was boosting all Norah's stuff and selling it off. Maybe there was no niece and nephew. Maybe Shelley had just persuaded Norah to say there was. The poor old soul was a bit hazy about whether or not she had a brother, wasn't she? Maybe Shelley was acting all kind and neighborly and quietly paying off her mortgage thanks to Claypole's auctions.

Opal was beginning to like this idea. Her thoughts tumbled forward, meeting no resistance, until her eyes lit on the photograph in front of her again. She shook her head and almost laughed. Right. Shelley had a picture of Opal from twenty-odd years ago. Sure thing.

Time for bed.

She dragged herself to her feet, checked the back door, checked the front door, fastened the front and back windows (trying not to think about what an oven the house would be by the morning), and went upstairs. She needed to butt out of Fishbo's past, in case it was Pep who was threatening her. She needed for sure to butt out of looking for little Craig, in case it was Zula or Mrs. Pickess or the Reids (it couldn't be!), and she needed to keep the extreme hell away from her new neighbor, whether or not threatening notes were in his repertoire along with smashing toys and buying kiddie-snacks that went straight in the wheelie-bin.

But at least she could go full steam ahead with Miss N Fossett, the little bed girl. Bad things bloody well shouldn't happen to little girls and even if they did, someone had come along and found out, and now she knew.

She put the photograph of the wild-haired little girl with the beaming smile next to the note from the quiet little girl who couldn't stop saying sorry. She fastened her window, thinking about Norah's window and the thick black bars. She pulled a chest of drawers across in front of her door, thinking about Norah's door with its little brass bolt, and then, imagining Norah safely tucked up with the prayer book on the table beside her, door latched and windows barred, she climbed into the high, safe ship of her own bed. And even after everything she had been through that long hot horrible day, she was asleep while the air in the sealed room was still cool and sweet around her.

THIRTY-FOUR

"RIGHT THEN, MY FLOWER," she said. Norah giggled. "I've seen the kitchen and I'm going to say two things. One: don't make porridge—it's obviously not your strong point. And two: would you like some toast and a cup of tea?"

"Toast and tea," said Norah. "Yum-mee."

"You are very low maintenance in your way, Norah Fossett," said Opal. "If we ignore the oatmeal you've got welded to the cooker, anyway."

Once she was installed in the chair in the morning room with her plate of jammy toast and Billy Smart's fireworks exploding over the screen, Opal made her way upstairs. She had thought about taking a duster and a can of polish with her in case Shelley turned up. But who was she kidding? Shelley wouldn't fall for a duster and polish; she'd be more likely to think Opal was trying to hide something than if Opal offered no excuse at all. Besides, it was Sunday lunchtime; Opal reckoned Shelley fitted Miss Fossett in around her family—she wouldn't be doing spot checks and sneak raids on a Sunday.

On the landing, she stood and looked around, wondering if the other half of Norah's bed would be in the attic or in one of the other rooms. Try the rooms first. She opened a door opposite the head of the stairs and looked in.

It was stuffed with furniture. Good dark mahogany, from what Billy and Tony had taught her. Two enormous tables with marble tops and arrangements of mirrors that looked like something from the front of a church instead of somebody's bedroom. A chest of drawers with at least eight drawers in it, higher than Opal's shoulders, and a mirror, full-length, standing on dumpy legs carved out of wood to look like bird's feet clutching gold balls. There were even two bedside tables of the same dark mahogany, with glassed over tops to stop teacups leaving rings on the wood. What *wasn't* there was a bed. There was just a space on the floor between the two nightstands and a brighter, darker oblong where the bed had protected the carpet from the sun.

"Bugger me," said Opal.

She went back down to the morning room and stood behind Norah's chair. That had worked better the last time than confronting her head on.

"Norah, love?" she said in a soft voice. Norah kept watching the horses, but she took her thumb out of her mouth—Opal noticed that it was stuck here and there with little morsels of chewed toast—and made a small sound. "Where's the bed from the room with the big mirror?" She had to hope there wasn't a big mirror in every room. "The mirror with the bird feet."

"Ball and claw," said Norah. "Mother's room."

"Really?" said Opal. "Okay. Well, where's your mother's bed, love?"

239

"They took it back," said Norah. "When she died."

Opal suppressed a sigh. Not *them* again. She was sick of *them*.

"Did they?" she said, keeping her voice very light. "Where did they take it back to?"

"To the hospital," Norah said.

Opal rolled her eyes, looking down at Miss Fossett's pink parting. Maybe she wasn't going to get any sense out of her today. Then she blinked and thought again. Maybe Norah was talking the whole plain truth. "They" brought Norah's dinners and did her personal care. And maybe the same "they"—roughly—really had come for the bed her mum had died in to take it back to the hospital again. She crossed her fingers.

"Not the hospital bed," she said. "The one before she was ill. Where did you put it when the hospital bed came?"

"In the attic," said Norah. "Men came. Look, she's going to stand up on his back now." On the screen, a woman with thighs like a gladiator had scrambled up to stand on the back of a black horse, one hand holding onto a long rein and the other hand high above her head. Miss Fossett raised her own hand getting just the same flourish into her fingers, bringing the thumb with its little lumps of chewed toast very close to Opal.

"Is it still up there?" said Opal. Miss Fossett put her arm down. She said nothing.

"Norah? Is your mum's bed still in the attic?"

"Mm-hmm," said Miss Fossett. She had put her thumb back in her mouth again.

"And where's the hatch?"

"Hatch?"

"The way into the attic."

"I'm not allowed up there."

Opal laughed and ruffled her hair. Norah turned round and gave her a smile so surprised and so sweet that Opal could have hugged her.

"And it's definitely still up there?" Opal said and got only a frown. Norah had forgotten what they were talking about again. "Your mother's big bed? It's in the attic?" Norah nodded and turned back round to face the television screen. She spoke so softly that, if Opal hadn't been bending to kiss her, she might have missed it.

"Half of it is," she said and then in went her thumb and she sat back to enjoy the show.

Opal raced back upstairs, scanned the landing and, seeing no hatch there, started opening one door after another. She knew there was no real rush, but she couldn't help herself. The thought that it was so close! One of the doors was locked, but all the others revealed rooms with smooth, bare, plaster ceilings. She checked above the highest shelf in the linen cupboard, piled to the top with crumpled sheets and stinking of mothballs. She took a good long look at the panels in the one white-tiled, cold-floored bathroom with a wooden cistern high up on the wall and a smell a long way worse than mothballs.

When she had been right round she sat down on the top step of the stairs, frowning at that one locked door, absently pulling at the matted clumps of cobweb in the fretwork of the banisters. How could Norah not know what a hatch was? What else would you call it? A trap door?

Then Opal got a flash in her mind from some old black-and-white film or something, of a white-haired housekeeper in a long white nightie and a candle in her hand, opening a door and going up a set of creaking stairs. Of course! A house like this wouldn't have a hatch in the ceiling and a ladder. It would have a proper attic staircase, room to spare.

So where was it? She looked again at the only locked door and went to squint through the keyhole. It wasn't a dark stairway behind there. It was another broad, sunny bedroom, at least twenty feet to the bay window where the daylight was pouring through.

So where the hell was it? Think, Opal. In one of the bedroom cupboards? But it couldn't be because if there was a staircase behind a false cupboard door, the next room along would have a crooked ceiling, like her kitchen, and none of the rooms in the hou—

She slapped her head and made her way along the landing to the turn in the corridor where the carpet turned into lino, to Norah's little room. Of course, if someone was going to be bothered with people shoving suitcases up and down into the attic, it would be the maid, not the bosses. (No matter what Norah had said about her little place being the nursery, Opal was sure that it had started out its time as the maid's room way back when.)

And there it was. Opposite the door, half-covered over by the dressing chest, there was another door and above it the ceiling was boxed in around the stairs the door led to. Opal dragged the chest out of the way, stopped and dragged the little bedside table out of the way a bit too to make more room, and finally got the door free and clear. It was locked, but the key was in it and it turned fairly smoothly. So smoothly, in fact, that Opal took it out and wiped it on her palm to check. Yep, there was fresh oil there. Feeling worried, she trotted up the narrow stairs into the dim heat of the attic.

There was just one skylight, small and dusty, and Opal would have loved to find a bulb to switch on. This place was seriously creepy. It had little off-shoots and corners, dead-ends and unexpected spaces. She couldn't work out at first why a big square house would have such

242

a complicated attic with all these bends and turns, until she thought a little harder and realized it was the bedroom chimneys that made it into such a maze.

But that wasn't the only reason she hated being up here. Worse than the thought of getting lost, there was the fact that everything was … shrouded. That was the only word for it. Anonymous shapes stood around or lay on the floor, all wrapped in brown sacking. Trunks and cupboards, she assured herself, and—Oh, help! A tailor's dummy—but she couldn't stop the sweat beginning to trickle down her neck as she imagined a hand lifting up from the side of one of the bundles and plucking the sacking away.

She took a few deep breaths to calm herself and flapped her hands in front of her face to try to cool herself down, then she started, trying to be as methodical as she could, to look for a mound of sacking the right shape and size. When she had been right round twice and was absolutely melting, sweat coursing down the insides of her bare arms and darkening her back, when her hair was itchy and must be as frizzed as it had been in the photograph of the girl on the step, when her nostrils and eyes and even her mouth felt full of little needlelike fibres of sacking—she was forced to conclude that Norah was having her on. The damn thing wasn't here, wasn't anywhere. She lifted her top and wiped her head with it, then she tutted—she had probably just put a dirty smear on it. She held it out, this way and that, trying to see, but she was standing in a deep shadow. She looked up to see what was causing it, and that's when she saw what she'd been looking for.

It had been shoved up over the beams and balanced there. About four or five feet wide and at least as tall. The only part of it that she could see sticking out of its sackcloth wrapping was the legs—two bulbous legs, thicker than her own thighs with little brass casters on the ends.

243

"Gotcha!" Opal said. "Hah! At bloody last. Right then."

She couldn't even dream of getting it down, but then she didn't really want to. Oh, she would tell Billy and Tony that she had found it and then if they wanted to try to talk it out of Miss Fossett, getting it down would be their problem. All she wanted to do was get up there with it, unscrew the orbs and get the two missing parts of Norah's prayer.

She could reach the beams with a bit of a jump, even get her hands round one and swing, but she wasn't a commando; there was no way she could haul herself up there. She looked around again for something light that she could drag over, and settled on a wicker hamper about the size of a washing machine lying on its side that trundled over the floor easily enough and took her weight with just a bit of creaking when she clambered up onto it. Now she could get her elbows over the beam and, ignoring the rough scrape of the wood against her chest and armpit, she managed to drag herself up until she was pivoting at the waist and she could swing one of her legs up and over. She straddled it, gripping as hard as she could with her thighs, and glanced over to where the headboard rested, wrapped in its sacking. It looked really far away—she had chosen to come up a couple of beams over so she had space to move around, but now she was regretting it. She shuffled up until she was opposite and then, swearing softly, she got very carefully up on her hands and knees and crawled over, not letting her breath go until she was safely straddling a beam again, holding on tighter than ever.

She took hold of the sacking and pulled. Nothing. Which she supposed was better than the whole thing moving and crashing to the floor but wasn't exactly ideal. She gripped harder and pulled again. Absolutely nothing. At this side, the sacking was tucked under with the join at the bottom, the whole weight of the headboard holding it in place. She should have gone downstairs for a pair of scissors or a knife as soon as she saw it was wrapped, but too late now.

And anyway, at the other side, there was a flap of sacking on the top. If she could get over there, she could just push it back and once the unwrapping was started, surely she could find away to uncover as much as she had to. So, cursing herself and hating every second of it, freezing with every squeak and creak, wondering if she was only imagining that the beams were moving underneath her, she crawled onto the flat side of the wrapped headboard and made her away to its far edge and the flap of loose wrapping. It flipped back without protest—Opal had had a flash of worry that it might be stitched up—and there was the elaborate carving she had grown so used to seeing every day. She hauled at it a little more and felt it begin to slip away from the top of the post, revealing the bulges and baubles and feathery pennants there.

THIRTY-FIVE

"Fuck!" said Opal. Then again. "Fuck it to buggery." The words were absorbed into the muffled sacking womb of the attic, not as if she had shouted them at all.

What she had found, what was she was sitting on, what she had worked so hard to uncover, was the bloody footboard to match her bloody headboard. It was the wrong half of the wrong bed. She had forgotten there even *was* such a thing.

She flipped the sacking back over and, all fear of heights gone in her anger, she slithered down to hang from her hands and then dropped lightly onto the floor.

Of course she looked around the rest of the attic, peering up at the beams, but there was nothing. And so she made her way back down the stairs to Norah's little white bedroom, and closed and locked the door.

It was when she was dragging the dressing chest back into place that she realized just how filthy she was. She saw the brown marks her hands left on the white-painted wood and then looked at herself in the mirror and laughed. She looked like the creature from the Black Lagoon, her hair and face coated with dust and sacking fibres and her top smeared all over with it too and sticking to her with sweat. So she left Norah's room, went into that cavernous, rank bathroom, and scrubbed her face and hands, leaving some of the smears all over Norah's grubby little hand towel.

When she opened the door again to go back and finish shifting the furniture, though, she heard something that made her turn to stone.

"Woo-hoo," came a voice from downstairs. "Sorry, I'm late, but wait to see what I've brought you."

Bloody Shelley! Opal retreated into the bathroom doorway. But the head she saw go past the foot of the stairs wasn't Shelley's straightened and highlighted one; this head had dark hair held up in a long comb and the walk was wrong too, bouncing and a bit flustered.

Would Norah say there was someone upstairs? Would she even remember? Should Opal just go into one of these rooms and wait for whoever that was to leave again? Not the bathroom—that was the one place a visitor was most likely to go—but one of the bed-rooms, maybe.

Only… what if Norah said that her friend was upstairs and that woman came to check. Or if she said someone was upstairs but she didn't know who it was or what they were doing. Opal made a deci-sion. She went over to the big cistern and pulled the chain. Then she turned her vest-top inside out—cleaner, even if it meant her label was showing—and went downstairs in her best carefree saunter.

"Thanks, Miss Foss—" she was saying as she opened the morn-ing room door, then: "Oh! Sorry. I didn't hear you. Did you knock? I was at the toilet."

"Who are you?" said the woman. She was standing in front of Norah's chair with one hand in her shoulder bag, frozen mid-rummage.

Norah turned round and beamed at Opal. "Hello, my pretty flower," she said.

The woman opened her eyes very wide and then she smiled too. "Well, whoever you are, Auntie Norah seems to like you! I'm Sarah Fossett."

"Norah's niece!" said Opal. "Of course."

"Well, great-niece, whatever. But I've always just called her Auntie Norah."

"I'm Opal Jones. I'm … it's hard to explain. We met one day, out on the street, and I brought your auntie home and then I popped in again and … one thing led to another."

"That's nice," said Sarah. "Neighbor, are you?"

"No, you're thinking of Shelley," Opal said, but Sarah frowned. "Oh no, I know *Shelley*," she said.

"Shelley!" said Norah. "Shelley had a party and I went."

"Yes, nobody escapes Shelley," Sarah said. Opal raised her eyebrows, and Sarah went on. "I shouldn't. She's very good but … you know. We all better eat our vegetables." This was such a good summary of everything Opal had ever thought about Shelley that she burst out laughing. Norah started laughing too and clapped her hands, and Sarah finally managed to find what she was fishing in her bag for and produced it. "Tah-dah!" Norah put out her hands and took it, inspecting it very closely. It was a DVD. *Moscow State Circus*.

"A different one?" Norah said, turning troubled eyes up to Sarah and Opal.

"A *new* one," Sarah said. "We can watch it together, and if you like it, I'll leave it for you. If you don't like it, I'll take it away."

"All right," said Norah, still frowning but nodding too, turning the shiny case over and over in her hands.

"And now, a cup of tea!" said Sarah. "Opal, is it, did you say? Do you want to help me?"

Opal followed her down the hall to the kitchen.

"That was really great, the way you handled her there," she said.

"Practise, love," said Sarah. "I'm a geriatric nurse. So Auntie Norah is just what I need on my day off!"

"It's Alzheimer's she got, innit?" said Opal. She watched Sarah attacking the porridge pan Opal herself had decided to leave soaking. Sarah looked up and see-sawed her head this way and that before she answered.

"A touch," she said. "Probably. But … I dunno. I think Auntie Norah has always been a bit strange."

"You *think*?" said Opal. "Haven't you always been close then?"

Sarah shook her head.

"Didn't know anything about her until my dad started doing the family tree," she said. "That was about, oh, fifteen years ago."

"So your dad's not her brother?" Opal said, telling herself it wasn't likely, hoping she wasn't going to have to tell this woman—so friendly—that her dad had been … whatever Martin Fossett was.

"No," Sarah said. "Norah's brother died yonks ago. So Dad said. Died young."

"Your granddad?"

"No," Sarah said again. "To be honest"—the kettle had boiled and she broke off to swirl out a teapot with hot water and dash it down the sink before she went on—"I never saw the family tree Dad was at. I think there was some kind of tale he didn't want told. Years ago and everyone dead and gone, but Dad still buried it." Opal nodded. "I lost touch with Auntie Norah again after that. Well, I was getting married and had a family to run about after. You know how it is, or you will soon enough." She twinkled at Opal, and Opal tried very hard to smile back, not to let her face freeze the way it wanted to. "Then when I got divorced, I came round to see Auntie Norah and I was shocked to see the change in her, the state she was living in. Felt ashamed of myself for leaving her on her own for years, knowing she's got no one else."

"So … you don't have brothers and sisters?" said Opal.

"One sister in the states," Sarah said. "Been there years."

"Only Miss Fossett said she had a nephew."

"She says a lot of things!" said Sarah. "No, there's just me and Norah. Two Miss Fossetts. I took my maiden name again." She shook her head. "Norah's funny about men. Men in the family anyway."

"You can say that again," said Opal, softly.

Sarah put three cups and saucers on a tray then stopped and looked out of the window into the wall of the tunnel three feet away.

"Ooh, I hate that stupid walkway," she said. "Why would anyone put that right through their back garden? You know what it makes me think of? The secure ambulance drop for Ward Four. Locked ward, you know." Opal nodded. From what Shelley had said about Norah's life, it wasn't too far from the truth.

"It could be a new lease of life for Auntie Norah, getting out of this place at long last." Opal nodded again. "You could put your tuppence-worth in," said Sarah. "She might listen to you." She was looking round the kitchen, shaking her head. "If I could finish getting this place cleared and sell it, she'd be in the best of private nursing homes for the next twenty years." Opal nodded but she couldn't help her eyes narrowing. "Oh, don't you start!" Sarah said, but she was smiling.

"Sorry," said Opal. "You just hear … "

"You do," said Sarah. "But I don't want this place and I don't want the money from selling it either. I've got my home and my kids and my job—I'm quite happy. I don't even play the lottery, me. I just don't want to be lying my bed every night worrying about her. I'd move in if it didn't mean shifting the kids' school, and they've had enough up-heaval with the divorce and everything."

Opal believed her, but something she'd said before was niggling away and she had to check it, couldn't just leave it dangling.

"So you're clearing the place, yeah?"

"Started," said Sarah.

"Only ... that stuff in the morning room ... "

"Oh my God," Sarah said. "But hasn't Norah told you? That's not hers. That's *theirs*!"

"Oh, yeah, *them*!" said Opal. "I know *them*."

"And you know what? I don't think that's Alzheimer's at all," Sarah said, not really laughing now. "I think, like I said, that's just Norah. 'It's not mine. I've never been away. I didn't do that. I didn't make the cocoa—it was *them*." She sighed. "So I'm clearing out very gradually, starting with the attic, not moving anything Norah's going to miss, you know. I'll do a bit more today if I can settle her."

"The attic?" Opal hoped that her eyes hadn't flashed when the panic flared up in her. Norah's bedroom was still messed up from when Opal had been up there. Sarah lifted the tray and, edging round the table past Opal, left the kitchen.

Outside the morning room door, though, she turned.

"Can you take this in, love, while I nip upstairs?"

"To the attic?" said Opal.

Sarah gave her a look and spoke to her in the voice Opal supposed she used at work to her geriatric patients. "To the toilet," she said.

Opal grappled the heavy tray into her hands and watched Sarah bound up the stairs to the first floor. She went into the bathroom—Opal could hear the bolt shoot across as she locked the door. What an idiot! Sarah was hardly going to go up the attic stairs right now, with a cup of tea waiting for her down here. She put her shoulder against the morning room door.

"*Magnificent men on the flying trapeze,*" Norah sang, which didn't sound quite right to Opal, although she couldn't work out where it was wrong.

"Nothing's ever exactly what it should be with you, Norah," she said. "I found the bed. In the attic."

"Mother's bed," Norah said.

"Yeah. That's not the one I was after, though. I want the one with the roses and chrysanthemums. The one with the plume things."

"Fleur de lis," said Norah, and Opal's heart leapt.

"Could be, could be," she said. The name sounded familiar, although she'd have to ask Billy and Tony to be sure. "Where's that, then?"

"Gone," Norah said. "Half of it anyway." Opal's heart leapt like a fish, but she tried to keep watching the circus and talking in the same soft way.

"Half of it gone, eh?"

"*Ohhhhh,*" said Norah, along with the crowd, as the man torpedoed through the air, spinning like a bobbin, and was caught by his partner on the other swing. "Martin got too tall and Father took the footboard off and put it away."

"Riiiiight," said Opal, thinking *yes, yes, yes!* It was Martin's bed. The footboard went in the attic, and Sarah sold it. She crossed her fingers. "So where's the headboard, Norah my flower?"

"Martin's room," said Norah.

"And where's Martin's room?"

"Next to mine." Opal frowned.

"Your little room?" she said. "Or your big room?" Norah said nothing. Surely, Opal thought, trying to picture it, the locked room—the only locked room—*was* next to the empty room Norah had pointed to through the banisters on Friday. Is that what Norah was saying? The missing headboard with the secret compartments and the other two halves of the note were in that locked room up there?

"Norah?" she said. "Answer me. Is your brother's room next to your big bedroom with the green tiles round the fire?"

"No!" said Norah. "I didn't. I'm sorry. I never. I haven't got a brother, I never had a brother, I don't want a brother."

"Sh-sh-sh," said Opal. She had heard the cistern gurgling. "Hush now. Woooo—look at the clever men on the trapeze, Norah. Sh-sh-sh." And both of them were watching the two men, listening to the snare drums rattle and the cymbals crash, joining in with the gasps of the crowd, when Sarah came back into the room.

"I'd best be off," Opal said when she had drunk enough of the tea to be polite, scalding her mouth, gulping it down. "See you soon, Miss Fossett. Nice to meet you, Miss other Fossett!" Sarah laughed but groaned a little too.

"Maybe I should be Ms.," she said, "but I don't know—*Ms.*, eh?"

Opal looked down at her hand and frowned. "I must have … Did you see a ring lying on the washbasin? I must have left it up there."

"Didn't spot it," said Sarah.

"I'll check on my way out," Opal said. She sped up the stairs and crept along the passage to the back, into Norah's little room, where she finished dragging the chest over and repositioned the bedside table too. She wondered how fussy Norah was about where her prayer book sat. Had Opal knocked it out of place? She moved it more to the middle and frowned, wondering if that looked better or worse, if it mattered anyway.

Then something about the whole morning seemed to settle like a weight on her neck. What was she doing running around like some lame girl hero from a storybook? Upsetting Norah, conning Sarah Fossett, who couldn't have been nicer. She had left sweaty finger marks on Norah's book too. She picked it up to wipe it and it flopped open, showing a dedication on the inside cover and a bookmark embroidered with a cross and doves in a ray of sunshine. *Given to me, Norah Anne Fossett, on my birthday by my father who loves me very much, 17 July 1938* said the dedication in thin spidery writing that had faded to a shade of brown just darker than the yellowed paper it was written on. Opal stared at it, troubled but unable to say what it was about the message that was troubling her. Then, thinking that she couldn't spin out looking for a ring any longer, she left the room and softly closed the door.

She took just one peek through the keyhole of the locked bedroom on her way past, but all she could see was the panelling under the window opposite and a shadow, which might have been cast by a chair or a bed or anything, and then she clattered back down the stairs.

"Found it," she called out. "See ya!" and she left by the kitchen door.

Sarah's right about this tunnel, she thought, hurrying along it. It was beyond weird and she was glad to get back out into the lane between the row of garages, even gladder to get back on the main street, under the green shade of the trees. That creepy feeling in Norah's bedroom wasn't guilt because she shouldn't be meddling; it was the heebie-jeebies because she absolutely should. There was something wrong in that house. She looked back over her shoulder at the mouth of the lane, and something moved in the corner of her vision. She turned round even farther to see what it could be, then whipped her head back to face the front again.

Franz Ferdi from next door was standing half-hidden behind one of the trees, watching her.

THIRTY-SIX

HAD HE SEEN HER notice him? She quickened her pace until she reached the corner and then, out of sight, she broke into a run. He'd followed her! He'd followed her to a dead-end lane and then waited over an hour for her to come out again. She risked a look behind. No sign of him, but she didn't stop running.

So *was* it him who put the photo through her door? Must have been. And how did he have it? She couldn't bring herself to think about that one. Still no sign of him at the next corner and now she was on a busy street with plenty people. She slowed down to a fast walk and kept on, putting another meter and another meter of distance between him and her, trying not to think about when she was home again and all that separated them was one layer of bricks that he could huff and puff and blow right down, at least with that whistling hammer of his anyway.

She didn't see the upside until she was almost home. Then, imagining what everyone would think if they saw her panting and ragged, fleeing up Mote Street and fumbling for her key, she realized that if it was Franz Ferdi who was threatening her, she didn't need to worry what Margaret and Denny, Pep and Fishbo, any one of the Joshis, or even Mrs. Pickess saw. Maybe she should even tell one of them, tell everything she knew, and she was still trying to decide who to talk to first when she rounded the corner of the street and ground to a halt there. There was an ambulance parked in the middle of the road right in front of her with its back doors open.

"Opal, my soul!" Margaret had spotted her and came shuffling down the pavement on her worn-out slippers to clamp Opal hard against her. She hadn't taken her cigarette out of her mouth and Opal heard a few strands of her hair fizz and snap as it singed them. She pushed Margaret back to arm's length.

"Denny?"

"Fishbo!" Margaret said, with her lip trembling. Opal took the cigarette out from between her lips and threw it on the ground.

"And still you're at these filthy things! Is he … ?"

"He's hanging on," Margaret said. Two tears, magnified by her glasses, swelled and fell onto her cheeks where they hit the first of her many deep wrinkles, and ran away towards her hair. "No one's nagged me about smoking since Karen stopped coming," she said. "Oh, Opal. The colour of him. Pep asked me in to see should he call the doctor, and the colour of him was like nothing on this earth I've seen."

"He was bad enough yesterday," Opal said. "Kind of grey."

"Purple he was this morning and turning himself inside out with the coughing." They both turned at the sound of feet in the open corridor and saw two ambulance men carrying a stretcher towards the door. On it, Fishbo lay strapped under a green blanket. At least, his head was there at the top of the stretcher. If not, you'd have sworn there was only the blanket under the strapping; his body made no bulge in it at all. He had a plastic mask held to his face and his eyes were closed and fluttering. Pep came trotting out after him, carrying a pair of slippers and a collection of prescription boxes.

"I shouldn't have bathed him," he said. "I thought I was helping."

"Now, Mr. Kendal," said one of the ambulance men. "We told you. This is pneumonia, proper pneumonia. Nothing to do with a hot bath."

"It was cool," said Pep, dropping one of the pill boxes, hardly noticing. "I thought it would refresh him."

"It probably did," said the ambulance man. "It's pneumonia. If anything made it worse than it was always going to be, I'd say it was chemical irritants. His bed smelled like a branch of Boots, that's what got him coughing."

Opal whimpered, but no one heard her. Pep was putting the armload of boxes into a plastic sack the driver gave him and climbing into the back, telling Margaret about the keys and asking her to phone the rest of the boys. It wasn't until they had pulled away that she managed to speak.

"It was me, Margaret," she said. "I put Shake-n-Vac on his mattress when I was changing his bed and I forgot to hoover it out again. And I squirted everything in the room with—"

"Away and get off," Margaret said. "Chemical irritants!" But of course a woman who went around in a cloud of bleach and Elnet would say that.

"The paramedic *said*," Opal insisted.

"He's a van driver," said Margaret. "What would he know? The man has pneumonia from the germs in that dirty trumpet of his. I've seen him empty it out—makes me heave."

"That's condensati—"

"And you'll have done him a power of good cleaning his room for him, Opal. They're a dirty lot, men on their own. But I should be struck down for my hard heart. Talking that way when one's at death's door and one's heartsick with worry." She patted her pocket but then took her hand away quickly and looked to see if Opal had seen her. "I can't pack up smoking today, when I'm all upset," she said. "But I'll wait a while before I have one."

"I tell you what *would* help," Opal said. She was disgusted with herself for how quickly she'd thought of it. "Instead of just locking up why don't you and me go in and give the place a right good going over. When you see what it's done to the paint you'll not be so quick to light up again."

"That'll be the best thing we could do for them," said Margaret, nodding. "And I love to have a clean at something good and manky."

Opal couldn't help putting her arm round Margaret's skinny little shoulders and hugging her.

"Just us two though?" she said, nodding at Mrs. Pickess's door. "Where is she, in fact? Not like her to miss something."

"Church," said Margaret. "Where we should all be."

"I didn't know Mrs. Pickess was one for church," Opal said. "Mind you, she dresses like it and she's a big enough misery."

"She's been going ten years," Margaret said.

"Ten years, eh?" said Opal.

"I took it she went to pray for Craig when she started," Margaret said. "I never talked to her about it, but I'll own it touched me. I should be kinder to her really. On her knees, praying for my little lost boy."

Opal said nothing. She could believe that Craig disappearing might have had something to do with Vonnie Pickess getting religion, but she wasn't so sure it was Craig and Karen, Margaret and Denny,

259

that Mrs. Pickess was praying for. (Except, if it was Franz Ferdi threatening Opal with old photos and following her, what did Vonnie Pickess have to pray for?)

"Margaret?" Denny's voice came through the open window. "Are you ever coming in here and tell me how he's doing?"

"I'll get my vac and stuff and meet you in there," Opal said and, by hurrying, by throwing into her mop bucket everything she could possibly need and wearing the mop across her shoulders like she was a milkmaid, she did it in one trip and was in Fishbo's bedroom with the wardrobe pulled half over the door before Margaret arrived. Because no matter what Margaret said about trumpet spit, the paramedic—he wasn't a van driver; he had a stethoscope on—had said "chemical irritant," and Opal owed it to Fishbo now more than ever to do something good for him in the time he had left, however little that might be. And now she was sure that Pep hadn't warned her off with that photograph through her door, there was nothing to stop her.

"I've shifted the furniture," she called through the door at Margaret's timid shouting of her name. "I want to get this place done first, and then we can divvy up the rest of it after."

"Okay, my soul," Margaret called back. "I've just seen the bathroom anyway, dear God in heaven, so I've plenty to keep me busy."

Opal unwrapped the tissue from the frame on top of the pile. It was a photograph; she had known it would be. A posed studio portrait of a very beautiful young girl, with the hairdo of a film star in old black-and-white movie times, if there had been black film stars back then. She was smiling broadly, just short of grinning, and there was a light in her eyes that seemed to suggest she wasn't far from laughing out loud. Opal studied her, her painted-on eyebrows, her cupid's bow mouth (also painted on, and a good quarter-inch inside the real edges of her mouth, the rest of her lips covered with makeup and powdered down). Fishbo's childhood sweetheart, most likely. Or it could be his sister, she supposed, but why would a sister be twinkling and giggling that way? She turned the picture over but there was nothing written on the back of it, so she laid it aside and unwrapped another.

A family group this time. Two stony-faced, middle-aged parents and a range of children from their twenties down to one who was still a baby. A grandchild maybe, or a big surprise. The beautiful film-star girl was here, one of the oldest ones, looking less well-groomed in this picture but just as happy. She was holding one of the smallest ones, and standing between two of the other eldest children. Opal studied their faces and gasped. One of them was definitely Fishbo. It was hard to say which, the family resemblance was so strong, but one or the other, it had to be. Hilarious, flattened-down hair with a center parting and a collar and thin tie that was almost as funny, but no mistaking him: the broad shoulders poking his jacket out as if it was still on a hanger and all the rest of his clothes just draped over his skin-and-bone figure, the same at twenty as he was today. Again she turned the picture over, but this time she was lucky. The names were on the back.

Eugene Sr., Isabella, Eugene Jr., George, Samuel, Samantha, Cleora, Little George, Little Samantha. 17 May 1960.

Opal flipped it back and forward a bit, trying to work out who was who, but the main point was that Little Samantha and Little George were babies then and they would definitely be alive today, even if the rest were gone. Then she frowned. There couldn't be two brothers called George and Little George, could there? Or two sister Samanthas. She didn't think so, although she supposed things could be different in New Orleans from how they were here. But probably that meant that Little George in Cleora's or Isabella's arms was a grandchild.

The next picture added another piece to the puzzle. Cleora wasn't a daughter of the family at all, because here was a wedding picture of her standing beside George, Eugene at his elbow as best man and looking even more like him in their identical formal suits. Cleora was beautiful in a lace dress that pressed her figure in at the top and then spread like a tutu to her ankles and showed off slim, pretty feet in high-heeled white sandals. A flower girl that Opal thought was the sister Samantha was slightly out of focus on the other side as if she was moving when the camera clicked, scratching at her tight satin dress maybe or just squirming, hating to be dolled up that way and asked to stand still.

Right. So Fishbo had two brothers and a sister and at least one niece and nephew. Probably more if Samuel had met a Cleora of his own or if Samantha had got over her dislike of tight satin and had her own wedding day.

Opal listened and could hear Margaret singing in the bathroom, her voice growling on the low notes and soaring out of all control on the high ones. Was it a hymn? Opal cocked her head. Michael Bublé. She smiled and went back to the pile of papers that waited under the picture frames.

She meant to go right past the *Evening Posts*—they would tell her about life here in Leeds and it was New Orleans she needed to study up if she was ever going to find them, but she couldn't help herself. Craig Southgate's face stopped her dead, and she couldn't move past it without looking. There was Karen, Robbie at her side, divorce forgotten for the moment. Opal felt a lurch when she looked at Robbie Southgate. In her real memory of him he was just a voice and a pair of jeans, but there was his face and hairstyle and the little bluebird tattoo on his forearm; she had forgotten he had that. And she thought he should have rolled down his sleeves so it didn't show in the picture; it was just wrong to have it displayed that way. For a sliver of a moment, Opal thought about why that might be, then her mind scuttled away, kept moving, fast and light, never stopping until the thought was a distant smudge far behind her.

THIRTY-SEVEN

AND THERE ON ANOTHER front page were Margaret and Denny, Margaret with darker hair and fewer lines and Denny unrecognisable. Or rather the Denny that Opal would have recognised anywhere instead of the man he was now. They were looking into the camera with stricken faces—she checked the date; it was less than a week after Craig had gone, and so the whole Reid family must have been reeling between grief and worry and the secret they had just begun pressing down. All of them except Robbie, that is, and right enough he didn't look like the rest of them. He stood tall and glared at the camera with a look of pure righteous anger in his eyes that made Opal shiver even ten years on. She didn't look at his arms, didn't want to see.

Then there was the paper she couldn't account for even though she skimmed right through every page before moving on.

And the reviews for the band. She flicked through them.

Until there was only one *Evening Post* left. From 1970 it was. March 1970 and there in the double-page section right in the middle of the paper, where a montage of photographs was gathered, she saw three familiar faces, all beaming: Fishbo, George, and Cleora standing on a dockside, dressed in thick winter coats and with hats on. She blinked and read the caption: "Yorkshire lads and lasses! Eugene, George and Cleora Gordon, jazz trio, arriving at Hull after sailing from Kingston. 'By 'eck, it's good to be 'ome.'"

Opal could only stare. Three of them? Fishbo's brother and sister-in-law had come with him? From Kingston? Were they still here? Was Fishbo lying in hospital gasping for breath and wishing for family when some of his family was a phone call and a quick car run away? She couldn't begin to imagine why that would be.

Opal bundled up the newspapers—all those copies of the *Daily Gleaner*—and put the tissue paper back around the photos. She quickly hoovered the mattress and reset the sheets then dragged the wardrobe away from the door and looked around. Let Margaret think that was her best shot at gutting a bedroom, she decided. She couldn't spend any more time in here without it looking dodgy. So she just picked up the few tissues he'd used overnight and left.

Margaret was on her knees scrubbing herself out of the bathroom door, out of breath and pink in the cheeks, like a young girl.

"Are you all right?" she said, craning over her shoulder at Opal. "You don't look well."

"I'm fine," Opal said, but her voice was husky and her eyes were filling.

"You look like fine's cousin that doesn't get on with him," Margaret said.

"Maybe that driver was right after all about the Shake-n-Vac," Opal said.

But Margaret would have none of it, just set Opal to work in the kitchen saying that hard work cured most things and cabbage water helped with the rest of them. And she was still going at the frying pan with a Brillo pad—onto the third one—when Big Al rat-a-tatted on the back door and walked in.

"Hello, lovey," he said. "What's the news from upstairs then?"

Opal only stared back at him.

"Fishbo," Al said. "Any better?"

Margaret came powering into the room, still holding her scrubbing brush in one hand. She had lit a cigarette, Opal saw.

"Jesus, Mary, and who's the other fella," she said. "I was supposed to call you and it flew right out of my mind. He's in hospital, Al, he's off to St James's in an ambulance with Mr. Kendal. I was supposed to call you all."

"I thought he was on the mend," Big Al said, patting his pockets until he found his phone. "Thought the grog was working." Opal shrank at the words, but Big Al had turned away and noticed nothing. "Jim?" he said. "Aye, I'm there now. No—listen, don't come. The old fart's only gone and ended up in Jimmy's. Pep's there now. Can you go round and … Aye, that's what I were thinking. No, there's no use, they don't let you have them on. Mucks up the machines. You get round, and I'll call Hoadley."

He hung up and dialled again. One button, speed dial.

"Jimmy D's only round the corner," he said to Margaret and Opal while the phone rang. "When did he go in?" But then the phone was answered and he turned away again.

"Now then, H," he said. "You've not to get in a state, right? Is Stella there? Right, well, I'm going to tell you summat and don't take on."

Opal and Margaret exchanged a look then. They all really cared about Fishbo, this bunch of men. Big Al was talking like he was giving bad news to a loved one. And when they heard the raised voice coming over the phone, a squawk of fear, they knew that Mr. Hoadley

266

(who Opal had always thought was the very strangest of a pretty strange bunch) was just as rocked on his heels as the rest of them.

"I will, I will," said Big Al. "He is. I've already called him. He's on his way. Aye, well, you could. Or come here and wait for him with me. Come here, H. We'll wait together." He put his phone back in the breast pocket of his Hawaiian print shirt and blew out a big sigh, puffing his cheeks, rolling his eyes, rubbing his hand on his trousers as if he had been gripping the phone tight enough to get sore.

"I hope Pep's got some beers," he said. "And summat to eat wouldn't go wrong."

Margaret opened the fridge and clucked her tongue. "Slim pickings," she said. "He's not been thinking on shopping, with Fish so ill. And it *would* be Sunday night too." Then the house phone rang, and Big Al went to answer.

"It's Pep," he called through to the kitchen. "He's on his road home."

"How's—" Margaret and Opal both shouted.

"Stable. Critical," he called. Then into the phone, "How can he be both?"

"Can I go and see—" Opal said.

Big Al shushed her and listened to Pep on the other end of the phone, then he shook his head. "ICU," he said. "No visitors except family." He turned away. "They're cleaning. Aye well, I'll tell them. Okay. But hang on for Jimmy and he'll run you over. H is on his way too."

He hung up and came back to the kitchen door.

"Doesn't sound too good," he said. "No visitors except family! What's a man like Fishbo supposed to do then? Talk to the wall?"

"Did Pep tell them his family's in Louisiana?" Margaret said.

"Kingston," Opal said. She spoke softly, but Big Al heard her. He rolled his eyes and smiled.

"Pep said to stop cleaning and start cooking. He said he hasn't eaten a bite since yesterday and not a proper meal since Thursday teatime."

Kingston. Inside her head, the word was deafening.

Margaret was still standing in front of the open fridge. She bent down and peered in as if she might still see something she'd missed before.

"Men!" she said. "How can you not even have a bit of bacon to save your life?"

"Don't look at me," said Big Al. "My wife buys bacon by the ton." He patted his front, making a solid smacking sound. "This isn't just the wind blowing up me shirt, you know."

"I'll go to Zula," said Opal. "She'll help out, I'm sure she will. With the food anyway, not so sure about the beers."

"What? Are you kidding?" said Big Al. "Sunil likes his pint. That end garage of his is like a cash and carry."

She reeled out of the door and stood in the yard, shaking. Kingston. There was only one Kingston that Opal had ever heard of. The one that people left in the Sixties to come to England. And it wasn't in Louisiana. If she looked at all those copies of *The Daily Gleaner* up there in his wardrobe, she knew she'd find it was printed in Kingston, Jamaica, and it would be full of birth, marriage, and death announcements for the Gordon family who lived there.

That was what Pep Kendal was on about all those times he said plenty without speaking a word. Fishbo wasn't a jazz man from New Orleans. It was total hogwash; it was his patter, and he'd been at it so long he'd almost forgotten it wasn't true. That accent that never faded and always sounded the same, no matter how long he lived in Leeds. All that guff about the hurricane! And then when Opal said she'd find his family, he couldn't think up one good reason to stop her. She almost laughed. He'd rather die without seeing his own bloody family than have anyone find out he was bogus? Then suddenly she felt as if she'd never laugh again. He'd rather die than have his fantasy revealed for the pose it was until along came Opal Jones, meddling, threatening to find them. He was ill and tired and she'd made him anxious, put him under strain. And then she'd squirted poisonous chemicals in his bed, and now he was in hospital and might never get out again.

THIRTY-EIGHT

AND SO IT WAS that, as Pep and Jimmy D arrived from the hospital, Pep leaning hard on the younger man's arm and Big Al rushing forward to offer another, and as Mr. Hoadley belted up the road from Morley, Opal found herself knocking on the Joshis' door and asking Zula if she could reduce the Mote Street pizza mountain by taking some supplies down to the other end, where the Boys were gathering for some kind of vigil or practise wake or something. And Zula pressed her hand to her heart and said she couldn't believe it—she knew Mr. Fish had a bit of a cough, hadn't seen him for weeks, knew he was in bed trying to kick it, but surely it hadn't gone that far. Really and truly? And nothing would do but she took the pot of meat stew she was cooking for the boys' dinner—carried it down the street with her oven mitts on, the steam wafting after her—and then came back for bags of chips and tubs of ice cream, punnets of strawberries she'd got for nearly nothing if Opal could believe that (with it being such great strawberry weather), and Sunil was packed off to the end garage for beer and some pink wine for Zula and Margaret, and then he went to get Denny, because Margaret could no more leave the men to muck up the kitchen and waste Zula's curry that she could bear to think of her husband sitting all alone. So Denny Reid left the house for the first time since Easter, and they gathered in the music room with the door open to where the phone was in case the hospital called: Sunil and Zula, Denny and Margaret, and four out of five of the Mote Street Boys.

But not Opal. When Zula was flying round her kitchen, Opal saw a laptop open on the table and just asked, on the off-chance, if Zula would mind …

"Now?" she said.

"I want to do a bit of research on pneumonia, have something to tell Pep, stop him worrying."

"You youngsters and your Internet," Zula said. "But as long as you don't find out the worst of the worst and come down the street shouting about it."

"No, I want to reassure them all," Opal said. Of course, what she really wanted to do was try to see if there was any word that George and Cleora Gordon or their children anyway were still in Yorkshire. There couldn't be too many Cleoras, surely. Even in Leeds. Certainly not in Hull, anyway.

"Aye well, you crack on," Zula said. "You can tell Vik where his dinner's gone for me."

Opal got herself a long drink of cold water and sat down. She was pretty sure she was doing the right thing. She had been wrong to start—dead wrong—but since she *had* started she couldn't stop now. If he really was dying at least he could see a familiar face, hear his brother's voice, or Cleora's, or someone calling him Uncle Gene and reminding him of home.

"Cleora Gordon" got nothing in the UK. "Cleora Gordon" worldwide turned up seventeen hits, and Opal's heart soared. Genealogy, it was. Just like how Sarah Fossett's father had found Cousin Norah again. Strange abbreviations and little numbers sending you off somewhere else with more Gordons and more abbreviations, but they were all in Kingston, anyway. And then Opal began to wonder if the reason that Fishbo had joined the Mote Street Boys when he used to be in a Gordon trio was that he had stayed and George and Cleora had gone back again. There was no sign of Little George and Little Samantha in that photo at the docks. Maybe their mum and dad were just visiting and it was only Fishbo who was here for good.

The more she thought about it, the more sense it made. They wouldn't leave their kids, and Fishbo would hardly start putting it about that he was a Louisiana jazzman if his brother was right here in Yorkshire and could blow the story sky high. She didn't know much about the jazz scene in Yorkshire, but it couldn't be a big one.

Then Opal wondered if Kingston was the kind of place that had online phone books, like America, or the kind of place like England where nobody knew anybody's number and if you lost your phone your friends thought you'd dropped them and then they dropped you. "Online Phone Book, Jamaica" she typed. And "Kingston" and "Kingston, Jamaica" and all she got were towns all over Ohio and Kansas named after both of them. So she typed "Online phone book, Kingston, Jamaica, West Indies" with a last gasp kind of feeling. If there was a little town in Minnesota called the West Indies, she was giving up and going down the road for some curry.

But there it was—bingo! The White Pages for Kingston, Jamaica, West Indies. Opal typed in Gordon and then watched, heart sinking, as the screen filled up with them and the end of the list disappeared out of view, the little blue bar at the side showing how many screens there were. She scrolled down and looked at the Georges—over a screenful just of them!—and was scrolling back up to the top again when she saw it. Saw *them*. But only three of them.

Cleora Gordon. One, two, three.

And there was a phone sitting right there on Zula's table. Opal told herself Zula and Mr. Joshi must never be done calling overseas and they'd never notice, then she looked up all the extra numbers to punch in in the right order to call someone that far away and she punched them in and waited, listening to the phone ring, thinking—too late—that she didn't know what time it was over there and she might wake someone up and make them worry that it was bad news. Only of course it *was* bad news—exactly the sort of news you'd think it might be when the phone woke you in the middle of the night. And someone was answering.

"Morning!" said a woman's voice. She didn't sound groggy or annoyed.

"Hi," said Opal. "Can I speak to Cleora Gordon, please?"

"That's me," said the woman. She still didn't sound annoyed, but she didn't sound a day over twenty-five either.

"Um. Are you George Gordon's wife, Eugene Gordon's sister? Sister-in-law?"

"I'm nobody's wife," said the woman with a rich, rolling laugh. "You got the wrong lady, I'm glad to say."

The next Cleora Gordon answered the phone with the same sunny greeting, sung out. "Morning!"

"Hi," said Opal. She raised her voice to make it heard above a babble of music and children on the other end of the line. "Is that Cleora Gordon?"

"That's me. Who's asking?"

"My name's Opal Jones. But listen, are you the Cleora Gordon who's related to Eugene and George? Little George and Little Samantha's mother?"

"Little George?" said the woman, and her voice had risen to a shriek of hilarity. "Little George is a grandpa! Who is this?"

Opal took the receiver away from her ear and stared at it, unbelieving. She had found them. Found Fishbo's family. Found Cleora anyway.

"Opal Jones," she said again. "I live in Yorkshire. In Leeds. And I'm afraid I'm calling with some bad news."

The kids and music carried on, but the woman was silent.

"It's Eugene," said Opal. "He's ill. He might be dying."

Still there was silence and then the sound of bumping and shifting as the woman took the phone somewhere away from the noise, shutting a door, dulling the happy sounds down to a mumble.

"Eu*gene*?" she said. "Eu*gene* is back in Leeds again? You jesting me? He *hated* it there. We both did. *Leeds*? And he's dying? Who are you?"

"I'm just a friend," Opal said. "A neighbor. He's in hospital."

"In Leeds?" It was like she was saying *on Mars*. "Is he visiting George?"

"No," said Opal. "He lives here. He's been here for … well, twenty-five years anyway." Opal's lifetime.

"Huh?" said Cleora.

"I know you must have lost touch," Opal said. "I thought you'd want to know. I know he's only your brother-in-law, but it was your name I found."

"Huh?" said Cleora again. "My brother-in-law?"

"If you've got George's number, I could get on to him. Fishbo's never mentioned him, but if he's still in Leeds—"

"Whoa," said Cleora. "Back up, slow down. Who's Fishbo?"

"They must have lost touch."

And now the woman was laughing again.

"Someone got their boots on the wrong feet here, baby, and either it's you or it's me. My brother-in-law, George Gordon, stayed in Leeds when Gene and I came home. We couldn't stand it there."

"George? But his name's Eugene."

"Eu*gene*, my husband, left me for the first time thirty-five years ago and the last time I saw his no-good backside was twenty years ago now. But he told me he had gone to America. Came back here flashing green dollars at the kids and the grandkids, Mr. Big Shot."

"Fishbo's your husband?"

"I don't know who this Fishbo is you keep talking. Eu*gene* is my husband. Now, he might be dead and he might be dying, but trust me he's not doing it in Leeds."

"Why would George pretend to be Eugene?"

"I don't know that and I can't tell you, baby," said the woman. "Why would my husband pretend to live in California, USA, if he lived in England in the cold and the rain?" Opal considered telling her that England was sizzling in another day of steamy sunshine, but she decided Cleora wouldn't believe her anyway.

"I don't know," she said.

"Because those Gordon boys are all the same, that's why," said Cleora, and she was laughing again. "Stories and music and dancing and *more stories*." She sighed and sang a little tune as she let it go.

"Right," Opal said.

"I've got my kids and my grandkids and my great grandbaby," said Cleora. "Those days are a long time ago. A lifetime ago. You tell George Cleora said hello, baby. And if Eu*gene* shows his sorry face, you tell him Cleora said plenty but you didn't understand those bad words."

"I will," said Opal. "I'll do that. Sorry to have bothered you."

"It was nice talking," Cleora said. "You be a good girl and stay away from bad boys."

"I really will," said Opal. "What's the baby's name? Your great-grand-baby? I'll tell Fishbo he's got a … "

"Great-grand-nephew," said Cleora. "Jeez-*um*—another Gordon boy. Just what the world needs right now. He's called Travon. You tell Uncle George."

But as Opal hung up the phone, she was sure she wasn't going to be telling George he had a nephew. She would have bet a month's pay she'd be telling Eugene he was a grandpa again. And at last she understood why Fishbo didn't want anyone trying to find his family. It wasn't just that Louisiana was a big fat fib; it was that he had left his wife and children. He wasn't a single man who lived for his music. He was just another useless deadbeat bastard who never thought about anyone but himself.

Except, if that was true, where was George? Where was the brother-in-law who liked it in Yorkshire if Fishbo was the husband who hated it but came back anyway? Who visited Kingston twenty years ago and told Cleora he lived in California. Well, at least that bit sounded just like Fishbo.

———

She didn't go back to Pep's. Why should she? They were only neighbors—the band weren't even that—and she had too much on her mind to go to some knees-up or sit-in or whatever it was.

There was tomorrow's task, for one thing: getting a hold of a key to that room where the other half of the bed was.

Then there was the new big worry. Franz Ferdinand was following her, and he had written a threat on a picture and put it through her door. He had been on Mote Street all those years ago. Or he was just following her and someone else was threatening her—she didn't know if that was worse or better.

And there was the even newer, even bigger worry of having maybe killed Fishbo with Shake-n-Vac. Finished him off with it, at any rate. If she really still cared as much about Fishbo anymore. He wasn't who he said he was, and he had left his family. Opal didn't think much of men who upped and left their families, especially when they went on and on to little neighbor girls about being like a grandpa.

And of course there was the biggest worry of all: Nicola's outhouse was full of Zula's cement. Nic herself was full of Mrs. Pickess's brandy. And little Craig Southgate was gone.

So she went home, on her own, shut the doors, shut the windows, tried to think it out, tried not to think at all, very nearly poured herself a brandy until she imagined how it would feel to wake up in the morning in this sealed and sweltering house with her mouth glued up and her dry breath whistling inside her nose. She was just telling herself that she could keep the upstairs windows open when she heard him coming home. He was thumping and clattering out in the yard, and she went up to the back bedroom to look out and see what he was smashing up this time, but he was only moving stuff around in the outhouse, clearing space, bringing a ladder and a workhorse out into the yard. What was he moving in then? He lifted the workhorse into the back porch but the ladder—a bulky thing, folded in fours, looked heavy—he left in the yard, chained and padlocked around one of the washing poles. *Who's going to run off with a great article like that?* Opal thought, then she realized that wasn't the point. The point was that unless a ladder was chained up anyone could come along and open it, put it against a house wall, climb in, and rob the place blind or strangle someone in her sleep. And of course if Franz Ferdi had a ladder ...

With a sigh that was almost a groan, Opal shut the back bedroom window. She even went up to the attic and shut the skylight there—that ladder looked long enough for sure. The front bedroom window could stay open, though. No one was going to set up a ladder in the street, where all the neighbors could see. Not on Mote Street. There was Vonnie Pickess coming home right now in a blue print dress and a short-sleeved white cardigan that showed her old-lady elbows, grey-pink spirals of skin. She stood outside her door, looking around, sniffing for news, hearing only silence. Margaret and Denny's telly was off, no sign of life at the Joshis, all quiet at No. 1. Her glance flicked over to Opal's house, and the look on her face was nothing that Opal could put a name to. Then she went inside and closed her door.

The open front window did no good at all. By two o'clock in the morning, Opal was twisted in her sheets, throwing her head from side to side, panting.

Someone was crying, locked in a room where the floor came halfway up the door and the bed was only a headboard and nowhere to sleep unless you balanced along it, and there were children and grandchildren and great-grandchildren too, but Opal didn't know their names and she was supposed to tell the newspaper who they were for a photograph they were printing, but she was locked in a van where the floor came halfway up the walls and she was supposed to play the trumpet at the hospital but the mouthpiece was stuck in the concrete and only the horn was free and no matter how hard she pulled it wouldn't come out, and she was coughing and bleeding and trying to hide the sheets inside a wardrobe full of frames wrapped in tissue with no pictures because she was hiding from someone—someone's mother or someone's daughter or sister. And a little girl could see her and she kept driving past, and Opal told her she was too young to drive the car and she should go home, and the girl said her daddy was driving and Opal looked and so he was, one arm on the steering wheel and one arm holding Opal in the seat beside him, two bluebirds, and they moved when he stiffened his arm to hold her down when she tried to open the door and run away, but she couldn't open the door because she was locked in an outhouse where the floor came all the way up to the ceiling and tasted like iron and she was drowning.

"Leave me *alone*," said Opal, waking and sitting in one snap. She waited in the quiet for a moment or two, gulped in three breaths that hurt her chest and didn't draw any air down into her, then she curled up and put her hands over her head and began to rock, the old bed creaking and popping like a sailing ship all around her. *Someone will come along and they will find this*, she thought to herself, but the prayer of the little bed girl wasn't working tonight. It sounded like a curse in her ears and yet she couldn't stop it playing and replaying now that it had begun. *Our Father*, she whispered to herself, and then stopped. *In a cottage, in a wood*. But she had never heard that before Jill in the salon sang it to her.

"Help me, help me," the rabbit said.

"No!" said Opal, out loud.

The outhouse, the outhouse, the hold your nose and shout—

"*No!*" She screamed it, and in the silence that followed she heard a loud click then nothing more. "Go away," she said in a loud voice. "Leave me alone. Two times one is two, two times two is four, two times three is six."

Halfway through the eleven times table she fell asleep, and "sixty-six" was the last thing he heard her say. He listened for a while, then walked away from his open window—separated from hers by only five feet—got into bed, and clicked his light off again.

THIRTY-NINE

SARAH FOSSETT HAD CLEANED the kitchen, and Norah hadn't had time to muck it up again. Or rather she had had plenty of time but couldn't drag herself away from her new DVD, so all her dinners were still in their tubs in the fridge and the cooker top and sink were still buffed and gleaming.

"She's lovely, your Sarah," Opal said.

"Mm-hm," said Norah, without moving her eyes away from the screen. She was barricaded into her armchair again.

"Norah?"

"Mm-hm."

"Where do you keep the spare keys? The keys to the rooms upstairs?"

"I'm not supposed to touch the keys," Norah said. "I'm not allowed to."

"But *I'm* allowed to," said Opal. "Where are they?"

"Mother keeps the keys," Norah said.

Opal couldn't help her face twisting up to hear Norah talking about her mother that way. If Opal hadn't seen the empty rooms with her own eyes just yesterday, she'd be afraid to go up there.

"But *where* does she keep them, Norah love?"

"In a drawer, in her desk, in her room, in her house," Norah said.

In a cottage, in a wood. Opal shook it out of her head. She didn't know that song. She must have let out a sound, because Norah tore her eyes away from the screen and took her thumb out of her mouth.

"Sorry," she said. "Sorry, sorry."

"Sh-sh-sh," said Opal. "You haven't done anything wrong. You watch your clowns and don't mind me."

She started right there in the morning room, since that was where the photograph albums and jewelry boxes were. In a desk in the corner with a roll-top, there were dozens of compartments Opal thought were ideal for storing keys, but there was nothing but letters and papers there. And pipe cleaners.

"I'm not allowed to touch Father's desk," Norah chipped in from across the room.

"Right," said Opal. "Okay. It was your dad that smoked a pipe. Obviously. So where's your mum's desk then, eh?"

"Mum," said Norah as if she had never heard the word.

"Mummy?" said Opal. Surely no one said *Mother* even back when they were a little tiny girl.

"You're not supposed to say that," Norah said. Opal thought that she was in a very obedient mood today and it was getting pretty annoying. She wondered if Norah had ever done anything naughty in her entire life. "Norah," she said. "Do you want to help me do something secret?" Norah said nothing. "I want to hide a surprise in Mother's desk. Do you want to help me?"

Norah stared, glanced at the door, looked back at Opal, and nodded. "A nice surprise?" she said.

"A lovely surprise," said Opal. "Come on. You help me. I'll pause the disc for you."

Norah was already pushing away her tray table. She leapt up and trotted over to the door. Opal threw down the remote and followed her. Followed her along the corridor into the kitchen. From there through a door of dark wood with glass panels into a sort of little office with nothing in it except a chair set in front of double cupboard doors. Norah took hold of one in each hand and swept them open. She gasped, a small nervous sound, and turned troubled eyes to Opal.

"Where is it?" she said, but Opal was looking at the desk that was fitted into the cupboard, built in there. A household desk or something. Exactly where the lady of the residence would sit and write out her shopping lists and make up brown envelopes of money for her servants' wages.

"It's right there," she said. Norah turned back and then faced Opal again.

"Gone," she said.

"What's gone?"

"Silver," said Norah. "Mother's silver. The turret … the soup … turret."

"A tureen?" Opal said.

"And the candelabrum," Norah said. "And all the boxes! Oh. Oh. Mother's cake slice. I'm not allowed to touch it. And the spoons and knives and forks. I'm not allowed to touch them. I didn't touch them."

Opal shushed her, holding her little hand and swinging it, trying to calm her. She looked at the empty shelves reaching high up above the desk all the way to the ceiling. Then she reached out and ran a hand along one. It was smooth and dust-free and her fingers, when she brought them to her nose, smelled of polish. Burglars wouldn't polish the shelves once they'd swiped the silver.

"Sarah," she said softly.

"I didn't touch it," said Norah. "I didn't. We never had any silver. Mother doesn't like silver. We haven't got any. Men came. They took it away. They came and took it."

"Sh-sh-sh," Opal said. If Sarah wanted to sell Norah's stuff to get the money together for a good nursing home, it was none of her business, but surely she should at least have tried to let Norah know. Or maybe she did. After all, Norah had forgotten all about it now. She was sitting on the chair—an old-fashioned desk chair that swivelled round and round on its single leg—swaying from side-to-side.

"Do you want to watch the circus?" Opal asked, and Norah leapt up and scurried off—silver forgotten, surprise for Mother in her desk forgotten, everything blown away like seeds off a dandelion.

It gave Opal a wriggling feeling inside every time. She kept upsetting Norah, right from the first day they had met out on the street. And then she threw her little treats like she was training a puppy and made her forget again. It wasn't right and she would be glad when it was over.

But right now it was worth it. If Norah was going into a home, at least the people there would know about her, once Opal had found the evidence that would prove what had happened. The staff would know just how careful and tender they had to be and if it was a *really* good nursing home, Norah might be happier there than she had ever been anywhere. And anyway the last little trick—"Let's hide a nice surprise in Mother's desk for her!"—had definitely been worth it. Because there they were: a fat bristling bunch of keys, right there in the top drawer. Opal took them, restarted the circus, and went upstairs, telling herself she was helping. Not like Sarah was helping—helping get Norah into a nice, neat old folks home—and certainly not like Shelley was helping—helping her struggle on day after day. Opal was hacking through a forest of vines trying to get Norah out of the tower where she'd been asleep for a hundred years. Or that's what it felt like anyway.

On the landing, she sat down on the carpet and started working methodically through the bunch of keys. Some were too big and some were too small, but more than she had expected were just right, fitting in and moving a bit, sometimes quite a bit. Then she thought, *of course they do.* Those were the keys for all the other doors, and so they were all the same size. Then she put one in that turned a bit more than the rest and with an extra twist turned all the way. She left the bunch hanging in the door, pushed it open and walked into the room.

"Oh bloody hell, I don't believe it!" she said. She went as far as stamping her foot on the bare boards between the hall runner and the carpet on the bedroom floor.

It was all there, the chest of drawers, the dressing table with the marble top, the dressing table with the wooden top, the bedside pot stands, the wardrobe with three doors, all of them absolutely covered in roses and chrysanthemums in the pattern Opal knew so well. And where the bed should have been, just like before, just like in Mother's room, a bit of rough wallpaper where it had scraped and a patch of dark carpet where it had shaded and no fucking bed. Again.

"Where is it *this* time?" Opal demanded, loud enough to set the lampshade ringing. And she took the stairs three at a time and went to stand in front of the television, ignoring Norah's cry of distress and attempts to lean out far enough to see round her.

"Norah," she said. "Where is Martin's bed?"

"Sorry, sorry, sorry," Norah said.

"No," said Opal. "Nuh-huh." She wagged her finger. "You told me he got so tall that the foot part went to the attic. Okay, I get that. And when Sarah started clearing out, she saw two halves and didn't see the bit that was in the rafters. And she took the two bits and sold them. Starting with the stuff in the attic and cupboards, she said. I get that. Because you wouldn't miss it. But where is the top half of Martin's bed? Hm?"

"Sorry, sorry, sorry," Norah said. "The bed and the silver and foxy and the glasses. I didn't touch them. I'm not allowed to. We didn't have any. Mother doesn't like them."

"What glasses?" Opal said.

"In the dining room," said Norah. "Men came." She pointed a finger out of the morning room door, her hand clutching a tissue, wavering a bit as she did so.

"Men came?"

"In my room," Norah said. "I'm not allowed to."

"You're driving me bananas today," Opal called over her shoulder as she left the room and opened the dining room doors on the other side of the hallway. More of the same heavy, blood-red furniture, even heavier with the blood-red velvet upholstery and dark-gold silk-papered walls. Opal went to a sideboard against the long wall, a beast of a thing, and opened one of the doors. Empty.

"It's for a good cause," she said to herself, but she wondered if Sarah had asked Norah's doctor what he thought about the idea of sneaking things away when Norah wasn't looking. Because if it happened in Opal's house it would freak her right the hell out, and she had all her marbles.

"But glasses are glasses and silver's silver," she said, going back to the morning room. "What happened to the other half of Martin's bed. When did 'men come'?"

"One man," Norah said. "He's very strong."

"He must be. Right. It's gone then. If it's gone, it's gone."

"Gone," Norah said. "I'm not supposed to—"

"Okay, okay. It would have been good to have all the evidence, but I bet if you try, you'll remember. It's safe to remember."

"Sorry, sorry," Norah said, and deep down inside Opal a huge solid boulder of fear and revulsion turned over like a hippo in a mud hole. She swallowed.

"Norah, my love, I'm going to sit down now and talk to you and I don't want you to get upset. Okay?"

"Okey-dokey," Norah said. "And then I'll watch my tape. I've got a tape of the circus. And I've got a new one too."

Opal nodded, waiting for silence.

"Do you remember writing secret notes and hiding them?" Norah blinked. "Where did you hide them? Can you remember?" Norah said nothing. "Okay, let's start with this one. Did you write in your prayer book?"

"No!" Norah said. "I didn't. I didn't scribble in my special boo—"

"No, no, no," Opal said. "I know you didn't scribble. I don't mean scribbling. Did you write your name inside the cover?"

"Yes," Norah said. "Sorry?"

Opal shook her head. "No, you're a good girl, Norah. You wrote a lovely thing inside your prayer book, didn't you?" But just like when she had been looking at it something about that little dedication bothered her again now. She shook the thought away. "Okay. Now. Do you remember writing a note? Four notes? North, south, east, and west?" Norah was watching her closely, but she said nothing. "I thought at first you hid them in your bed. But you didn't, did you? You hid them …" she waited "… in Martin's bed, didn't you?"

Norah put her head down and started in her smallest, quietest voice to say sorry.

"Did you sleep in Martin's bed, Norah?" Opal said. She couldn't see the crumpled little face, but she watched two tears drip down onto Norah's lap. "Poor little love," she said. "Did you write notes and hide them when you slept in Martin's bed?"

"I never," Norah said. "I didn't. I didn't want a brother and I never had a brother and I didn't. I'm sorry, I'm sorry, I'm sorry."

"I know, sweetheart," Opal said. "I'm sorry too. But you'll forget all about it in a minute again. So I'm going to ask you. Norah? Norah, listen to me. Where is Martin now? I need to know if he can hurt anyone or if he's—"

"St. Michael's and All Angels," Norah said. Her voice had dropped to a whisper.

"He's dead?" said Opal. And when Norah said the next thing it was more like a snake's hiss.

"*Safe in the arms of Jesus, where you will never be.*"

"Eh?" said Opal. Norah looked up and blinked.

"Mother told me," she said. "Safe in the arms of Jesus, where I will never be."

"Fu—Blimey," said Opal. For a moment they sat looking at one another, one blinking, one staring without blinking until her eyes were dry.

Then Opal roused herself. "I'm going to make sure someone hears about all of this, Norah my love."

"Can I watch my circus tape?" Norah said.

FORTY

AND SO HE WAS ten minutes' walk from Opal's own house, was he? St. Michael's and All Angels Church was just down the road and Opal knew it well, or knew its name anyway, loved its name, had spent hours saying it over to herself when she was a little girl. Not that she had ever been inside the place—Nicola didn't go much for churches—but it was right opposite the Skyrack, and Nicola certainly went for pubs, even student pubs—*especially* student pubs in September when they all had lots of money and no sense and could be flattered and embarrassed into buying a drink for anyone who asked them. So she used to leave Opal sitting on the steps of the monument halfway between the church gate and the pub door, sitting there with her bag of crisps and bottle of pop, and Opal used to read the name on the board and imagine that St. Michael and all the angels too might be in the pub as well as her mum and the students, or else why was it called the *Sky*rack? Which she thought of as a kind of tiered arrangement of seats where the angels could all sit for a good view of Michael himself. She wished she was old enough to go inside the pub and sit on the rack beside them, get a look at him.

Inside the churchyard, it was clear right from the off that Martin must have been dead a fair while; all the gravestones were old mossy lumps, the writing nearly worn away on some of them. *Good*, Opal thought. Maybe he died before Sarah Fossett was born, certainly before her daughter was. Maybe he had never hurt anyone ever again after Norah, especially if his own child was a boy—which he had to be if Sarah's maiden name was Fossett, actually.

"Can I help you with something?" The voice just behind her made Opal jump, and she turned to see an elderly woman, tall and broad, standing with her feet planted wide apart on the path behind her.

"Oh God!" said Opal. "What a fright. Sorry, I didn't hear you."

"Well?" said the woman.

"What?" said Opal.

"What are you doing in here?" Opal blinked.

"Is it private?" she said. "The gate was open. Who are you?"

"I'm a member of the congregation and the chairman of the committee on—"

"And *is* it private?" Opal said.

"It's …" to give the old woman her due she didn't come right out and say it.

So Opal said it for her. "It's not for taking drugs or having a cuddle, yeah. Actually I'm looking for a gravestone. I'm looking for someone who might be buried here."

"Ahhhh," said the old woman. She let go of the strap of her handbag, which she had been gripping as hard as she could with her gnarled old knuckles. "Genealogy, eh? Family tree?"

"Yeah, well, no. The tree's been done already. I'm just following up sort of thing. Interested. It's someone called Fossett. Martin Fossett."

At the sound of the name, the woman's eyes flashed and, firmly planted as her feet were, she took a steadying step to one side.

"What's your interest in *that* family?" she said.

"They're an interesting family," said Opal. The woman gave her a hard look but then nodded and beckoned her to follow.

It was at the shadowy side of the church, quite far from the path, a tall block of grey stone with a cross shape on the top. *Martin William Fossett*, it said, *1931–1943. Beloved son of William and Anna Fossett. Also William Fossett 1899–1945, beloved husband of Anna and father of the late Martin.* And at the bottom *Safe in the arms of Jesus.* Just like Norah had said.

"So you know about the scandal," the woman said to Opal. She was whispering, even though there was no one else around and the sound of the traffic out on the road would have covered their voices anyway.

"I do," said Opal.

"I don't know the whole story," said the woman. "I was just a girl, and it was all hushed up."

"So I see," said Opal. "Beloved son. Blimey."

"They'd never get away with it now, of course, but who's to say it wasn't better that way?"

Opal said nothing for a moment, although she was thinking plenty. She read the inscription again.

"Is Anna in there too?" she said. "Why's she not on the stone as well?"

"Oh no," said the woman. "Mrs. Fossett only died a few years back. Well, gosh, it must be twenty! But there haven't been burials in the church grounds for a lot longer than that. There wasn't even a ceremony here, as I remember. Just the crematorium. She wouldn't have liked it, but there was no one to say different. No one to make sure things were done nicely for her."

"What about Norah?" Opal said. "In fact … " she turned round and read the names on the headstone again. It had only just struck her.

"Well, the daughter …" said the woman. "She's hardly …" Opal turned to look at her and saw that her face was screwed up as if she had smelled something nasty.

"You know what?" Opal said. "There *is* something wrong with taking care of it all in the family. All hush-hush. He's got a headstone, and she's like some dirty little secret."

"Oh, you young ones," said the woman, flapping a hand at Opal.

"Yeah, but Martin's own children and grandchildren didn't even know about Norah until someone did the family tree. She had relations all these years and she didn't even meet them."

"Martin's children?" said the woman. She frowned. "Martin Fossett didn't have any children. How could he?" She held her hand out, inviting Opal to read the headstone again. And it was only then that Opal looked properly at the numbers. *1931–1943.* Martin Fossett was only twelve when he died.

"So who's Sarah?" said Opal, stupidly. How was this woman supposed to know? "Oh my God. Who the hell *is* Sarah?"

"Please!" said the woman. "Language."

"She's wiggled her way in and she's stripping the place. I bet she's got Norah to change her will. And no bloody wonder—"

"Please!"

"—she didn't go apeshit when she saw me in there. She couldn't risk starting a pissing contest about who had the right to be pals with Norah. It was Shelley who was normal—all suspicious and that. Nicey-nicey Sarah should have set my alarms bells ringing, but I was so chuffed not to get chucked out I never wondered why. I've been a bloody fool. Bugger it. Look, I've got to go."

"Yes," said the woman faintly. "Please. Go."

"Sorry," said Opal. She looked up into the canopy of the trees and said it again—"Sorry"—to St. Michael and all the angels, whose ears must be stinging.

———

Shelley. Shelley, who Opal thought was her enemy, would be her ally now. But all she knew was that Shelley was a neighbor. And she didn't even know whether she was a neighbor from one of the other eight house on the cul-de-sac or if she lived somewhere out the back near the garages. Probably at the back, since that was the way she'd come in both times Opal had seen her, but there was no way of knowing which house, and Opal couldn't remember her surname (if she had ever heard it). And there was no point in trying to explain to Norah. So she just let herself in to Norah's kitchen, read Shelley's number off the sign tacked up there, and called her.

No answer. Opal left a message, trying to make it sound as calm and reasonable as she could get it. *Not very calm at all*, she thought; the more she spoke, the more paranoid she seemed. So she said good-bye and hung up, leaving her number. Then she wrote down the details of the social service contacts that were printed out on the other signs, because she wasn't going to rely *just* on Shelley. She would phone in the morning as soon as the offices opened, maybe even phone Citizen's Advice, get a lawyer on it. Sarah wasn't going to get away with it anymore.

And she had another idea too—it came to her on the way home. She was on fire now, fuelled by an anger she couldn't explain but that was burning inside her with a fierce power, making her feel more alive than she had been for weeks, for all of these long, sweltering weeks of remembering no matter how hard she tried to forget.

It was Martin Fossett's headstone that did it; the way the bare facts were written there, chiselled there, literally written in stone. Fishbo wouldn't have kept a newspaper in his wardrobe for nothing. That *Evening Post* from 1990 that she couldn't account for? It had a death notice in it. It must have. There used to be two Gordon brothers and now there was only one. And Cleora had said she'd last seen her husband twenty years ago. And 1990 was twenty years ago. What Opal didn't know was whether it would be George or Eugene whose death was reported there. It would make sense to think that Eugene Gordon died and that was when his wife stopped hearing from him. But Eugene was Fishbo. But Eugene hated Leeds, and Fishbo still lived there. But if it was George who died, why would Eugene never contact his wife again?

She knocked on Pep's door but got no answer. He must be at the hospital visiting Fishbo. So she tried Margaret, who always used to have all the keys when Opal was little. She was like the street janitor back then.

"Mother of God," said Margaret when she opened the door. "What's happened."

"Nothing," said Opal. "Eh?"

"You look—I thought you'd had bad news about Fishbo."

"No," said Opal.

"So what's upset you?" said Margaret. Opal thought about it. *Nobody is what they seem and someone is after me and something terrible happened in that place I will not think about in my own backyard, and I'm trying so hard not to remember, but it's coming, it's coming, the memory's coming back and I can't stop it. Like when you go from feeling sick to starting to heave and there's no way back and here it comes and…*

"I'm just hot," she said. "Can I borrow Mr. Kendal's door key?"

"What are you going to do?"

"I'm just going to finish off cleaning," Opal said.

"Ah, right enough we might have left a present for the pixies in the music room," said Margaret. "I can't remember clearing up anyway. Do you want a hand?"

"I'll manage on my own."

"Good," said Margaret. "I have a head on me today like a bag of bent nails." She looked behind the door to where Opal assumed Denny was sitting. "What was that muck Sunil was pouring down us by the end, Dennis my soul? Some Indian firewater like you never imagined, Opal."

"Polish honey liqueur," said Denny's voice. "And you *asked* him to open it."

Margaret unhooked a key from the board by the door and Opal left them to their hangovers. They were enjoying them anyway in that way people do, knowing that they'd get another good sleep that night and be back to normal in the morning. Not like Nicola's daily cycle from the shaking, sweating, retching, coffee, and ciggies to the first drink and the long haul up to the plateau that lasted an hour or two or maybe all afternoon but never beyond; then the skittering off away to the wilds of the night again, schemes and plans and parties with whoever was there, laughing and kissing, dancing, cackling, screeching, shouting, giving back as good as she got, crying, shoving, slapping; the reeling out into the night, the threats, the phone calls, the gulping, streaked with makeup, trying to get to a basin in time, the promises, stories, confessions, the lists longer every time of what had gone wrong and who it was and why it wasn't, slower and dryer silences stretching, until she was sleeping again.

Opal unlocked the front door and went in, ignored the music room, went up to Fishbo's bedroom, and opened the wardrobe.

She was wrong about the death notice. There was no Gordon there. She checked the births and marriages too—nothing. But she couldn't believe that this one paper was here for no reason. She took it and spread it open on the bed, sat down prepared to read every word on every page until she found it.

And find it she did. There it was, page twelve, two paragraphs, no pictures. No wonder she had missed it before. "Two Die in Leeds Cab Crash," the headline said.

The driver of one vehicle and a passenger in the other both died in a head-on collision between a registered taxi from Joshi Cabs of Leeds and a private car in Kirby Moorside in the early hours of Saturday morning.

The victims, 23-year-old Cathy Hawesdon of Bradford and 44-year-old James Drury, a father of three from Meanwood, were both pronounced dead on arrival at Leeds General Infirmary. The driver of the cab, Eugene Gordon, was unharmed. Mr. Drury was travelling in the front seat of the taxi and was not wearing a seatbelt at the time.

FORTY-ONE

OPAL READ IT AGAIN and again and again. Then she folded the paper closed and put it back where she had found it, going to stand by the window and look out when she was done. He really was Eugene, then. And he had left his wife and children. And he had survived a crash that killed a young girl and a father of three. And after that he had never seen his wife or spoken to her, even written to her, ever again. Was it guilt? Did he cause the crash and he was the only one who knew it because the others had died?

But wouldn't something like that more likely drive him towards his wife instead of away from her? Opal was so lost in her thoughts that she had spent quite a few minutes watching the vague movements across the street without really taking in what they were. Just a shadow passing over and back behind the net curtains in one of the front bedroom windows. Then she gasped and stepped back, her eyes snapping wide. It was the front bedroom of No. 6, Someone was in her house. Someone was in her bedroom, moving around.

She let herself out of Pep's front door and locked it, then stood staring at her window, not knowing what to do. If she crept in she might be able to trap whoever it was, but then she'd have to deal with them. If she made enough noise at the front door, they might leg it out the back, but then what? A car came round the corner, windows down, music thumping, engine snarling, and she stepped right out and flagged it down.

"Lift home from here, love?" said Sanjit, and he rubbed his chin, sucking the air in over his teeth. "It'll cost you."

"Ha-ha," said Opal. "Sanj, there's someone in my house. I just saw them walk past the bedroom window."

Sanjit craned his neck and peered up from under the shade strip along the top of his windscreen.

"Seriously? It's not just the curtains moving?"

"Seriously. Will you come in with me?"

"Will I come up to your bedroom?" he said, wiggling his eyebrows.

"Sanj, for God's sake. There's someone in my house. And two nights ago someone put an anonymous letter through my door. I need you to help me."

"Okay," said Sanjit, pulling his brows down. He got out of the car and slammed the door.

"Sh," said Opal.

"Oh, yeah, right," Sanj said. "So are we trying to catch them or scare them off?"

"I don't know," Opal said. She was crossing the road and digging her key out of her bag. She fitted it and opened the door. The door between the living room and kitchen was shut, and for a moment they both stood and listened to the silence, then came the sound of the back door slamming and feet thundering away across the yard.

"Fucking hell, there's somebody there!" shouted Sanjit, diving for the kitchen door and tugging at it.

"What did I *say*?" Opal shouted after him. "Push it! Sanj, push! It opens the other way." And he was gone, across the kitchen, out the back door, across the yard, out through the gate and away. Opal pounded up the stairs to the door of her bedroom and then stopped. Did she really want to see? But she couldn't help herself. She pushed the door open and stepped in.

Nothing written on the walls, nothing scrawled on the mirror, no letters or photos, no envelopes propped up anywhere. Her wardrobe doors were closed and all her drawers too. She walked over towards the bed and that's when she saw it, curled up with its nose under its tail. A cat with the handle of a knife—Opal's own bread knife—sticking out of its back, the whole blade deep inside.

Opal felt her stomach rise and turn, but then she took another step closer. How could a cat look so comfortably curled up when it was stabbed? She heard noises downstairs again.

"It's me," came Sanjit's voice. "I lost him. Where are you?"

"Up here," Opal said, and he bounded up the stairs and came into the bedroom.

"Fucking hell!" he said. "Oh Christ."

"It's not real," said Opal. She walked over and picked the cat up off the bedcover. It stayed in its curled-up pose with the knife sticking out, just the same. "It's one of those fake ones. Real fur. You get them at the market."

"Oh, right, yeah," said Sanjit, rubbing his stubble again, trying to get back his cool. "But you don't usually keep your bread knife in it, right?"

"It's not mine," Opal said. "I mean, it's not my fake cat. It's my bread knife, I think. But he brought the cat with him." Then she made a big sound that she hadn't meant to, and she couldn't say whether it was a sigh or a sniff or some new kind of sound from out of a new part of her body she'd never used before. Sanj came over and put an arm around her shoulders, pressing a little too hard and hurting her collar bone, but it was welcome.

"Did you see where he went?" Opal said.

"Never saw him at all," said Sanjit. "He was out the gate before I was through the kitchen. I went down to the canal path, but he could have gone any way really. You need to call the police, you know."

"No!" said Opal, breaking free from the painful comfort.

"Do you know who it was doing it?"

"I think so," Opal said. "There's been someone following me anyway."

"Following?" His eyes were like gobstoppers. "Bloody hell, Opal, what's going on?"

"I don't know. Every time I think I've found something out, it gets more confusing. I just don't know. But ... Sanj, did you hear someone running? I know you said you didn't see anyone, but did you hear footsteps disappearing into the distance or anything?" Sanjit shrugged and frowned, not understanding. "Only I think maybe whoever it was didn't actually go all that far. I think it might be one of the neighbors, actually."

His frown deepened. "Not one of us?"

"No," said Opal.

She went over to the dressing table where the two notes and the photograph were and showed the photo to Sanjit. "Turn it over," she said. "That's what came through the door."

"Well it wasn't Margaret or Mrs. Pickess," Sanjit said, when he had read it. "He was off like a rocket."

"Yeah, but that's what I'm saying," Opal said. "Was he? Did you hear him running or could he maybe just have bobbed in the next gate? Dammit, I wish I'd come up and looked out the back window."

"You should phone the police," Sanjit repeated. He gave the photo back and wiped his hand just like Opal had found herself doing the first time she touched it.

"I hate the police," Opal said.

"Yeah, me too," said Sanjit. "I'm going to go and get Mum and Dad. You trust *them*, don't you?"

"Yeah," said Opal, hoping it sounded sincere. "'Course I do."

She listened to him go downstairs then watched him cross the road, and only when he had gone inside did she notice the sound of thumping coming from the backyard. Was Franz Ferdi unbolting the ladder? Was he going to set the ladder up and come back into her house through her window now? She went to the back bedroom, but the ladder was still folded and chained to the pole. He was setting up some kind of table or work bench. It must have been him dragging it that she had been hearing. And now he was uncoiling an orange extension cable from his back door and plugging it in. He pulled a pair of plastic goggles down over his face and fiddled with a switch, setting a round disc on the edge of the work bench spinning.

It was, Opal realized, a saw—some kind of cutting machine anyway—and she shivered to see the wink of the spinning metal blade as Franz Ferdi went back into the outhouse and then re-emerged with a long heavy log of some pinkish wood in his arms. Opal had forgotten that the first time she'd met him he had left sawdust all over her step, but she supposed if he came home from work covered in sawdust he was probably a carpenter. And if he was a carpenter by trade, it might be his hobby too.

She watched him for a while. He had a pencil behind his ear and a cloth hanging out of his back pocket and, through the closed window she could just hear it, he was whistling. Could that man really just have been snooping around her house? Could a whistling man with a pencil behind his ear really have pushed that photo through her door? But the crying was real, and she had seen him smashing up that red and blue plastic.

Eventually, when her stomach started growling, she turned away from the window and went downstairs. But as she came into the kitchen, the front door banged open and Zula Joshi, followed by Sanjit, burst in.

"Not even locked!" she said and turned to smack Sanjit over the back of his head with her open palm. "I was out, Opal. Sanjit told me when I got in. Didn't think to call." She turned again to swat, but he ducked and she missed him. "Did you leave the back open when you were out?"

"Don't think so."

"Was it forced?"

"I never even thought of that," Opal said, and she turned to look at the lock of the back door just behind her. "Nope. Not forced. It must have been someone with a key."

"And who's all got a key? We've got one and Margaret . . . you should change the locks."

"Don't be daft," Opal said.

"And give us copies of the new one!" Zula said. "It's not neighbors breaking in and leaving knives."

"Well, *someone's* not pleased I'm back," Opal said. She couldn't help remembering Sunil hissing at his wife that day, asking her why she was being friendly, saying that Opal asked too many questions.

"Who?" said Zula.

"I think—" Opal dropped her voice as she said it. "It might be the new bloke next door."

"Him?" said Sanjit. "He's only been here ten minutes."

"Yeah, no, but that's the thing," Opal said. "I think maybe he took the photo, Sanj. I think he was here before."

"What photo?" said Zula. "Sanjit said a note."

Opal still had it in her hand, and she held it out to Zula now.

"My God," Zula breathed. "Opal, what is going *on*?"

"Dunno," said Opal. "I've got no proof of anything. So don't tell me to go and accuse him, and don't tell me to go to the police." She turned and looked out of the kitchen window at the outhouse, at the piece of cardboard she had shoved into the frame where she'd smashed the glass away. "I just need to keep my head down. I've been ... interfering in things that are none of my business."

"Like what?" Zula said.

"Like more than you'd believe," said Opal, thinking about the message she'd left for Shelley, raking through Fishbo's wardrobe not even an hour ago, stalking Karen Reid like some kind of cartoon detective in a trench coat. "I thought I could help."

"Help who?" said Zula.

"Fishbo. Margaret and Denny."

"Help with what?"

"Plus this other friend of mine. You don't know her."

"Help with what?" said Zula again and that look was back on her face, that sideways look like the first time she had edged the conversation so carefully around to Opal's storage needs and possible renovation plans without ever actually mentioning it. *The outhouse, the outhouse, the hold your nose and shout house.*

"Opal?" said Zula. "Are you singing? Are you okay?"

"Was I? I didn't mean to do it out loud."

"What did you think you could help Fishbo with? Or Margaret and Denny?"

"Believe it or not," Opal said, "I thought I could find little Craig." Zula was staring at her, completely still, like a waxwork of herself. "And I thought I could maybe find Fishbo's family and get them together while there was still time." She laughed, one single bark of laughter. "And my other friend. She is so past helping, I can't even tell you. But I was going to do it all. Me! Ha. *Me!*"

"Find Craig?" said Zula, and the words sounded like two gobs of mud dropped into a pond.

"Yeah, I know."

"And Fishbo's ... family."

"Yeah, I know about that too. Luckily, he doesn't know I know."

"You should be careful, Opal," Zula said. "And you shouldn't be alone. I'll go back and get a sleeping bag. Stay here and keep an eye on you."

"Keep an *eye*?" Opal said.

"Not like that." Zula's hand fluttered around her neck, patting straight the chain she wore there. She smiled at Opal. "I mean, look out for you, look after you. You know what I'm saying."

"Like you did for Mum," Opal said.

"Exactly. Good, then," Zula said. "In fact, why don't you come over with me now? So I can 'keep an eye on you' even better." She was sending herself up, making a joke of it to cover the slip, maybe. Opal shook her head.

"I've had a long day. I just need a bit of peace and quiet to myself really. If I've started singing without knowing it, I definitely do!"

"Good luck then," Sanjit said. "Peace and quiet wise."

"I know," said Zula. "What *is* that horrible noise?"

"Wood saw," said Opal. "Him next door. He's a carpenter, you know."

And when they had gone, she went back upstairs to see how he was getting on with his log, see if he'd turned it into a totem pole by now.

He'd turned it into something. Opal could hardly believe what he'd done in the time she'd been talking to Zula. What had been a plain boring round log like a telegraph pole was now sinuous and curvy like some kind of gigantic banister rail, or not really a banister rail, but more like a—

Opal put her head against the glass and stared at it. It looked so familiar and yet she couldn't think what it reminded her of. A ball at one end, a straight bit, then in and out, in and out, and a big ball near the other end with an uneven lump left right at the tip.

"For carving," Opal said to herself and as the words rung in the silence around her she could see it, the unborn ghost of it, hiding inside the vague shape of the log he was turning and turning and turning. And once she had seen it she couldn't unsee it. Franz Ferdinand was making a copy of her bed.

So it *was* him in her bedroom and he *had* run next door when Sanjit disturbed him, but why was he copying the bed? The photograph with the threatening note, the cat with the knife in it—those things made some kind of sense if he was trying to scare her, but why would he copy her bed? That was madness. That couldn't really be happening. She was losing touch with what was real. She was losing her mind. She blundered down the stairs, out into the yard, the lane, the yard next door, and he stopped the saw when he caught sight of her.

"What are you doing?" Her voice sounded hoarse in her ears as if she'd not spoken for days.

"Sorry, love," he said, pushing his goggles up onto his head making a white path through the red dust stuck to his brow. "Aye, I suppose it's getting a bit late for all that noise."

"But what are you doing?" Opal said. "Are you making a bed?"

"I'm making half of one," he said. "The other half's missing." Opal felt the ground shift underneath her feet. "Are you all right?"

"But you shouldn't know that," Opal said. "You had no right to be in my house, and you had no right to be snooping around my bedroom copying my bed. What are you doing to me?"

"*Your* bed?" said Franz Ferdi. "I'm not copying your bed. What are you on about?" He took his goggles off completely and pointed into the open door of his outhouse. "I'm copying that bed there, love. Making the other half of it anyway."

Opal turned round and peered into the dark interior. There, leaning against a blanket tacked onto the wall, was the headboard, six feet high, five feet wide, roses and chrysanthemums and funeral plumes. She turned back to face Franz Ferdi.

"Did you get that from Billy and Tony?" she asked him.

"Who? Here, you need to sit down, you look right peaky."

"Why is Martin's bed in your outhouse? Nobody's bed should be in there."

"How do you know about Martin?"

"It's not right. It's filthy in there."

"It's not great, I'll give you that. Look, love—"

"*The outhouse, the outhouse, the hold your nose and shout house,*" Opal mumbled. Franz Ferdi put his head back and laughed a laugh that rang out across the yard and echoed back from over the lane.

"I haven't heard that for donkey's years!" he said. "*Hold me by my left hand, flush me down the muck pan.*" He turned—"Hey!"—and rushed forward, but he was too late.

Opal had slithered to the ground before he could catch her, knocking her head hard against the stone flags just inside the outhouse door.

FORTY-TWO

IT WAS A SMELL that came back first, even before her eyes fluttered open: the smell of damp stone and standing water, the smell of mice and rusting metal, and darkness and secrets and … sweat. She opened her eyes.

"Lay still," said Franz Ferdi's voice. "Don't move too quickly."

His work shirt was bundled under her head, stinking sharply of fresh sweat and the oily perfume of new sawdust.

"Promise me you won't move while I get you a drink of water."

"Promise," Opal said. And she kept it, lying flat on her back staring up at the outhouse ceiling, the undersides of the tiles overlapping on top of the beams, just the same, just the same, and it made her pull her knees up to her chest and hug them hard, rocking on the stone flags even though it bruised her backbone every time she moved.

"Here, love," said Franz Ferdi, kneeling down beside her with a cup in his hand. "Hutch up a bit and drink some of this down. Then tell me what's the matter. It can't be as bad as all that."

"Did you find the notes?" Opal said when she had swallowed two mouthfuls of water and held her breath until she was sure it would stay down. But Franz Ferdinand only frowned at her, so she struggled to her feet, using the headboard posts to haul herself upright. She gripped one hard and twisted, feeling it start to shift right away.

"Blimey O'Reilly," said Franz Ferdi. He came over and stood right behind Opal. "I never even noticed that. That graining is absolutely perfect." He ran a nail over the join that was almost invisible until you knew it was there.

"My bed's good at catching people out," said Opal. "It's got form." She lifted off the top part and there, inside the brass-lined compartment, was a folded piece of paper just like the other two.

"How did you know this was here?"

"Wait a bit," Opal said and started on the other one.

"And why d'you keep saying it's your bed?"

Opal unscrewed the second post and took out the last piece of folded paper.

"Not this half," she said. "Come with me." And she led him into her house and upstairs to her bedroom. Or rather he led her, holding her elbow, steadying her, helping her move in a straight line even when the pounding in the back of her head threatened to topple her. He let go of her at the bedroom doorway.

"Now, how in the name of Christ did you get the other half of Auntie Norah's—"

"*No way.* You're Norah's nephew?"

"Did Sarah sell you that bed?" he said. "Did she hide *notes* in it?"

Opal hesitated then.

"Sorry," she said at last. "I know it's your family and it's not very nice. But Norah wrote those notes when she was a little girl. I've had two of them for a month and I've been trying to find the other two. I'll burst if I don't read them."

"Go ahead," he said. "It's not my family anymore."

"Huh?"

"We're divorced. She'll take the walls down round the old girl's ears, and I can't do a thing to stop her."

"Ahhh! Right!" said Opal. "You're Sarah's *husband*!"

"Ex," he said emphatically.

"Norah said it: a niece and a nephew and a great-niece and a great-nephew. And I couldn't work out why Shelley—that's Norah's neighbor—didn't know the nephew! But that's you and Sarah and your kids, right?"

Franz Ferdi's face puckered up. "That's right. Two kids."

"And they were supposed to visit you, weren't they? But they didn't come?" *He'd bought games for them to play with and everything*, she thought. Plastic toys that he'd smashed to bits with a hammer.

"She's told me if I try to get power of attorney with Auntie Norah or tell anyone what's going on in that house, I'll have to go to the courts for visitation."

"Is that why you moved here?" Opal said. "To be near Norah?"

Franz Ferdi gave her a screwy look, one eyebrow up and one down.

"I moved back to Leeds to be near the kids when Sarah moved here. *She* moved to be near Norah. Soon as she found out the state Norah was in, she was in like Flynn."

"I know!" said Opal. "At least, I worked out she must be. Only that was when I thought she was no relation at all. And she really moved here to … She told me she didn't want to move the kids' schools."

"She tells people a lot of things."

"She seemed really nice," said Opal.

"Oh aye," Franz Ferdi said. "Whenever there's a divorce it's always some poor suffering woman and some bastard hurting her. And you can tell I'm a bastard, by the way, because who else would choose to live on Mote Street and expect his kids to come visiting here?"

"I can't *believe* you're on Mote Street," Opal said, missing the point completely. "Right next door to me. And this bed." She knocked her knuckles against it. "It went all the way to Northallerton. To Claypole's."

"Yeah, she's careful not to use the same place twice."

"And I only found it because I was lost." Then she looked back at him and shook her head. "I can't believe you're right here."

"I'm here cos I couldn't afford to be anywhere else. Little kids disappearing keeps the price down just lovely. How about you?"

"And Sarah really gave you a hard time just for that?" She couldn't help the thought that was seeping in at the back of her brain: if she ever chipped away at the concrete behind her outhouse door, this guy would never see his children again.

"She said if Finn and Charlie were here overnight, she'd not sleep for worrying."

"Shows she's got a heart," Opal said. "Once she knows the whole story about Norah, she'll never just chuck her in a council home."

"The whole story?"

"The notes," said Opal. "At last. All four of them." She got up, swaying a bit and feeling the back of her head pulse with pain, and brought her two folded notes back to the bed and opened them.

South: *because bad things happen to little girls*

East: *when someone finds this after I am gone*

He was reading them over Opal's shoulder.

"God Almighty," he said.

"It was Martin," said Opal. "Her brother."

311

"Bloody hell, how do you know?"

"Because Norah won't even admit she had a brother most of the time. Won't even say his name. And it was all hushed up, whatever he did to her. She was just kept at home, as if she had done some kind of disgusting thing. Shelley said it—she was like a prisoner."

"That was the way back then," Franz Ferdi said. "Poor old Norah. No wonders she's so ... "

Opal was unfolding the other notes.

North: S*he will be punished for what she has done*

"Where does that fit then?" Franz Ferdi said. Opal opened the last one.

West: *who do what Norah says she will do to me.*
MWF. 1st August 1939

She shuffled them first one way and another until they could both read the message as plain as day.

She will be punished for what she has done when someone finds this after I am gone because bad things happen to little girls who do what Norah says she will do to me.
MWF. 1st August 1939

"Martin William Fossett," said Opal. "He was eight when he wrote that."

"Kids," said Franz Ferdi, and his voice sounded unsteady. "It might be nowt."

"But she did it," Opal said wonderingly. "She did what she said she would. It's true."

"How d'you mean?"

"He died when he was twelve."

"Of what?"

"It was all hushed up," Opal said. "A scandal, but they dealt with it in the family, and Norah was kept locked up at home and she doesn't even admit she ever had a brother unless you catch her just the right way."

"But you don't know it for sure," Frank said.

"I just assumed ... poor little Norah saying sorry, sorry, sorry. I never thought for a minute she had something to be sorry *for*. Like you just said."

"Some poor suffering woman?"

"And some bastard hurting her. You just said it, and it's true."

"Auntie Norah?"

Opal shook her head.

"That's another thing I can't work out. Sarah and you both say Auntie Norah, but if Norah's only brother died when he was twelve, how can she be anyone's auntie? I used to think maybe her dad had left and got married again and had a new family—like mine did—but I saw his gravestone and he did die during the war, just like Norah said. When she was away."

"Away where? You said she'd been in the house her whole life."

"Oh, yeah," said Opal. "That's right. That's what Shelley said. Oh my God—Shelley! I left a message on her phone saying Sarah was no relation and she was stealing Norah's stuff."

Franz Ferdinand started laughing. "She is! I hope Shelley gives her what for. And if she wants to prove she's a relation, she should produce this famous family tree my ex-father-in-law was working on all those years, that suddenly disappeared without anyone seeing—" He stopped talking and cocked his head. "Visitors?" he said.

Opal's front door had slammed open again.

"Opal?" Zula's voice came up the stairs.

"Up here," Opal called.

Zula arrived, panting, and then plunged forward with her hands out to grab Franz Ferdinand's neck.

"Get away from her, you animal!"

"No!" Opal threw herself in front of Zula, elbowing Franz Ferdi's middle. "Zula, I got it wrong. It's fine."

"Eh?" said Franz Ferdi, rubbing himself.

"Sorry," Opal said. "Zula, Franz Ferdinand is nothing to do with the knife or anything."

"Franz Fer … ? It's Frank," he said.

"Frank, right," said Opal. "Sorry. I only knew FF, and I—"

"Francis Findlay," said Franz Ferdi. "That's bad enough."

"Are you *sure* you're okay, Opal?" Zula asked again. She had come forward and was staring hard into Opal's eyes.

"Probably not," said Franz/Frank. "You need to go to the hospital. You need looking at for concussion." He stood and held his hands out for Opal.

"That's what I came to tell you, Opal," Zula said. "Pep just phoned. He says if you want to see Fishbo, you better come straight away."

FORTY-THREE

"CONCUSSION?" OPAL SAID, AS the van pulled away. "Do you really think so?"

"You've been talking a load of bollocks, love," Frank said.

"Well, yeah, but that's not just since I bumped my head, is it?" said Opal. "Just like how it's not all Alzheimer's with Auntie Norah. Not nearly." Then they were quiet again. "I knew there something up with her prayer book," Opal said, at last.

"Yeah? Not the praying kind?"

"No—well, that too, yeah—but it was the writing. It was nothing like the writing on the bedpost notes, and it never occurred to me. Plus the question of why a dad wouldn't write a dedication in his daughter's present instead of her having to write her own. That makes sense too now. I just thought he must have been one of those don't-care dads." She glanced at Frank from the corner of her eye. "Sorry. There it is again, eh?" He said nothing. "Man, that really hurt when I looked out of the side of my eye."

"Shut them," Frank said. "Rest them. Don't want you keeling over on Fishbo's deathbed. The nurses don't allow it."

Opal wanted to say she thought he must be a great dad, but didn't know how to put it, and didn't know, now she'd met him properly, if he was actually that much older than she was, didn't want to offend him. And even thinking about it was making her feel sick—dads and brothers and Fishbo, Cleora and Steph and Sandy, and Norah going away and—

"Hey! Hey," Frank was reaching over across the middle seat, shaking her and she opened her eyes and looked at his arm, seeing bluebirds that weren't really there. "You were moaning."

"I had a nightmare."

"I'm definitely getting you looked at," Frank said. "Here we are." He swung the van into the hospital gates and headed for the car park.

"But Fishbo first," said Opal. "Just in case."

———

"Baby Girl," said Fishbo, lifting his eyelids about half an inch for about half a second, as if they were made of lead. He was wearing another oxygen mask over his face and it was hissing so loudly she had to bend close to hear his croak of a voice over it.

"Mr. Fish," she said. "How are you feeling?" She took hold of one of his hands, cold and stiff.

"Cuttin' loose," he whispered. "Shaking the dust off my heels and breakin' free."

"Don't say that!"

"Let him speak, love," said Pep Kendal, who was sitting in a chair on the other side of the high bed. He looked just about as tired as Fishbo and twice as grey.

316

"Can't they help you?" Opal said. "What is it anyway?" She could hear her voice rising and getting shaky. She knew she shouldn't cry, should stay calm for him, but...Mr. Fish!

"Streptococcal pneumonia," said Pep Kendal. "Both lungs."

"But you can't die of pneumonia," said Opal.

"Cain't say they owe me!" said Fishbo. "I done wore these lungs out, blowin' that ole horn." He spread his lips as far as they would go under the mask, the old beaming Fishbo smile.

"Pep," Opal said. "Can I have a minute on my own?"

Pep looked as if he wanted to say no, but he also looked as if he needed to lie down on a row of chairs and sleep for a week, so in the end he got up and left them.

"One minute," he said, pausing at the door. "And don't you upset him."

Opal listened to the hiss of the oxygen for a moment or two once they were alone and watched the double hitch of Fishbo's bony chest as it rose and fell.

"I spoke to Cleora," she said. Once again, Fishbo's eyes fluttered. "She sent you her love."

"Me?" Fishbo said.

"You," said Opal. "Eugene Gordon. She sent all her love. And she said you've got a new great-grandson. What was his name...? Travon."

"Ayyyyyy, Baby Girl. What you been at, huh?"

"Sorry."

"Eugene Gordon is long gone."

"I know, but she still loves you." *Where's the harm*, Opal thought, *in letting him think that now?*

"Eugene was my brother, but he's gone on ahead of me."

"You're...George?"

317

"I'm George. Cleora is a fine woman and if she'da been mine, I'da hung on to her."

"Why did you pretend to be Eugene?" Opal asked. There was nothing but the hiss of the oxygen for a long, long time. Then at last he drew in a hard, hurting breath and spoke.

"Eugene had a license," he said.

"For what?" said Opal.

"Drive cab," said Fishbo. "No use to him back home, and I needed a job. Man's got to live."

"You . . ." Opal stared at him. "The crash? You didn't . . . ? I don't believe you." Fishbo lifted one eyelid just enough to let a slit of light show.

"You wanna believe I left Cleora, Samantha, and Little George?" he said.

"No," said Opal.

"Cain't have both," Fishbo breathed. "Pick one, Baby Girl."

"No," said Opal again. "You're confused, that's all."

"Thass right," said Fishbo. "I'm confuse. And iss all over now."

Opal waited to see if he meant it literally, but in a second or two, he was speaking again.

"You still there, Baby? Iss dark in here."

"I'm here, Mr. Fish."

"I wann you play, hear me? Mooon Reeeebahhhh. Play for me."

"I haven't got a trumpet," Opal said. "And the nurses would probably kill us both."

"He doesn't mean now, you daft lump," said Pep's voice from the doorway. "He means at the funeral. He's been going on and on about it. That's why I asked Zula to bring you."

"Right," said Opal. She turned back to the bed. "You have got a deal, Fishbo," she said. "I'll play."

318

Pep was wiggling his eyebrows at her and so she stood, kissed Fishbo on his cheek to one side of the mask and then on the head where it wasn't so crowded, and went back to the waiting room.

"What are *you* doing here?" she said, when she saw them all. Vonnie Pickess was sitting between Margaret and Zula, in her blue print dress with her white cardi folded on her knee.

"I've known that man since before you were born," Mrs. Pickess said. "Who put you in charge? I was here when it was your mother too, you know, which is more than I can—"

"Come on with you both," said Margaret. "This isn't the time. Hang on and you can have a proper punch up at the wake."

Opal laughed in spite of everything, but she could see Franz Ferdi—Frank, she would have to start calling him—giving Margaret an odd look as if he couldn't quite fathom her.

"Will you come round to casualty now, Opal?" he said. "If you've said your goodbyes."

"In a minute," said Opal. "I need to talk to … " she looked at the three of them sitting there " … all of you really."

"I'll just … " said Frank and walked away.

Opal sat down opposite the three women and leaned back very slowly. Her head felt as if it would split right down the back so she leaned forward again.

"I could understand why *you* didn't want to tell the police when Craig went missing, Margaret," she said. "You and Denny and Karen would have been up in court. Maybe in jail. But I couldn't understand why Zula kept the secret. Until now."

"What are you talking about, Opal my soul?" said Margaret. "Mr. Gilbert said you had a bang on the head."

"George Gordon," she said, and she saw Zula stiffen, "didn't have a driving license, and he caused a crash. And you covered it up. So

319

years later you didn't want the police poking into everyone's past and finding out that Eugene wasn't really Eugene. Is that it?"

"That's it," Zula said, exhaling loudly. "We had our five boys to think of. If Sunil and I had been tried and convicted, what would have happened to our boys?"

Opal nodded and then winced. "But what about you, Mrs. Pickess?" she said. "Why did you buy my mother's brandy?"

"I don't know what you're talking about," said Mrs. Pickess, but her hands were twisting her folded cardigan as if she was kneading dough.

"Vonnie?" said Margaret, turning. Mrs. Pickess didn't meet her gaze, and Opal didn't blame her.

"Two of my pals from Tesco at Roundhay are willing to swear that you did," she said.

"She was an addict," Mrs. Pickess said. "It was a kindness, really."

Opal waited. Margaret waited, staring at Mrs. Pickess, her damp eyes enormous behind her bifocals. Zula waited too, but she was thinking furiously, couldn't hide the fact that she was.

"She was better off after a drink," Mrs. Pickess said at last. "When she sobered up, she started all kinds of nonsense. On and on about that blessed outhouse." Opal felt her insides shift. Zula put her hand over mouth. Margaret just kept staring, but her jaw was trembling now. "'Poor little kiddie, locked in the outhouse,'" she used to say. She used to say she wanted to tell someone. She was going to *tell* someone."

"Whose outhouse?" Margaret said.

"Mine," said Mrs. Pickess. "And I chased him out. Margaret, I'm sorry. I'm so sorry. I've prayed for forgiveness. He was hiding in there, and I chased him away. I had just given it all a coat of fresh emulsion and he'd gone in and scuffed it."

"Right!" said Opal. She put her hands against both sides of her head to stop the pounding. "He was covered in paint! You thought if they found him in my mum's outhouse, they'd know he'd been in yours."

"Margaret, I'm so sorry," Mrs. Pickess said again.

"How could they find him in your mother's outhouse?" Margaret said.

"Because that's where he was," said Zula. "That's where he's been all this time."

Opal nodded. "And because you believed that, you gave her the stuff to fill in the floor. And when she'd died you kept an eye on the place, didn't you?"

"Didn't want bailiffs poking round," said Zula.

"And you tried to make sure I came back so that new people wouldn't come and dig it up again."

"We'd have bought it if you hadn't come."

"And you did it on the quiet so that no one would know you were involved. And you told me time and again that you would help if I ever started working on the place. Right? But can I ask you something? Why did you think he was in there?"

"Because he was," said Zula. "He is. Like Vonnie said. Nicola talked about it all the time. The kiddie in the outhouse. Locked in. 'All the blood,' she used to say."

"Oh, Lord, so she did," said Mrs. Pickess, and she put her hands over her face and started rocking.

Margaret was shaking now as if she was holding onto a pneumatic drill. Her heels rattled against the floor and her arms shook at her sides.

"Craig," she said. "In your mother's yard? All this time? Little Craig?"

"He isn't," said Opal firmly. "He never was." Her head felt like a peeled egg, just a membrane holding it together and like it would burst any minute. "The kiddie in the outhouse with all the blood? That was me."

"Ladies?" One of the auxiliaries had been watching them from the nurses' station. "Is everything okay? Are you feeling ill, love?" They all looked at her to see which one of them she was talking to.

"Just upset," said Zula. "Tired out."

"Do you want me to ask how your..." she ran out of words, looking round the four of them wondering what relation they could all possibly have in common.

"Although Opal here needs to go and have a check for concussion, don't you, my soul?"

Opal put her hand up to the back of her head and felt the lump there. Then the auxiliary nurse did the same and her eyes widened.

"You better had," she said.

"I'll take her." Frank was back, with four plastic cups of tea. "Save one of those for Mr. Kendal, eh?"

But when they were on their way, walking through the corridors, following the painted lines that showed the route, Opal started arguing.

"It's not concussion," she said. "It's not my head, it's my brain. Listen, can we just sit down and I'll try to tell you?"

So they got another two plastic cups of tea from another machine and sat on a windowsill on a long empty corridor and Opal tried to tell him: about Gene and George Gordon, about Friday night not Saturday morning, and the little boy who hid in vans and outhouses and got paint on himself, and the brandy and the concrete and the kiddie in the outhouse who wasn't Craig Southgate at all—it was her, Opal Jones.

"Only … God, I can't explain it. I know it was me, but all I can remember is Robbie's arm with the bluebird tattoos. I've been having nightmares about them."

"Who's Robbie?" said Frank.

"Craig's dad. My mum's boyfriend. But there's something I've forgotten." She shook her head, frustrated.

"Hang on, love," said Frank. "Are you saying Craig Southgate's dad did something to you in your outhouse that you can't remember? Or that he made you promise not to tell? You need to go to the police. They need to find that little boy's body, for his mum and his granny's sake, and if you know that his dad was the kind of man who'd—"

"No, no, no," said Opal. "That's not right. It's not what you think. Even Karen Reid said her ex-husband would never hurt Craig. Hurt any kid, really. She was so angry with me for even saying his name."

"So what is it that happened then?"

"I can't remember, but it wasn't when I was tiny. It was just before I left and went to Whitby. I was twelve. It was a few years before Craig went missing. How can I not remember something that happened when I was a great big girl of twelve?"

"A great big girl of twelve?" said Frank and there were tears in his eyes. "Opal, love, listen to yourself. What are you saying? My Charlie's twelve, and she's a baby."

"Can we go and see Norah?" Opal said. "I'm so sure if I talk to her, I'll remember what it is I've been trying so hard to forget. I know I sound crazy. But Norah sounds crazy too half the time. I think she could help me."

FORTY-FOUR

She was in the morning room, tucked up in her chair with the tray table pulled in front, watching her circus.

"You!" she said. "And you too! Both together."

"Hiya, Norah," Opal said. "Yes, both together today. And I bet you can't guess where I've been since I was here earlier on. God, was that really today? It feels like a week ago."

"I'm not allowed to bet," Norah said.

"I've been down to St. Michael and All Angels," Opal said. "I went to see Martin."

"Sorry," said Norah. "Sorry, sorry, sorry."

Frank shifted from foot to foot, and Opal knew what he was thinking. It was a long time ago, no way of knowing what really happened, and this sweet little thing would melt a heart of stone. But Opal had been a sweet little thing once too, and she wasn't so easy to fool as him.

"He died, didn't he?" she said.

"I haven't got a brother," said Norah.

Opal signalled to Frank to move out of view behind the armchair and she moved too, leaned over the back and waited a moment or two while Norah watched the screen.

"How did he die, Norah?" she said.

"A rope," Norah said.

"Were you there?"

"I didn't do anything," Norah said. "I was only playing."

Opal heard Frank catch his breath, and she held her hand out to him to keep him quiet a little longer.

"Is that why you went away?"

"I didn't go away," Norah said. "Martin went away. And he never came back, ever again. I haven't got a brother, I never had a brother, I don't want a brother."

"But you were away when Father died, weren't you?" Opal said.

"*They* sent me away," Norah said. "It was them."

Opal looked down at the top of her head, wondering what to ask next. There was no point in saying 1943 and 1945 to Norah, trying to talk about when Martin died and then her father. But it occurred to her that she didn't know how old Norah was. If she could tie Father dying or Norah's trip away from home to an age in her girlhood, maybe Norah would remember.

"Was he your big brother or your little brother, Norah love?" she said.

"Big," said Norah. "Little. They sent me away when he was born."

Opal gripped the back of the armchair so tightly that her knuckles cracked.

"Well, we'll get off then," she said. "Do you want anything? Cocoa again?"

"Cocoa," said Norah with her thumb in her mouth, and Opal beckoned to Frank to follow her as she crept away.

"So," he said in the kitchen, as the milk boiled. "She got sent away when the new baby came and twelve years later she got her own back by … what? Hanging him?"

"Or tricking him into hanging himself," Opal said. "She's no angel, little Norah. But you got the first bit wrong. She didn't get sent away when *Martin* was born in 1929. She'd have been tiny herself then. She got sent away after he had died, when he was twelve, in 1941. She got sent away when her 'little brother' was born, when she was in her teens. She got sent away for her 'little brother' to *be* born. *That's* how Norah can be an only child with nephews and nieces. That's what Sarah's dad found out in the family tree that made him stop looking."

Frank whistled long and slow between his teeth.

"Norah is really Sarah's granny? Finn and Charlie's great-granny? Grandpa unknown. Father unnamed on the birth certificate, to the Fossett family's eternal shame."

"Yup," Opal said. "Looks like it. And now I'm going to take her this cup of cocoa and say goodbye. I don't think I'll be back again."

———

"And did you remember the thing you thought Norah would help you remember?" Frank said, when they were back in the van.

"Yeah," said Opal. "Part of it anyway. And my headache's gone. I knew it wasn't concussion."

"What was it?"

"I did the same thing she did—no, scratch that! Sorry. But close enough. I said, at school in Whitby, that Michael, my half-brother, was my son. I told everyone. Told my guidance teacher, told the school chaplain that Steph and Dad had made me give him up and they'd adopted him and not told him who I really was. You would not believe the stink I caused. No wonder Steph hates me." She shook her head in wonder at all she'd managed to forget.

"Now why on earth would you do something like that?" Frank said.

"Exactly. I've finally remembered. Norah helped me." Frank swung the van round the corner of Mote Street. "But can we leave it for tonight?"

"Gladly," said Frank, parking. "I don't think I could take any more."

Opal opened her door. "Any chance you could bunk off work tomorrow?" she said.

"Why?"

"Would you give me a lift to Whitby?"

"What for?"

"Tell you when we get there, if it goes the way I'm hoping."

"Yeah, all right," said Frank, stepping down from the van and slamming the door. "Like you said—we've both had enough for today."

But there was just a little bit more. At the sound of the van door slamming, Sanjit had come out onto the pavement and was staring hard at Frank, with his fists clenched at his sides.

"Oh no, Sanj, yeah," said Opal. "I had that completely wrong." She turned and smiled at Frank, but he backed away with his hands up.

"Don't tell me," he said. "The hints are bad enough. I don't want to know."

"Okay," Sanjit said. "If you're sure." He turned round and called back into the house. "Opal Jones is here."

Sunil joined his son, squeezed his shoulder briefly, and then walked over towards Opal, putting out his hands and taking hers in them.

"Zuleika called from the hospital twenty minutes ago," he said, and he didn't have to say any more.

"Fishbo?" said Opal. "Oh, Mr. Fish! Oh, no."

FORTY-FIVE

THE FRONT SEAT OF a van was better than a bus on the country roads, and Opal was almost cheerful as they climbed up from Pickering to the high moor. As long as she only thought about little bits at a time, anyway, and that wasn't easy.

"Margaret says the funeral will probably be Friday," she said. "Three days—not counting today—to learn the trumpet part for 'Moon River.' I should have brought one with me, practised on the journey."

"I'm glad you didn't," said Frank. "This is not a big space. Are you going to tell me the rest now?"

Opal nodded. She owed him that much, but her hands were sweating and her mouth was full of water.

"It's all connected," she said. "Everything's joined to everything. You think you can keep things out of your head, if you concentrate hard. You think your brain's in charge. And then *Blammo*! Like from nowhere, one little thread starts to fray, one little rock gets lifted, and the light shines in. That's when you know it's your blood that runs the

329

show. Your bowels, you know? Your guts and your…. what do you call them?…your glands. When you're shaking so hard you can't talk and you're breathing so fast you can't think and all your…stories have…*Pfffffffff.*" She lifted her hand from her mouth like blowing a dandelion away.

"Tell me," he said, in his gentle voice as the van rocked along. There wasn't another car or house or sign of life in sight. The moor fog was coming down. "Start talking."

"Dunno where to start," said Opal. She looked at her watch. "Dunno if there's time."

"Make time," said Frank. "Talk fast. Tell me now."

"Okay…Okay…Well, it's all connected, see? That's the main thing. I see that now. The mum and the dad and the boy and the girl."

"Who's this?"

"And the little old lady and the poor old man. The baby that's lost and the baby that's…" She took a big breath, swallowed, tried again. "They're all the same."

"Start at the start and tell me it all," he said. "Keep on talking right till the end."

"The start?"

"When does it start?"

"I suppose…I dunno."

"So…once a upon a time," Frank said. The words made gooseflesh pop out on her arms.

"No!" She shivered. No more stories. Time for truth now. "It's… maybe a month ago."

"So…" he said, "once upon a month ago then."

She turned away from him and looked out at the fog drifting towards them. Beautiful, ghostly fog. Bloody cold too and murder on

330

your throat. "Three months ago really," she said. "I missed my mum's funeral."

"Margaret told me," said Frank. "As part of the general introduction to Mote Street, when she came to offer to keep a hold of my key."

"Good old Margaret," Opal said. "Yeah, I missed it. I had a hospital appointment. I didn't know if it could get it put back and I was scared to ask."

"Is that why we're going to Whitby now?" said Frank. "Have you got another one?"

"No," Opal said. "But it's sort of related in a roundabout way." She took a deep breath and turned so that she couldn't see him. "I was having an operation," she said. "A procedure."

"Uh-huh."

"A termination, as they called it. Except who the hell calls it that? I was having an abortion. And I couldn't put it off, because you've no idea what it was like trying to get the appointment for it in the first place. All the interviews and counselling and leaflets."

"It's just to make sure you're sure."

"Well, I *was* sure. Baz—he was my boyfriend—was off as soon as I told him. Which was a big surprise—never saw that coming at all. I'd imagined . . . had a name picked and everything. If it was a girl, leastways. Charlotte. But . . . stupid cow, as it turned out. Baz-shaped hole in the wall from him leaving so fast, you know? So I tried to get a loan of a caravan so I'd have some peace and quiet to think it through, but that didn't happen either, so I ended up in this bedsit and there was no way you could have had a baby . . . and anyway, the day I was booked in was the day that Nicola got cremated. So I missed it. So there you go."

Frank said nothing. They rolled on northwards along the moor, dry and brown from the weeks of no rain, the road kicking up dust behind them like something out of a cowboy film.

"What's that got to do with today, though, love?"

"I'm still 'love,'" said Opal. But she still kept her face turned away from him as she went on. "It started something off. I went back to Leeds because I hated the bedsit and I started remembering stuff I'd totally forgotten. Things started joining up, you know. Then I found out about Fishbo missing his family and I found Norah's notes in her bed—Martin's notes in his bed, as it turned out—and, of course, I heard about Little Craig and ... I really needed a distraction from the thing I didn't want to remember—so I started meddling, but it only made it worse, and then that song started ... "

"The outhouse song?"

"And the nightmares started ... "

"About the tattoos, is this?"

"And the thing I didn't want to remember got mixed up with the thing I couldn't stand thinking about until last night, when it all burst like a great big toxic boil."

"Lovely," said Frank.

"Sorry," Opal said.

"And what was it then?"

"In the boil? Sorry. It was what happened in the outhouse. I *thought* it was intuition telling me Craig was buried there, but it was a memory, like I said. It was about being pregnant."

"You mean, like the hormones made you remember ... What do you mean?"

"The first time I was pregnant," Opal said. "Before. I was twelve."

"Twelve?" Frank was staring straight ahead, but his jaw had dropped open.

"And it wasn't my mum's fault or my dad's, before you start. It just happened."

"My Charlie's twelve! How can you say it wasn't your mum and dad's fault?"

"It wasn't!" said Opal. "My dad wasn't even there. He'd been gone years by then. So *he* was hardly to blame."

"Oh, Baby Girl," said Frank.

Opal gaped. "That's what Fishbo always called me!" she said. "Anyway, okay. This is the bit." She breathed in very deep and held on to the breath until her chest started aching. "Okay, this is the tough bit. It's about Robbie Southgate. Craig's dad."

Frank hit the brake hard and pulled over to the side of the road. Another white van went past them with the driver leaning on his horn. Typical! Only other car for miles around and it nearly hit them.

"I'm turning round, love," said Frank, his voice sounding high in his throat. "We're getting the cops on it. Not that I wouldn't love to go and find him, but I'd end up in jail for murder."

"Eh?"

"It was Robbie Southgate who raped you?"

"God, no!" Opal said. "I wasn't raped. And it wasn't a man. It was my boyfriend. He was fifteen."

"Jesus! Finn's fifteen!"

"Yeah, you could be a granddad twice over by now," Opal said. Slowly, Frank pulled back out onto the road again. Opal waited until he had got up to top gear before speaking. "I wanted a boyfriend. Mum had one—always at least one—and I wanted one too. But I didn't want a baby. Not when I was twelve. So I tried to make it go away. On my own."

"In the outhouse," said Frank.

"On a Friday night. Mum's party. Thinking she'd be too busy to mind where I'd got to. So … I never even got my first-aid badge at Brownies and I would probably have killed myself if someone hadn't found me. It was one of mum's friends. Well, it was Robbie South-gate, is who it was. He was brilliant. He took me to hospital and stayed with me and he never looked down his nose at me or anything like that. He just looked after me. And all I remember was his arm when he was cuddling me in to him in the car—two bluebird tattoos on his arm. It was the only thing I could remember. Probably just as well." She scrubbed her hands over her face. "The rest of it—when it started coming back again—wasn't that fantastic, really."

"You poor little love," said Frank. "Do you want to stop? It feels dead wrong you saying all this and me watching the road."

"I'm not trying to get sympathy!" said Opal. "I'm just telling you. Keep going. We need to get there by chucking out time."

"Am I supposed to understand how all this fits together yet?" said Frank. "Because I don't."

"Listen," Opal said. "Karen Reid wouldn't hear a word against Robbie, right? And she stopped seeing her mum and dad. And when I grabbed her and said I wanted to talk about Craig, she was frightened."

"Yeah?"

"Don't you see? She was *frightened*. She shouldn't have been frightened. If her little boy had been missing for ten years and someone suddenly came up and talked to her about him she should have gone through the roof with … I dunno, hope or something. And I thought it was weird that she didn't look out of the bus window when all the school kids were going by. And I'll tell you something else, the thing that made her go completely nuts at me and start threatening me was when I told her where I grew up."

334

"Mote Street?"

"No, I mean, where I went to live when I *left* Mote Street: Whitby. She freaked when she heard that. And it was the next day that the photo came through the door. Taken from across the street—where Karen's parents live. From when I was a little girl, when Karen was always round with the baby. And if anyone could have a copy of a key to a house in Mote Street—say if they wanted to stick a cat with a bread knife in its back on someone's bed—it would be someone connected to Margaret. Like you said yourself, she's already come sniffing after one of your spares, hasn't she?"

"Karen Reid wanted you to stop looking for Craig?"

"And how weird is that?"

Opal directed him to the school gates, and they arrived in good time, ten minutes before the end of the day. But then five minutes after that, she looked in the passenger wing mirror and swore softly.

"I don't believe it," she said. "Steph's here. Don't tell me she still picks Michael up and takes him home." She got down from the van and went over to the parked car.

Stephanie got out before Opal reached her and stood with her arms folded, leaning against the car door.

"What are you doing here?" she said.

"I want to speak to Michael," Opal.

"Just as well I'm here to stop you then, isn't it?" She flicked a glance towards Frank as he came up beside them. "Who are you?"

"Frank Gilbert," he said, but he didn't put out his hand the way he had done when he met Opal. "Friend of your stepdaughter's." Steph raised her eyebrows but said nothing.

"I just want to ask Michael one very specific question," said Opal, "and then we'll go."

"What?"

"Remember when he joined that footie club." Immediately, blotches of angry pink began to bloom on Steph's neck.

"You're kidding," she said. "You must be joking. This again? That?"

"I know, I know," said Opal. "But listen. I just want to know if he knows—or if you know and then I don't even need to see Michael—where the coach lives."

"Eh?" said Steph, looking between Opal and Frank, frowning.

"Michael's coach from the club. Do you know his address? Or his phone number?"

"What's this about?"

"If you tell me, I'll get out of your sight," Opal said. All three of them turned as the school bell rang out in the building.

"It's Abbeville Avenue," Steph said. "Well I know it; I had to go round there and clear up all your bullshit. There and fifty other places."

"What number?"

"I can't remember the number. It's in the teens. A blue door with a stained glass lamp. Right. I've told you. So go."

Opal turned right away, but Frank stayed and said something to Steph, quite quietly, but Steph's answer was pretty loud.

He slammed into the van and glared at Opal.

"So that's your stepmother, is it?" he said. "She's like something out of fucking Disney."

Opal laughed, and Frank nearly laughed too.

"Poor Steph, you can't blame her. I made her life a complete misery. Right then. I don't know exactly where this is, but I'll do my best. If we get lost, we can stop and ask for directions."

"So why did your wicked stepmother go mad when you asked about your brother's football club?"

"That's when it started," Opal said. "I got given the responsibility of taking Michael to the club after school. And that's when I … flipped out and started saying Michael was my little boy that Steph and Dad stole from me. Only—believe it or not—I never put two and two together and worked out why I started saying it. I know now, of course."

"Why?"

"Robbie Southgate. I hadn't seen him since that night when I was twelve and I was eighteen by this time. I didn't actually recognise him, but I recognised the bluebirds on his arm. I started dreaming about babies. I started thinking about the fact that I couldn't actually remember anything about the whole summer when I moved here. I'd, like, I'd blocked it out? And Michael was exactly the right age you know. Twelve and half years younger than me."

"God almighty. So Steph was pregnant when you arrived after the … miscarriage?"

"No, actually," Opal said. "Michael's adopted. That's the whole point, see? He's adopted. And he obviously wasn't Steph's and Dad's real baby. He looks a lot more like me—complexion-wise, you know. So that's why people actually believed me. It's just like Norah, kind of."

Frank swerved the van and glared at her again.

"Opal bloody Jones," he said. "It's *nothing* like Norah. Norah hated her brother and pretended he never … Norah's nuts."

"I think we need to turn here," Opal said. "Yeah. Now, where's the … ? Oh, slow down, look. There's a coloured lamp and a blue door."

They parked, walked up the path, and rang the bell. Through the frosted glass they could see a figure approaching. A man it looked like, until the door opened and they saw that it was a boy, dressed in school uniform, with his tie undone.

"God, you look like your grandpa!" said Opal. "You won't remember me, but I used to babysit you when you were tiny." She stuck out her hand. "Craig, I'm Opal Jones."

EPILOGUE

IT WAS SO HOT that her fingers slid about on the stops, slick with sweat, and drops of sweat fell into her eyes and made her blink so she couldn't follow the sheet music, and her breath was all wrong because she was so near crying. But the other Mote Street Boys just played louder and louder, and she got through it. No one was listening to her anyway. Everyone gathered round the grave was listening to the absent echo of Fishbo's voice, craning to hear the ghost of it one more time.

Opal lowered her trumpet, Pep let his fingers fall from the keyboard, Big Al moved his sax to one side holding it like a rifle on an honour parade, Mr. Hoadley hugged his bass like a lover, and Jimmy D stilled the final flourish of his flare drum. Overhead, there was a rumble and the sky darkened. Pep cast a look at the socket of the orange extension cable that his electric keyboard was plugged into. It had either been that or try to wheel a proper piano over the grass, and this summer everyone had forgotten about rain.

The celebrant was speaking again. A nice enough woman from some church where they didn't go in much for God, but Opal couldn't pay attention to what was being said. She was looking at them all, ranged on the other side of the grave from where she had set up with the rest of the band.

Vonnie Pickess couldn't meet her eye, hadn't met her eye once since the showdown in the hospital waiting room. Opal would need to go and tell her it was okay. Nicola would have drunk herself to death sooner or later, and at least this way Mrs. Pickess had saved her ending up on the streets begging for change. Sunil and Zula were there in the front row too, Zula unable to keep shooting little sideways looks to where she wished she could turn round and stare with her mouth open. All five of the boys were there, reeking of aftershave and wearing enough hair gel to go round a regiment. They were the only ones who'd threatened to laugh at Opal's playing. Sanjit and Vikram anyway.

She should really have been practising every minute of the three days, but she'd been busy. She'd gone round to Walrus Antiques with Frank to get them to go and do a proper inventory of Norah's stuff—since Frank found out Auntie Norah was really Granny Norah, he'd started taking more of an interest in his children's stake in the estate, not so keen to let Sarah fritter it all away. So Billy and Tony were here today, Tony cleaned up in cords and a jacket and Billy well over the top in a jet-black funeral suit, black silk tie, and pointy patent-leather boots. They had come for the prospect of Opal playing the trumpet, but they couldn't keep their eyes off the five handsome Joshi boys, and Opal was looking forward to winding Vik and Sanj up about it in revenge for the smirking.

Margaret was there, in a black coat and mantilla that had to be sweltering her, and Denny was there in a wheelchair—an enormous wheelchair, but he'd made it. And Craig was there too, standing next to his granny, who was holding on so tight to his hand that Opal could see the tips of his fingers swelling up like red berries. Robbie was there too. But not Karen. If Robbie and Karen were ever be in the same place again, it would be a while yet.

"I found him," Robbie had said, when Frank and Opal were sitting in his living room in Whitby. "Wandering around the back lane, covered in paint. I was coming to see your mum, actually. And so I took him home and waited for Karen to phone me. And waited and waited and waited."

"I see," Opal had said.

"And then when she did get in touch, she lied. Said he'd only been gone an hour or two Saturday morning. So I thought I'd teach her a lesson. I wasn't going to admit I had him until she admitted how long he'd really been gone. But she never did. It was three days later I finally told her."

"You put her through hell," Opal said.

"She put me through it too," said Robbie. "And not only then, either. It was me that wanted kids, you know. Mad about kids—I still coach. Coach tennis all summer and football all winter. I had to talk Karen into having a baby at all. And when she left me, she cared more about me not getting him than about keeping him herself. Dumped him at Margaret's half the time, didn't she?"

"And so she gave him up to stay out of trouble?"

"We made a deal. He came to live with me, and I didn't tell on her."

"Didn't anyone recognise him? Wasn't everyone looking?"

"We spent that first summer up north fishing. With my sister. A man and woman and a kid—why would anyone look twice? Then we moved to Whitby when school started up again."

"But how did the teachers and all them not know?

"Changed our name," Robbie said. "We're MacDonalds now. My mum's maiden name."

"And you were right here all the time? In the same county, for God's sake?"

Robbie shrugged. "If someone had recognised him, it would be Karen in trouble, not me. Maybe that's what kept us safe: I didn't look guilty because I had nothing to look guilty over."

"So if I hadn't recognised you … And you didn't recognise me?"

"Michael Jones's sister? I didn't, no."

"And what about Margaret and Denny?" Opal said. "You said you had nothing to feel guilty about, but they've gone through worse hell than anyone."

"Karen said she'd told them where he was," Robbie said. "And she said they had fallen out with her and didn't want to see him anymore." He put his head in his hands. "I can't stand thinking about them not knowing. Ten years! How could I not check? They'll never forgive me."

"If you walk in with Craig, they'll forgive you anything," Opal said. "And if Karen brings little Jodie along, it'll be the same do." So they would all be back together, Margaret and Denny, Karen and Craig. One big happy family—except for the divorced ones who couldn't stand each other obviously. And Fishbo was gone where nothing would ever hurt him. And Frank would have Charlie and Finn, at least for a night after school every week and the odd weekend and holiday.

And what about Opal?

Sitting right there in a stranger's house, she bent over at the waist and a terrible honking, gulping sound came out of her.

"Mum," she wailed. "Mummy!"

342

And so Frank took her back to Steph's house and spent an hour talking to Steph in the dining room with the double doors closed over, and he had gone to the station that morning to meet the train. Opal looked across the grave and smiled at Michael, who rolled his eyes, because the funeral of some old bloke he'd never met wasn't his idea of a day out, but Frank had insisted.

"Opal needs her family," he'd said. "And you're it, pal. It won't kill you to be there for her for this one day."

"I quite like your Frank," Michael had said to Opal. "He just gives it straight."

Opal squealed. "He's not *my Frank*," she said, but she looked at him now standing behind Denny's wheelchair—him and Sunil together had shoved it over the grass, half-carrying it to stop it sinking into the ground—and she wondered if maybe he could be. He was the only person in the world who knew absolutely every stinking thing about her shithole of a life and he was still there, smiling at her.

And she couldn't forget the things he had said on the way home from Whitby, about how mothers weren't the be all and end all. And when she thought about what kind of mother Norah had been, and Nicola, and God knows Karen, she couldn't argue. As for fathers—her own, Fishbo, and Norah's too, if it was him who built the tunnel from the back door to the garage to hide her and sent his grandkid away—Frank was right about them too.

"As long as you're not alone," he'd said. "So long as there's someone, it doesn't matter who."

She smiled back at him. The Mote Street Boys lowered Fishbo's coffin into the ground and the celebrant called for a moment's quiet reflection. All the mourners were silent, but the sky rumbled again, crackled with a flash of light, and at last let go onto the parched ground the first enormous drops of cold, sweet rain.

Photo © Neil McRoberts

ABOUT THE AUTHOR

Catriona McPherson was born in Scotland, where she lived until moving to California in 2010. She is the author of the award-winning Dandy Gilver historical mystery series and is a member of Mystery Writers of America and Sisters in Crime. *As She Left It* is her first modern standalone. You can visit Catriona online at www.catrionamcpherson.com

ACKNOWLEDGMENTS

I would like to thank: everyone at Midnight Ink, especially Court-
ney Colton, Nicole Nugent, the lingering spirit of Steven Pomijie,
and the incomparable Terri Bischoff; Lisa Moylett, wonder agent;
Jess Lourey, for introducing me to Jessie Chandler for introducing
me to Terri; Diane Nelson, old pal and owner of Opal's house; Lou-
ise Kelly, old pal and third leg of the weekend that sowed the seed of
this story; Eileen Rendahl and Spring Warren, new pals and great
listeners; and Neil McRoberts.